TRISTAN STRONG
PUNCHES A HOLE IN THE SKY

THE GRAPHIC NOVEL

ADAPTED BY
ROBERT VENDITTI

ILLUSTRATED BY
OLIVIA STEPHENS

COLORING BY
LAURA LANGSTON

LETTERING BY
ARIANA MAHER

BASED ON THE *NEW YORK TIMES* BEST-SELLING NOVEL BY
KWAME MBALIA

RICK RIORDAN PRESENTS

D🌙SNEY • HYPERION   LOS ANGELES   NEW YORK

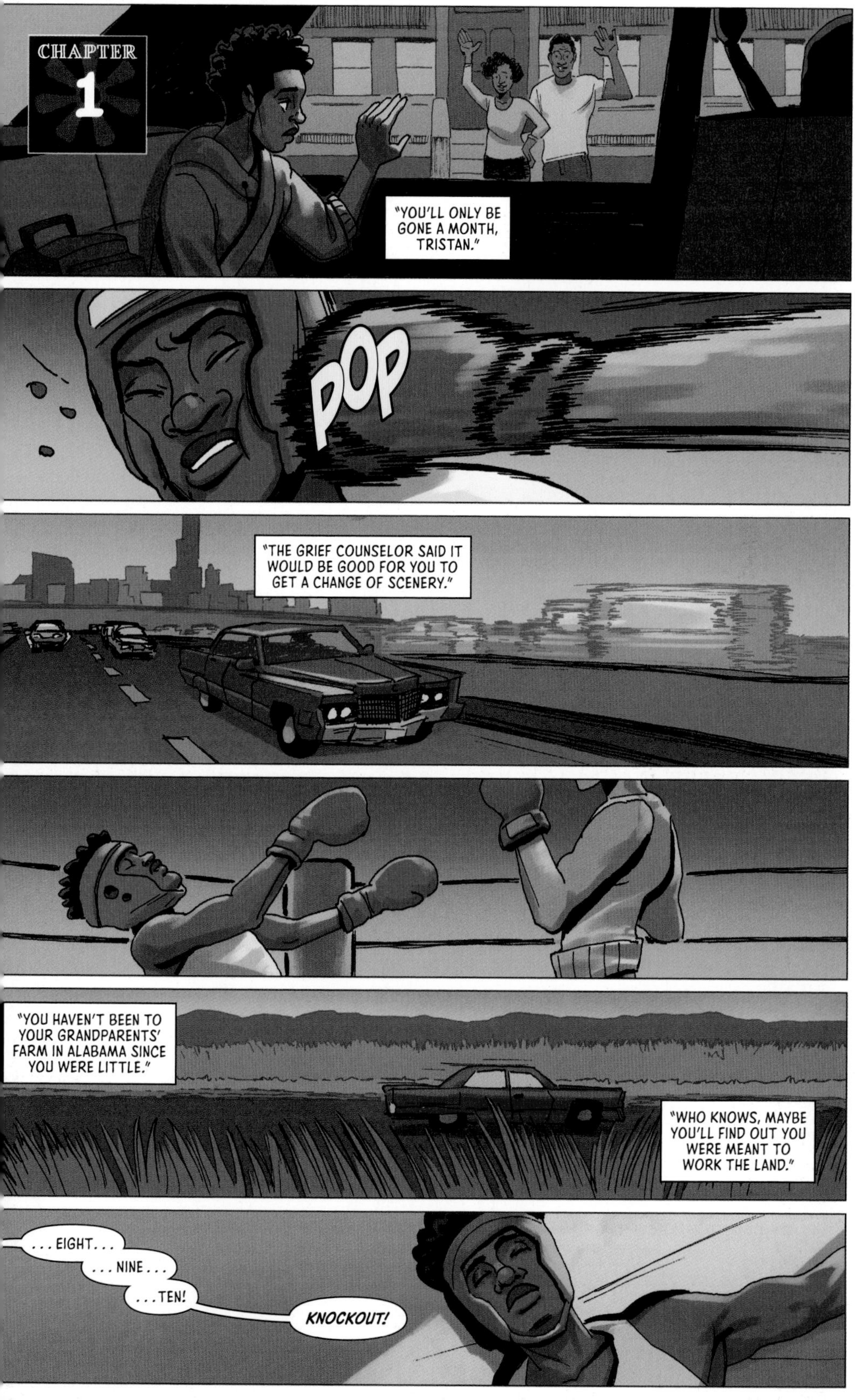
CHAPTER 1
"YOU'LL ONLY BE GONE A MONTH, TRISTAN."
POP
"THE GRIEF COUNSELOR SAID IT WOULD BE GOOD FOR YOU TO GET A CHANGE OF SCENERY."
"YOU HAVEN'T BEEN TO YOUR GRANDPARENTS' FARM IN ALABAMA SINCE YOU WERE LITTLE."
"WHO KNOWS, MAYBE YOU'LL FIND OUT YOU WERE MEANT TO WORK THE LAND."
. . . EIGHT. . .
. . . NINE . . .
. . . TEN!
KNOCKOUT!

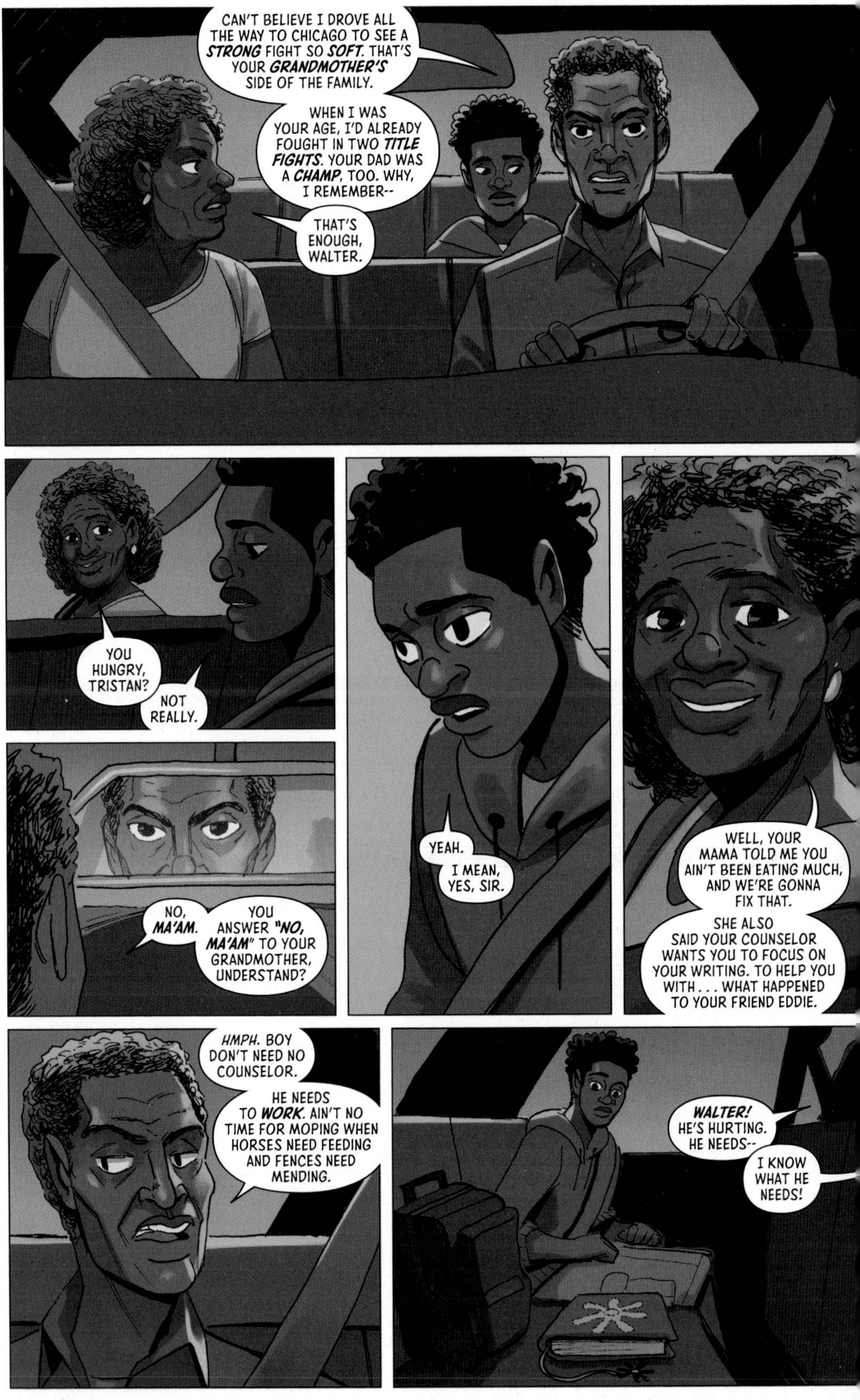
CAN'T BELIEVE I DROVE ALL THE WAY TO CHICAGO TO SEE A STRONG FIGHT SO SOFT. THAT'S YOUR GRANDMOTHER'S SIDE OF THE FAMILY.
WHEN I WAS YOUR AGE, I'D ALREADY FOUGHT IN TWO TITLE FIGHTS. YOUR DAD WAS A CHAMP, TOO. WHY, I REMEMBER--
THAT'S ENOUGH, WALTER.
YOU HUNGRY, TRISTAN?
NOT REALLY.
YOU ANSWER "NO, MA'AM" TO YOUR GRANDMOTHER, UNDERSTAND?
NO, MA'AM.
YEAH.
I MEAN, YES, SIR.
WELL, YOUR MAMA TOLD ME YOU AIN'T BEEN EATING MUCH, AND WE'RE GONNA FIX THAT.
SHE ALSO SAID YOUR COUNSELOR WANTS YOU TO FOCUS ON YOUR WRITING. TO HELP YOU WITH . . . WHAT HAPPENED TO YOUR FRIEND EDDIE.
HMPH. BOY DON'T NEED NO COUNSELOR.
HE NEEDS TO WORK. AIN'T NO TIME FOR MOPING WHEN HORSES NEED FEEDING AND FENCES NEED MENDING.
WALTER! HE'S HURTING. HE NEEDS--
I KNOW WHAT HE NEEDS!

IS THAT EDDIE'S JOURNAL? THE ONE HE USED TO WRITE IN?

YES, MA'AM. HIS MOM GAVE IT TO ME AT THE FUNERAL. IT HAS ALL HIS *STORIES*. EVEN THE FABLES YOU USED TO TELL US ON YOUR VISITS.

OUR END-OF-YEAR ENGLISH PROJECT WAS SUPPOSED TO BE A COLLECTION OF STORIES FROM OUR CHILDHOOD.

THAT SYMBOL. I HAVEN'T SEEN IT IN A LONG TIME.

YOU KNOW WHAT IT IS?

IT'S THE *SPIDER'S WEB*. AN OLD AFRICAN SYMBOL FOR CREATIVITY AND WISDOM. IT SHOWS HOW TANGLED AND COMPLICATED LIFE CAN BE.

BUT WITH A LITTLE IMAGINATIVE THINKING, WE CAN SOLVE MOST OF OUR PROBLEMS AND THOSE OF OTHERS.

Y'ALL NEED TO STOP FILLING HIS HEAD WITH THAT MESS.

THE BOY NEEDS TO STAY IN THE *REAL WORLD*.

WALTER, DON'T BE SO HARD ON HIM.

BOXING AIN'T GONNA JUST *HAPPEN!* HE GOT TO TRAIN HIS *BODY* AND *MIND!*

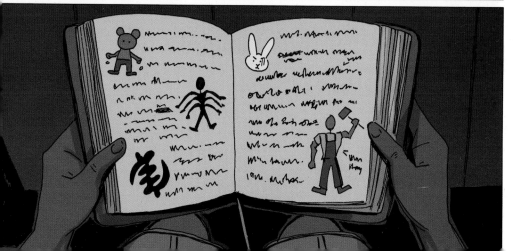

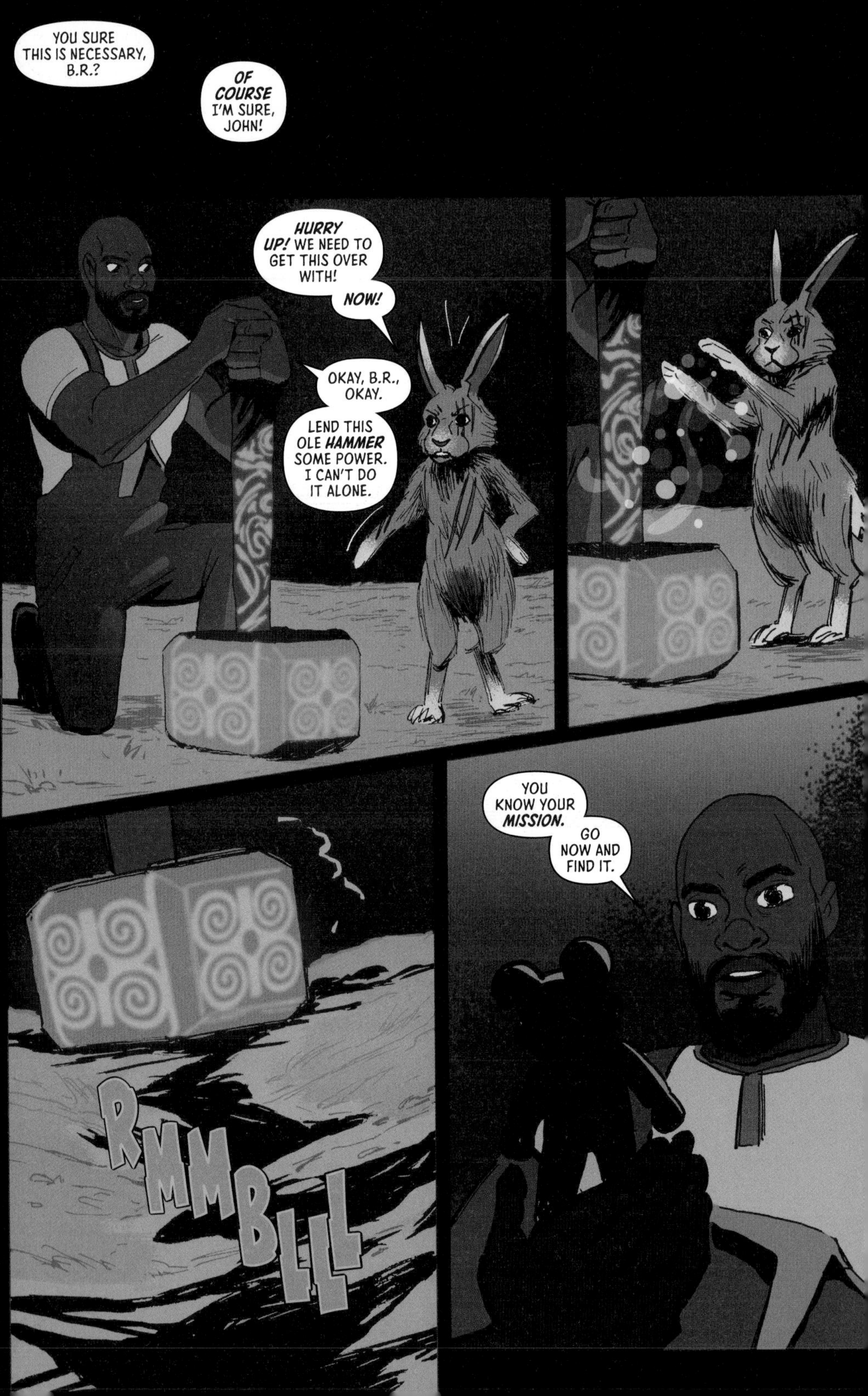
YOU SURE THIS IS NECESSARY, B.R.?
OF COURSE I'M SURE, JOHN!
HURRY UP! WE NEED TO GET THIS OVER WITH!
NOW!
OKAY, B.R., OKAY.
LEND THIS OLE HAMMER SOME POWER. I CAN'T DO IT ALONE.
RMMBLLL
YOU KNOW YOUR MISSION.
GO NOW AND FIND IT.

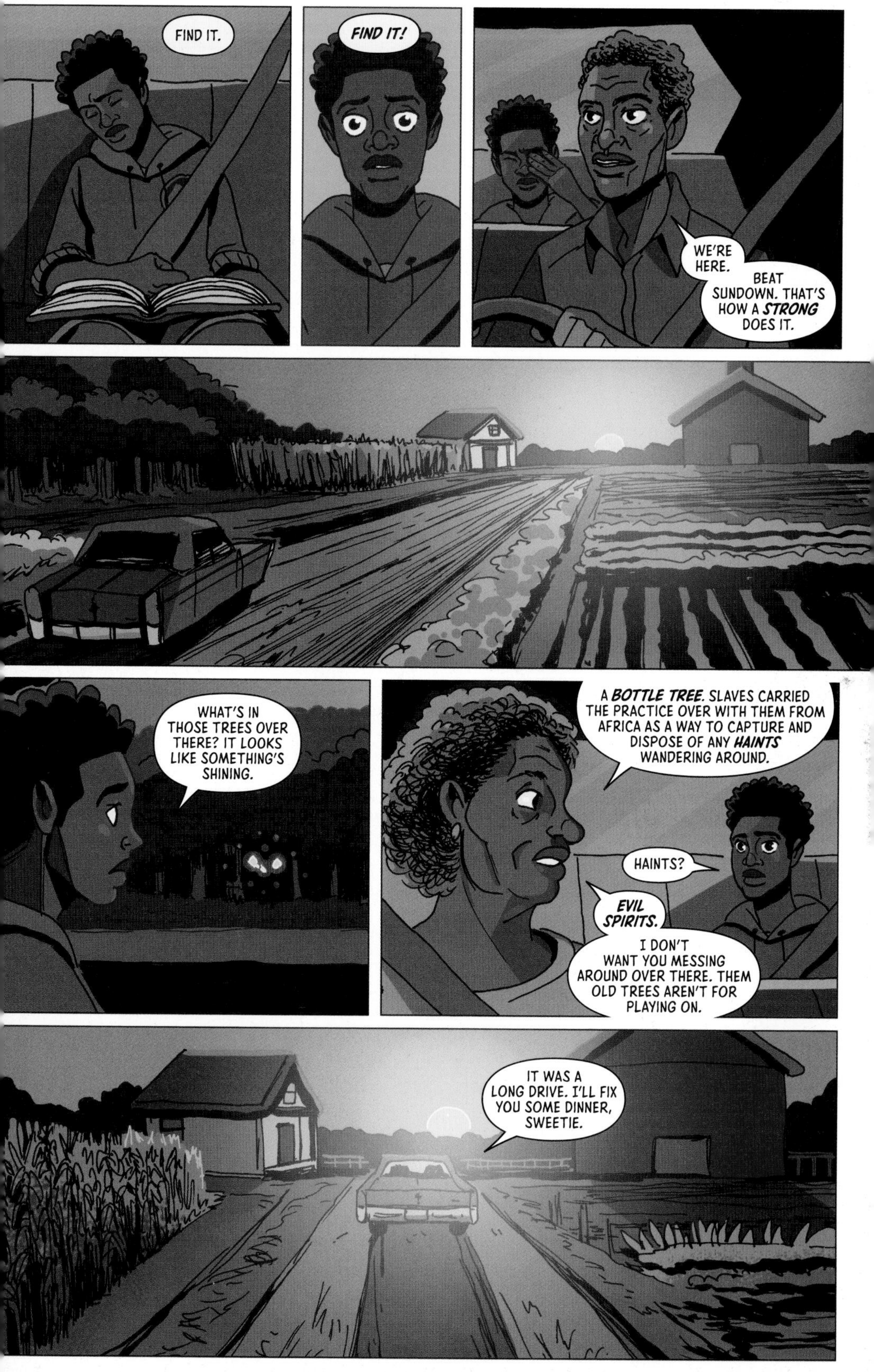

FIND IT.
FIND IT!
WE'RE HERE.
BEAT SUNDOWN. THAT'S HOW A STRONG DOES IT.
WHAT'S IN THOSE TREES OVER THERE? IT LOOKS LIKE SOMETHING'S SHINING.
A BOTTLE TREE. SLAVES CARRIED THE PRACTICE OVER WITH THEM FROM AFRICA AS A WAY TO CAPTURE AND DISPOSE OF ANY HAINTS WANDERING AROUND.
HAINTS?
EVIL SPIRITS.
I DON'T WANT YOU MESSING AROUND OVER THERE. THEM OLD TREES AREN'T FOR PLAYING ON.
IT WAS A LONG DRIVE. I'LL FIX YOU SOME DINNER, SWEETIE.

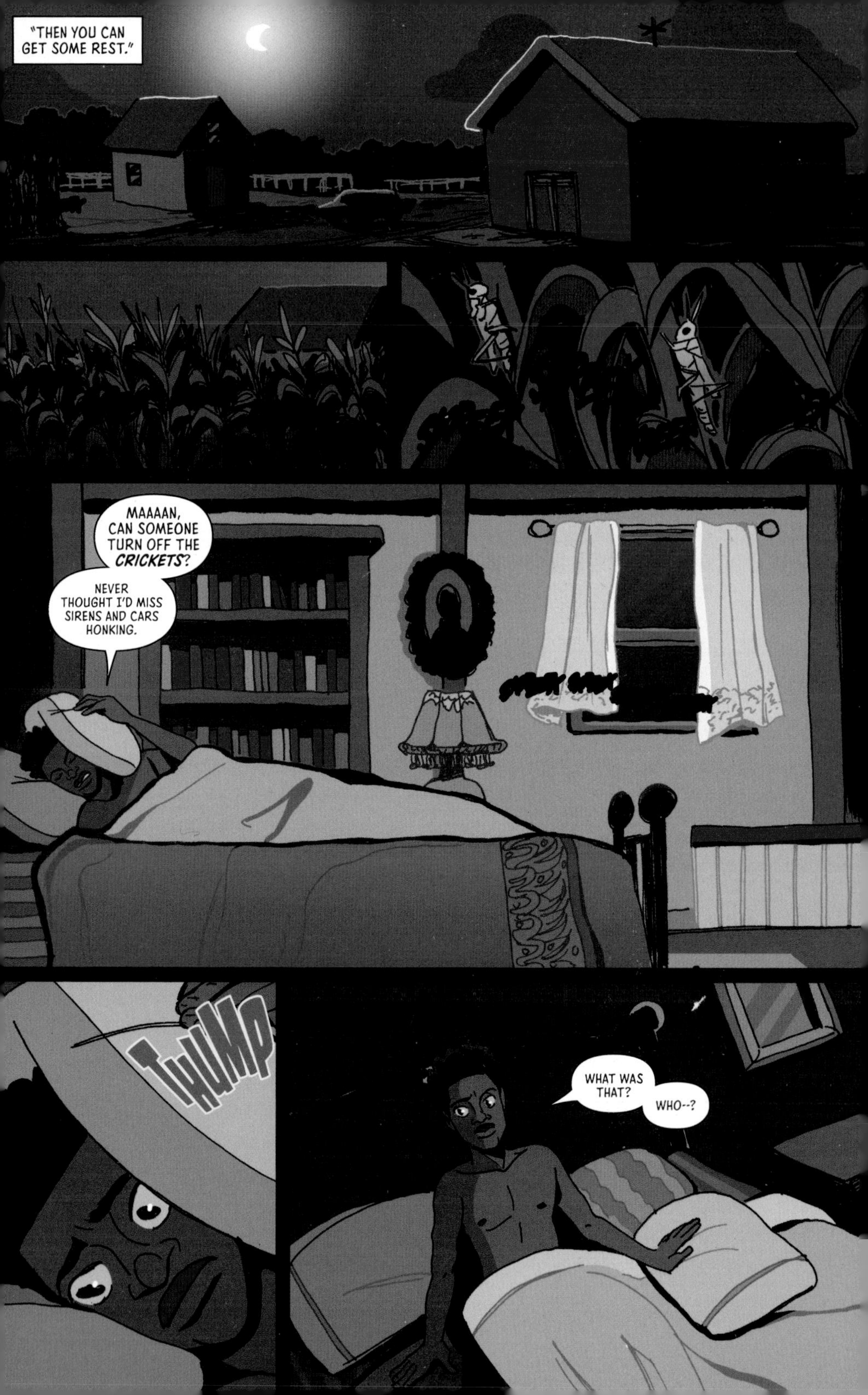
"THEN YOU CAN GET SOME REST."
MAAAAN, CAN SOMEONE TURN OFF THE *CRICKETS*?
NEVER THOUGHT I'D MISS SIRENS AND CARS HONKING.
THUMP
WHAT WAS THAT?
WHO--?

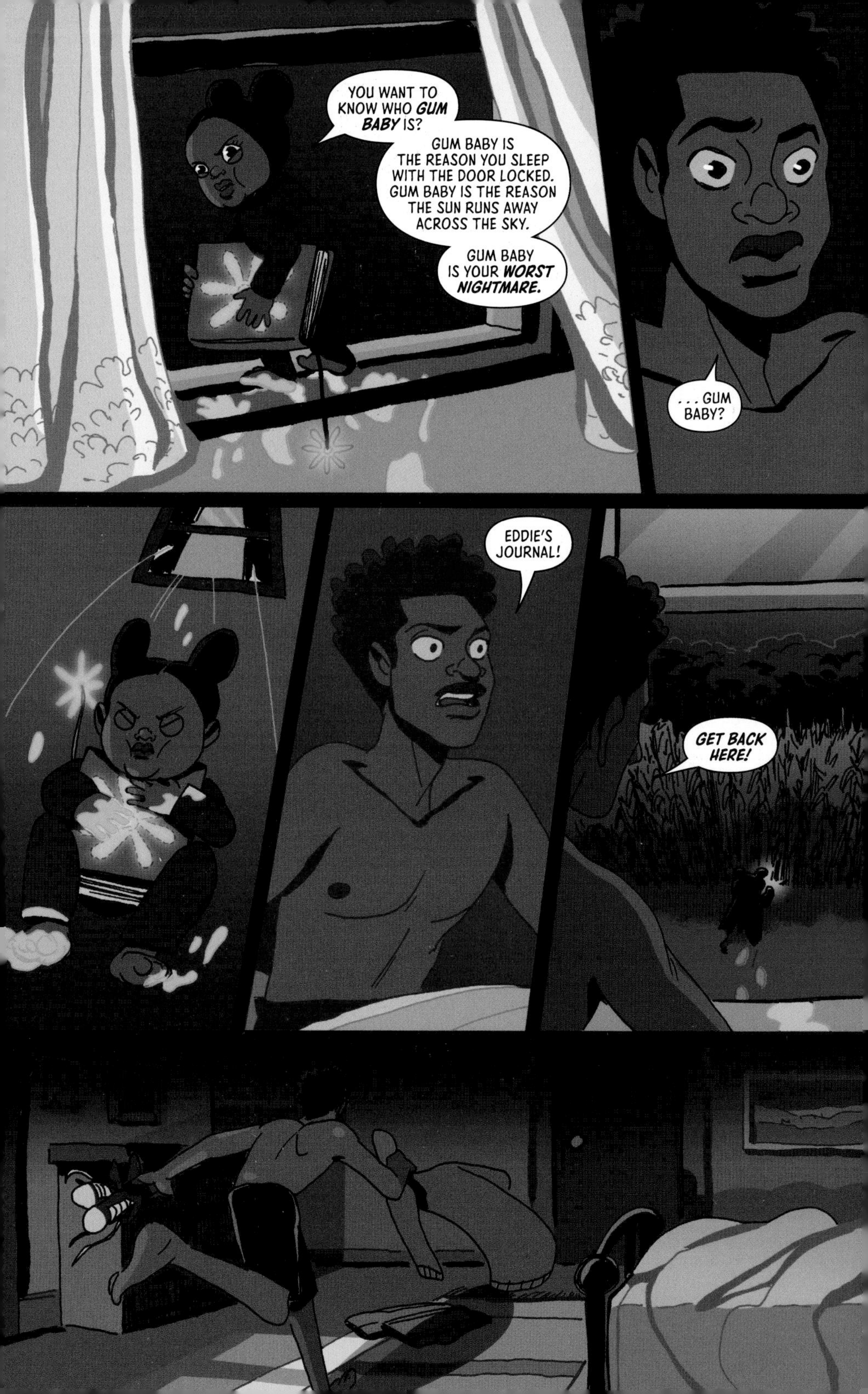
YOU WANT TO KNOW WHO GUM BABY IS?
GUM BABY IS THE REASON YOU SLEEP WITH THE DOOR LOCKED. GUM BABY IS THE REASON THE SUN RUNS AWAY ACROSS THE SKY.
GUM BABY IS YOUR WORST NIGHTMARE.
. . . GUM BABY?
EDDIE'S JOURNAL!
GET BACK HERE!

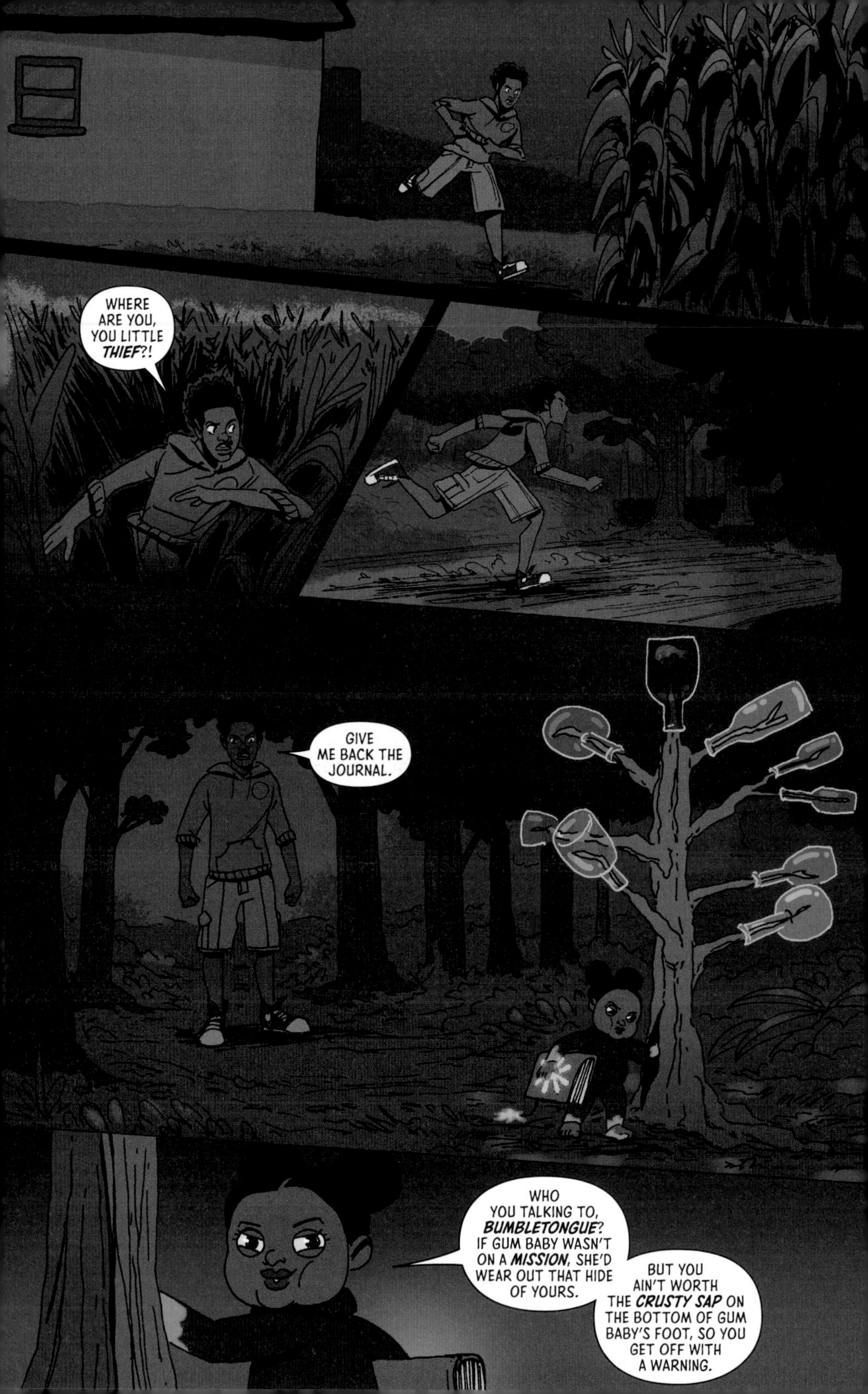

WHERE ARE YOU, YOU LITTLE *THIEF*?!
GIVE ME BACK THE JOURNAL.
WHO YOU TALKING TO, ***BUMBLETONGUE***? IF GUM BABY WASN'T ON A ***MISSION***, SHE'D WEAR OUT THAT HIDE OF YOURS.
BUT YOU AIN'T WORTH THE ***CRUSTY SAP*** ON THE BOTTOM OF GUM BABY'S FOOT, SO YOU GET OFF WITH A WARNING.

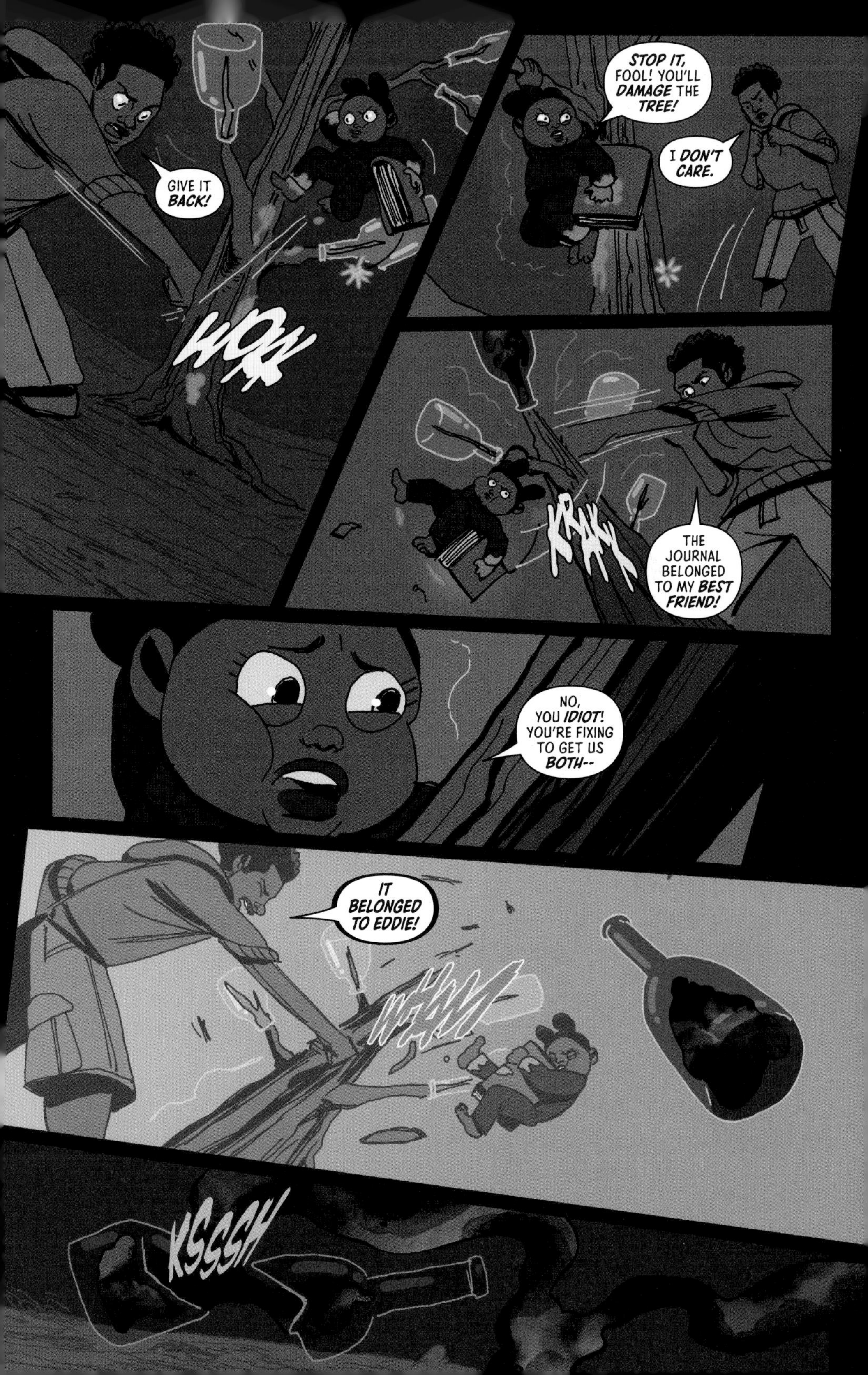
GIVE IT BACK!
WOK
STOP IT, FOOL! YOU'LL DAMAGE THE TREE!
I DON'T CARE.
KRAK
THE JOURNAL BELONGED TO MY BEST FRIEND!
NO, YOU IDIOT! YOU'RE FIXING TO GET US BOTH--
IT BELONGED TO EDDIE!
WHAM
KSSSH

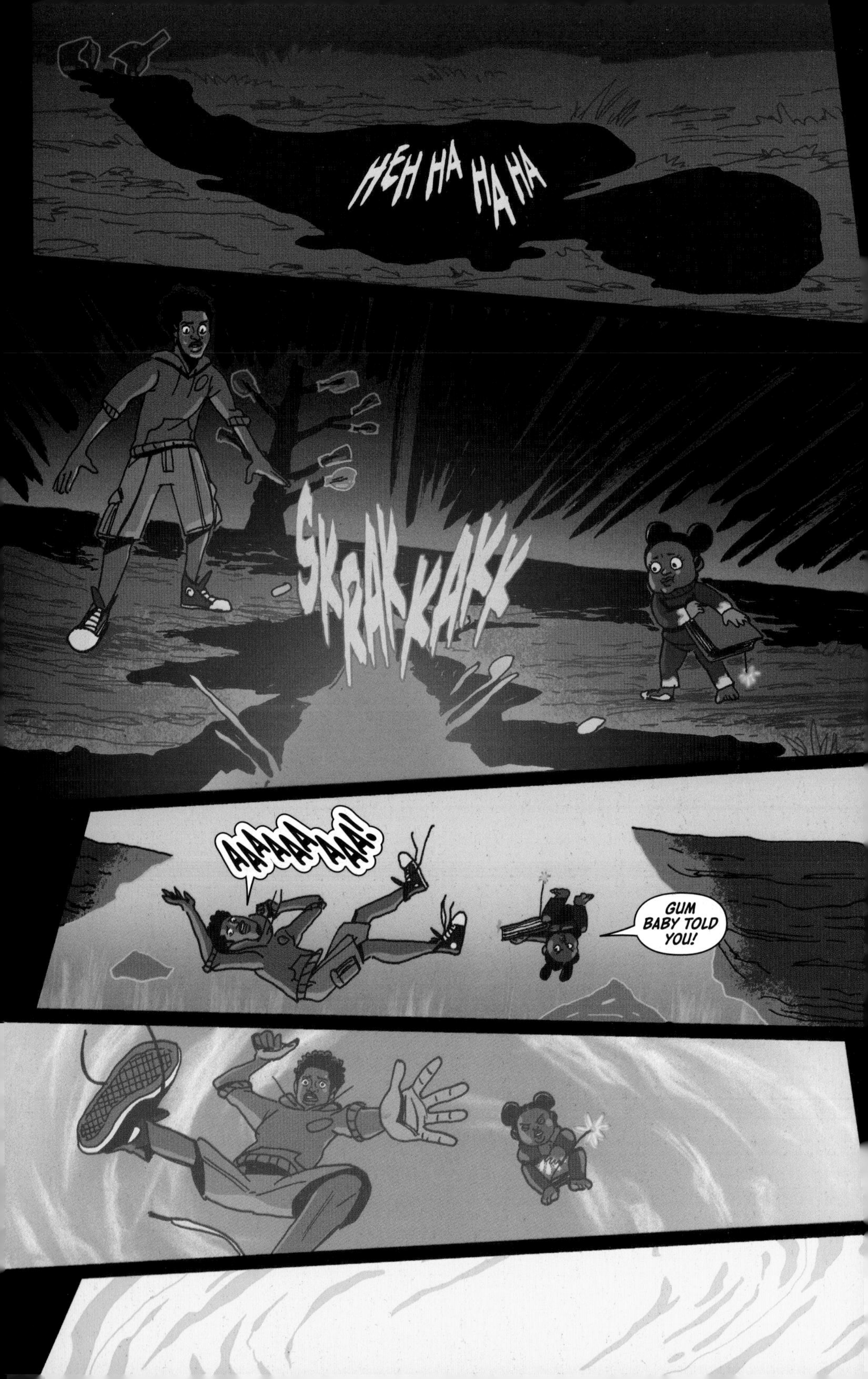
HEH HA HA HA
SKRAKAKK
AAAAAAAA!
GUM BABY TOLD YOU!

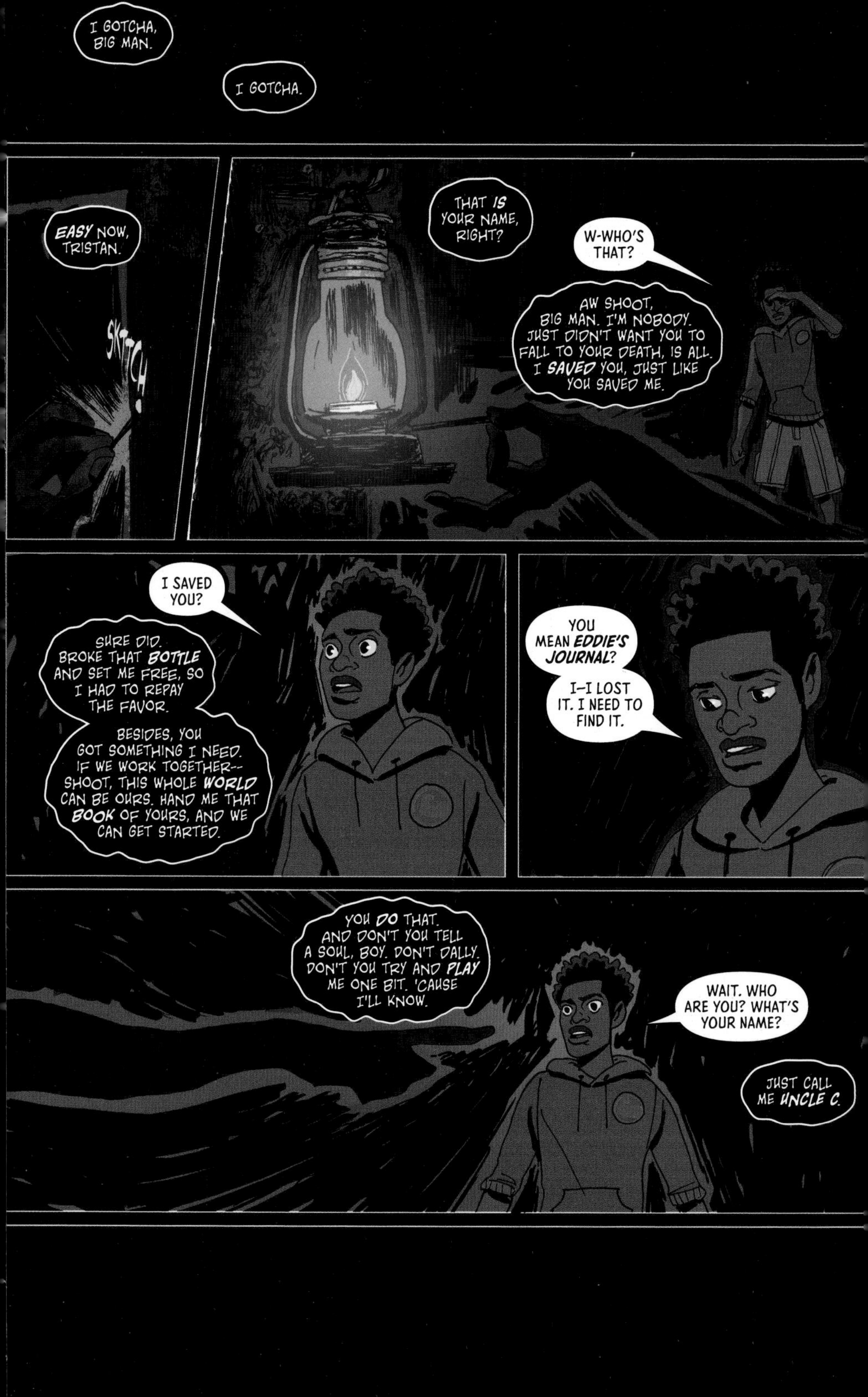

I GOTCHA, BIG MAN.
I GOTCHA.
EASY NOW, TRISTAN.
SKTTCH!
THAT IS YOUR NAME, RIGHT?
W-WHO'S THAT?
AW SHOOT, BIG MAN. I'M NOBODY. JUST DIDN'T WANT YOU TO FALL TO YOUR DEATH, IS ALL. I SAVED YOU, JUST LIKE YOU SAVED ME.
I SAVED YOU?
SURE DID. BROKE THAT BOTTLE AND SET ME FREE, SO I HAD TO REPAY THE FAVOR.
BESIDES, YOU GOT SOMETHING I NEED. IF WE WORK TOGETHER-- SHOOT, THIS WHOLE WORLD CAN BE OURS. HAND ME THAT BOOK OF YOURS, AND WE CAN GET STARTED.
YOU MEAN EDDIE'S JOURNAL?
I—I LOST IT. I NEED TO FIND IT.
YOU DO THAT. AND DON'T YOU TELL A SOUL, BOY. DON'T DALLY. DON'T YOU TRY AND PLAY ME ONE BIT. 'CAUSE I'LL KNOW.
WAIT. WHO ARE YOU? WHAT'S YOUR NAME?
JUST CALL ME UNCLE C.

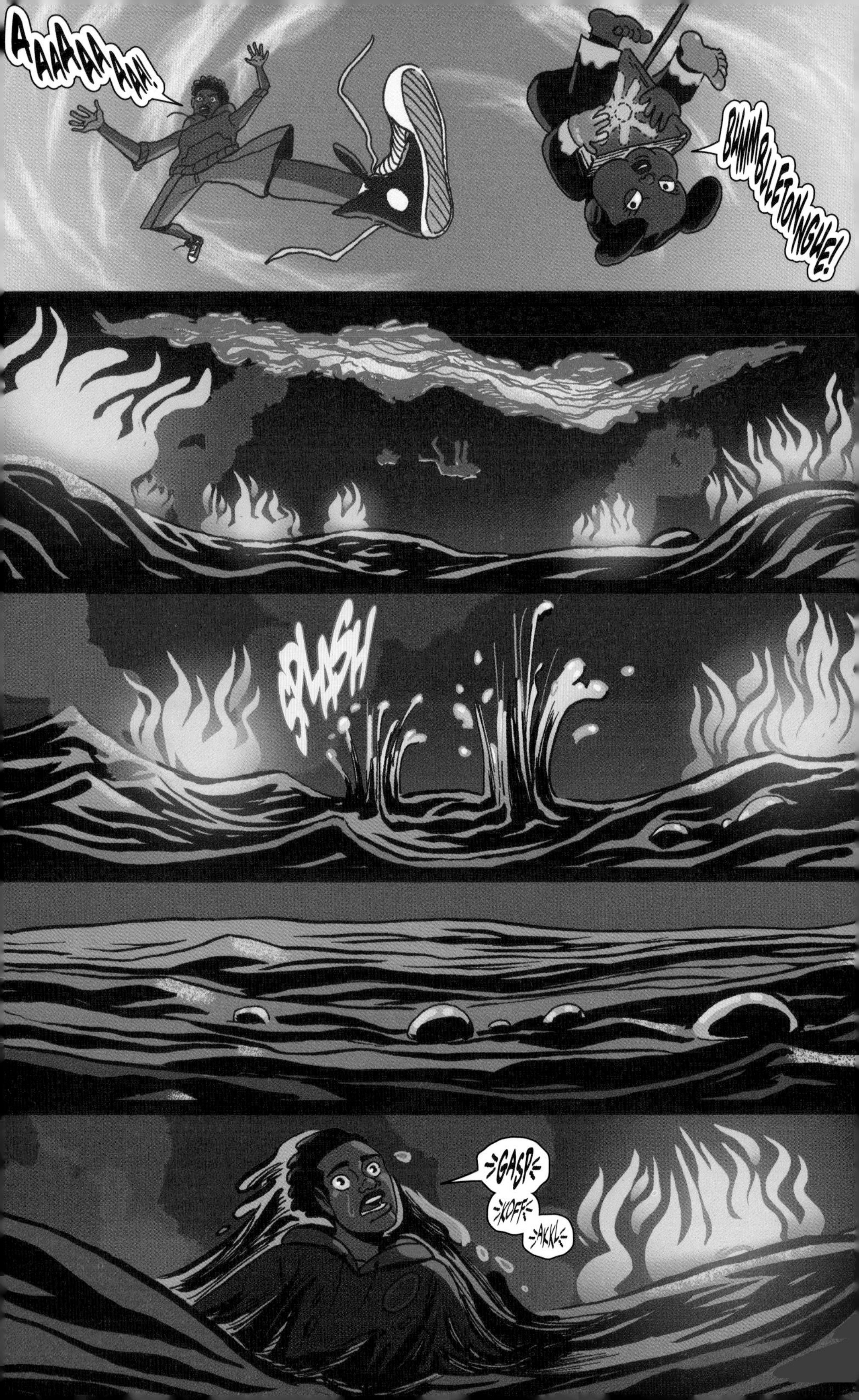
AAAAAAAAA!
BWAMBLETONGUE!
SPLASH
GASP
KOFF
AKK

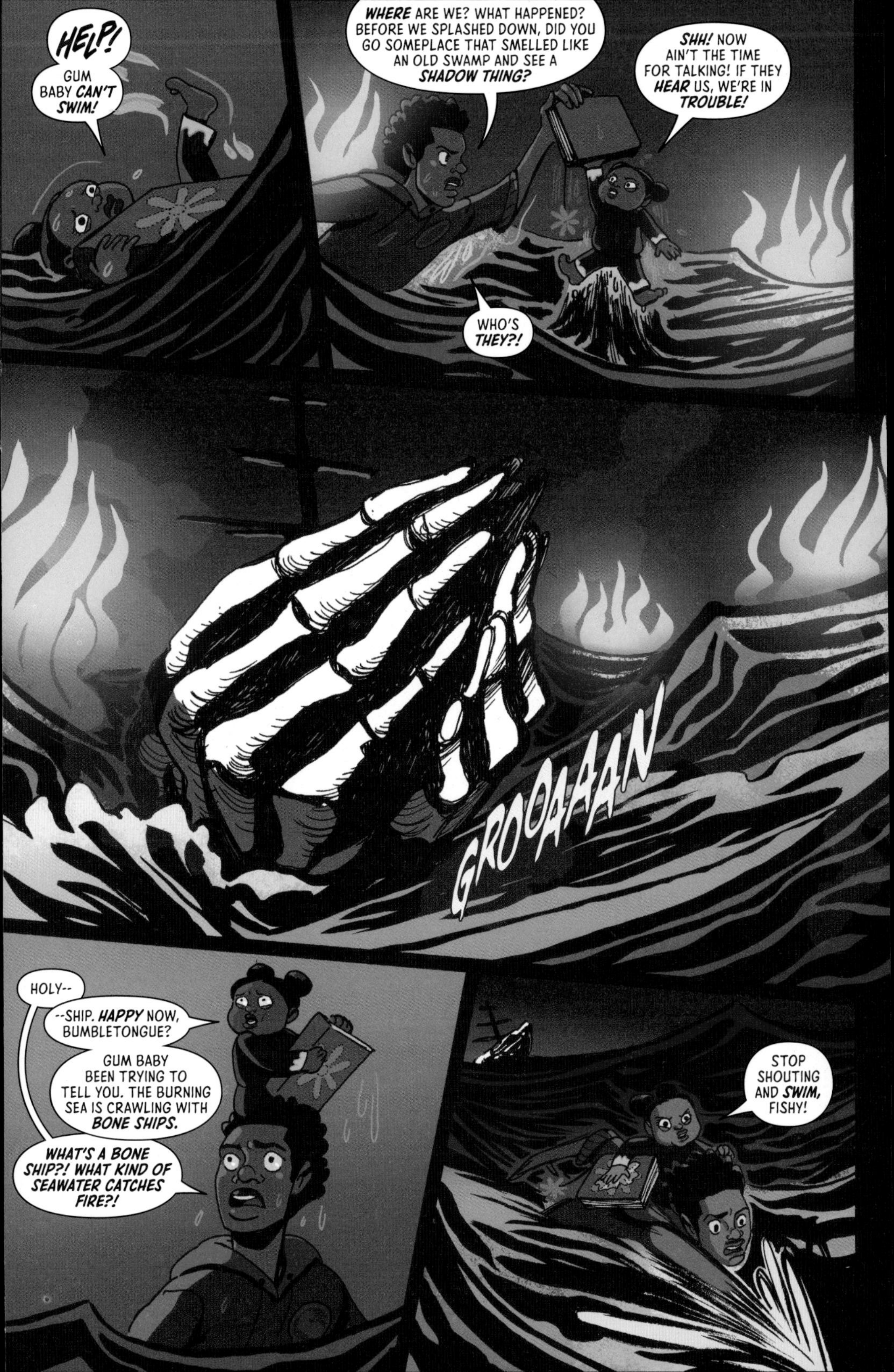
HELP!
GUM BABY CAN'T SWIM!
WHERE ARE WE? WHAT HAPPENED? BEFORE WE SPLASHED DOWN, DID YOU GO SOMEPLACE THAT SMELLED LIKE AN OLD SWAMP AND SEE A SHADOW THING?
SHH! NOW AIN'T THE TIME FOR TALKING! IF THEY HEAR US, WE'RE IN TROUBLE!
WHO'S THEY?!
GROOAAAN
HOLY--
--SHIP. HAPPY NOW, BUMBLETONGUE?
GUM BABY BEEN TRYING TO TELL YOU. THE BURNING SEA IS CRAWLING WITH BONE SHIPS.
WHAT'S A BONE SHIP?! WHAT KIND OF SEAWATER CATCHES FIRE?!
STOP SHOUTING AND SWIM, FISHY!

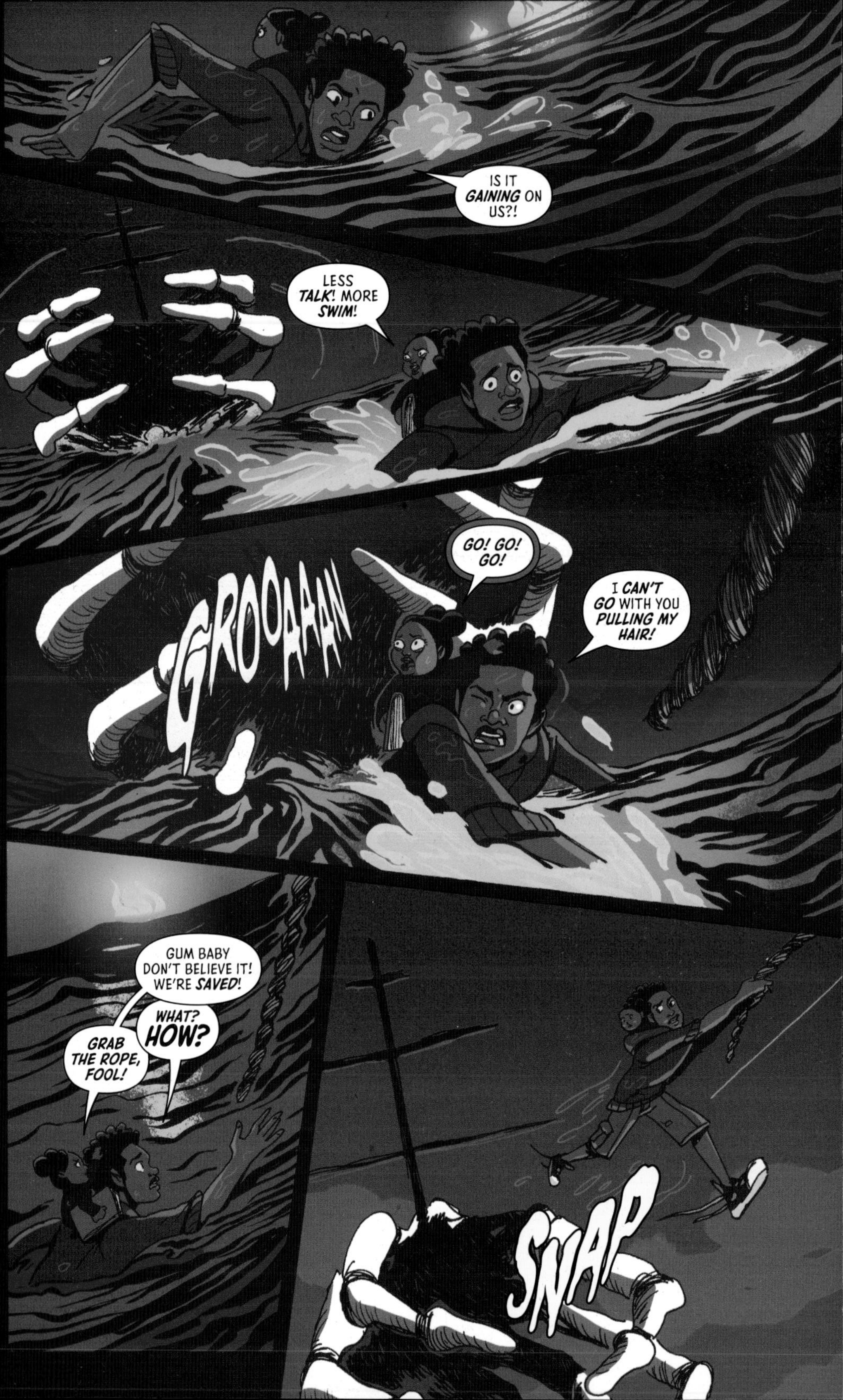

IS IT GAINING ON US?!
LESS TALK! MORE SWIM!
GO! GO! GO!
I CAN'T GO WITH YOU PULLING MY HAIR!
GROOAAAN
GUM BABY DON'T BELIEVE IT! WE'RE SAVED!
WHAT? HOW?
GRAB THE ROPE, FOOL!
SNAP

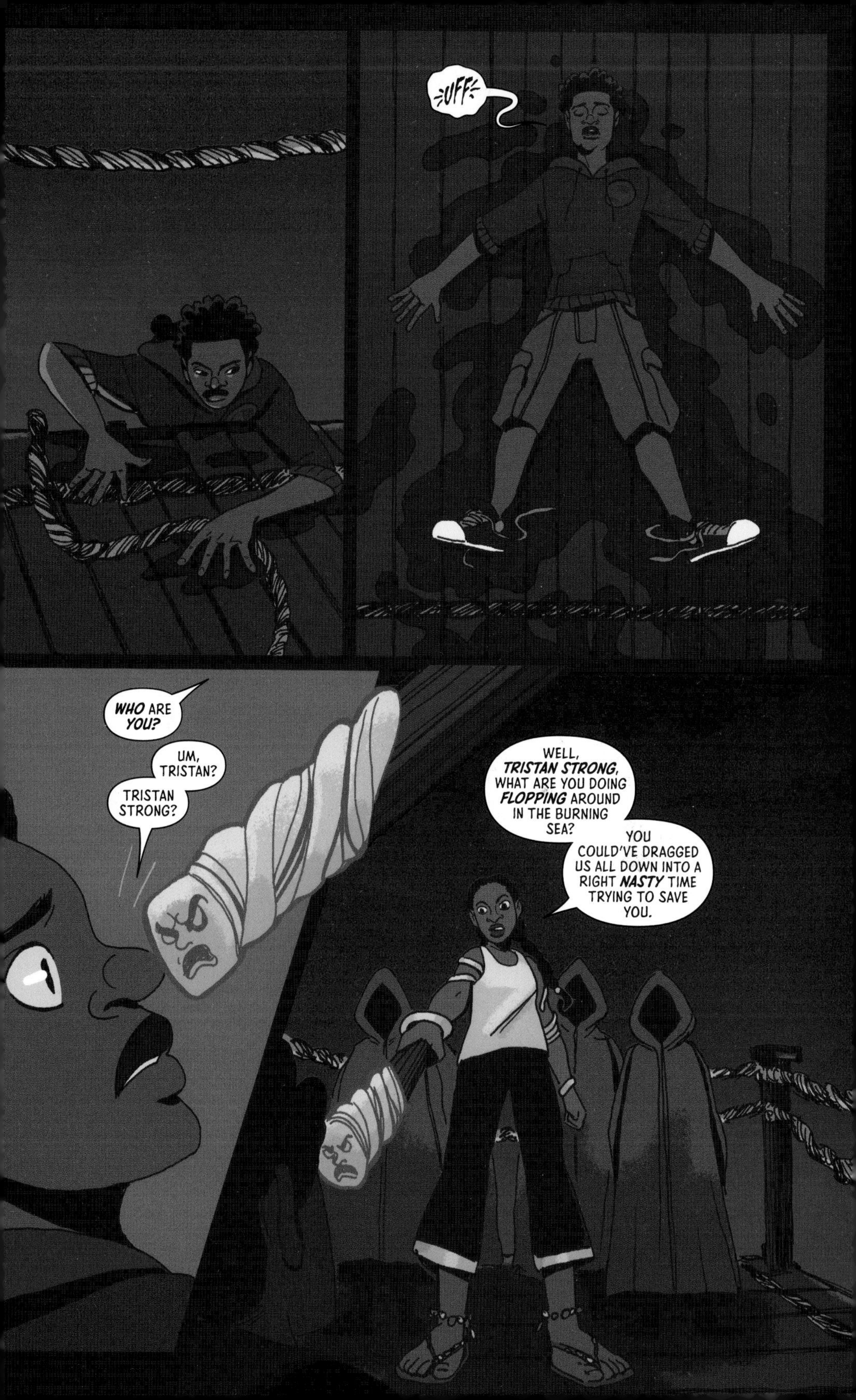

UFF
WHO ARE YOU?
UM, TRISTAN?
TRISTAN STRONG?
WELL, TRISTAN STRONG, WHAT ARE YOU DOING FLOPPING AROUND IN THE BURNING SEA?
YOU COULD'VE DRAGGED US ALL DOWN INTO A RIGHT NASTY TIME TRYING TO SAVE YOU.

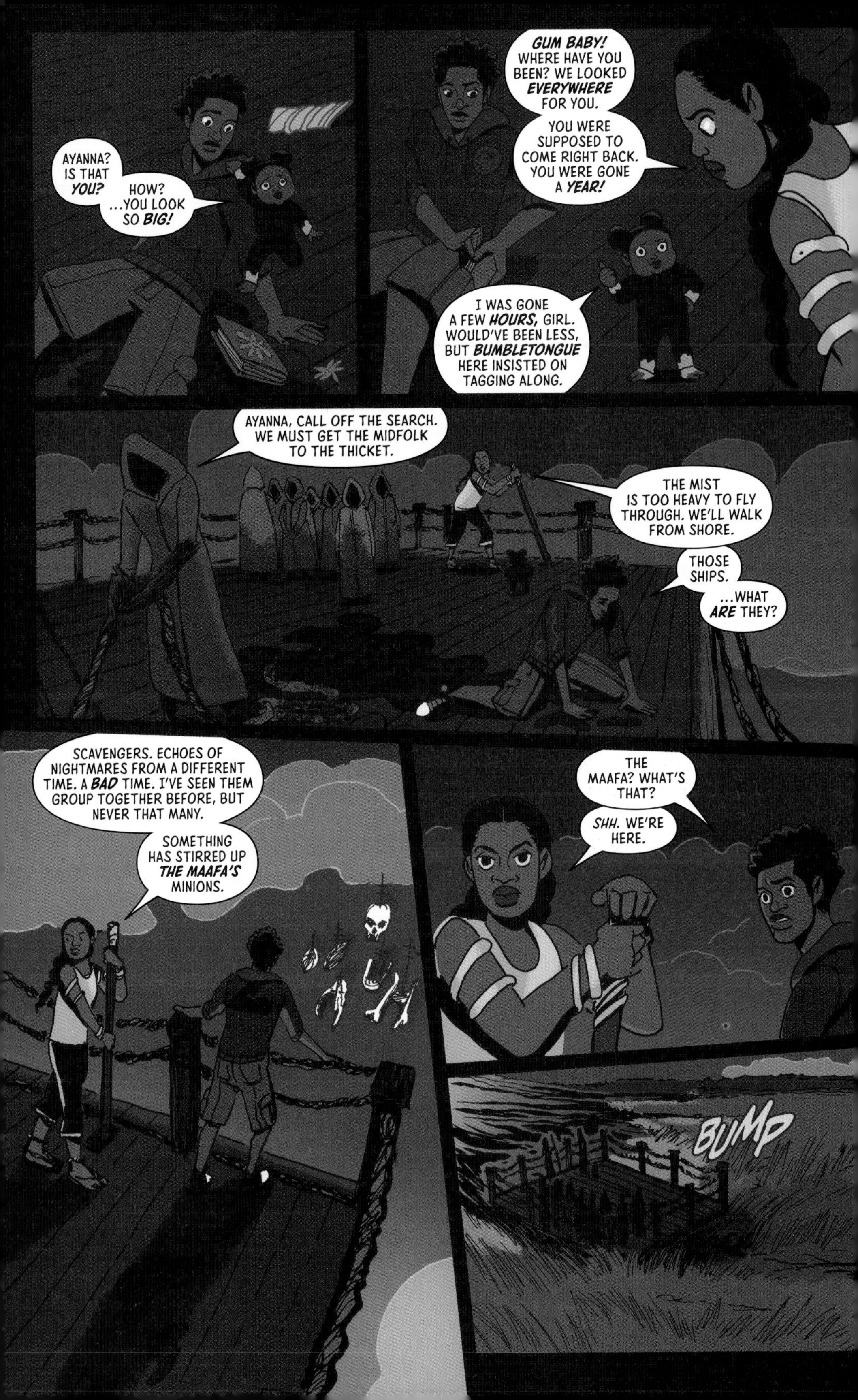
AYANNA? IS THAT YOU?
HOW? ...YOU LOOK SO BIG!
GUM BABY! WHERE HAVE YOU BEEN? WE LOOKED EVERYWHERE FOR YOU.
YOU WERE SUPPOSED TO COME RIGHT BACK. YOU WERE GONE A YEAR!
I WAS GONE A FEW HOURS, GIRL. WOULD'VE BEEN LESS, BUT BUMBLETONGUE HERE INSISTED ON TAGGING ALONG.
AYANNA, CALL OFF THE SEARCH. WE MUST GET THE MIDFOLK TO THE THICKET.
THE MIST IS TOO HEAVY TO FLY THROUGH. WE'LL WALK FROM SHORE.
THOSE SHIPS.
...WHAT ARE THEY?
SCAVENGERS. ECHOES OF NIGHTMARES FROM A DIFFERENT TIME. A BAD TIME. I'VE SEEN THEM GROUP TOGETHER BEFORE, BUT NEVER THAT MANY.
SOMETHING HAS STIRRED UP THE MAAFA'S MINIONS.
THE MAAFA? WHAT'S THAT?
SHH. WE'RE HERE.
BUMP

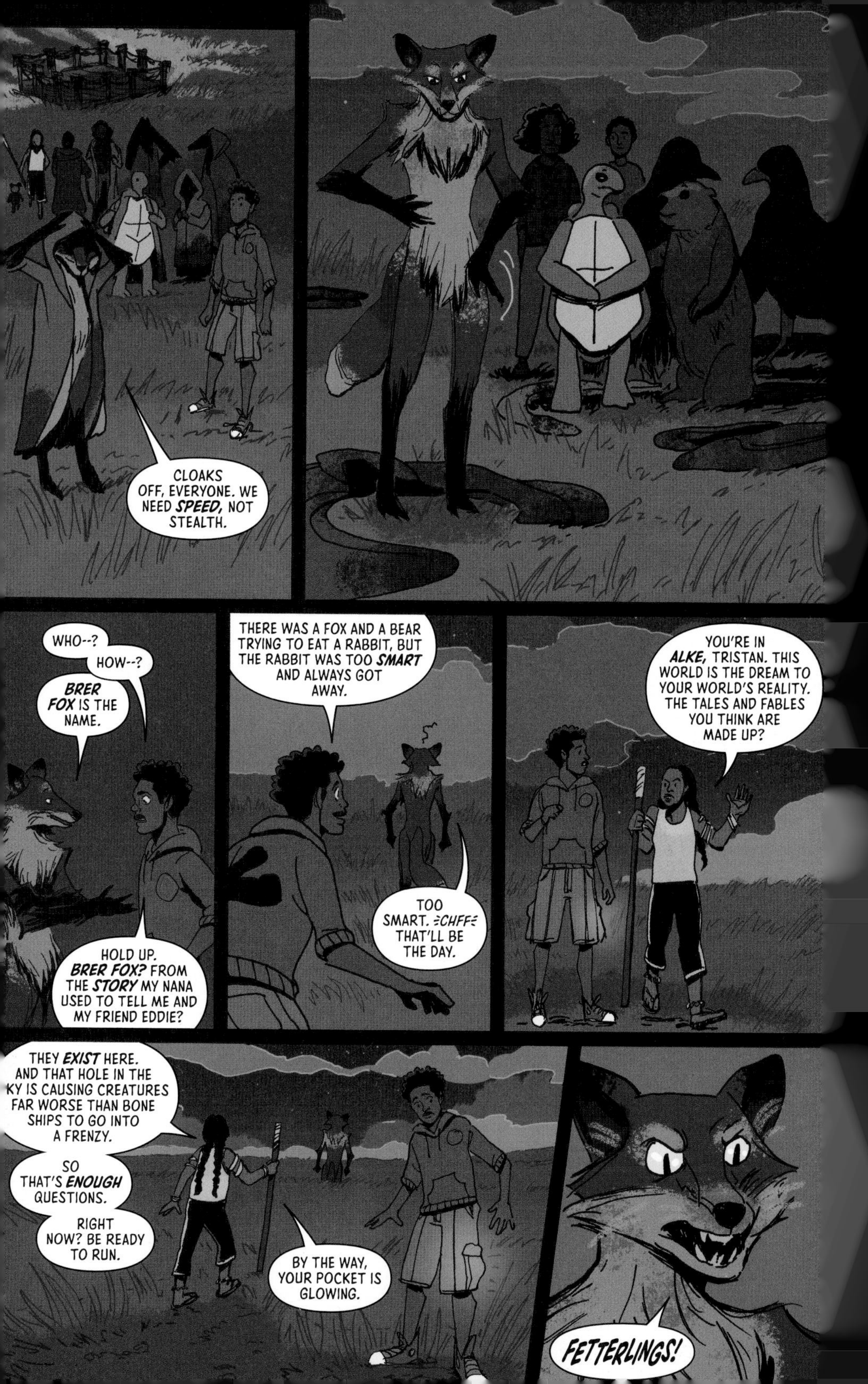
CLOAKS OFF, EVERYONE. WE NEED *SPEED,* NOT STEALTH.
WHO--?
HOW--?
BRER FOX IS THE NAME.
HOLD UP. *BRER FOX?* FROM THE *STORY* MY NANA USED TO TELL ME AND MY FRIEND EDDIE?
THERE WAS A FOX AND A BEAR TRYING TO EAT A RABBIT, BUT THE RABBIT WAS TOO *SMART* AND ALWAYS GOT AWAY.
TOO SMART. *=CHFF=* THAT'LL BE THE DAY.
YOU'RE IN *ALKE,* TRISTAN. THIS WORLD IS THE DREAM TO YOUR WORLD'S REALITY. THE TALES AND FABLES YOU THINK ARE MADE UP?
THEY *EXIST* HERE. AND THAT HOLE IN THE KY IS CAUSING CREATURES FAR WORSE THAN BONE SHIPS TO GO INTO A FRENZY.
SO THAT'S *ENOUGH* QUESTIONS.
RIGHT NOW? BE READY TO RUN.
BY THE WAY, YOUR POCKET IS GLOWING.
FETTERLINGS!

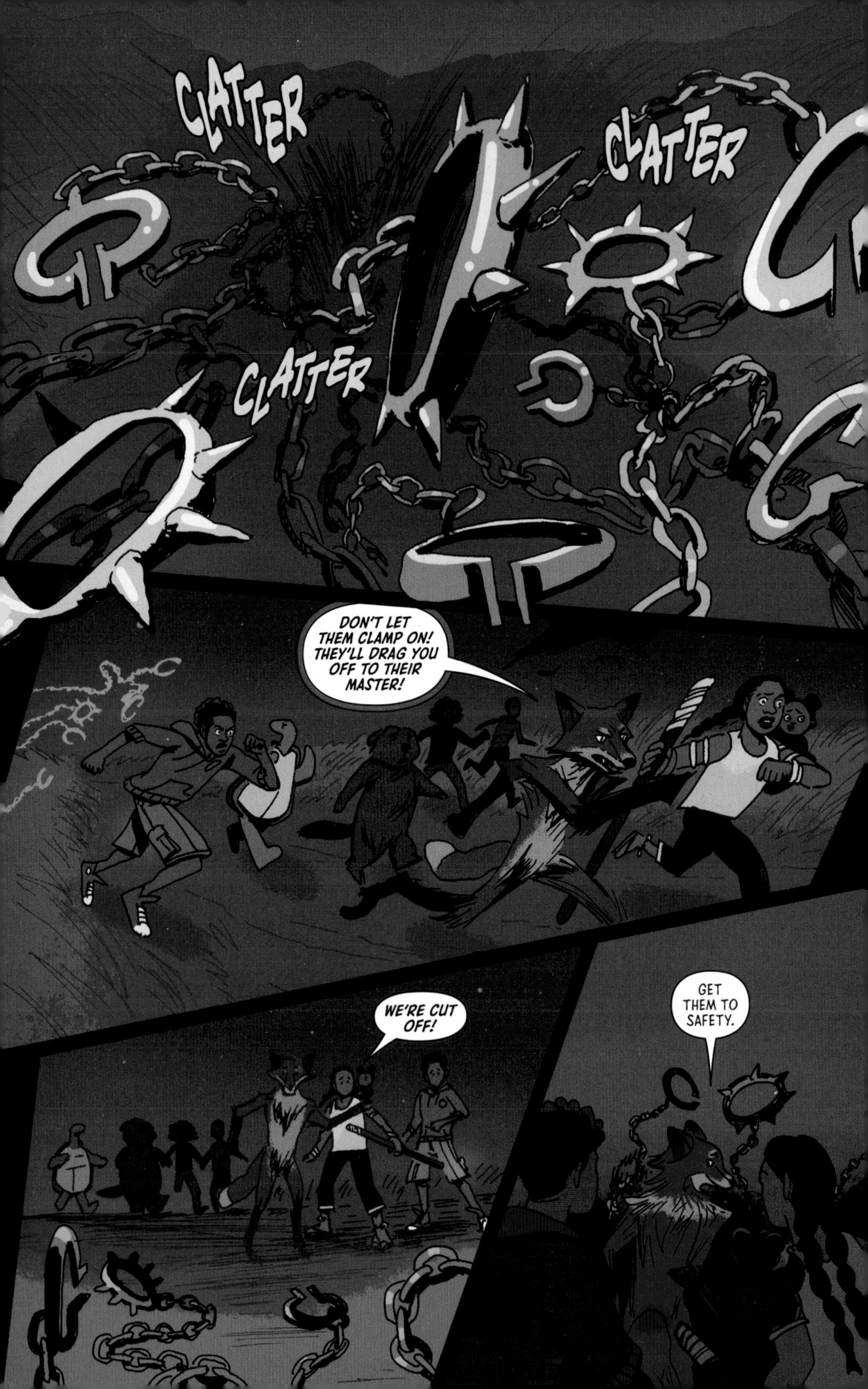
CLATTER
CLATTER
CLATTER
DON'T LET THEM CLAMP ON! THEY'LL DRAG YOU OFF TO THEIR MASTER!
WE'RE CUT OFF!
GET THEM TO SAFETY.

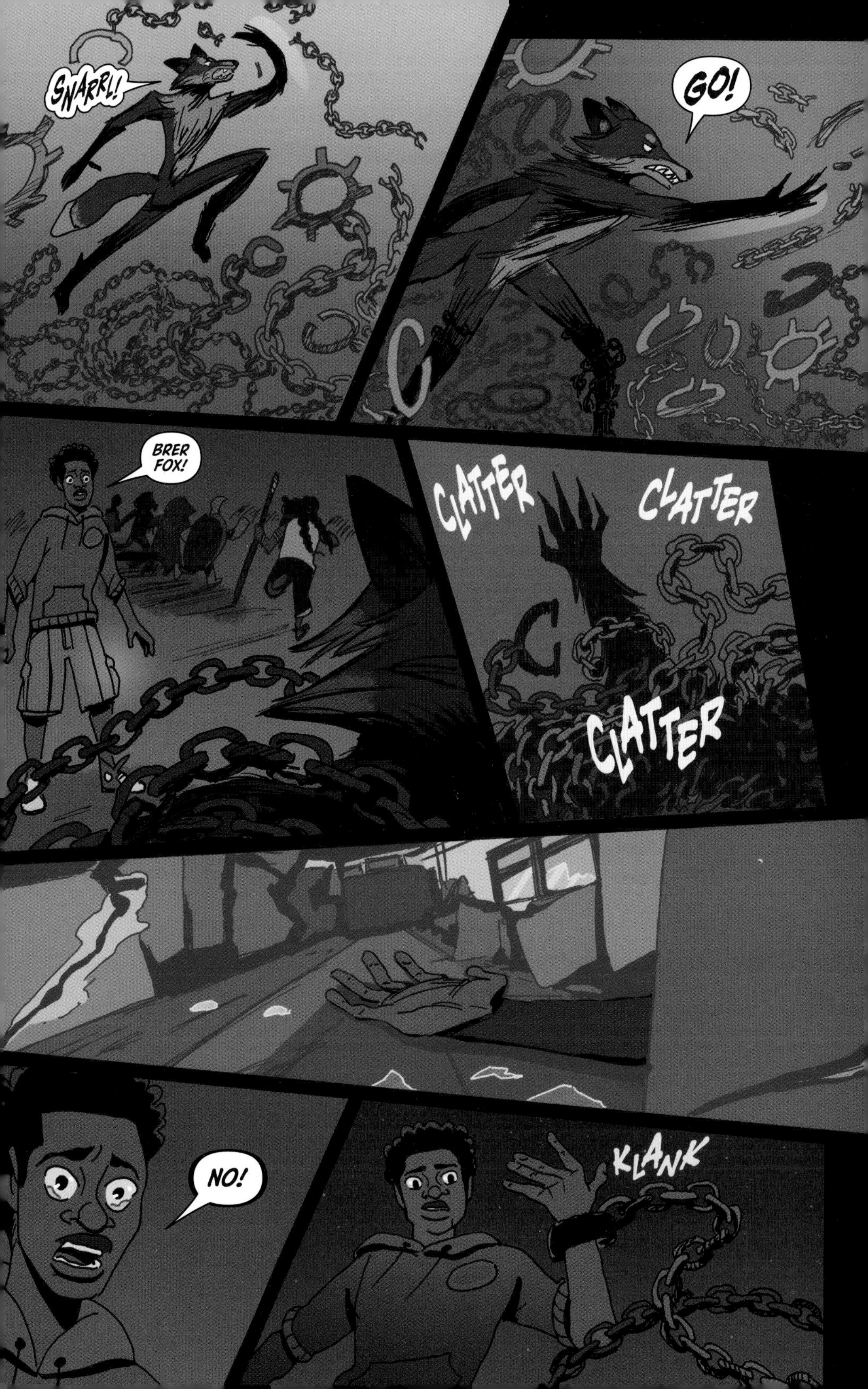
SNARRL!
GO!
BRER FOX!
CLATTER
CLATTER
CLATTER
NO!
KLANK

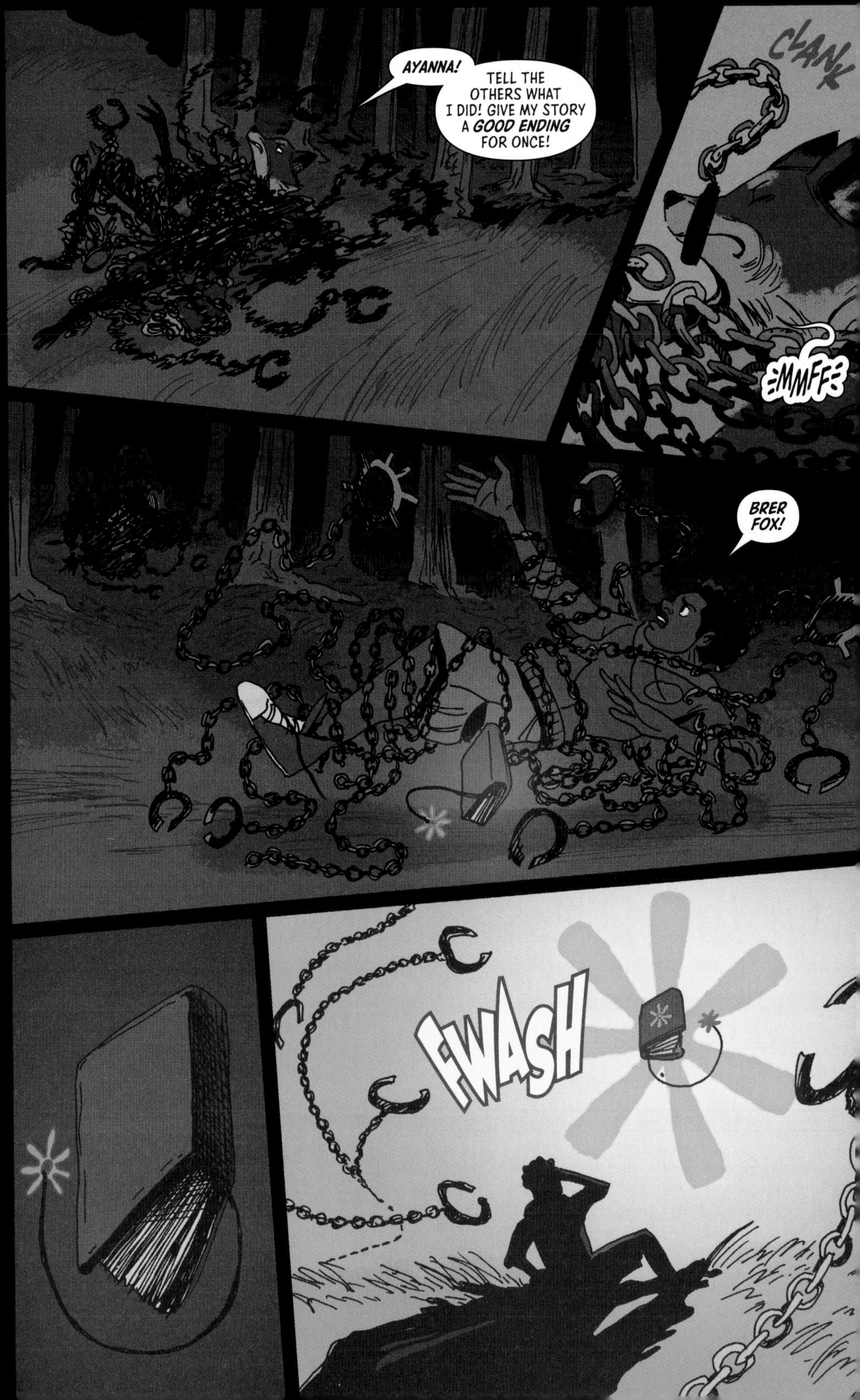
AYANNA!
TELL THE OTHERS WHAT I DID! GIVE MY STORY A **GOOD ENDING** FOR ONCE!
CLANK
MMFF
BRER FOX!
FWASH

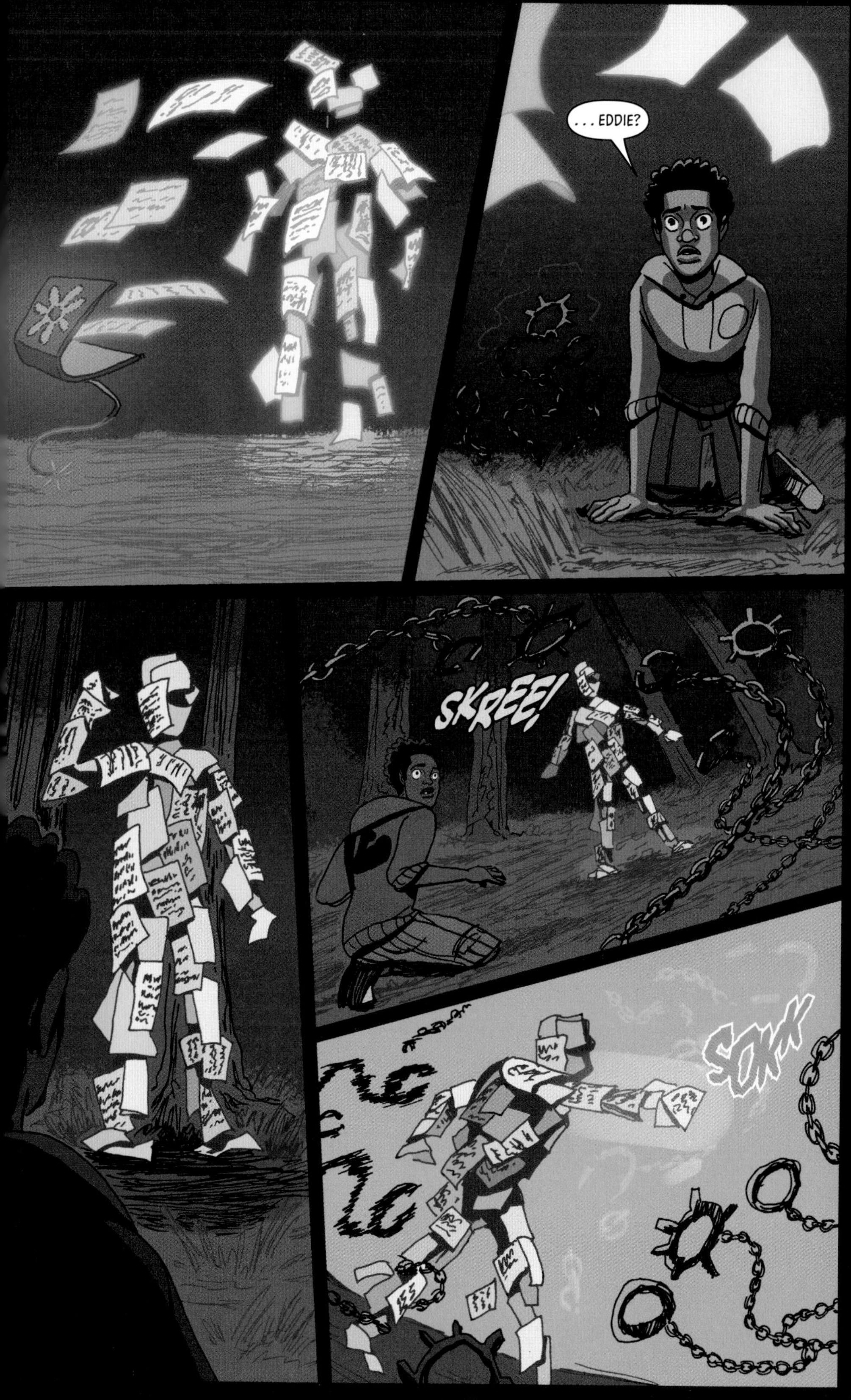
. . . EDDIE?
SKREE!
SOKK

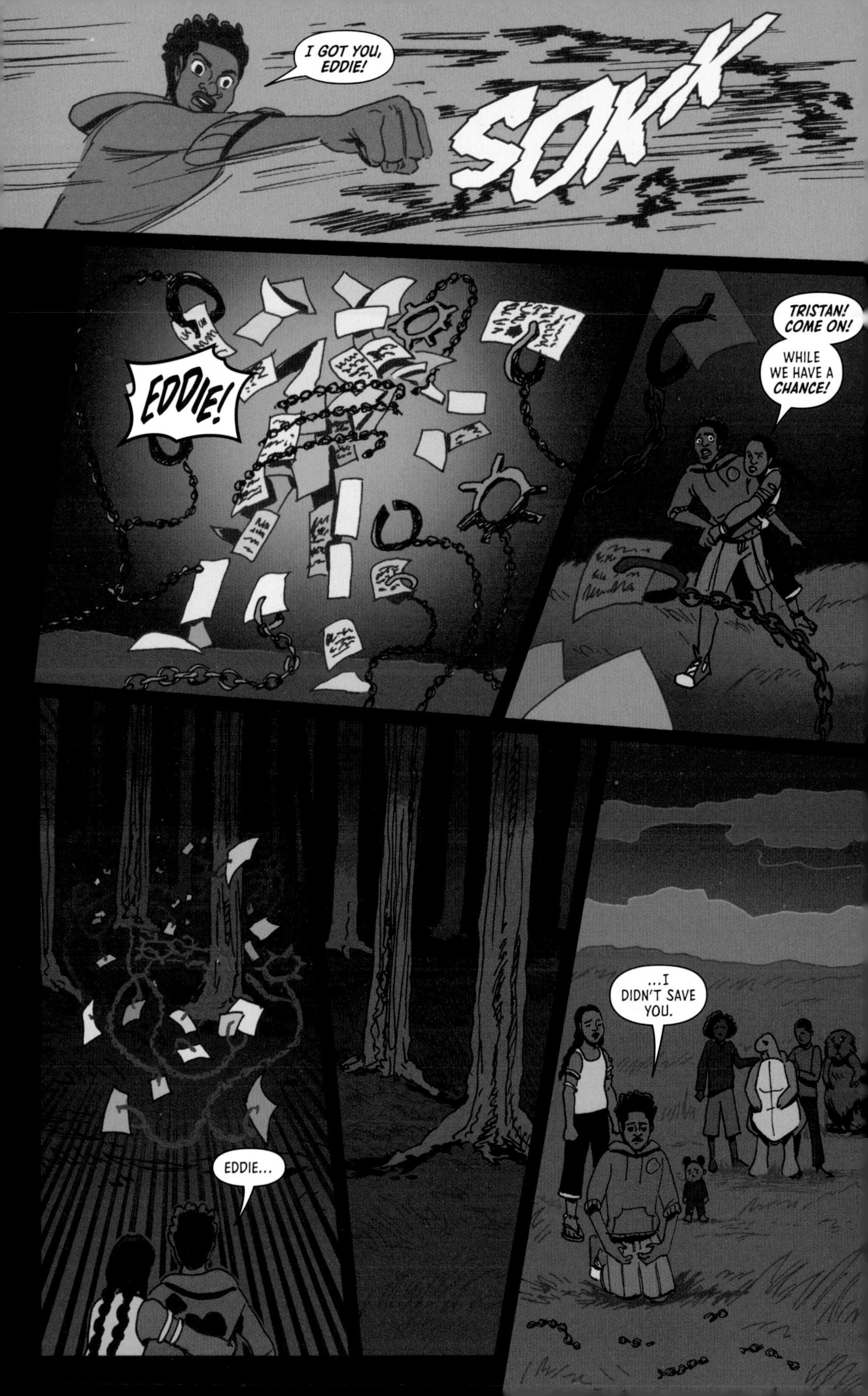
I GOT YOU, EDDIE!
SOKK
EDDIE!
TRISTAN! COME ON!
WHILE WE HAVE A CHANCE!
EDDIE...
...I DIDN'T SAVE YOU.

CHAPTER 2

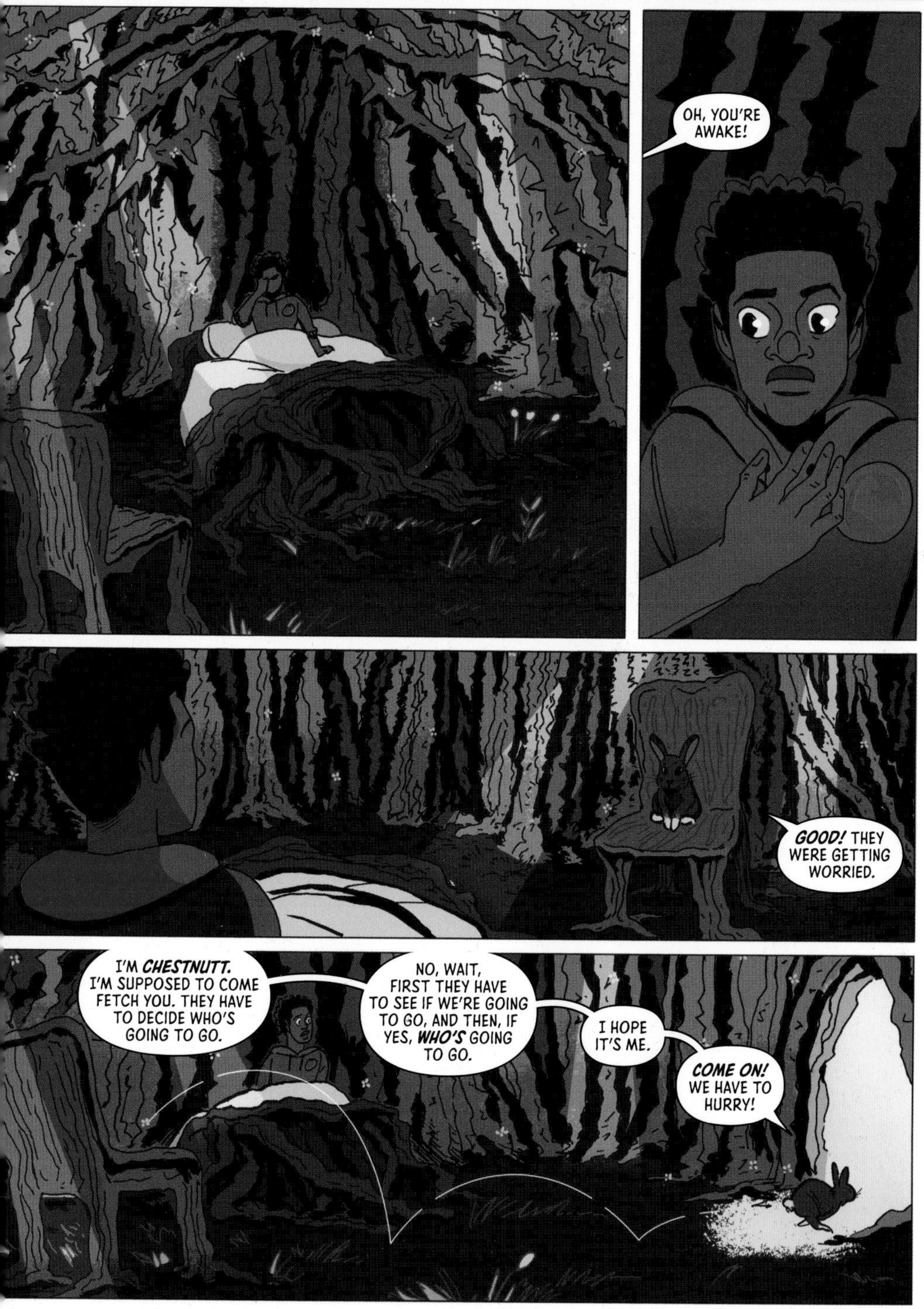
THANKS FOR THE BOOK, BOY.
OH, YOU'RE AWAKE!
GOOD! THEY WERE GETTING WORRIED.
I'M CHESTNUTT. I'M SUPPOSED TO COME FETCH YOU. THEY HAVE TO DECIDE WHO'S GOING TO GO.
NO, WAIT, FIRST THEY HAVE TO SEE IF WE'RE GOING TO GO, AND THEN, IF YES, WHO'S GOING TO GO.
I HOPE IT'S ME.
COME ON! WE HAVE TO HURRY!

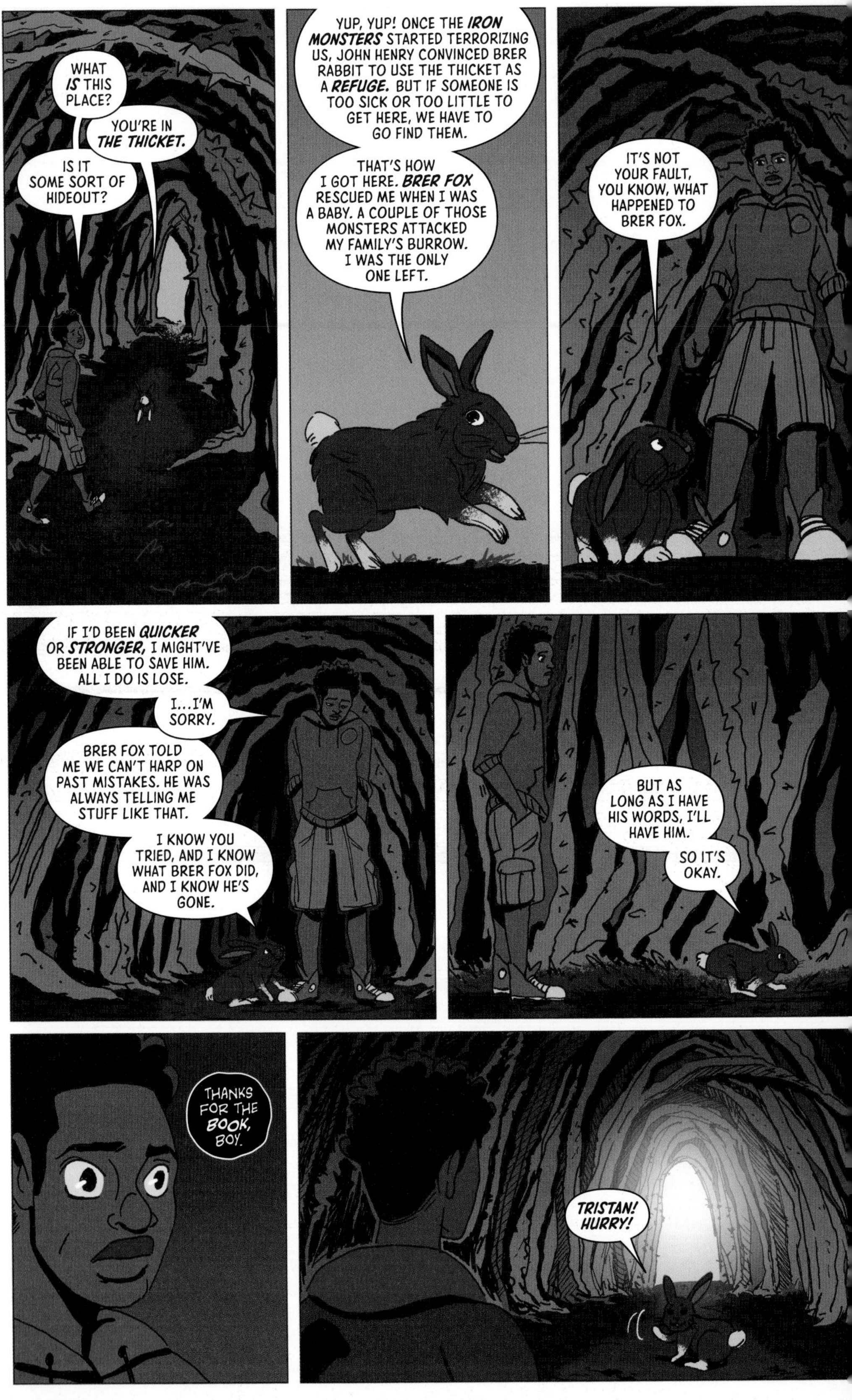
WHAT *IS* THIS PLACE?
YOU'RE IN *THE THICKET.*
IS IT SOME SORT OF HIDEOUT?
YUP, YUP! ONCE THE *IRON MONSTERS* STARTED TERRORIZING US, JOHN HENRY CONVINCED BRER RABBIT TO USE THE THICKET AS A *REFUGE.* BUT IF SOMEONE IS TOO SICK OR TOO LITTLE TO GET HERE, WE HAVE TO GO FIND THEM.
THAT'S HOW I GOT HERE. *BRER FOX* RESCUED ME WHEN I WAS A BABY. A COUPLE OF THOSE MONSTERS ATTACKED MY FAMILY'S BURROW. I WAS THE ONLY ONE LEFT.
IT'S NOT YOUR FAULT, YOU KNOW, WHAT HAPPENED TO BRER FOX.
IF I'D BEEN *QUICKER* OR *STRONGER,* I MIGHT'VE BEEN ABLE TO SAVE HIM. ALL I DO IS LOSE.
I...I'M SORRY.
BRER FOX TOLD ME WE CAN'T HARP ON PAST MISTAKES. HE WAS ALWAYS TELLING ME STUFF LIKE THAT.
I KNOW YOU TRIED, AND I KNOW WHAT BRER FOX DID, AND I KNOW HE'S GONE.
BUT AS LONG AS I HAVE HIS WORDS, I'LL HAVE HIM.
SO IT'S OKAY.
THANKS FOR THE *BOOK,* BOY.
TRISTAN! HURRY!

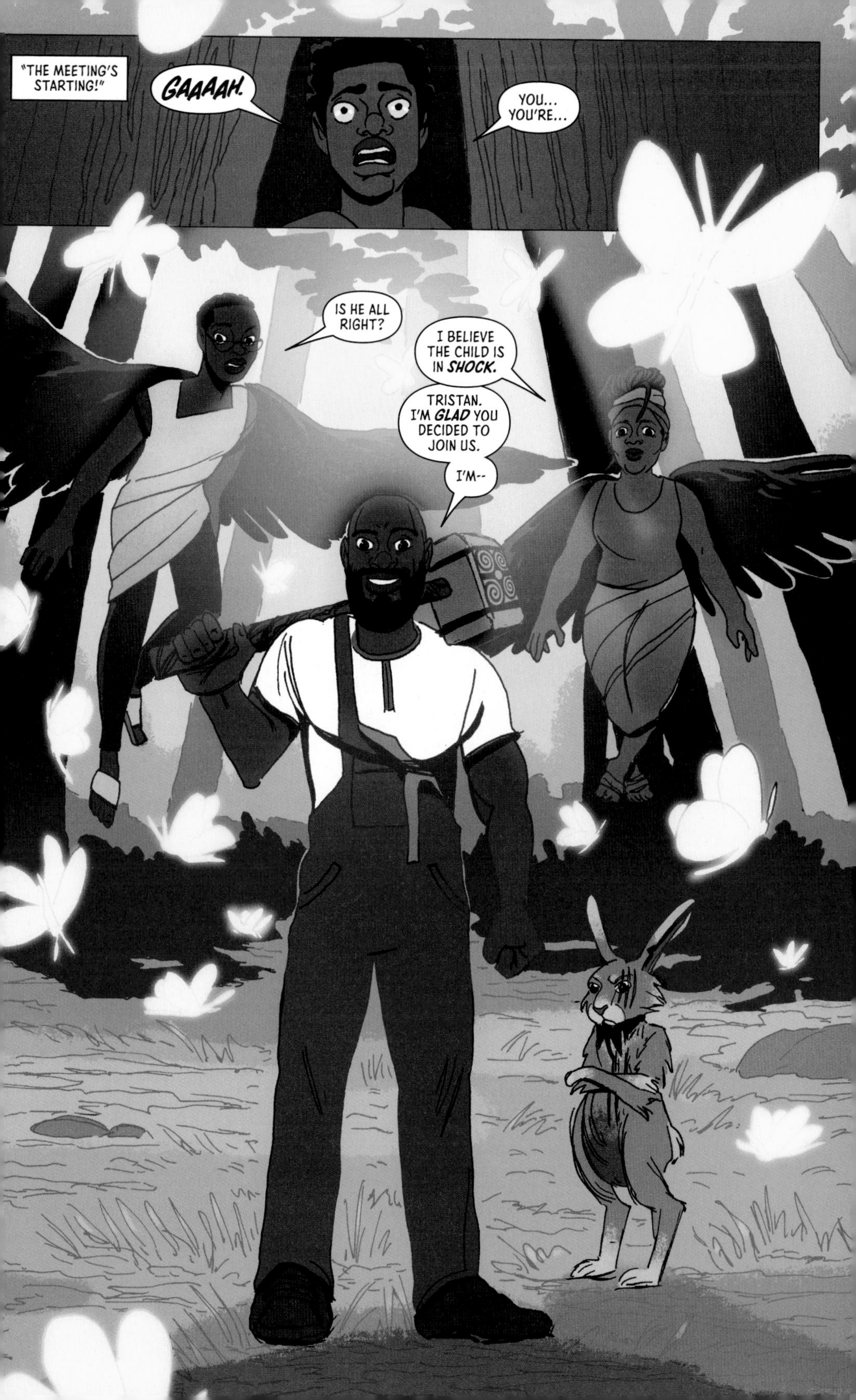
"THE MEETING'S STARTING!"
GAAAAH.
YOU... YOU'RE...
IS HE ALL RIGHT?
I BELIEVE THE CHILD IS IN SHOCK.
TRISTAN. I'M GLAD YOU DECIDED TO JOIN US.
I'M--

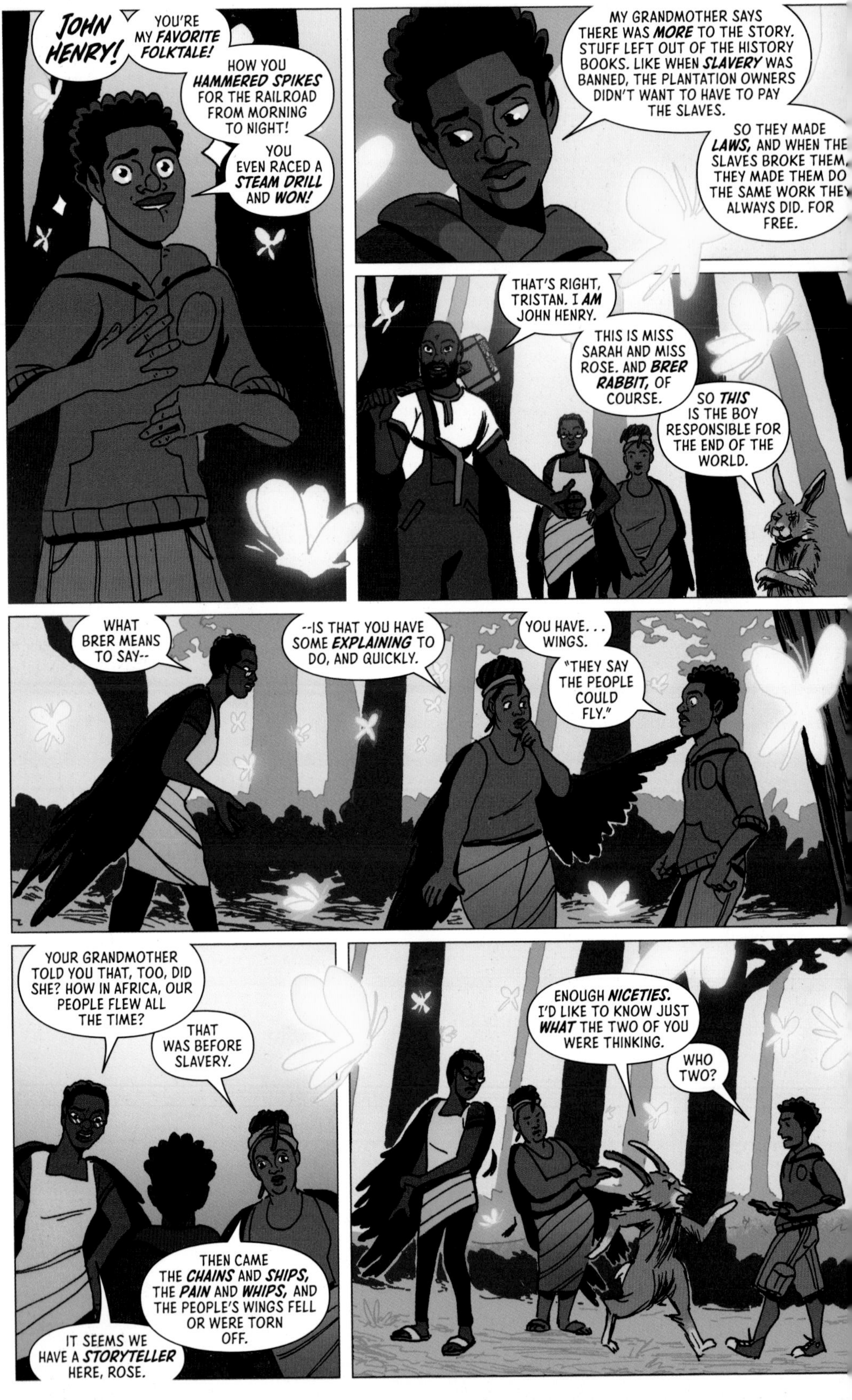
JOHN HENRY!
YOU'RE MY FAVORITE FOLKTALE!
HOW YOU HAMMERED SPIKES FOR THE RAILROAD FROM MORNING TO NIGHT!
YOU EVEN RACED A STEAM DRILL AND WON!
MY GRANDMOTHER SAYS THERE WAS MORE TO THE STORY. STUFF LEFT OUT OF THE HISTORY BOOKS. LIKE WHEN SLAVERY WAS BANNED, THE PLANTATION OWNERS DIDN'T WANT TO HAVE TO PAY THE SLAVES.
SO THEY MADE LAWS, AND WHEN THE SLAVES BROKE THEM, THEY MADE THEM DO THE SAME WORK THEY ALWAYS DID. FOR FREE.
THAT'S RIGHT, TRISTAN. I AM JOHN HENRY.
THIS IS MISS SARAH AND MISS ROSE. AND BRER RABBIT, OF COURSE.
SO THIS IS THE BOY RESPONSIBLE FOR THE END OF THE WORLD.
WHAT BRER MEANS TO SAY--
--IS THAT YOU HAVE SOME EXPLAINING TO DO, AND QUICKLY.
YOU HAVE. . . WINGS.
"THEY SAY THE PEOPLE COULD FLY."
YOUR GRANDMOTHER TOLD YOU THAT, TOO, DID SHE? HOW IN AFRICA, OUR PEOPLE FLEW ALL THE TIME?
THAT WAS BEFORE SLAVERY.
THEN CAME THE CHAINS AND SHIPS, THE PAIN AND WHIPS, AND THE PEOPLE'S WINGS FELL OR WERE TORN OFF.
IT SEEMS WE HAVE A STORYTELLER HERE, ROSE.
ENOUGH NICETIES. I'D LIKE TO KNOW JUST WHAT THE TWO OF YOU WERE THINKING.
WHO TWO?

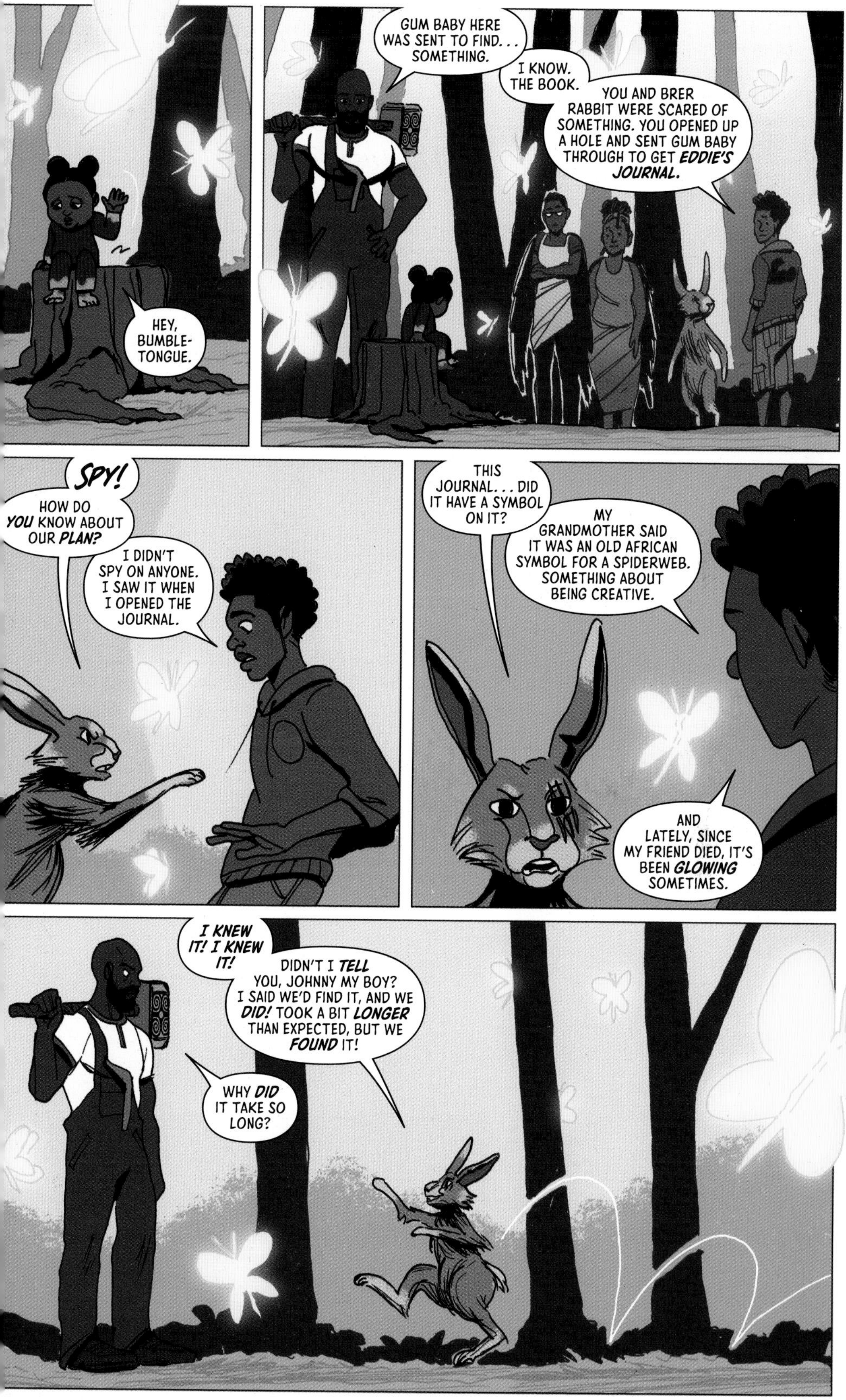
HEY, BUMBLE-TONGUE.
GUM BABY HERE WAS SENT TO FIND. . . SOMETHING.
I KNOW. THE BOOK.
YOU AND BRER RABBIT WERE SCARED OF SOMETHING. YOU OPENED UP A HOLE AND SENT GUM BABY THROUGH TO GET EDDIE'S JOURNAL.
SPY!
HOW DO YOU KNOW ABOUT OUR PLAN?
I DIDN'T SPY ON ANYONE. I SAW IT WHEN I OPENED THE JOURNAL.
THIS JOURNAL. . . DID IT HAVE A SYMBOL ON IT?
MY GRANDMOTHER SAID IT WAS AN OLD AFRICAN SYMBOL FOR A SPIDERWEB. SOMETHING ABOUT BEING CREATIVE.
AND LATELY, SINCE MY FRIEND DIED, IT'S BEEN GLOWING SOMETIMES.
I KNEW IT! I KNEW IT!
DIDN'T I TELL YOU, JOHNNY MY BOY? I SAID WE'D FIND IT, AND WE DID! TOOK A BIT LONGER THAN EXPECTED, BUT WE FOUND IT!
WHY DID IT TAKE SO LONG?

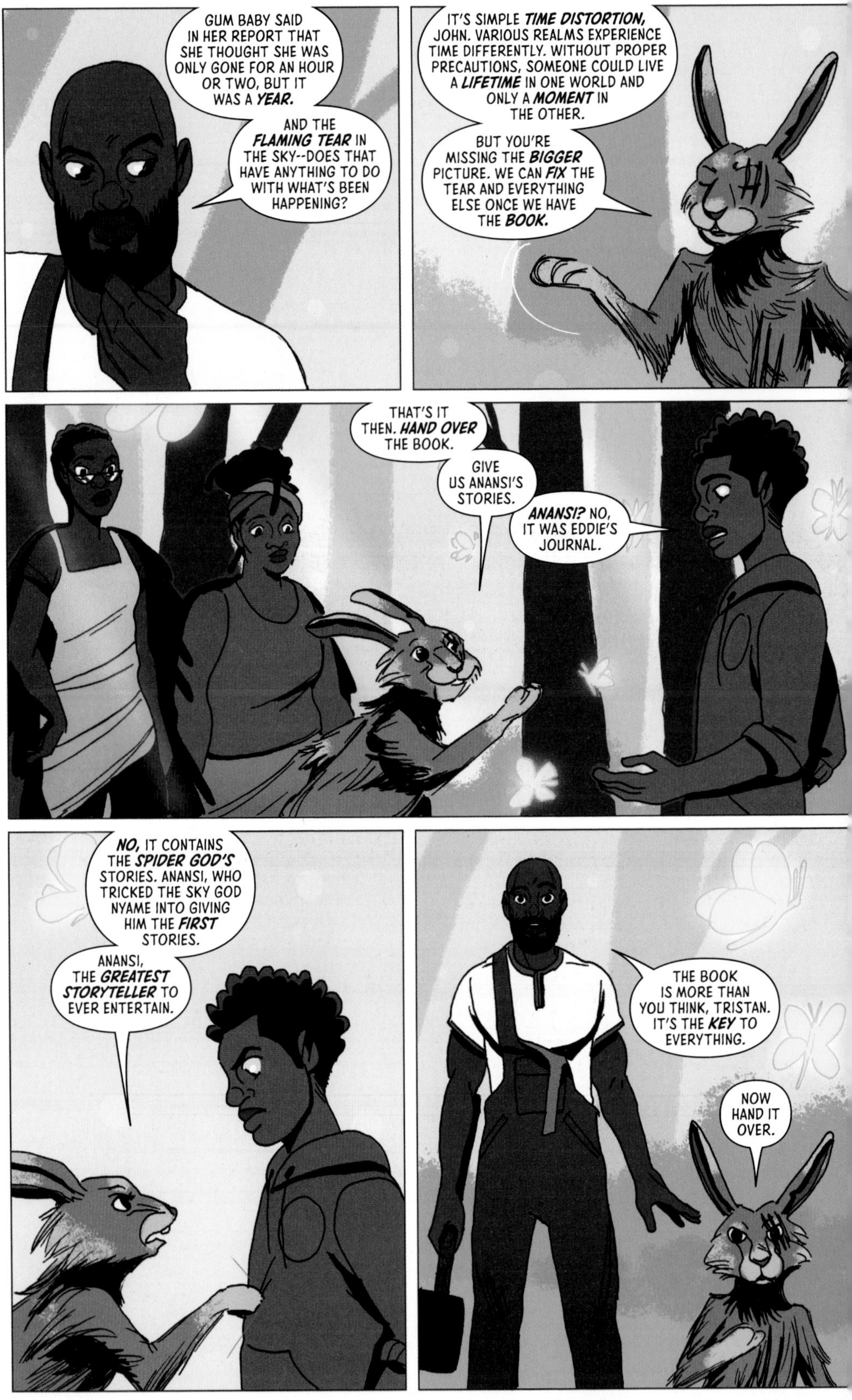
GUM BABY SAID IN HER REPORT THAT SHE THOUGHT SHE WAS ONLY GONE FOR AN HOUR OR TWO, BUT IT WAS A YEAR.
AND THE FLAMING TEAR IN THE SKY--DOES THAT HAVE ANYTHING TO DO WITH WHAT'S BEEN HAPPENING?
IT'S SIMPLE TIME DISTORTION, JOHN. VARIOUS REALMS EXPERIENCE TIME DIFFERENTLY. WITHOUT PROPER PRECAUTIONS, SOMEONE COULD LIVE A LIFETIME IN ONE WORLD AND ONLY A MOMENT IN THE OTHER.
BUT YOU'RE MISSING THE BIGGER PICTURE. WE CAN FIX THE TEAR AND EVERYTHING ELSE ONCE WE HAVE THE BOOK.
THAT'S IT THEN. HAND OVER THE BOOK.
GIVE US ANANSI'S STORIES.
ANANSI? NO, IT WAS EDDIE'S JOURNAL.
NO, IT CONTAINS THE SPIDER GOD'S STORIES. ANANSI, WHO TRICKED THE SKY GOD NYAME INTO GIVING HIM THE FIRST STORIES.
ANANSI, THE GREATEST STORYTELLER TO EVER ENTERTAIN.
THE BOOK IS MORE THAN YOU THINK, TRISTAN. IT'S THE KEY TO EVERYTHING.
NOW HAND IT OVER.

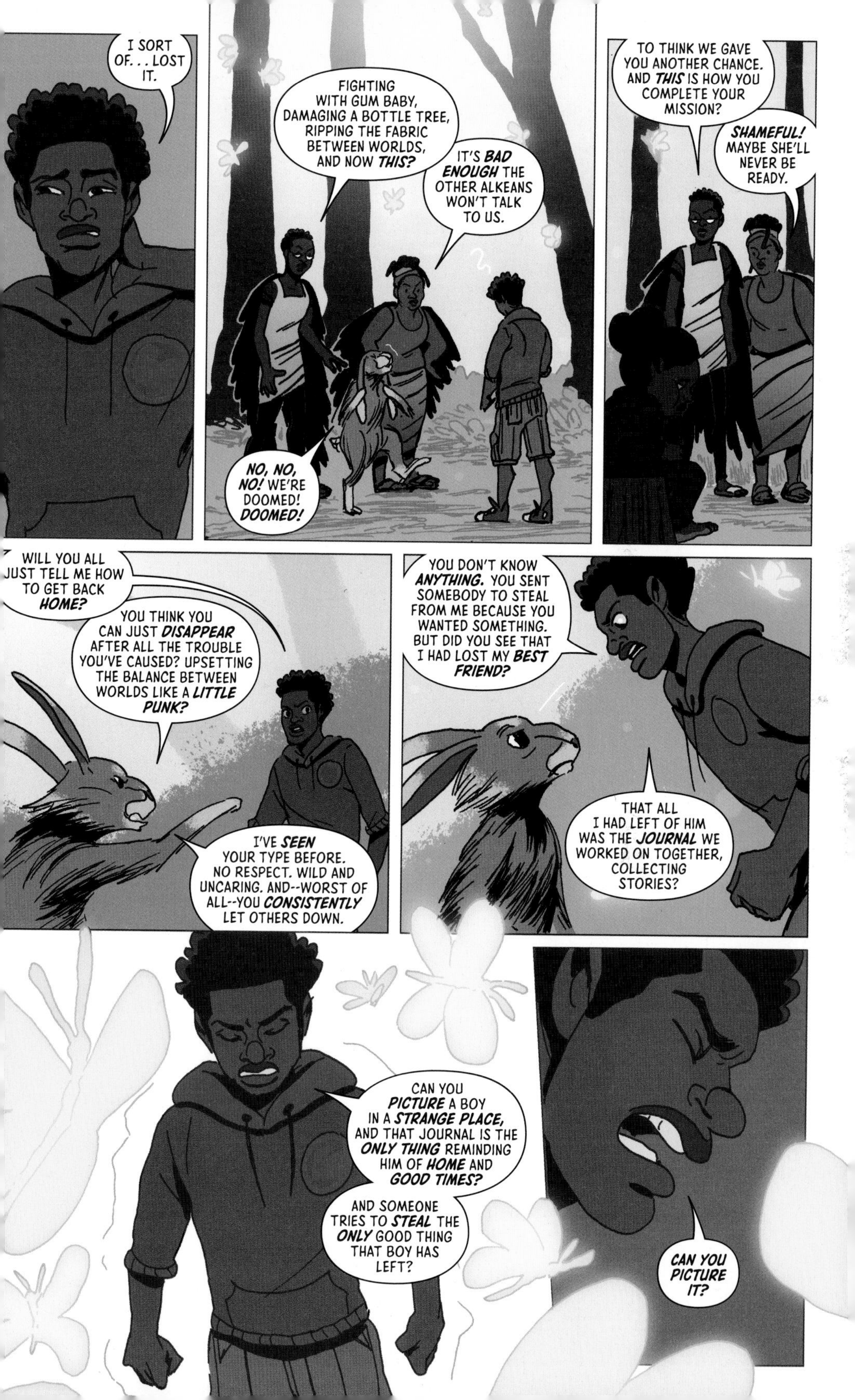
I SORT OF. . . LOST IT.
FIGHTING WITH GUM BABY, DAMAGING A BOTTLE TREE, RIPPING THE FABRIC BETWEEN WORLDS, AND NOW THIS?
IT'S BAD ENOUGH THE OTHER ALKEANS WON'T TALK TO US.
NO, NO, NO! WE'RE DOOMED! DOOMED!
TO THINK WE GAVE YOU ANOTHER CHANCE. AND THIS IS HOW YOU COMPLETE YOUR MISSION?
SHAMEFUL! MAYBE SHE'LL NEVER BE READY.
WILL YOU ALL JUST TELL ME HOW TO GET BACK HOME?
YOU THINK YOU CAN JUST DISAPPEAR AFTER ALL THE TROUBLE YOU'VE CAUSED? UPSETTING THE BALANCE BETWEEN WORLDS LIKE A LITTLE PUNK?
I'VE SEEN YOUR TYPE BEFORE. NO RESPECT. WILD AND UNCARING. AND--WORST OF ALL--YOU CONSISTENTLY LET OTHERS DOWN.
YOU DON'T KNOW ANYTHING. YOU SENT SOMEBODY TO STEAL FROM ME BECAUSE YOU WANTED SOMETHING. BUT DID YOU SEE THAT I HAD LOST MY BEST FRIEND?
THAT ALL I HAD LEFT OF HIM WAS THE JOURNAL WE WORKED ON TOGETHER, COLLECTING STORIES?
CAN YOU PICTURE A BOY IN A STRANGE PLACE, AND THAT JOURNAL IS THE ONLY THING REMINDING HIM OF HOME AND GOOD TIMES?
AND SOMEONE TRIES TO STEAL THE ONLY GOOD THING THAT BOY HAS LEFT?
CAN YOU PICTURE IT?

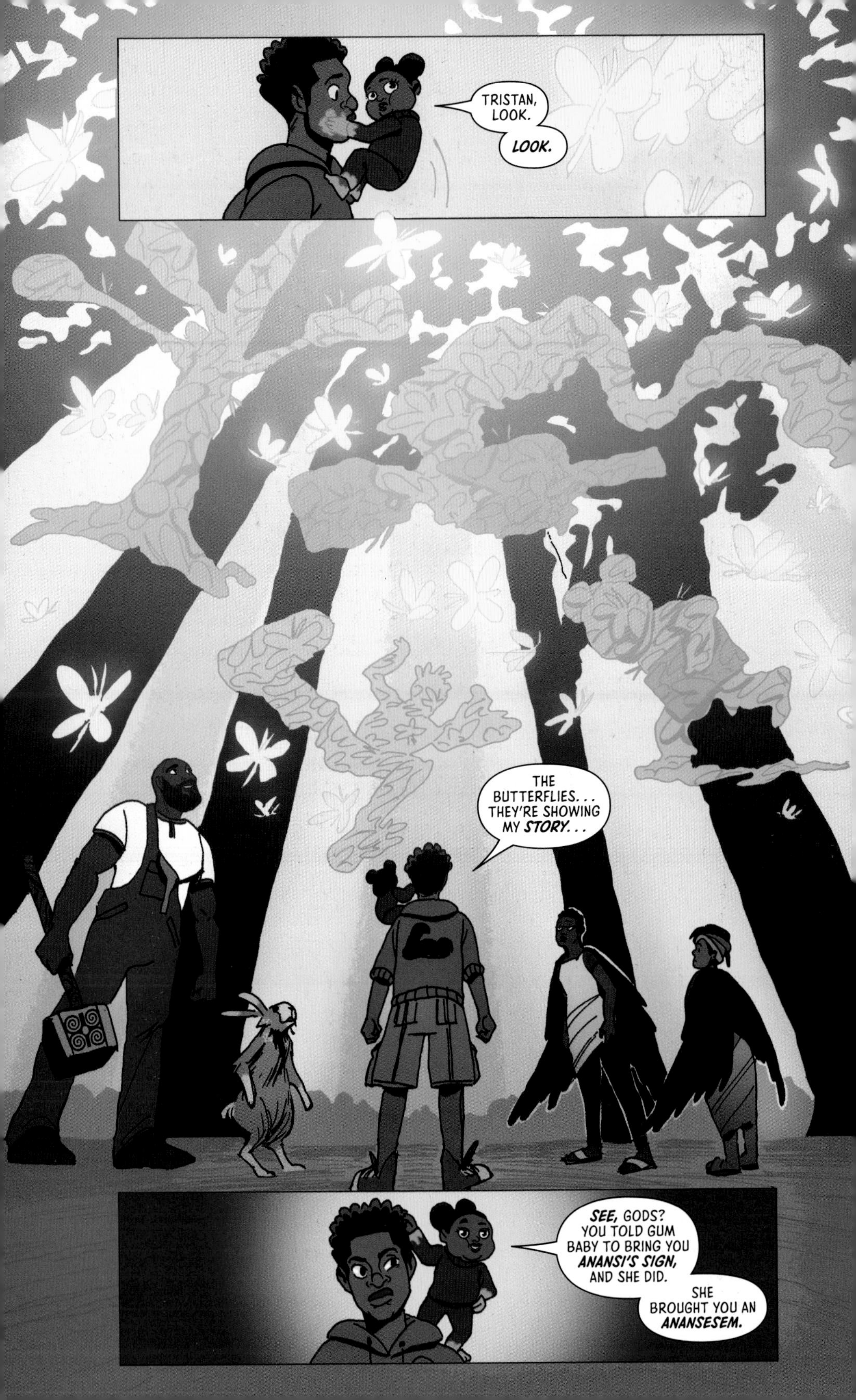
TRISTAN, LOOK.
LOOK.
THE BUTTERFLIES... THEY'RE SHOWING MY STORY...
SEE, GODS? YOU TOLD GUM BABY TO BRING YOU ANANSI'S SIGN, AND SHE DID.
SHE BROUGHT YOU AN ANANSESEM.

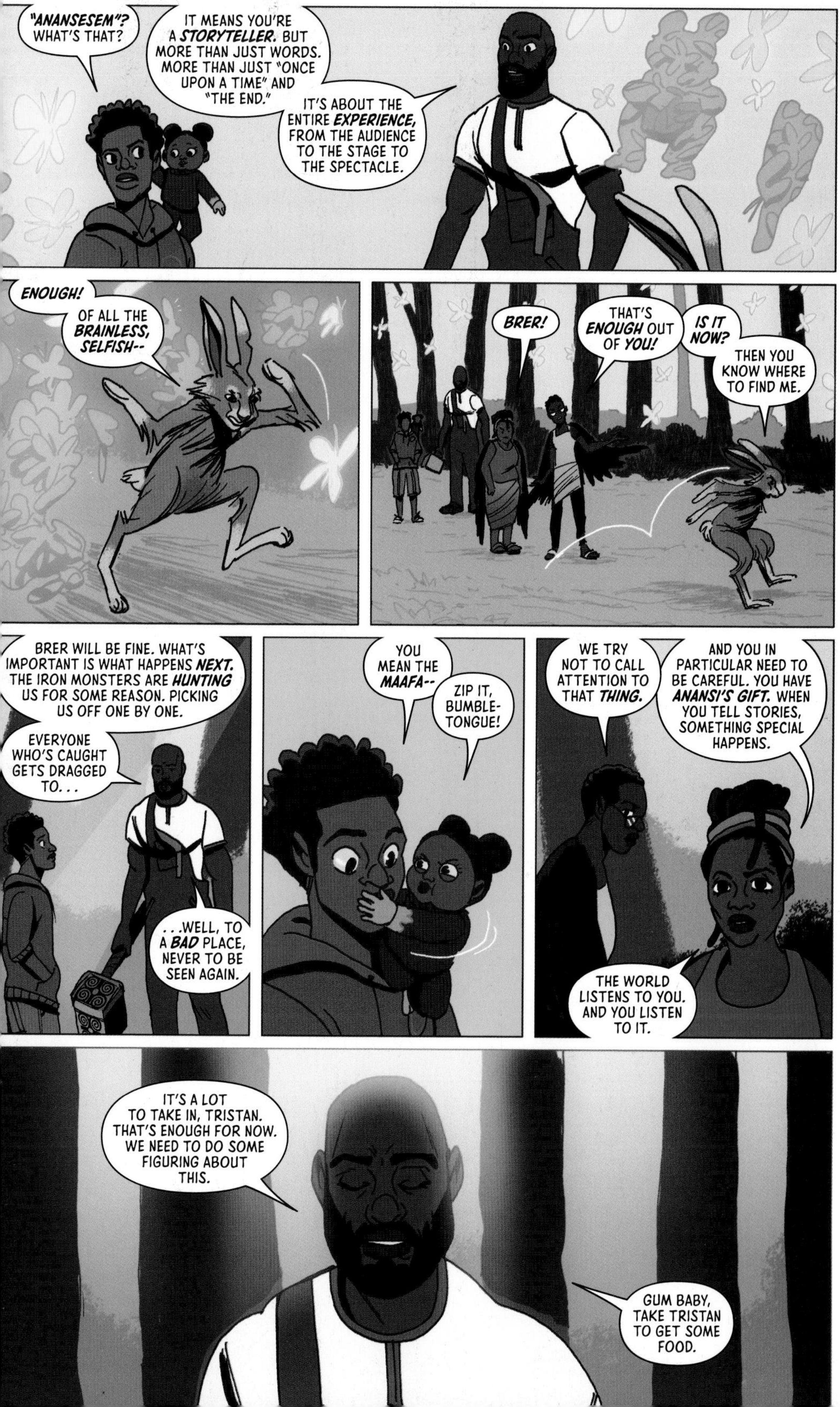
"ANANSESEM"? WHAT'S THAT?
IT MEANS YOU'RE A STORYTELLER. BUT MORE THAN JUST WORDS. MORE THAN JUST "ONCE UPON A TIME" AND "THE END."
IT'S ABOUT THE ENTIRE EXPERIENCE, FROM THE AUDIENCE TO THE STAGE TO THE SPECTACLE.
ENOUGH!
OF ALL THE BRAINLESS, SELFISH--
BRER!
THAT'S ENOUGH OUT OF YOU!
IS IT NOW?
THEN YOU KNOW WHERE TO FIND ME.
BRER WILL BE FINE. WHAT'S IMPORTANT IS WHAT HAPPENS NEXT. THE IRON MONSTERS ARE HUNTING US FOR SOME REASON. PICKING US OFF ONE BY ONE.
EVERYONE WHO'S CAUGHT GETS DRAGGED TO. . .
. . .WELL, TO A BAD PLACE, NEVER TO BE SEEN AGAIN.
YOU MEAN THE MAAFA--
ZIP IT, BUMBLE-TONGUE!
WE TRY NOT TO CALL ATTENTION TO THAT THING.
AND YOU IN PARTICULAR NEED TO BE CAREFUL. YOU HAVE ANANSI'S GIFT. WHEN YOU TELL STORIES, SOMETHING SPECIAL HAPPENS.
THE WORLD LISTENS TO YOU. AND YOU LISTEN TO IT.
IT'S A LOT TO TAKE IN, TRISTAN. THAT'S ENOUGH FOR NOW. WE NEED TO DO SOME FIGURING ABOUT THIS.
GUM BABY, TAKE TRISTAN TO GET SOME FOOD.

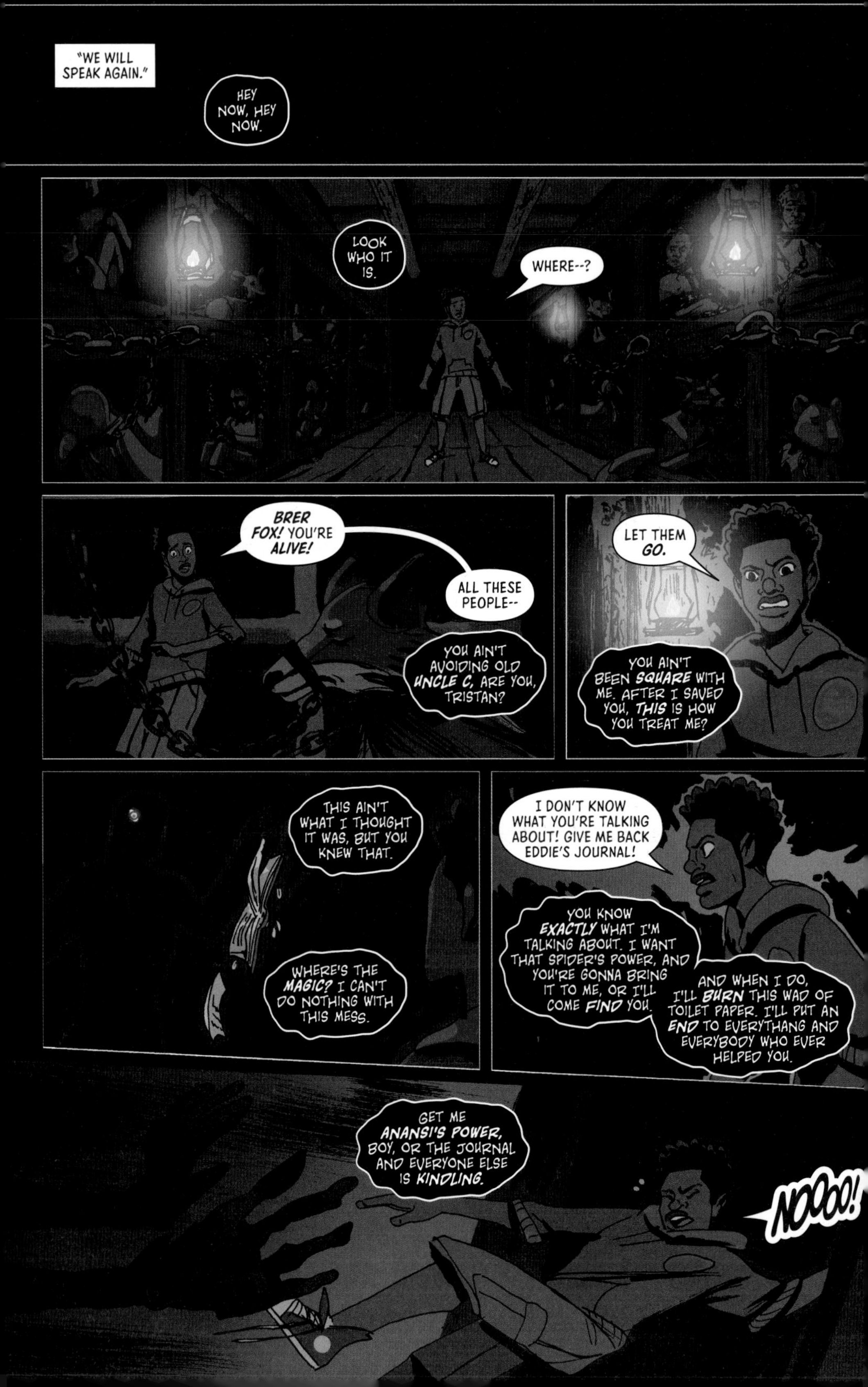
"WE WILL SPEAK AGAIN."
HEY NOW, HEY NOW.
LOOK WHO IT IS.
WHERE--?
BRER FOX! YOU'RE ALIVE!
ALL THESE PEOPLE--
YOU AIN'T AVOIDING OLD UNCLE C, ARE YOU, TRISTAN?
LET THEM GO.
YOU AIN'T BEEN SQUARE WITH ME. AFTER I SAVED YOU, THIS IS HOW YOU TREAT ME?
THIS AIN'T WHAT I THOUGHT IT WAS, BUT YOU KNEW THAT.
WHERE'S THE MAGIC? I CAN'T DO NOTHING WITH THIS MESS.
I DON'T KNOW WHAT YOU'RE TALKING ABOUT! GIVE ME BACK EDDIE'S JOURNAL!
YOU KNOW EXACTLY WHAT I'M TALKING ABOUT. I WANT THAT SPIDER'S POWER, AND YOU'RE GONNA BRING IT TO ME, OR I'LL COME FIND YOU.
AND WHEN I DO, I'LL BURN THIS WAD OF TOILET PAPER. I'LL PUT AN END TO EVERYTHANG AND EVERYBODY WHO EVER HELPED YOU.
GET ME ANANSI'S POWER, BOY, OR THE JOURNAL AND EVERYONE ELSE IS KINDLING.
NOOOOO!

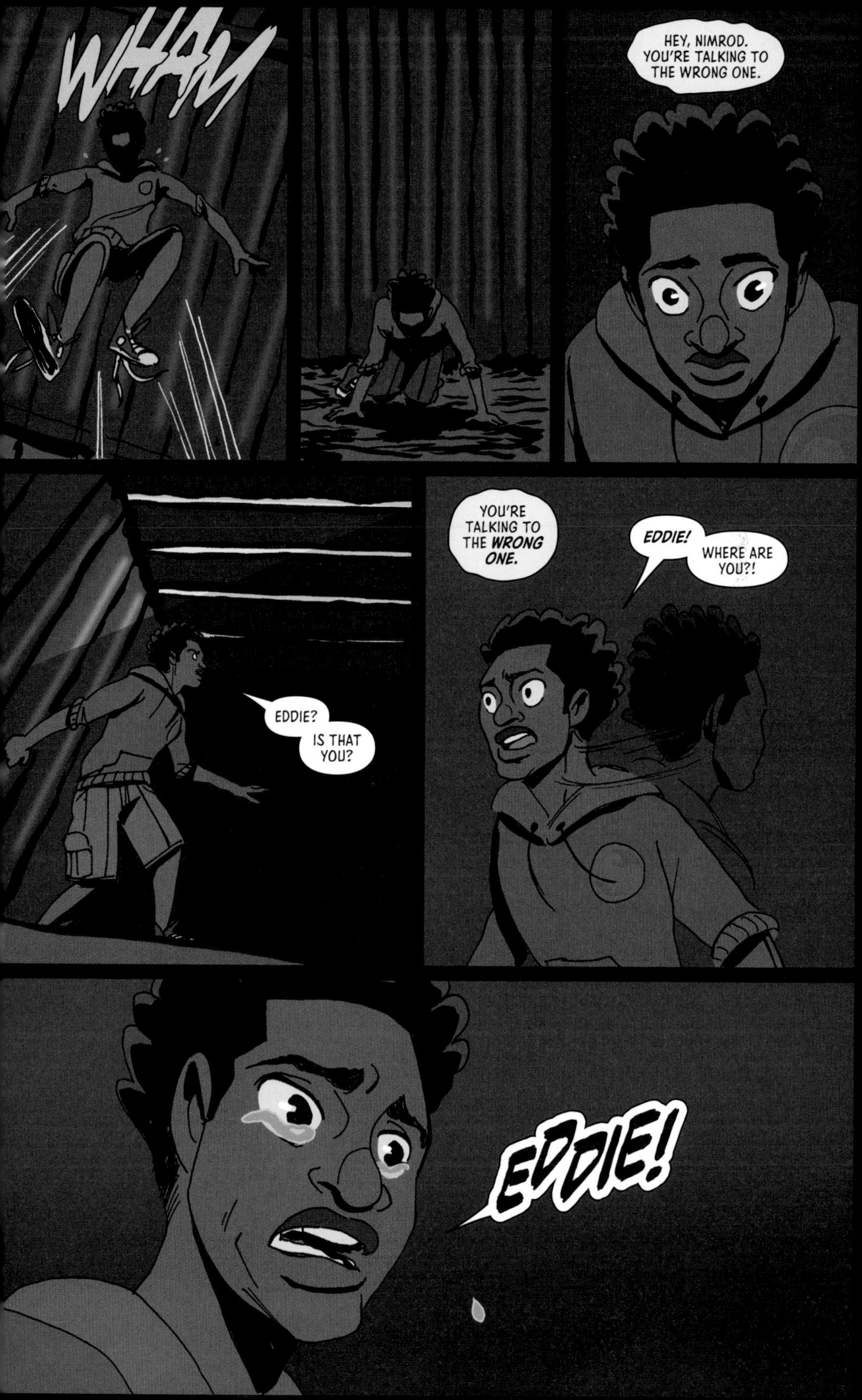
WHAM
HEY, NIMROD. YOU'RE TALKING TO THE WRONG ONE.
EDDIE? IS THAT YOU?
YOU'RE TALKING TO THE WRONG ONE.
EDDIE!
WHERE ARE YOU?!
EDDIE!

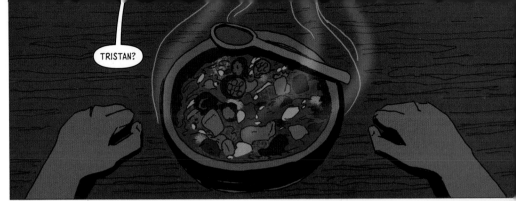

TRISTAN?

YOU ALL RIGHT?

OH, HEY, AYANNA. YEAH. I'M GOOD.

WHERE'VE YOU BEEN?

I HAD TO TELL SOME OF THE MIDFOLK FAMILIES THAT I WASN'T ABLE TO FIND THEIR LOVED ONES.

THEN I HAD TO TRY TO *CONVINCE* MISS SARAH TO LET ME GO OUT ON PATROL ONE LAST TIME. THERE ARE STILL MIDFOLK OUT THERE I CAN SAVE. I *KNOW* IT.

DID YOU REALLY DO IT? BRING THAT STORY TO LIFE. WITH *MAGIC?*

I DON'T KNOW. THAT'S WHAT THE GODS SAY.

I CAN'T EXPLAIN IT.

I HOPE THEY'RE RIGHT.

MAYBE, WITH YOUR HELP, WE CAN TIP THE BALANCE IN *OUR* FAVOR FOR ONCE.

I'M GOING BACK ON PATROL.

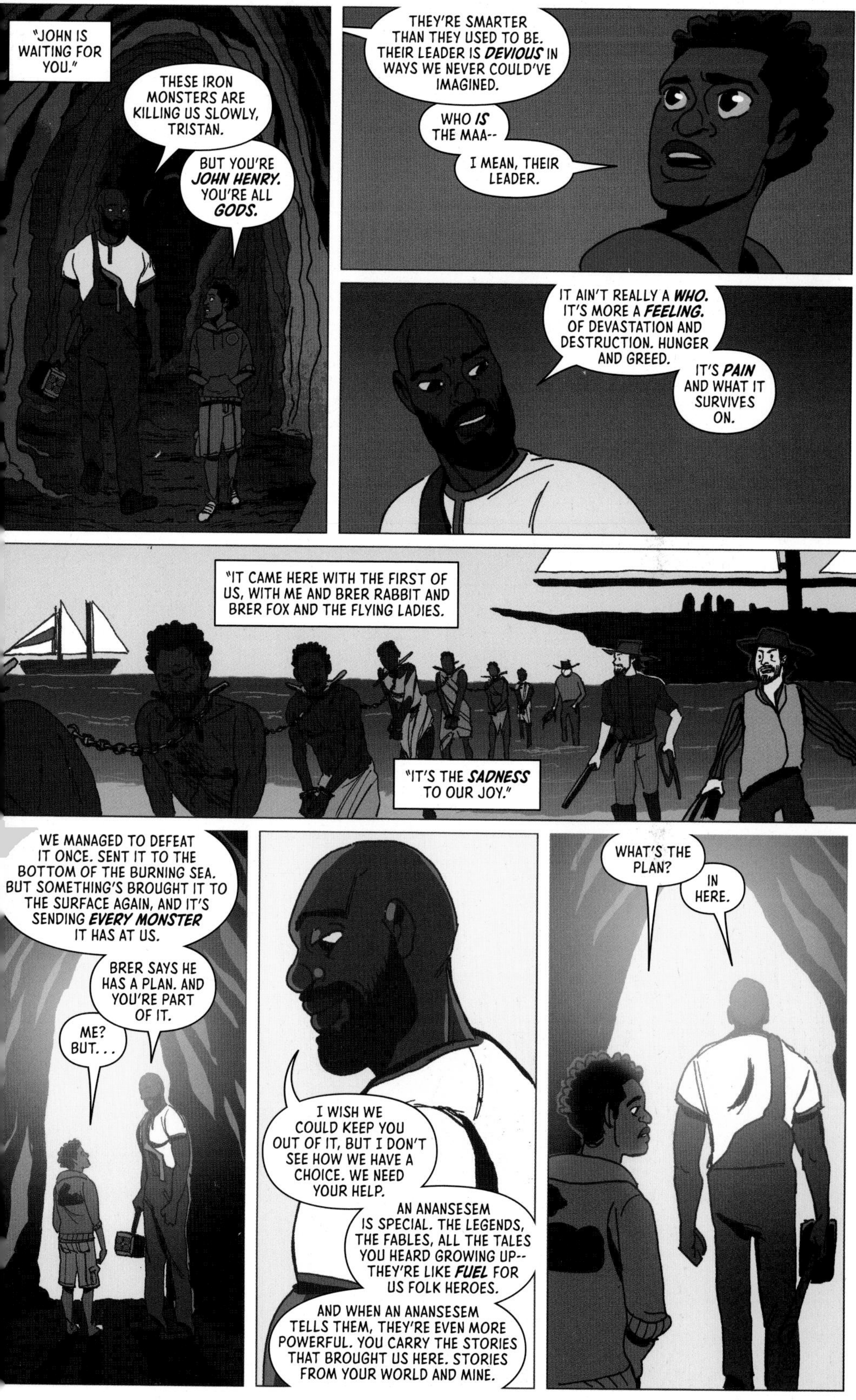
"JOHN IS WAITING FOR YOU."
THESE IRON MONSTERS ARE KILLING US SLOWLY, TRISTAN.
BUT YOU'RE *JOHN HENRY.* YOU'RE ALL *GODS.*
THEY'RE SMARTER THAN THEY USED TO BE. THEIR LEADER IS *DEVIOUS* IN WAYS WE NEVER COULD'VE IMAGINED.
WHO *IS* THE MAA--
I MEAN, THEIR LEADER.
IT AIN'T REALLY A *WHO.* IT'S MORE A *FEELING.* OF DEVASTATION AND DESTRUCTION. HUNGER AND GREED.
IT'S *PAIN* AND WHAT IT SURVIVES ON.
"IT CAME HERE WITH THE FIRST OF US, WITH ME AND BRER RABBIT AND BRER FOX AND THE FLYING LADIES.
"IT'S THE *SADNESS* TO OUR JOY."
WE MANAGED TO DEFEAT IT ONCE. SENT IT TO THE BOTTOM OF THE BURNING SEA. BUT SOMETHING'S BROUGHT IT TO THE SURFACE AGAIN, AND IT'S SENDING *EVERY MONSTER* IT HAS AT US.
BRER SAYS HE HAS A PLAN. AND YOU'RE PART OF IT.
ME? BUT. . .
I WISH WE COULD KEEP YOU OUT OF IT, BUT I DON'T SEE HOW WE HAVE A CHOICE. WE NEED YOUR HELP.
AN ANANSESEM IS SPECIAL. THE LEGENDS, THE FABLES, ALL THE TALES YOU HEARD GROWING UP-- THEY'RE LIKE *FUEL* FOR US FOLK HEROES.
AND WHEN AN ANANSESEM TELLS THEM, THEY'RE EVEN MORE POWERFUL. YOU CARRY THE STORIES THAT BROUGHT US HERE. STORIES FROM YOUR WORLD AND MINE.
WHAT'S THE PLAN?
IN HERE.

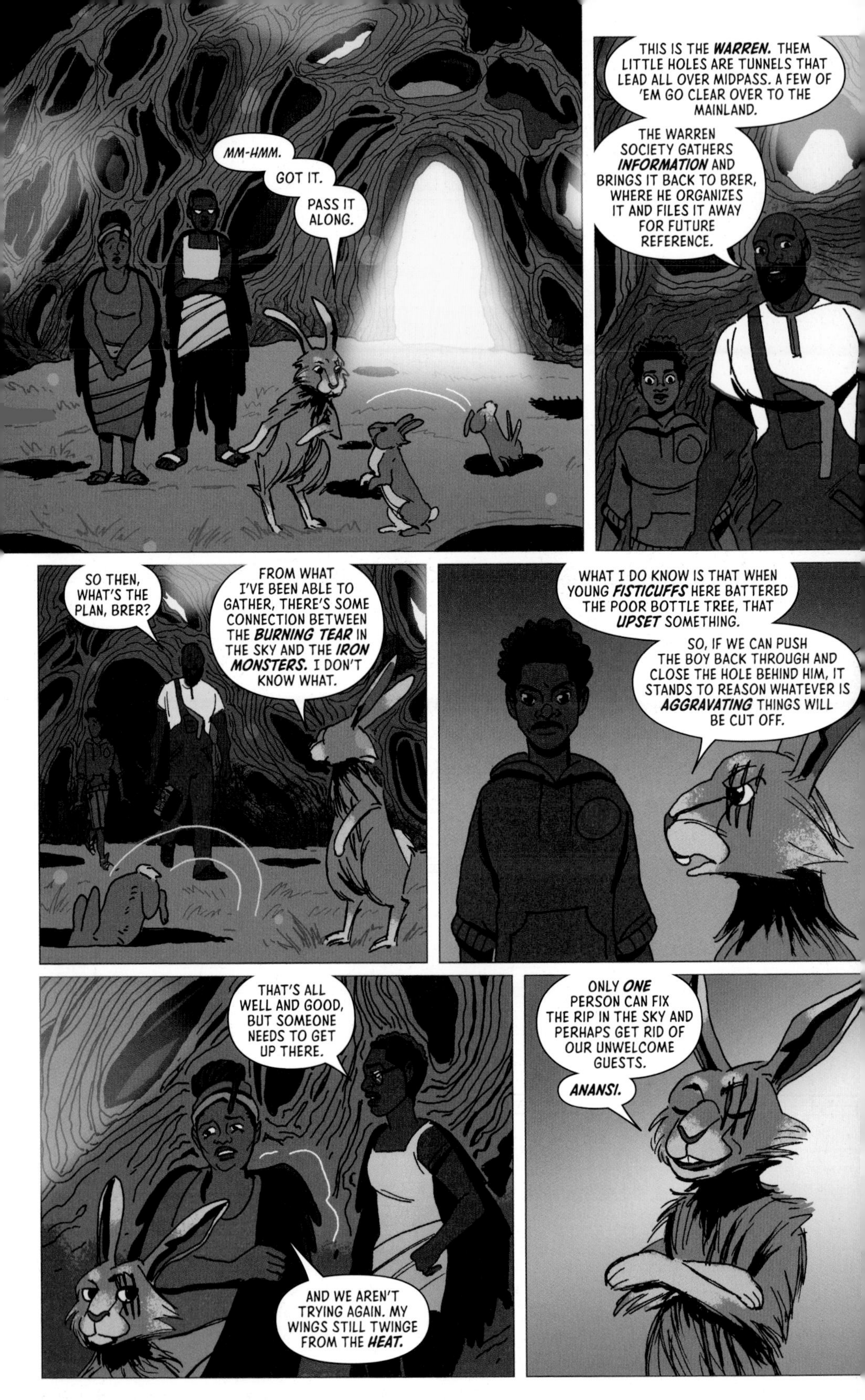
MM-HMM.
GOT IT.
PASS IT ALONG.
THIS IS THE **WARREN.** THEM LITTLE HOLES ARE TUNNELS THAT LEAD ALL OVER MIDPASS. A FEW OF 'EM GO CLEAR OVER TO THE MAINLAND.
THE WARREN SOCIETY GATHERS **INFORMATION** AND BRINGS IT BACK TO BRER, WHERE HE ORGANIZES IT AND FILES IT AWAY FOR FUTURE REFERENCE.
SO THEN, WHAT'S THE PLAN, BRER?
FROM WHAT I'VE BEEN ABLE TO GATHER, THERE'S SOME CONNECTION BETWEEN THE **BURNING TEAR** IN THE SKY AND THE **IRON MONSTERS.** I DON'T KNOW WHAT.
WHAT I DO KNOW IS THAT WHEN YOUNG **FISTICUFFS** HERE BATTERED THE POOR BOTTLE TREE, THAT **UPSET** SOMETHING.
SO, IF WE CAN PUSH THE BOY BACK THROUGH AND CLOSE THE HOLE BEHIND HIM, IT STANDS TO REASON WHATEVER IS **AGGRAVATING** THINGS WILL BE CUT OFF.
THAT'S ALL WELL AND GOOD, BUT SOMEONE NEEDS TO GET UP THERE.
AND WE AREN'T TRYING AGAIN. MY WINGS STILL TWINGE FROM THE **HEAT.**
ONLY **ONE** PERSON CAN FIX THE RIP IN THE SKY AND PERHAPS GET RID OF OUR UNWELCOME GUESTS.
ANANSI.

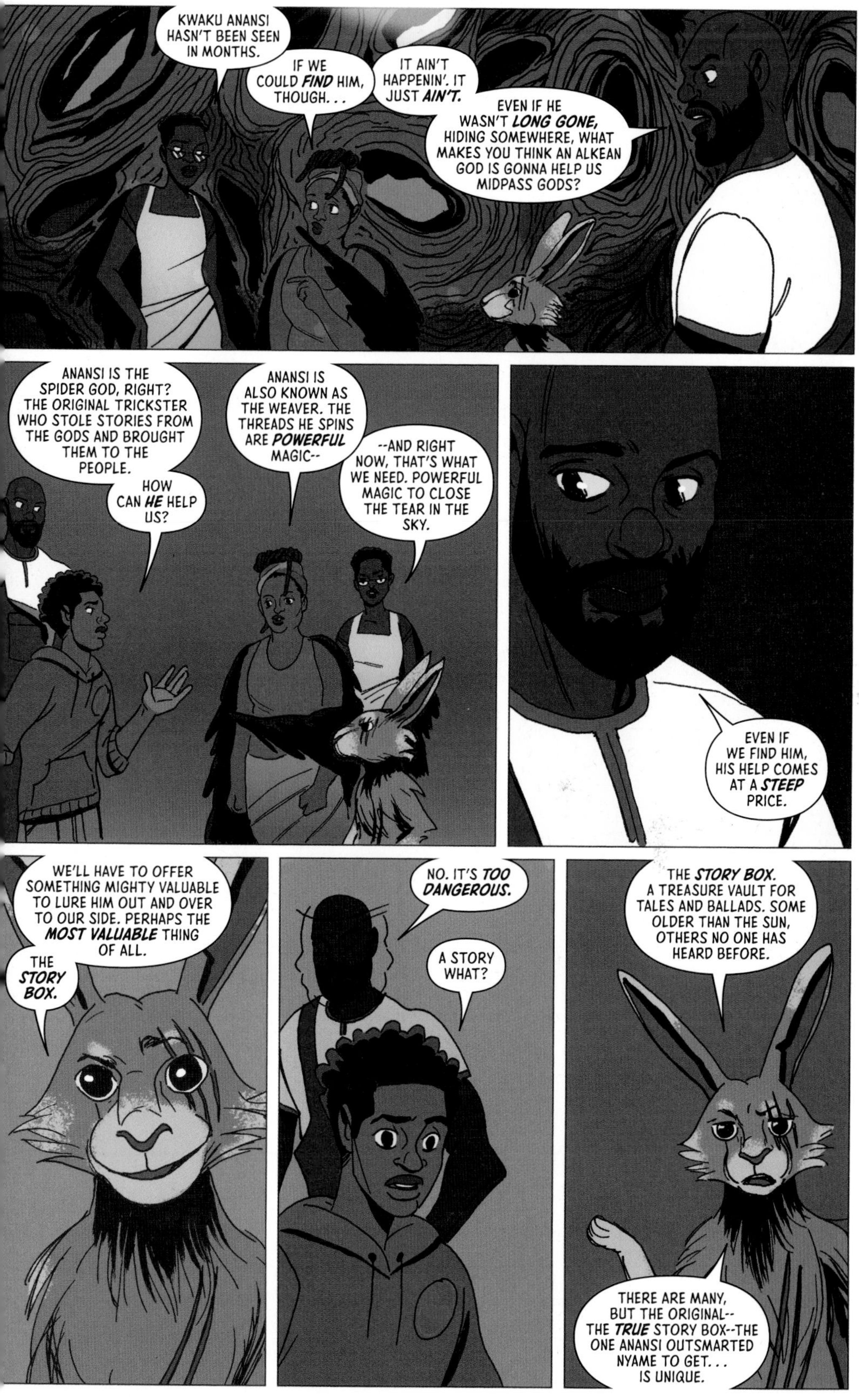
KWAKU ANANSI HASN'T BEEN SEEN IN MONTHS.
IF WE COULD FIND HIM, THOUGH. . .
IT AIN'T HAPPENIN'. IT JUST AIN'T.
EVEN IF HE WASN'T LONG GONE, HIDING SOMEWHERE, WHAT MAKES YOU THINK AN ALKEAN GOD IS GONNA HELP US MIDPASS GODS?
ANANSI IS THE SPIDER GOD, RIGHT? THE ORIGINAL TRICKSTER WHO STOLE STORIES FROM THE GODS AND BROUGHT THEM TO THE PEOPLE.
HOW CAN HE HELP US?
ANANSI IS ALSO KNOWN AS THE WEAVER. THE THREADS HE SPINS ARE POWERFUL MAGIC--
--AND RIGHT NOW, THAT'S WHAT WE NEED. POWERFUL MAGIC TO CLOSE THE TEAR IN THE SKY.
EVEN IF WE FIND HIM, HIS HELP COMES AT A STEEP PRICE.
WE'LL HAVE TO OFFER SOMETHING MIGHTY VALUABLE TO LURE HIM OUT AND OVER TO OUR SIDE. PERHAPS THE MOST VALUABLE THING OF ALL.
THE STORY BOX.
NO. IT'S TOO DANGEROUS.
A STORY WHAT?
THE STORY BOX. A TREASURE VAULT FOR TALES AND BALLADS. SOME OLDER THAN THE SUN, OTHERS NO ONE HAS HEARD BEFORE.
THERE ARE MANY, BUT THE ORIGINAL-- THE TRUE STORY BOX--THE ONE ANANSI OUTSMARTED NYAME TO GET. . . IS UNIQUE.

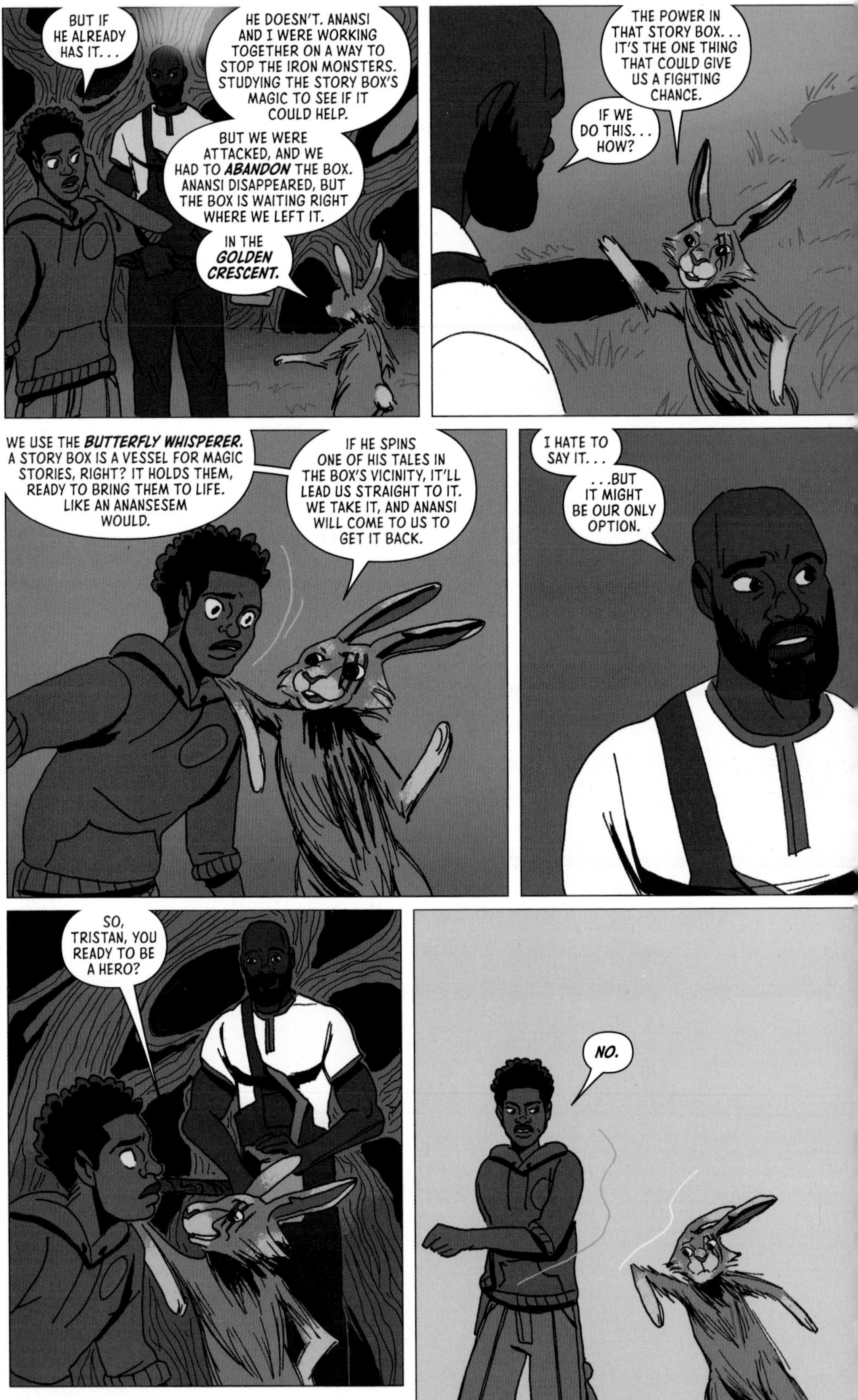
BUT IF HE ALREADY HAS IT. . .
HE DOESN'T. ANANSI AND I WERE WORKING TOGETHER ON A WAY TO STOP THE IRON MONSTERS. STUDYING THE STORY BOX'S MAGIC TO SEE IF IT COULD HELP.
BUT WE WERE ATTACKED, AND WE HAD TO *ABANDON* THE BOX. ANANSI DISAPPEARED, BUT THE BOX IS WAITING RIGHT WHERE WE LEFT IT.
IN THE *GOLDEN CRESCENT.*
THE POWER IN THAT STORY BOX. . . IT'S THE ONE THING THAT COULD GIVE US A FIGHTING CHANCE.
IF WE DO THIS. . . HOW?
WE USE THE *BUTTERFLY WHISPERER.* A STORY BOX IS A VESSEL FOR MAGIC STORIES, RIGHT? IT HOLDS THEM, READY TO BRING THEM TO LIFE. LIKE AN ANANSESEM WOULD.
IF HE SPINS ONE OF HIS TALES IN THE BOX'S VICINITY, IT'LL LEAD US STRAIGHT TO IT. WE TAKE IT, AND ANANSI WILL COME TO US TO GET IT BACK.
I HATE TO SAY IT. . .
. . .BUT IT MIGHT BE OUR ONLY OPTION.
SO, TRISTAN, YOU READY TO BE A HERO?
NO.

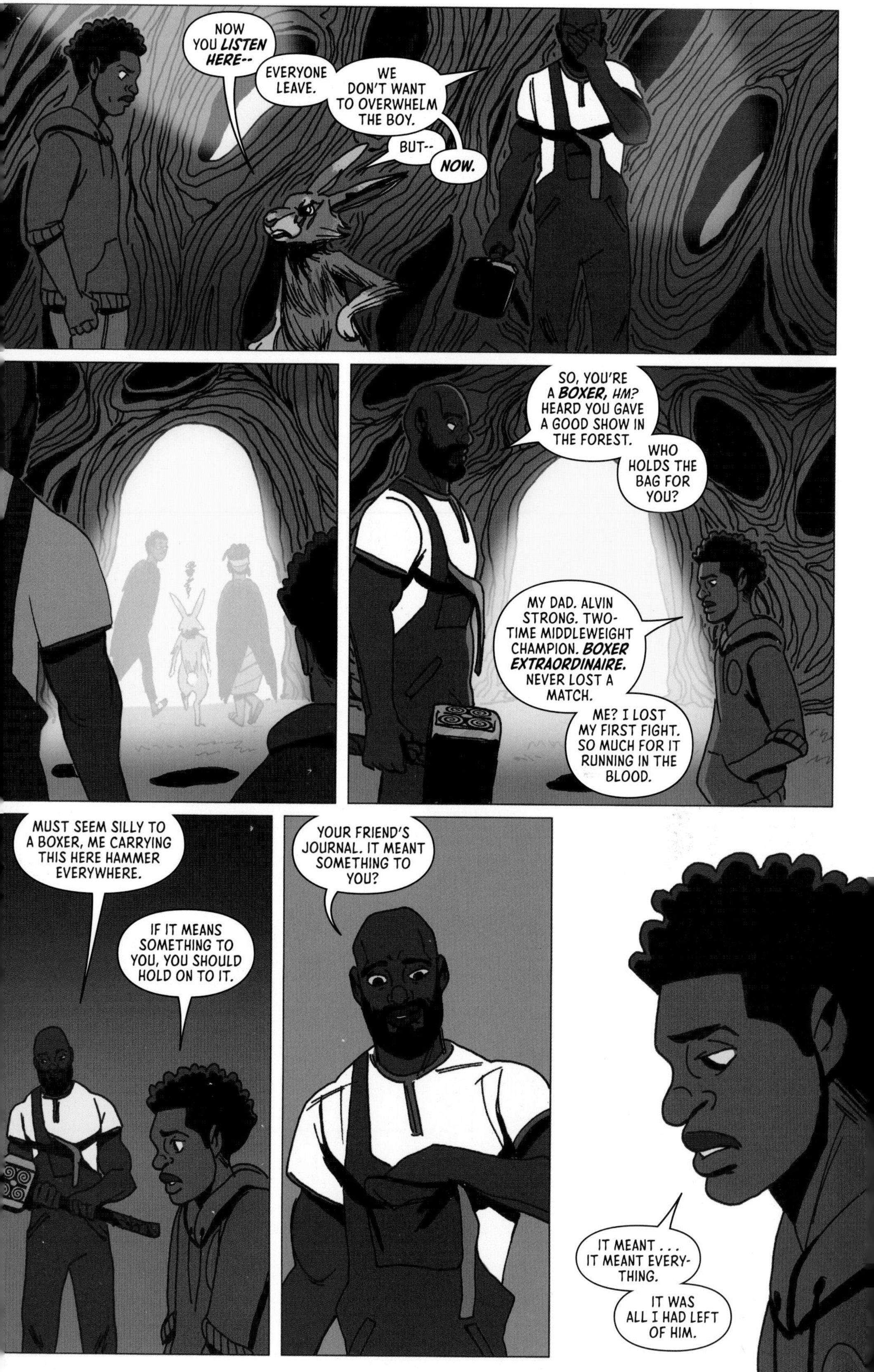
NOW YOU LISTEN HERE--
EVERYONE LEAVE.
WE DON'T WANT TO OVERWHELM THE BOY.
BUT--
NOW.
SO, YOU'RE A BOXER, HM? HEARD YOU GAVE A GOOD SHOW IN THE FOREST.
WHO HOLDS THE BAG FOR YOU?
MY DAD. ALVIN STRONG. TWO-TIME MIDDLEWEIGHT CHAMPION. BOXER EXTRAORDINAIRE. NEVER LOST A MATCH.
ME? I LOST MY FIRST FIGHT. SO MUCH FOR IT RUNNING IN THE BLOOD.
MUST SEEM SILLY TO A BOXER, ME CARRYING THIS HERE HAMMER EVERYWHERE.
IF IT MEANS SOMETHING TO YOU, YOU SHOULD HOLD ON TO IT.
YOUR FRIEND'S JOURNAL. IT MEANT SOMETHING TO YOU?
IT MEANT . . . IT MEANT EVERYTHING.
IT WAS ALL I HAD LEFT OF HIM.

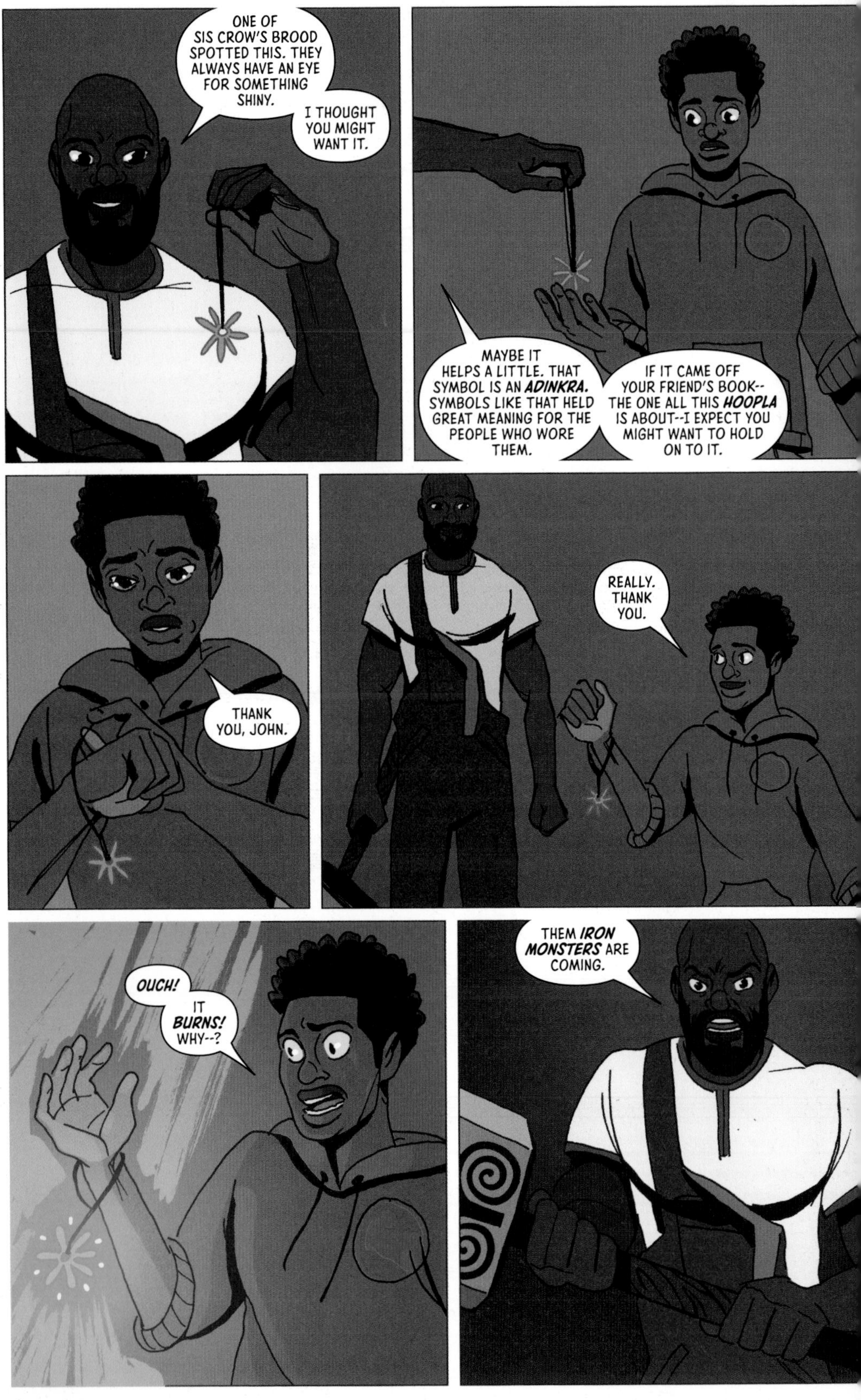
ONE OF SIS CROW'S BROOD SPOTTED THIS. THEY ALWAYS HAVE AN EYE FOR SOMETHING SHINY.
I THOUGHT YOU MIGHT WANT IT.
MAYBE IT HELPS A LITTLE. THAT SYMBOL IS AN *ADINKRA.* SYMBOLS LIKE THAT HELD GREAT MEANING FOR THE PEOPLE WHO WORE THEM.
IF IT CAME OFF YOUR FRIEND'S BOOK-- THE ONE ALL THIS *HOOPLA* IS ABOUT--I EXPECT YOU MIGHT WANT TO HOLD ON TO IT.
THANK YOU, JOHN.
REALLY. THANK YOU.
OUCH!
IT *BURNS!* WHY--?
THEM *IRON MONSTERS* ARE COMING.

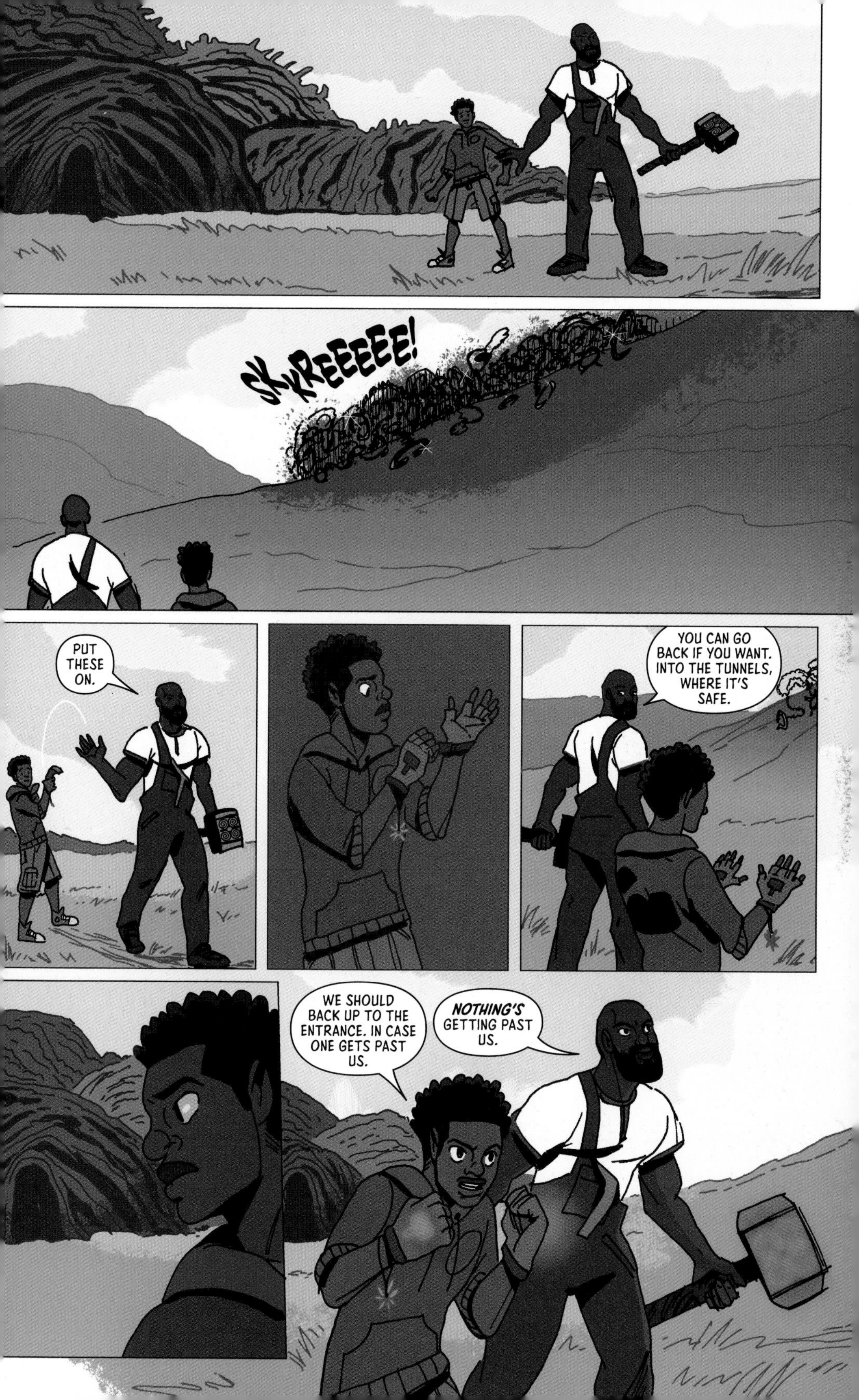
SKREEEEEE!
PUT THESE ON.
YOU CAN GO BACK IF YOU WANT. INTO THE TUNNELS, WHERE IT'S SAFE.
WE SHOULD BACK UP TO THE ENTRANCE. IN CASE ONE GETS PAST US.
NOTHING'S GETTING PAST US.

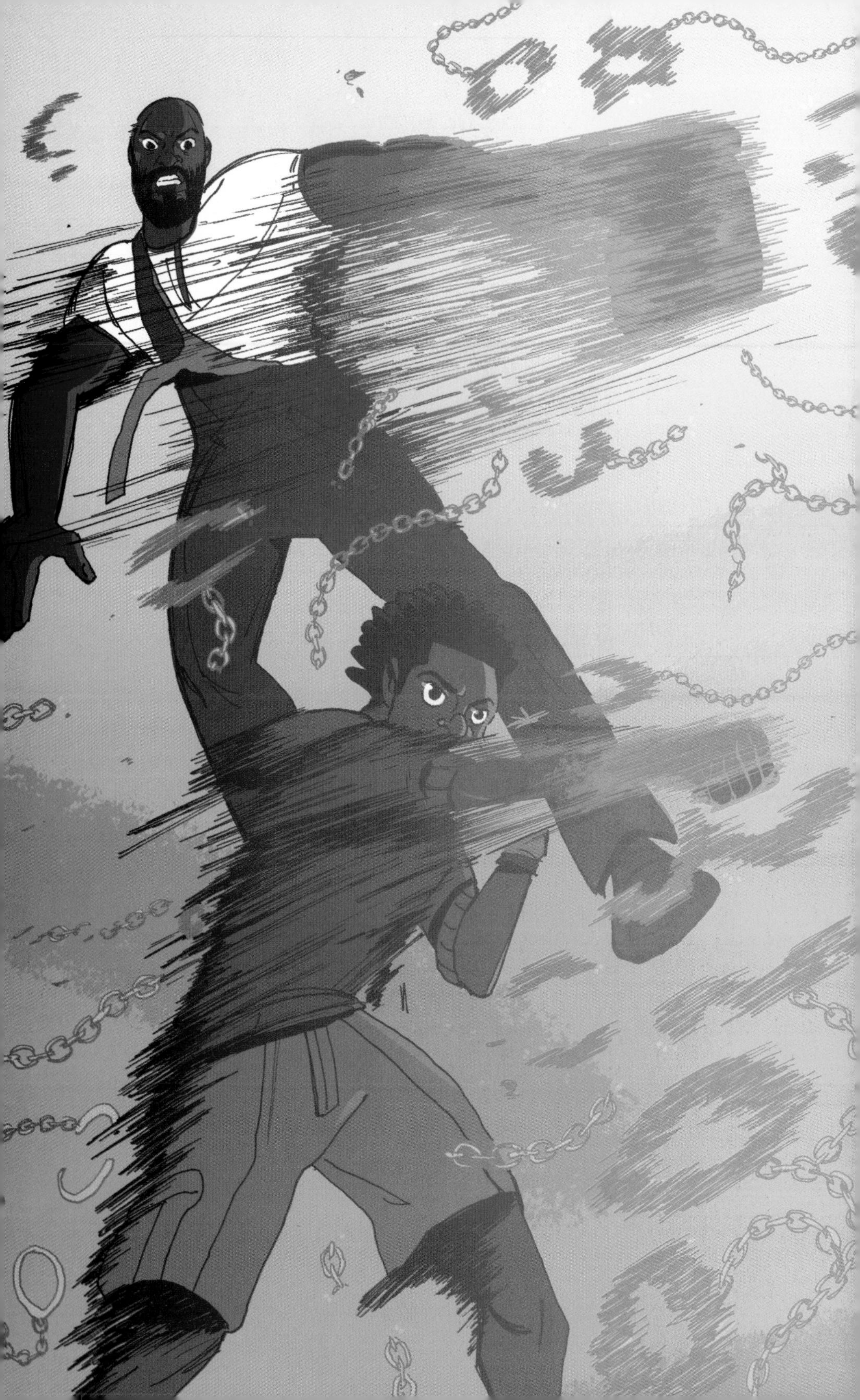

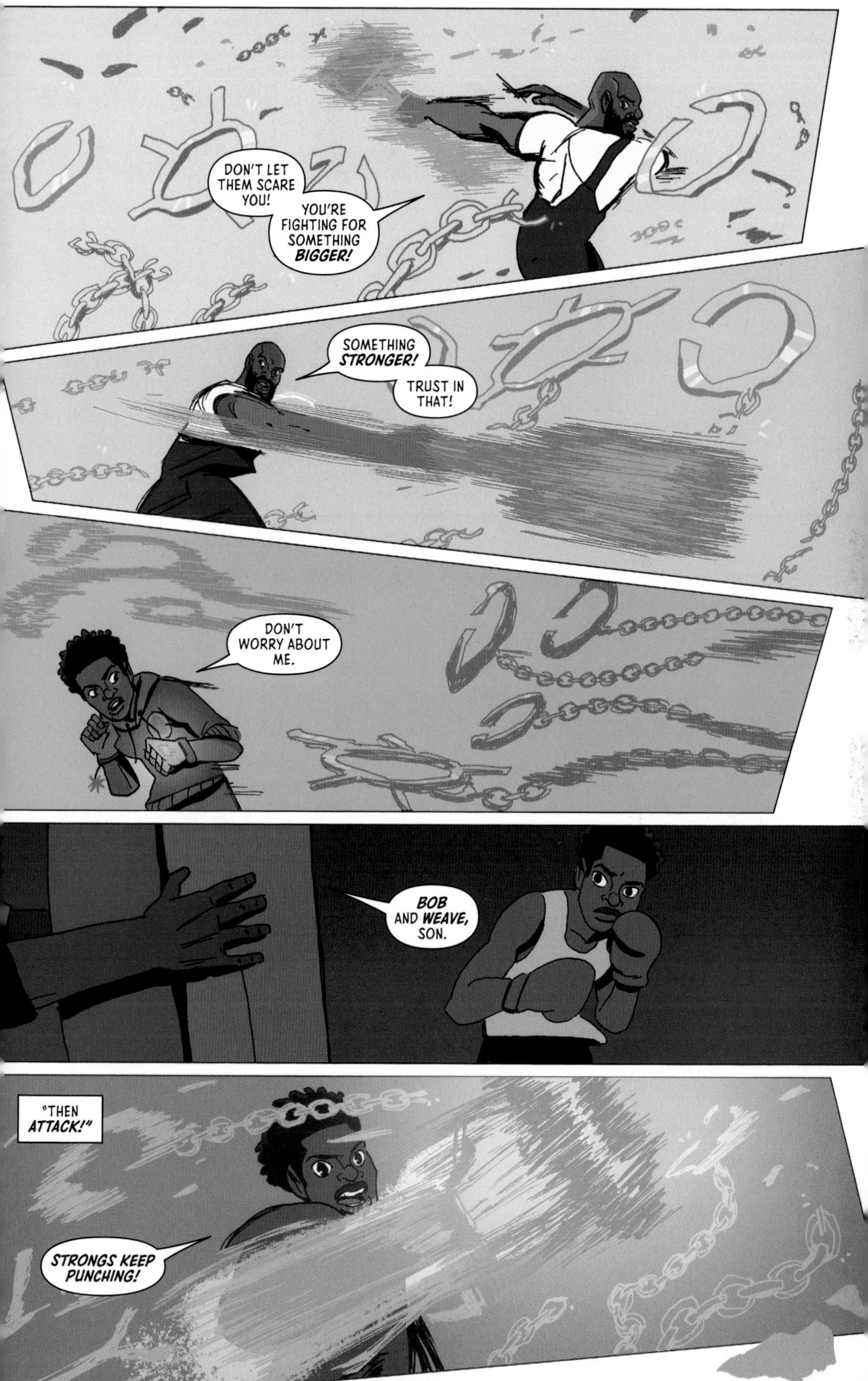
DON'T LET THEM SCARE YOU!
YOU'RE FIGHTING FOR SOMETHING **BIGGER!**
SOMETHING **STRONGER!**
TRUST IN THAT!
DON'T WORRY ABOUT ME.
BOB AND **WEAVE,** SON.
"THEN **ATTACK!**"
STRONGS KEEP PUNCHING!

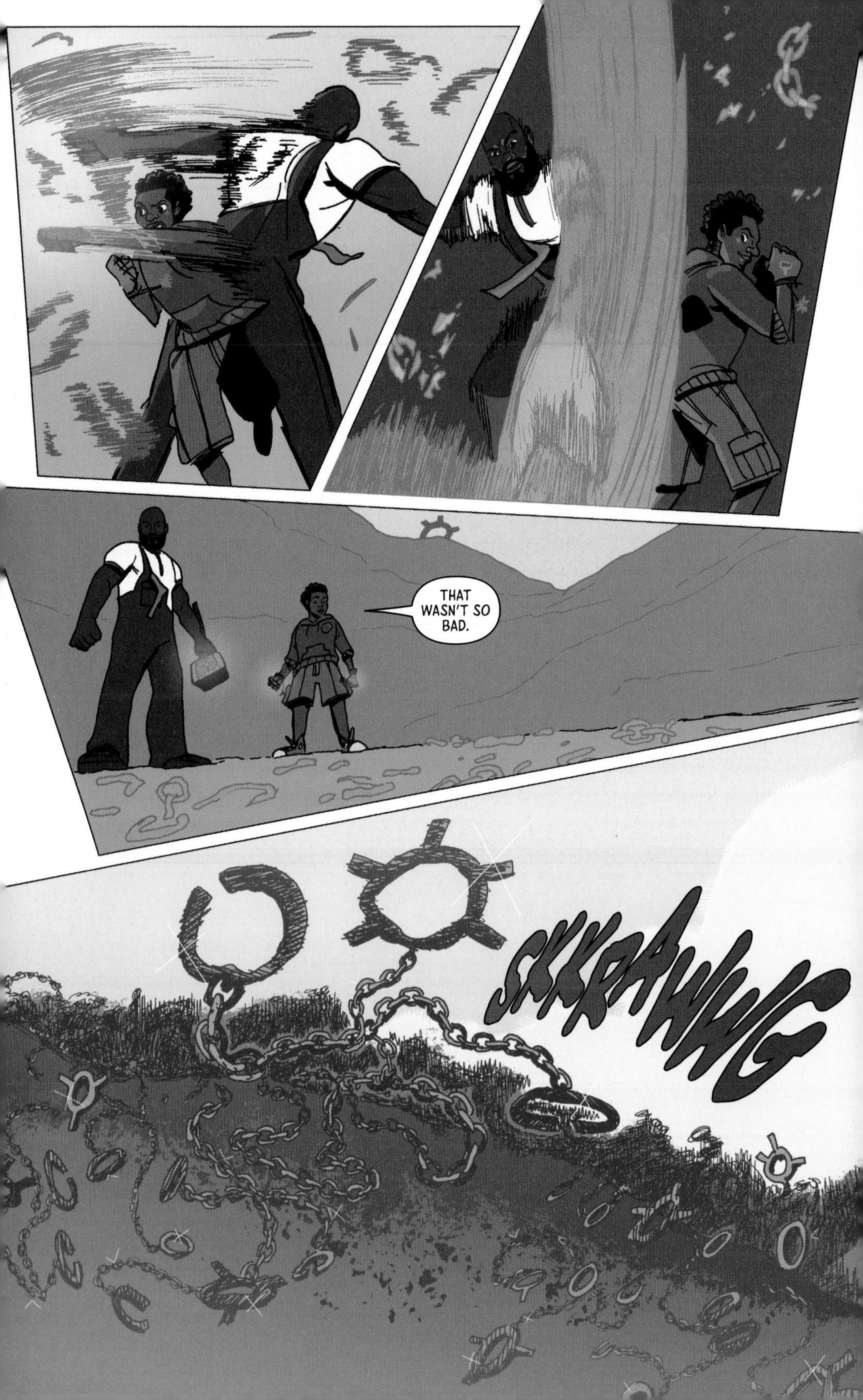
THAT WASN'T SO BAD.
SKKRAWWG

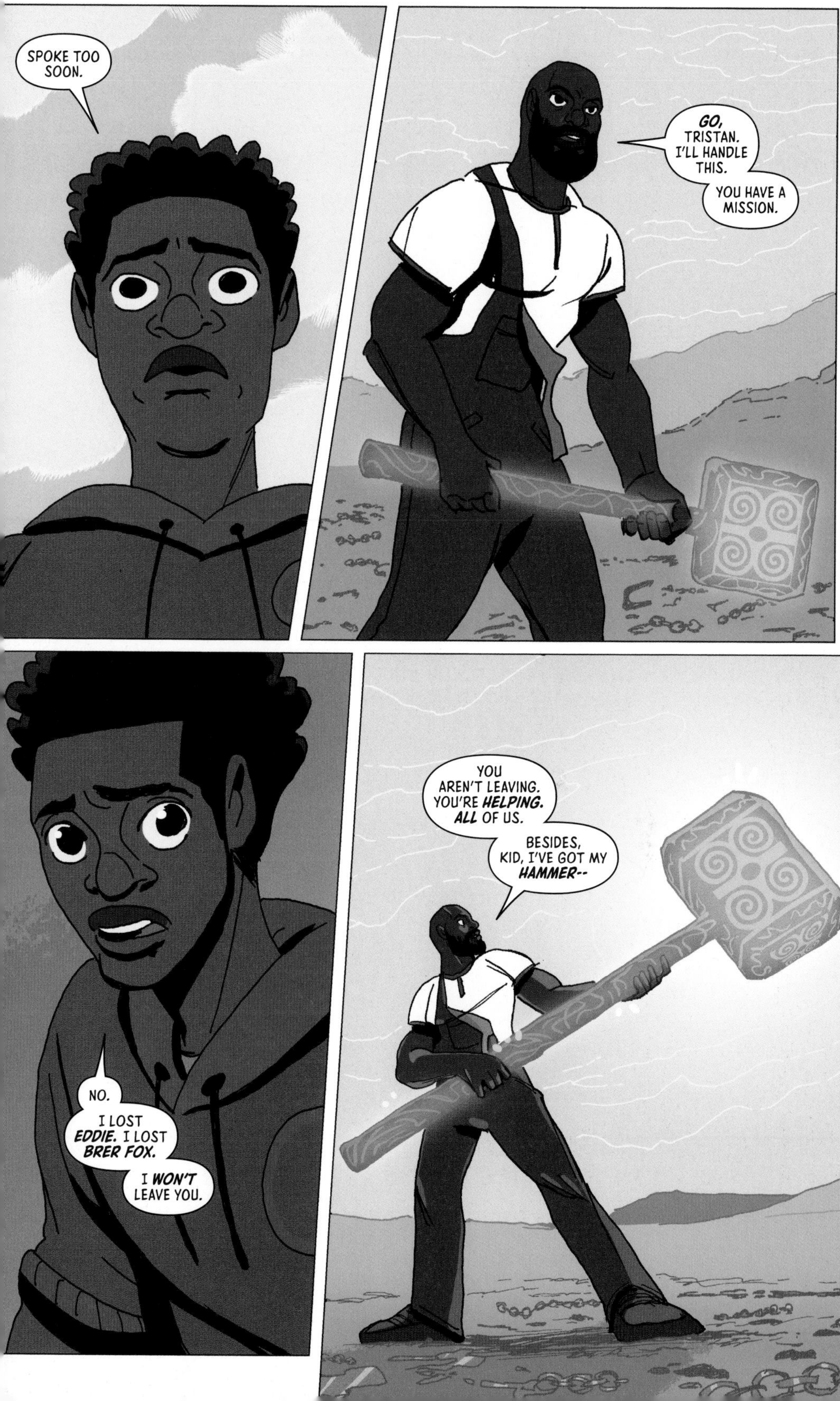
SPOKE TOO SOON.
GO, TRISTAN. I'LL HANDLE THIS.
YOU HAVE A MISSION.
NO.
I LOST EDDIE. I LOST BRER FOX.
I WON'T LEAVE YOU.
YOU AREN'T LEAVING. YOU'RE HELPING. ALL OF US.
BESIDES, KID, I'VE GOT MY HAMMER--

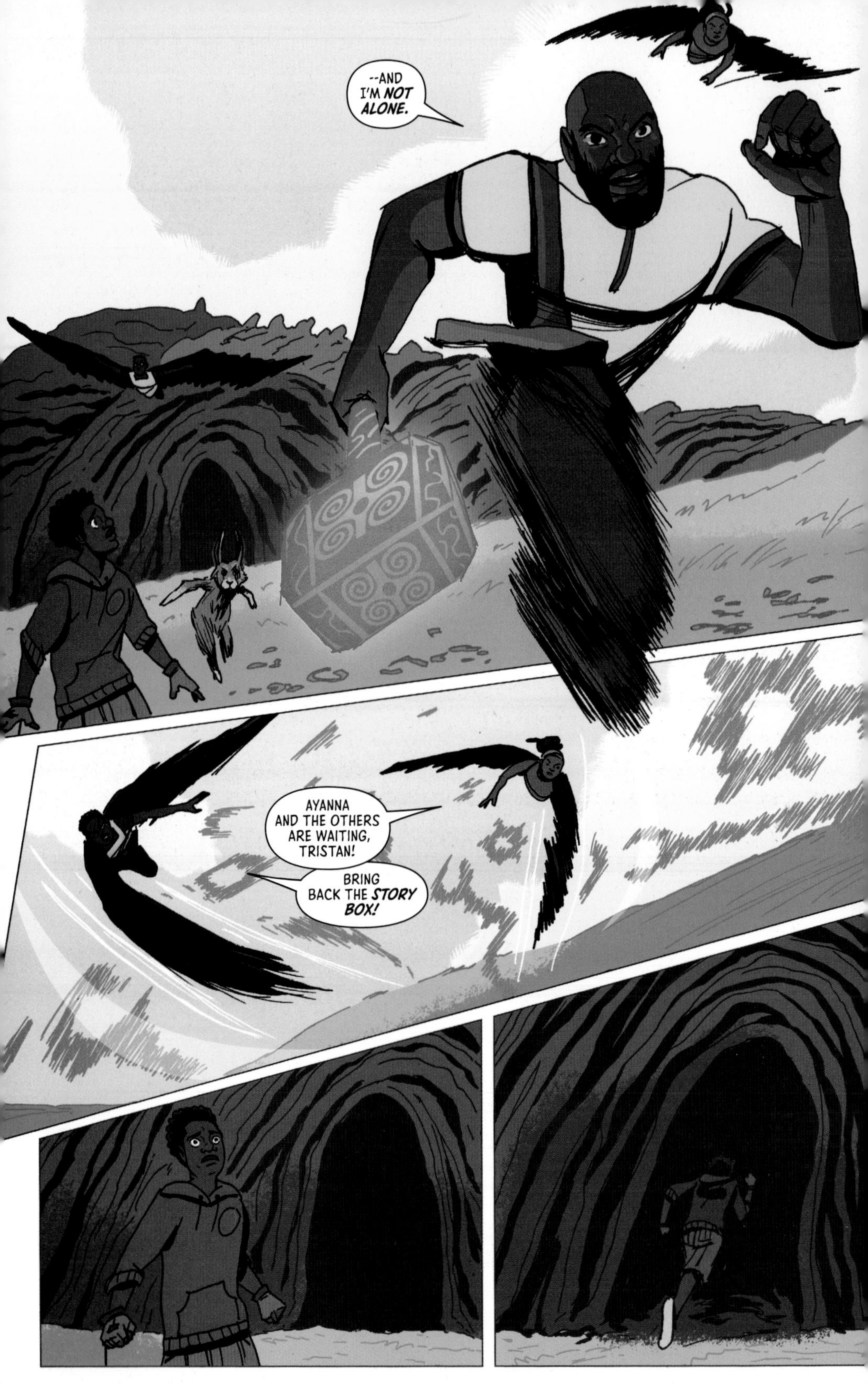
--AND I'M NOT ALONE.
AYANNA AND THE OTHERS ARE WAITING, TRISTAN!
BRING BACK THE STORY BOX!

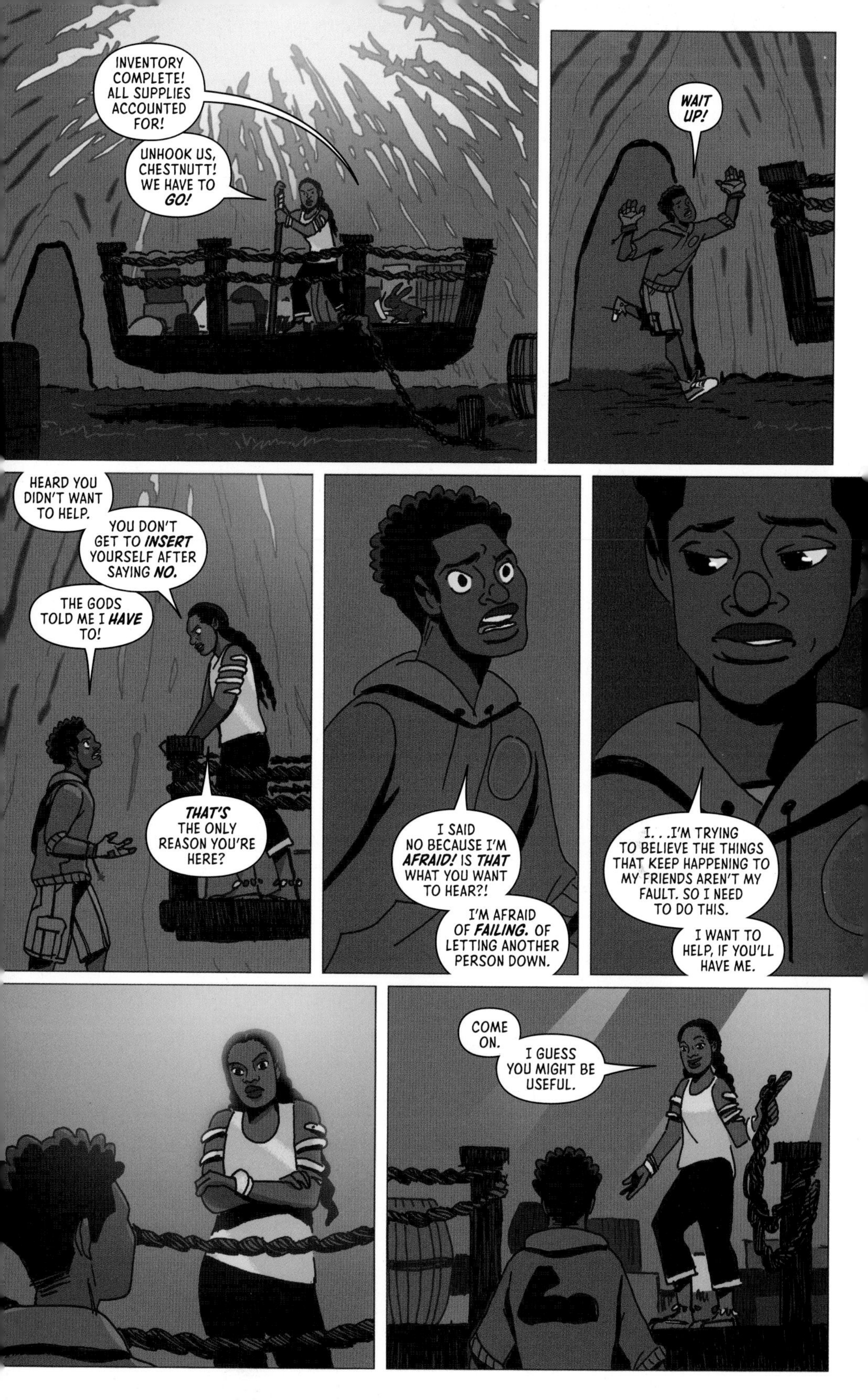
INVENTORY COMPLETE! ALL SUPPLIES ACCOUNTED FOR!
UNHOOK US, CHESTNUTT! WE HAVE TO *GO!*
WAIT UP!
HEARD YOU DIDN'T WANT TO HELP.
YOU DON'T GET TO *INSERT* YOURSELF AFTER SAYING *NO.*
THE GODS TOLD ME I *HAVE* TO!
THAT'S THE ONLY REASON YOU'RE HERE?
I SAID NO BECAUSE I'M *AFRAID!* IS *THAT* WHAT YOU WANT TO HEAR?!
I'M AFRAID OF *FAILING.* OF LETTING ANOTHER PERSON DOWN.
I. . .I'M TRYING TO BELIEVE THE THINGS THAT KEEP HAPPENING TO MY FRIENDS AREN'T MY FAULT. SO I NEED TO DO THIS.
I WANT TO HELP, IF YOU'LL HAVE ME.
COME ON.
I GUESS YOU MIGHT BE USEFUL.

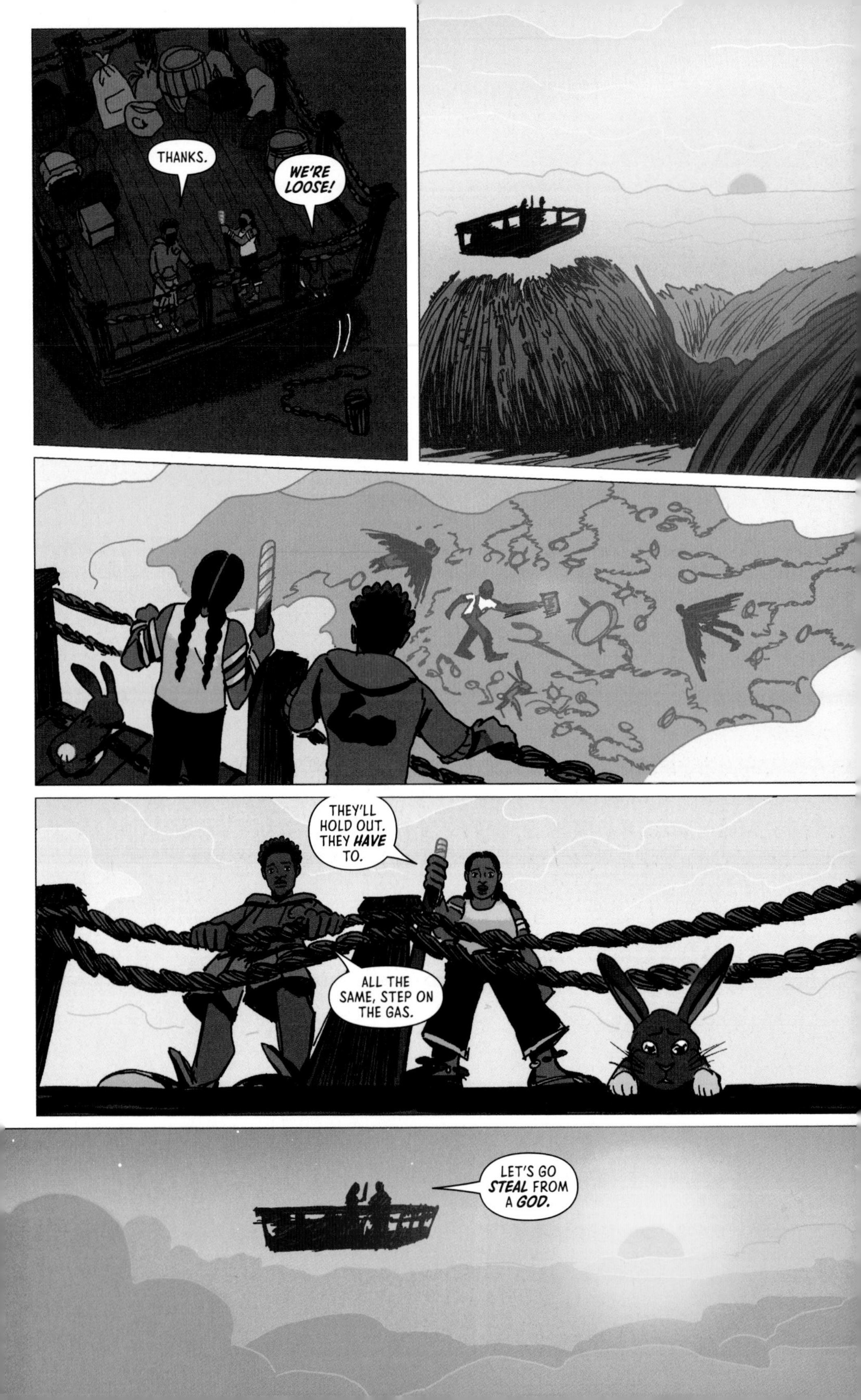
THANKS.
WE'RE LOOSE!
THEY'LL HOLD OUT. THEY HAVE TO.
ALL THE SAME, STEP ON THE GAS.
LET'S GO STEAL FROM A GOD.

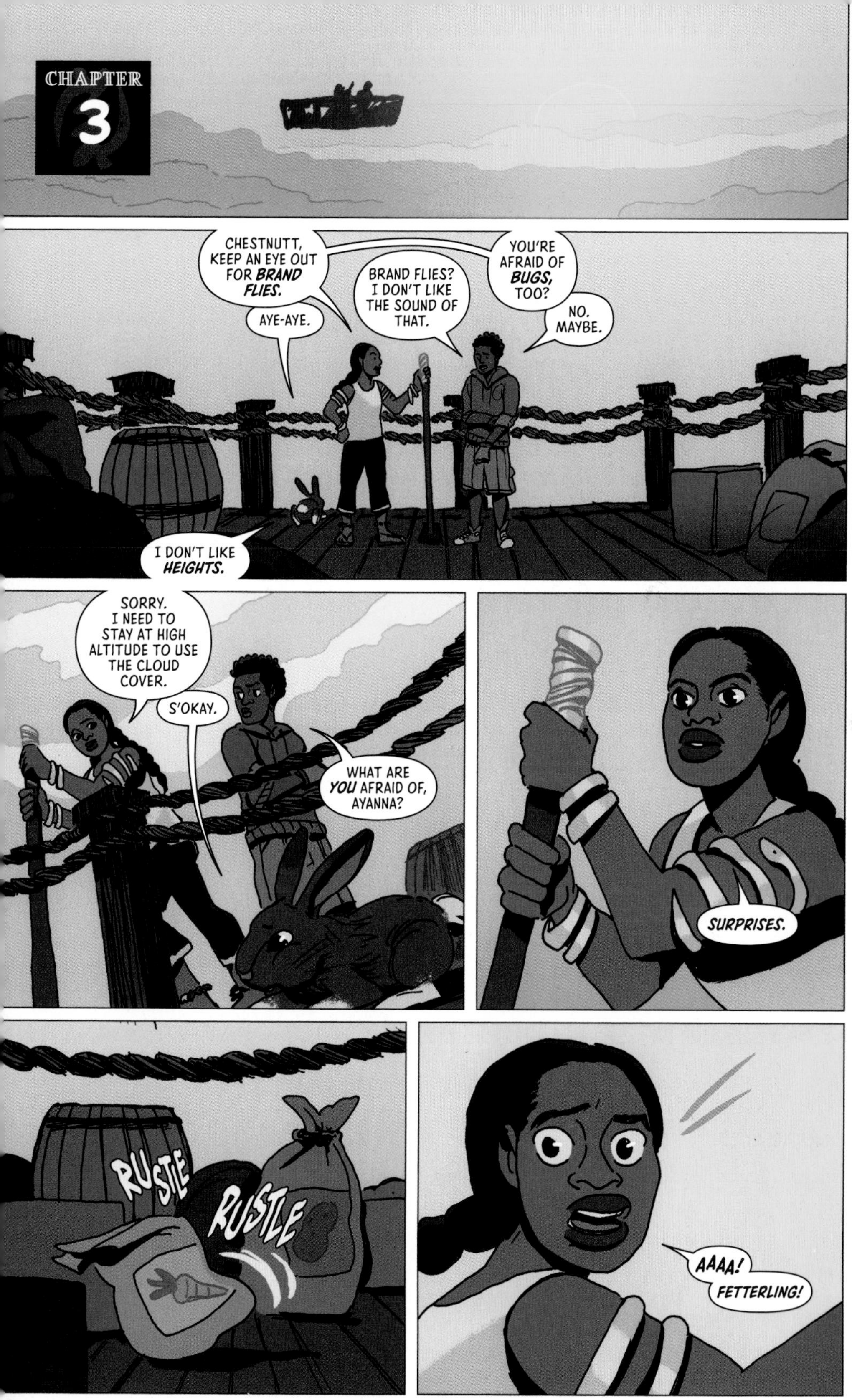
CHAPTER
3
CHESTNUTT, KEEP AN EYE OUT FOR BRAND FLIES.
AYE-AYE.
BRAND FLIES? I DON'T LIKE THE SOUND OF THAT.
YOU'RE AFRAID OF BUGS, TOO?
NO. MAYBE.
I DON'T LIKE HEIGHTS.
SORRY. I NEED TO STAY AT HIGH ALTITUDE TO USE THE CLOUD COVER.
S'OKAY.
WHAT ARE YOU AFRAID OF, AYANNA?
SURPRISES.
RUSTLE
RUSTLE
AAAA!
FETTERLING!

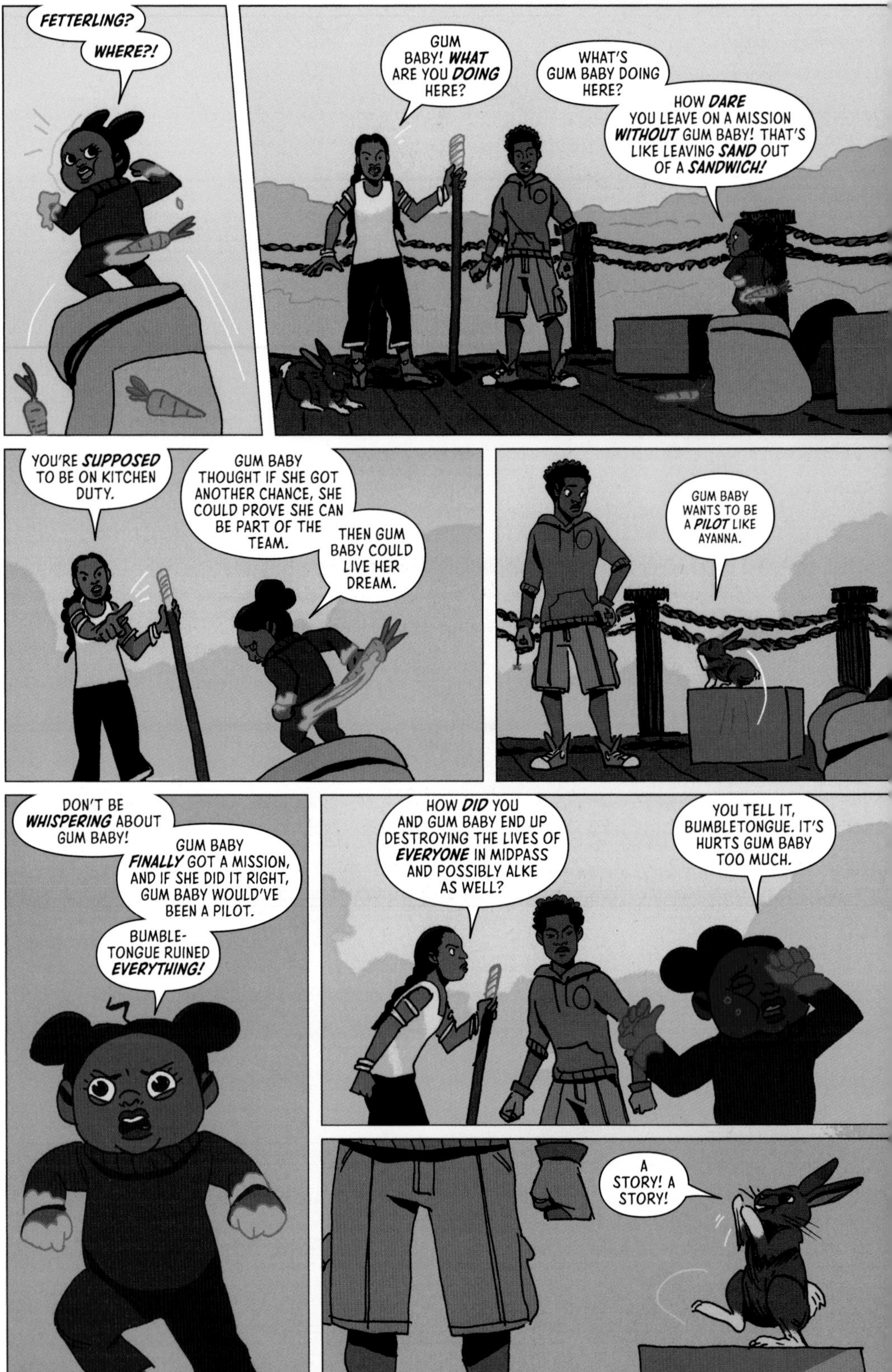
FETTERLING?
WHERE?!
GUM BABY! WHAT ARE YOU DOING HERE?
WHAT'S GUM BABY DOING HERE?
HOW DARE YOU LEAVE ON A MISSION WITHOUT GUM BABY! THAT'S LIKE LEAVING SAND OUT OF A SANDWICH!
YOU'RE SUPPOSED TO BE ON KITCHEN DUTY.
GUM BABY THOUGHT IF SHE GOT ANOTHER CHANCE, SHE COULD PROVE SHE CAN BE PART OF THE TEAM.
THEN GUM BABY COULD LIVE HER DREAM.
GUM BABY WANTS TO BE A PILOT LIKE AYANNA.
DON'T BE WHISPERING ABOUT GUM BABY!
GUM BABY FINALLY GOT A MISSION, AND IF SHE DID IT RIGHT, GUM BABY WOULD'VE BEEN A PILOT.
BUMBLE-TONGUE RUINED EVERYTHING!
HOW DID YOU AND GUM BABY END UP DESTROYING THE LIVES OF EVERYONE IN MIDPASS AND POSSIBLY ALKE AS WELL?
YOU TELL IT, BUMBLETONGUE. IT'S HURTS GUM BABY TOO MUCH.
A STORY! A STORY!

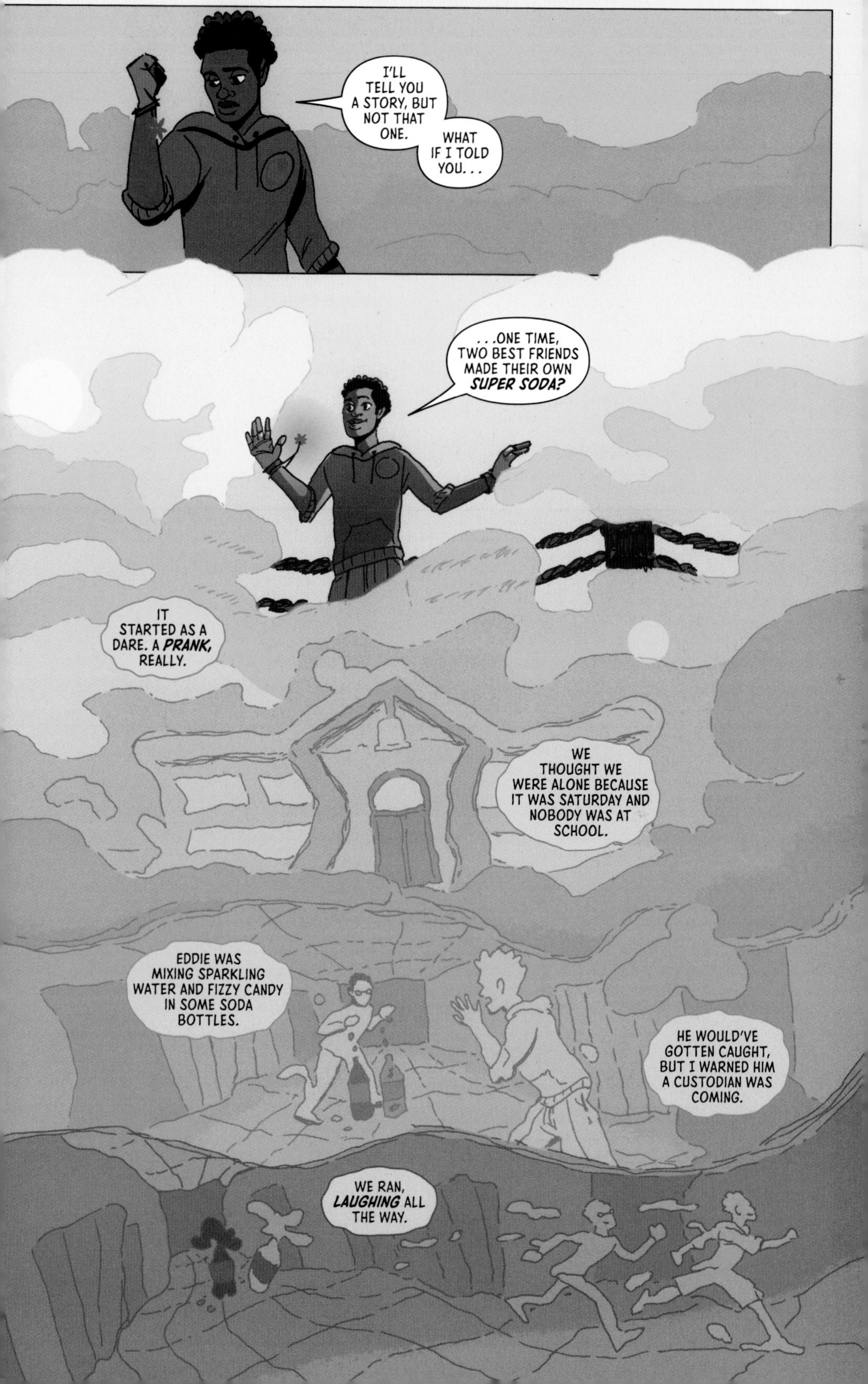
I'LL TELL YOU A STORY, BUT NOT THAT ONE.
WHAT IF I TOLD YOU. . .
. . .ONE TIME, TWO BEST FRIENDS MADE THEIR OWN SUPER SODA?
IT STARTED AS A DARE. A PRANK, REALLY.
WE THOUGHT WE WERE ALONE BECAUSE IT WAS SATURDAY AND NOBODY WAS AT SCHOOL.
EDDIE WAS MIXING SPARKLING WATER AND FIZZY CANDY IN SOME SODA BOTTLES.
HE WOULD'VE GOTTEN CAUGHT, BUT I WARNED HIM A CUSTODIAN WAS COMING.
WE RAN, LAUGHING ALL THE WAY.

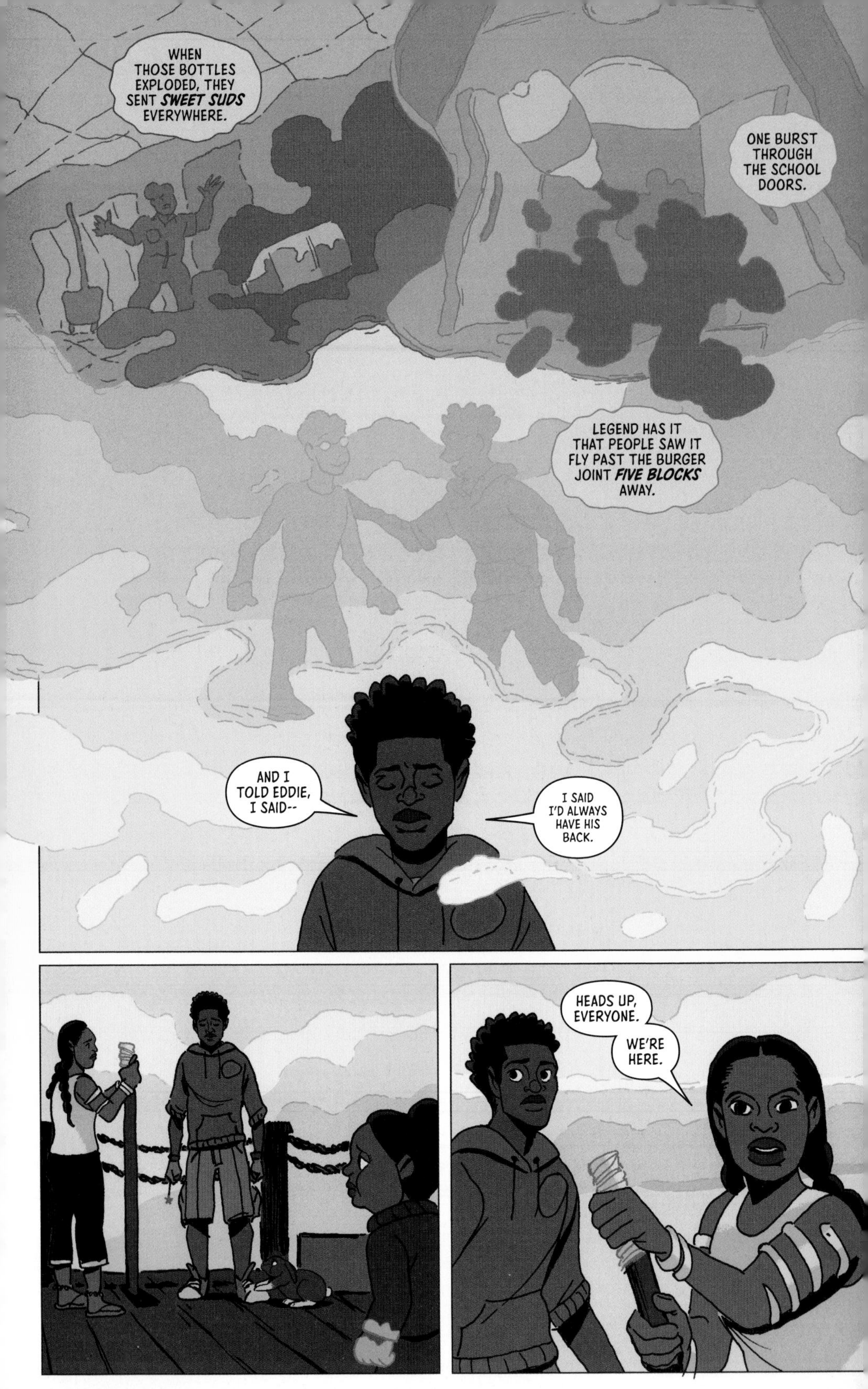
WHEN THOSE BOTTLES EXPLODED, THEY SENT SWEET SUDS EVERYWHERE.
ONE BURST THROUGH THE SCHOOL DOORS.
LEGEND HAS IT THAT PEOPLE SAW IT FLY PAST THE BURGER JOINT FIVE BLOCKS AWAY.
AND I TOLD EDDIE, I SAID--
I SAID I'D ALWAYS HAVE HIS BACK.
HEADS UP, EVERYONE.
WE'RE HERE.

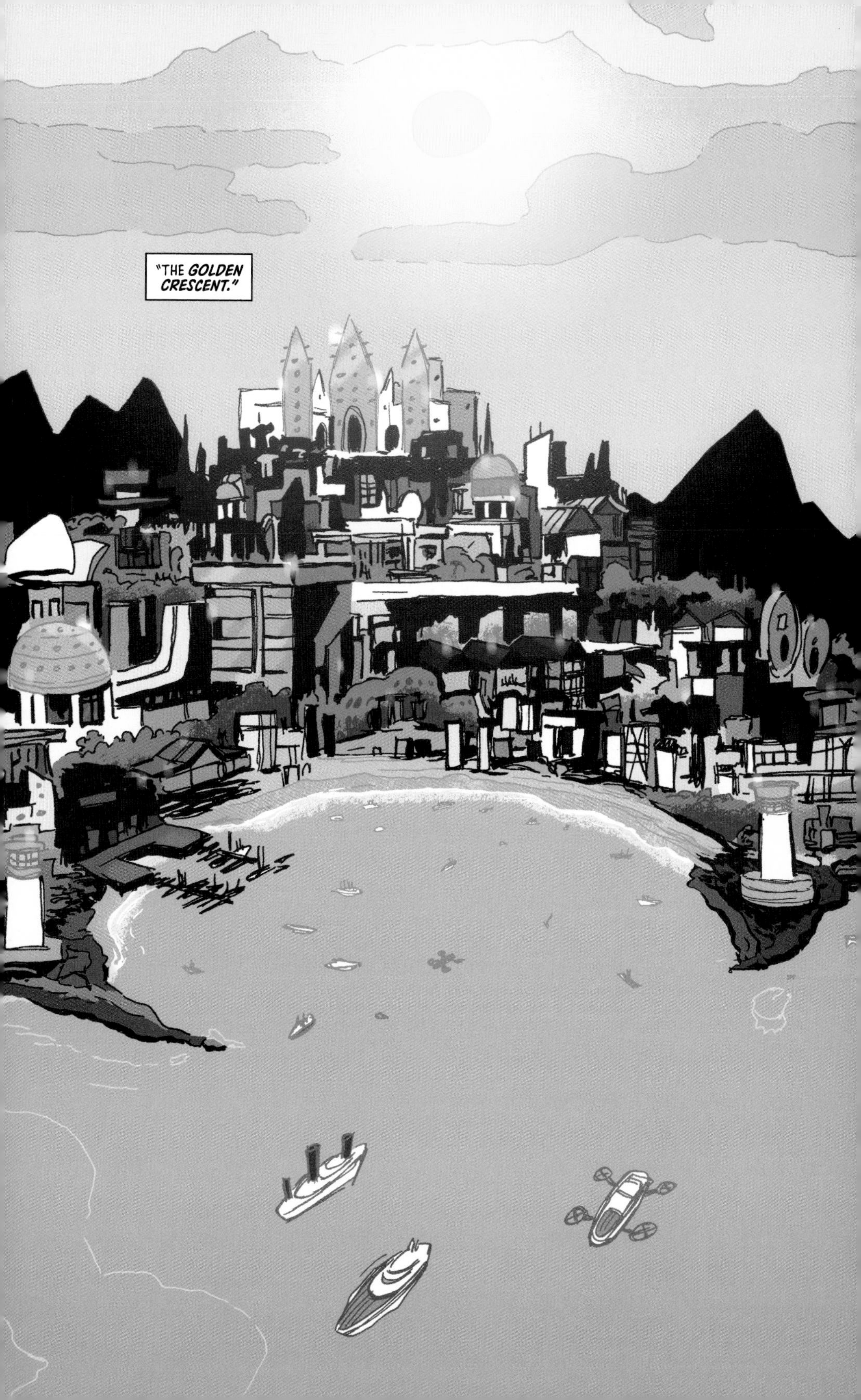
"THE *GOLDEN CRESCENT.*"

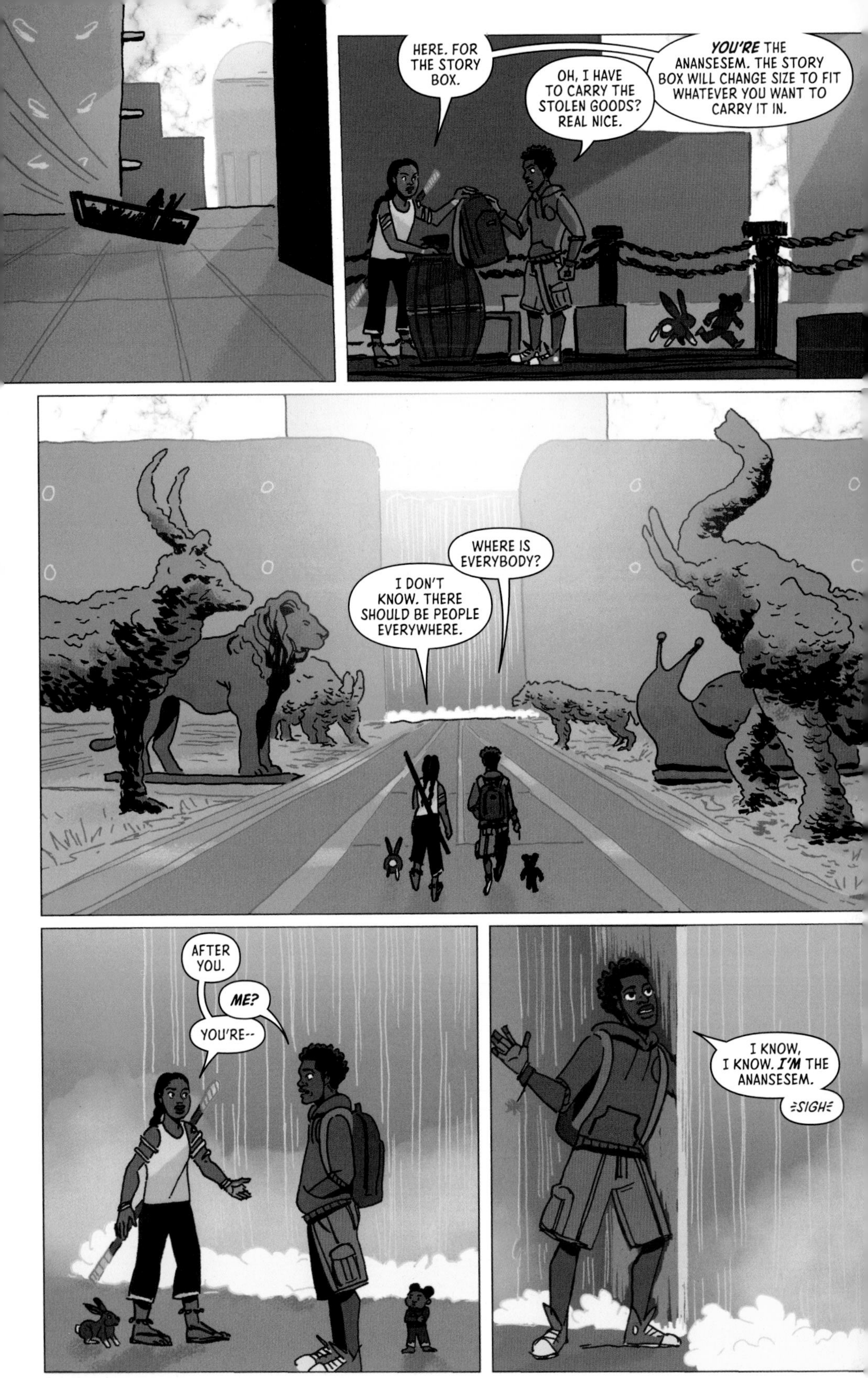
HERE. FOR THE STORY BOX.
OH, I HAVE TO CARRY THE STOLEN GOODS? REAL NICE.
YOU'RE THE ANANSESEM. THE STORY BOX WILL CHANGE SIZE TO FIT WHATEVER YOU WANT TO CARRY IT IN.
WHERE IS EVERYBODY?
I DON'T KNOW. THERE SHOULD BE PEOPLE EVERYWHERE.
AFTER YOU.
ME?
YOU'RE--
I KNOW, I KNOW. I'M THE ANANSESEM.
SIGH

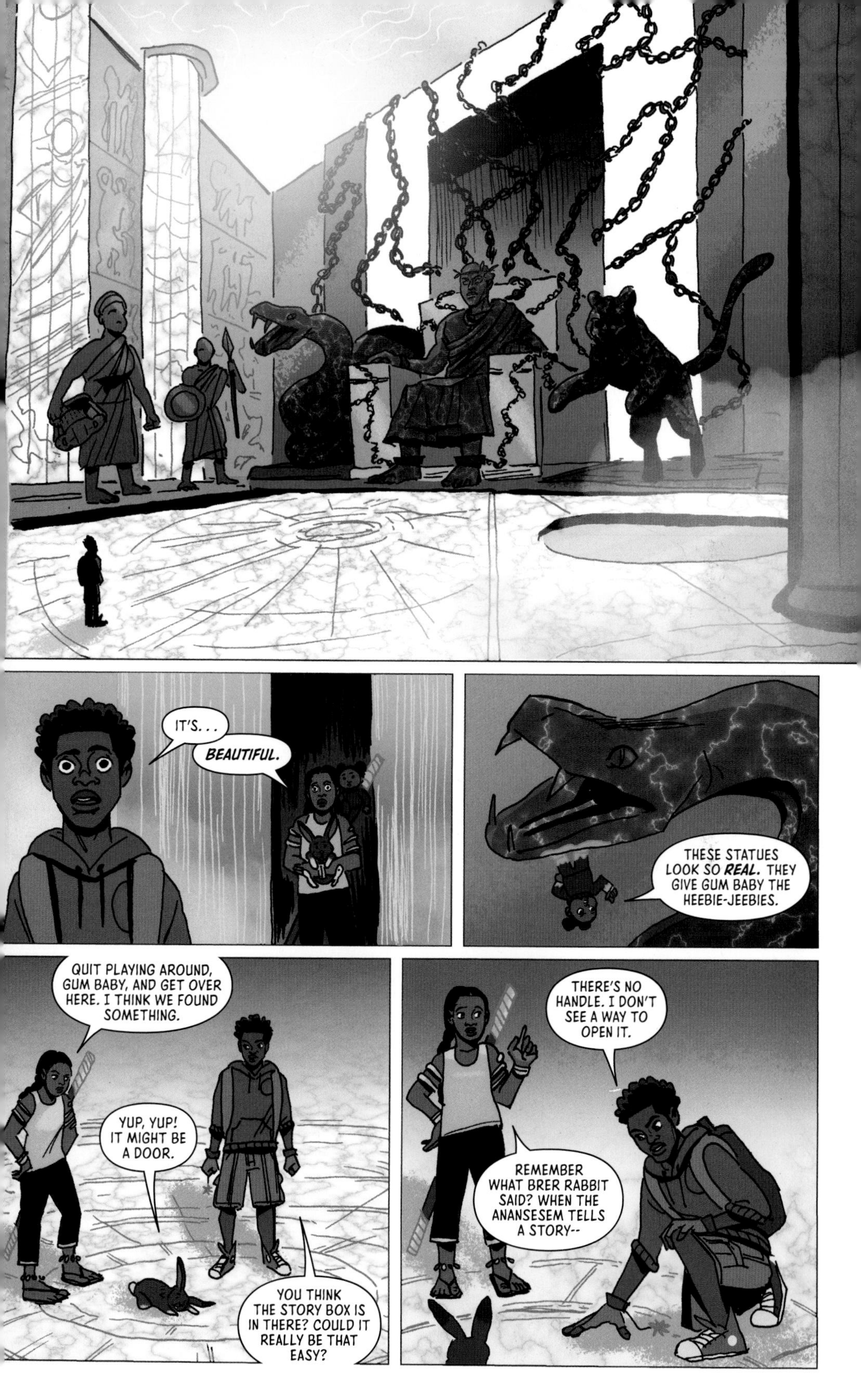
IT'S. . .
BEAUTIFUL.
THESE STATUES LOOK SO REAL. THEY GIVE GUM BABY THE HEEBIE-JEEBIES.
QUIT PLAYING AROUND, GUM BABY, AND GET OVER HERE. I THINK WE FOUND SOMETHING.
YUP, YUP! IT MIGHT BE A DOOR.
YOU THINK THE STORY BOX IS IN THERE? COULD IT REALLY BE THAT EASY?
THERE'S NO HANDLE. I DON'T SEE A WAY TO OPEN IT.
REMEMBER WHAT BRER RABBIT SAID? WHEN THE ANANSESEM TELLS A STORY--

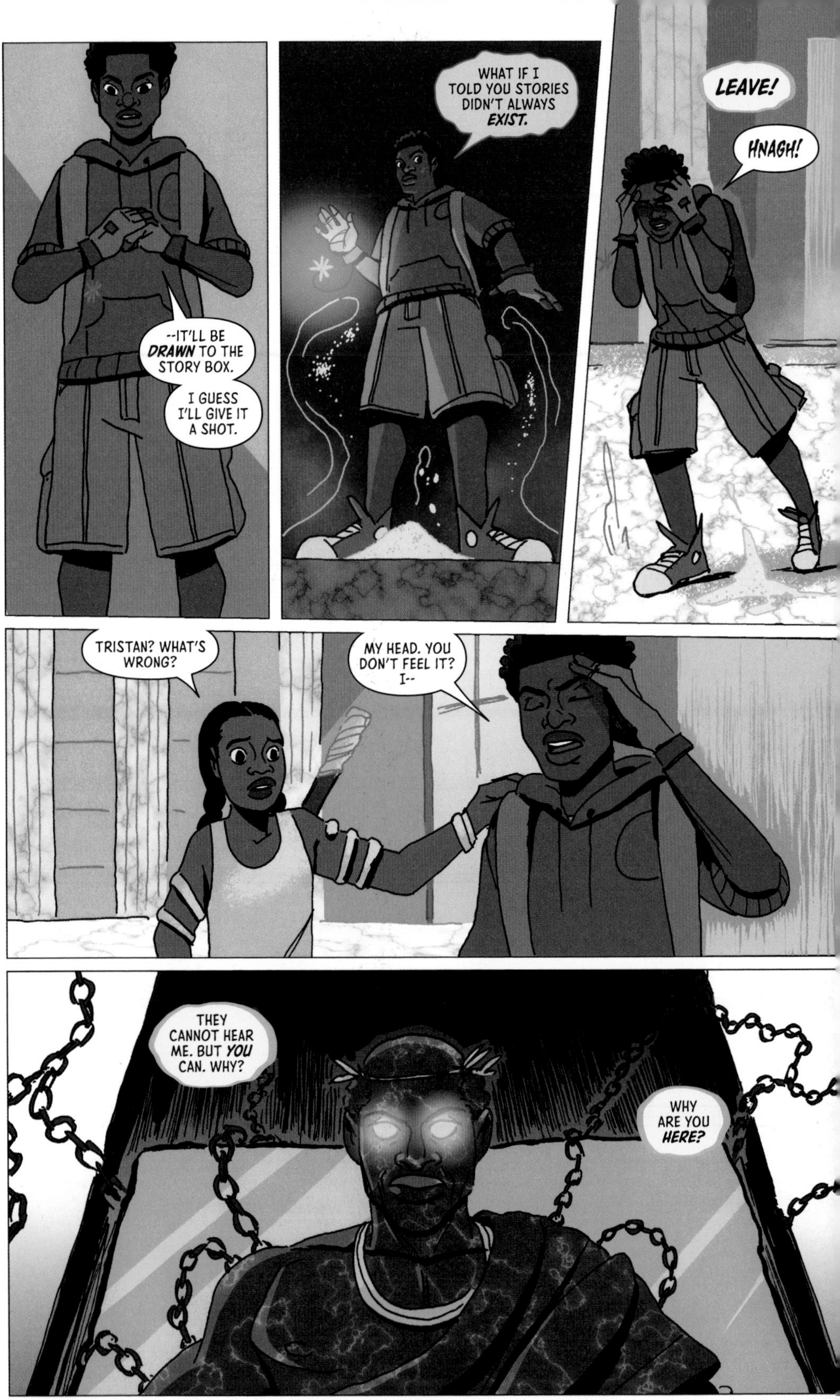
--IT'LL BE *DRAWN* TO THE STORY BOX.
I GUESS I'LL GIVE IT A SHOT.
WHAT IF I TOLD YOU STORIES DIDN'T ALWAYS *EXIST.*
LEAVE!
HNAGH!
TRISTAN? WHAT'S WRONG?
MY HEAD. YOU DON'T FEEL IT? I--
THEY CANNOT HEAR ME. BUT *YOU* CAN. WHY?
WHY ARE YOU *HERE?*

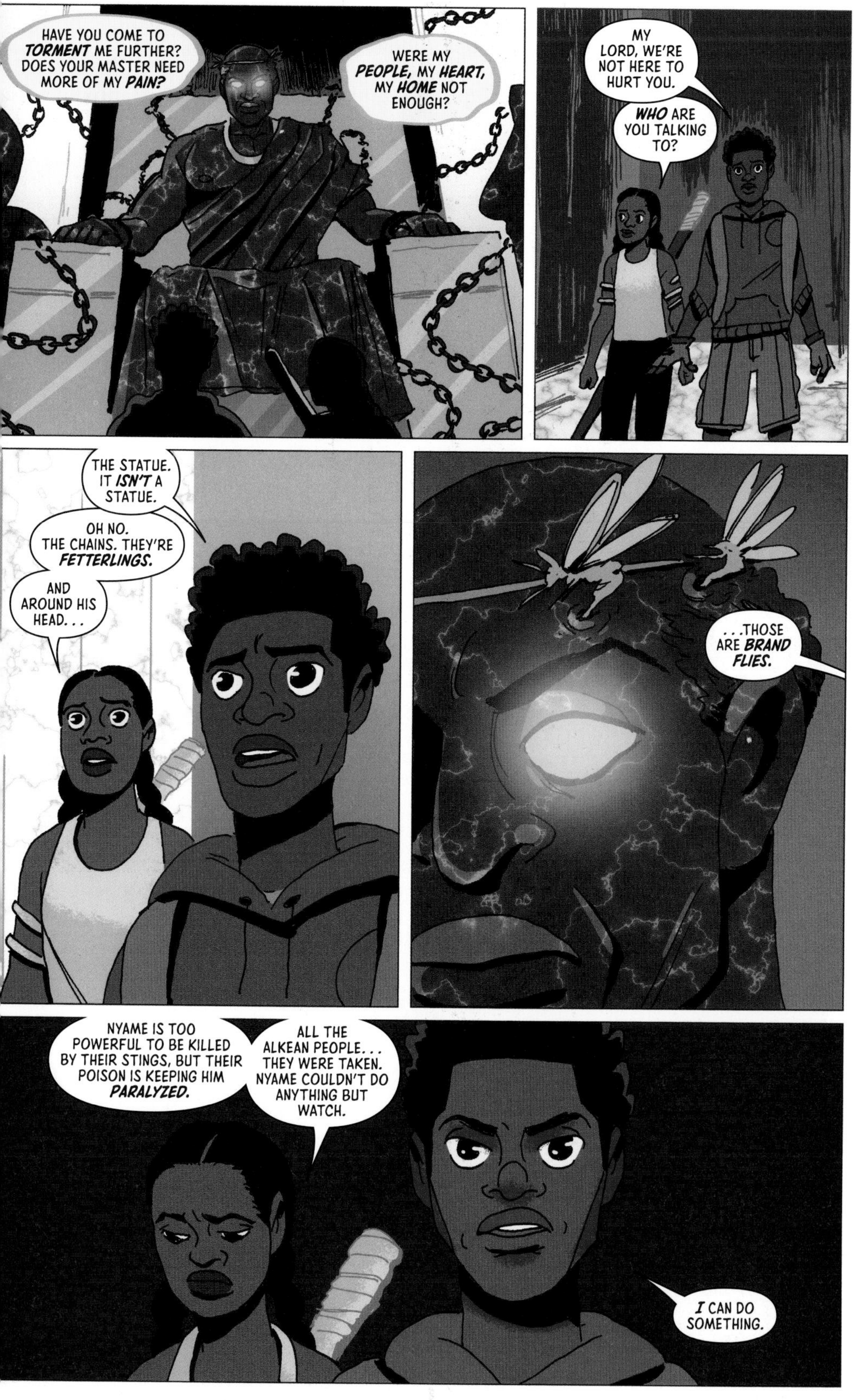
HAVE YOU COME TO TORMENT ME FURTHER? DOES YOUR MASTER NEED MORE OF MY PAIN?
WERE MY PEOPLE, MY HEART, MY HOME NOT ENOUGH?
MY LORD, WE'RE NOT HERE TO HURT YOU.
WHO ARE YOU TALKING TO?
THE STATUE. IT ISN'T A STATUE.
OH NO. THE CHAINS. THEY'RE FETTERLINGS.
AND AROUND HIS HEAD. . .
. . .THOSE ARE BRAND FLIES.
NYAME IS TOO POWERFUL TO BE KILLED BY THEIR STINGS, BUT THEIR POISON IS KEEPING HIM PARALYZED.
ALL THE ALKEAN PEOPLE. . . THEY WERE TAKEN. NYAME COULDN'T DO ANYTHING BUT WATCH.
I CAN DO SOMETHING.

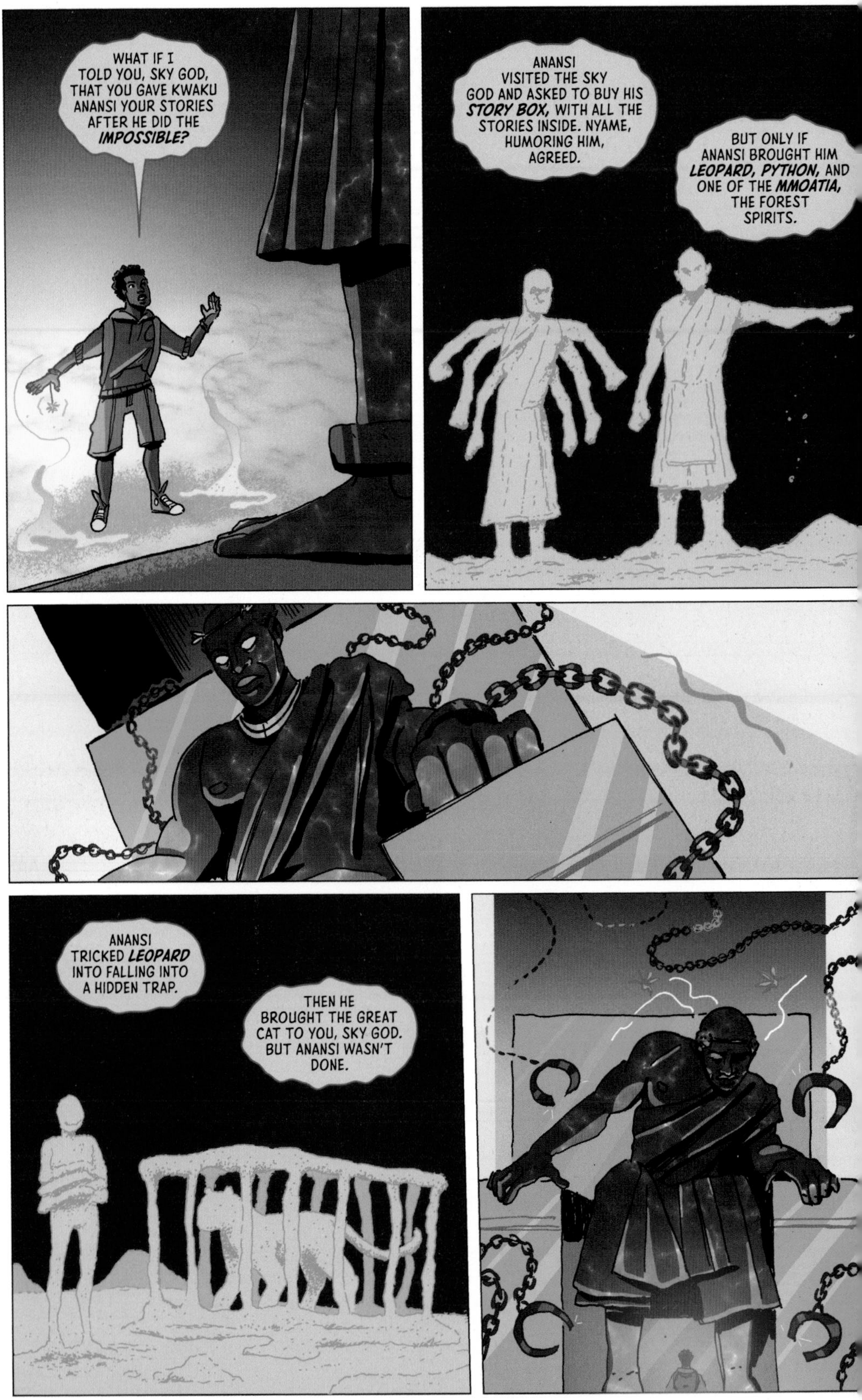

WHAT IF I TOLD YOU, SKY GOD, THAT YOU GAVE KWAKU ANANSI YOUR STORIES AFTER HE DID THE *IMPOSSIBLE?*
ANANSI VISITED THE SKY GOD AND ASKED TO BUY HIS *STORY BOX,* WITH ALL THE STORIES INSIDE. NYAME, HUMORING HIM, AGREED.
BUT ONLY IF ANANSI BROUGHT HIM *LEOPARD, PYTHON,* AND ONE OF THE *MMOATIA,* THE FOREST SPIRITS.
ANANSI TRICKED *LEOPARD* INTO FALLING INTO A HIDDEN TRAP.
THEN HE BROUGHT THE GREAT CAT TO YOU, SKY GOD. BUT ANANSI WASN'T DONE.

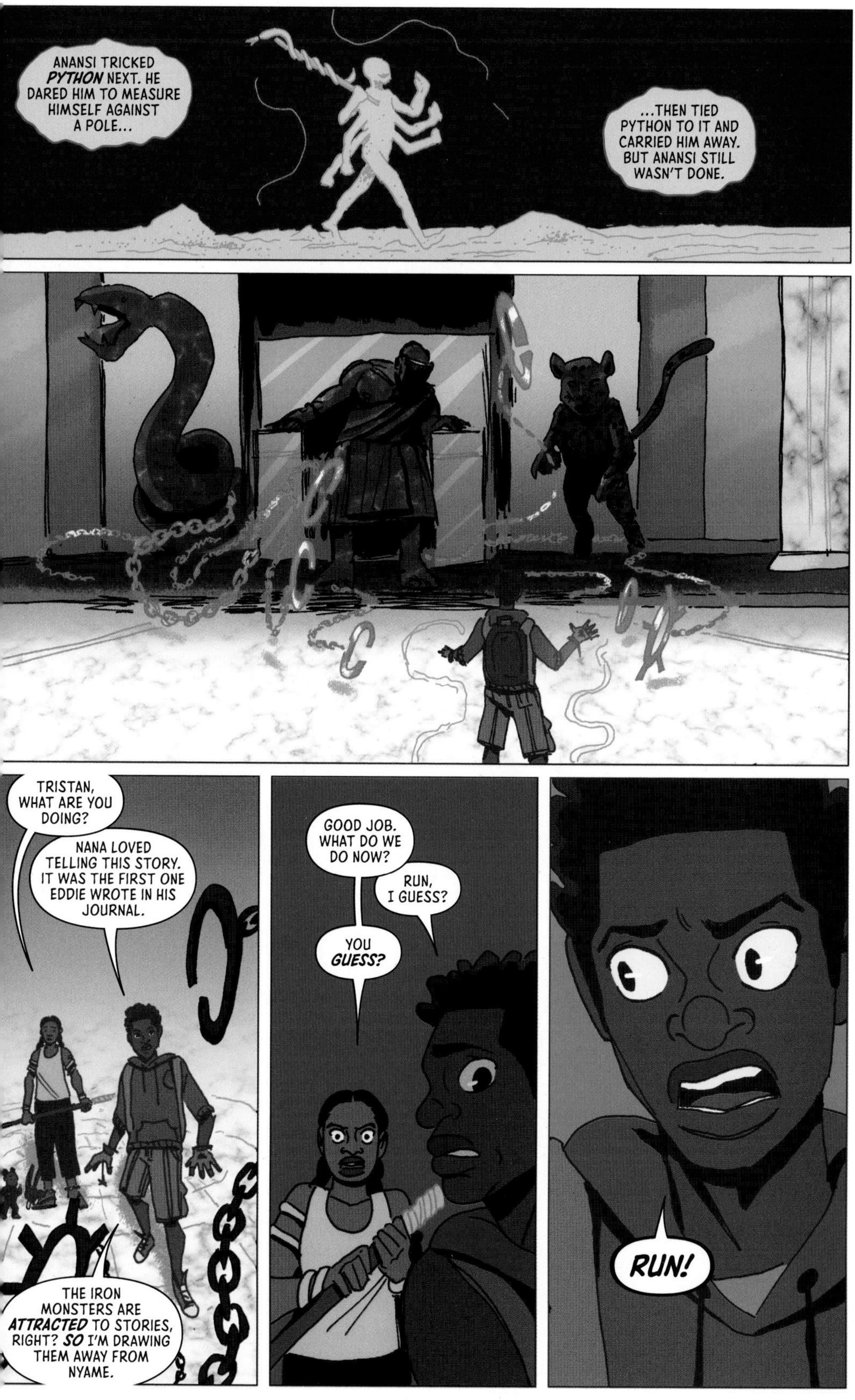
ANANSI TRICKED PYTHON NEXT. HE DARED HIM TO MEASURE HIMSELF AGAINST A POLE...
...THEN TIED PYTHON TO IT AND CARRIED HIM AWAY. BUT ANANSI STILL WASN'T DONE.
TRISTAN, WHAT ARE YOU DOING?
NANA LOVED TELLING THIS STORY. IT WAS THE FIRST ONE EDDIE WROTE IN HIS JOURNAL.
THE IRON MONSTERS ARE ATTRACTED TO STORIES, RIGHT? SO I'M DRAWING THEM AWAY FROM NYAME.
GOOD JOB. WHAT DO WE DO NOW?
RUN, I GUESS?
YOU GUESS?
RUN!

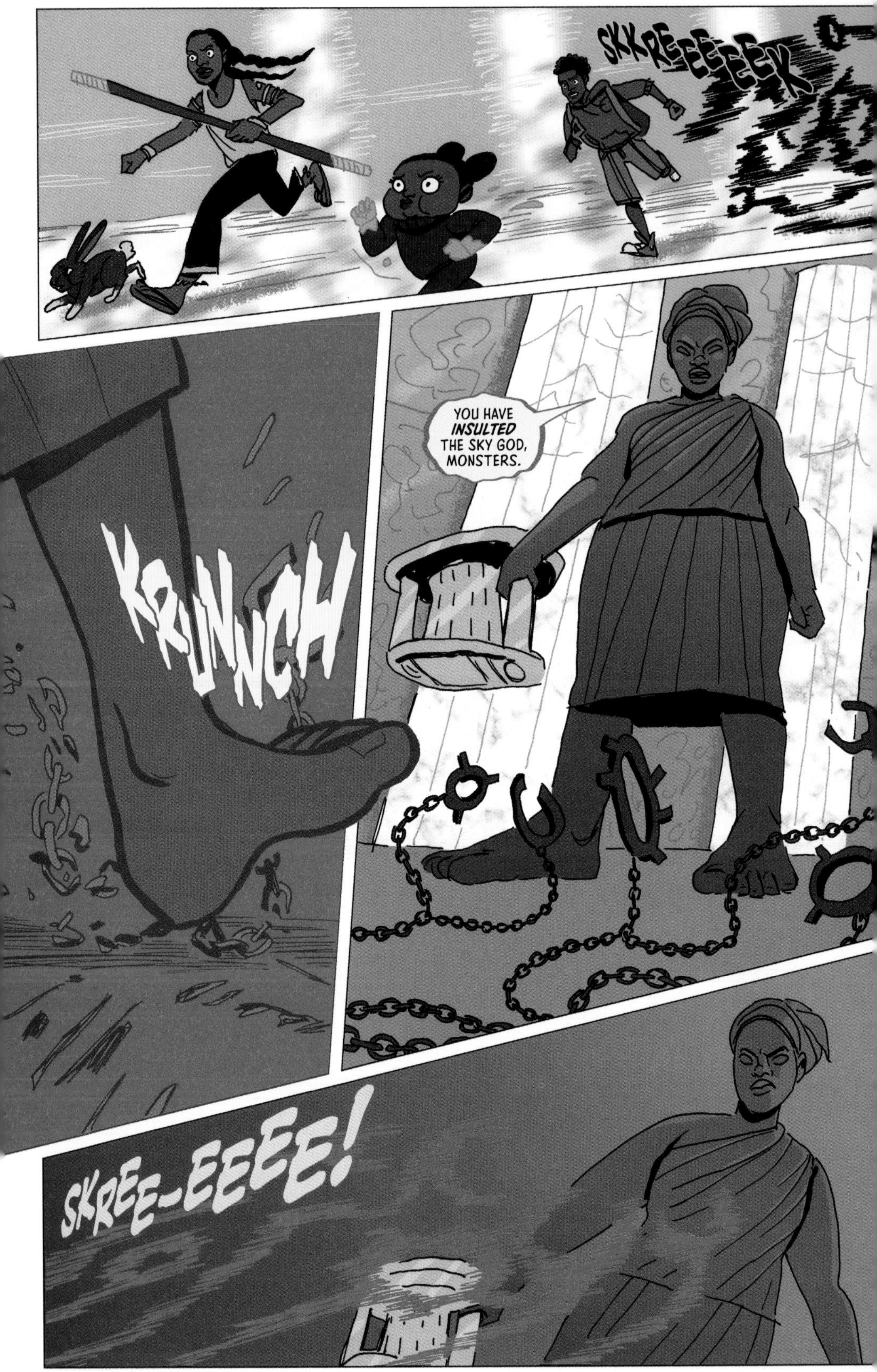
SKKREEEEEEK
KRUNNCH
YOU HAVE *INSULTED* THE SKY GOD, MONSTERS.
SKREE-EEEE!

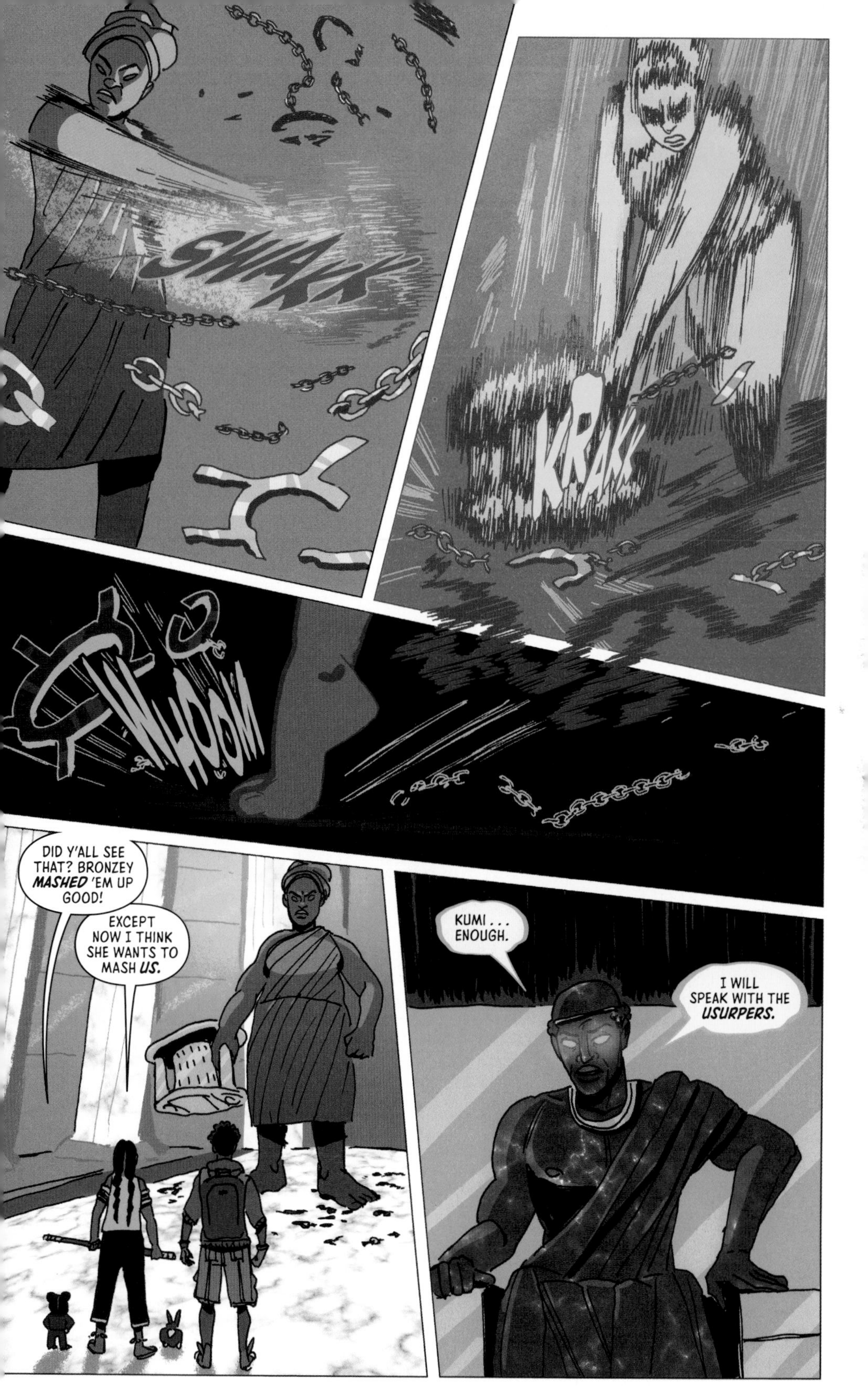
SHWAKK
KRAKK
WHOOM
DID Y'ALL SEE THAT? BRONZEY MASHED 'EM UP GOOD!
EXCEPT NOW I THINK SHE WANTS TO MASH US.
KUMI . . . ENOUGH.
I WILL SPEAK WITH THE USURPERS.

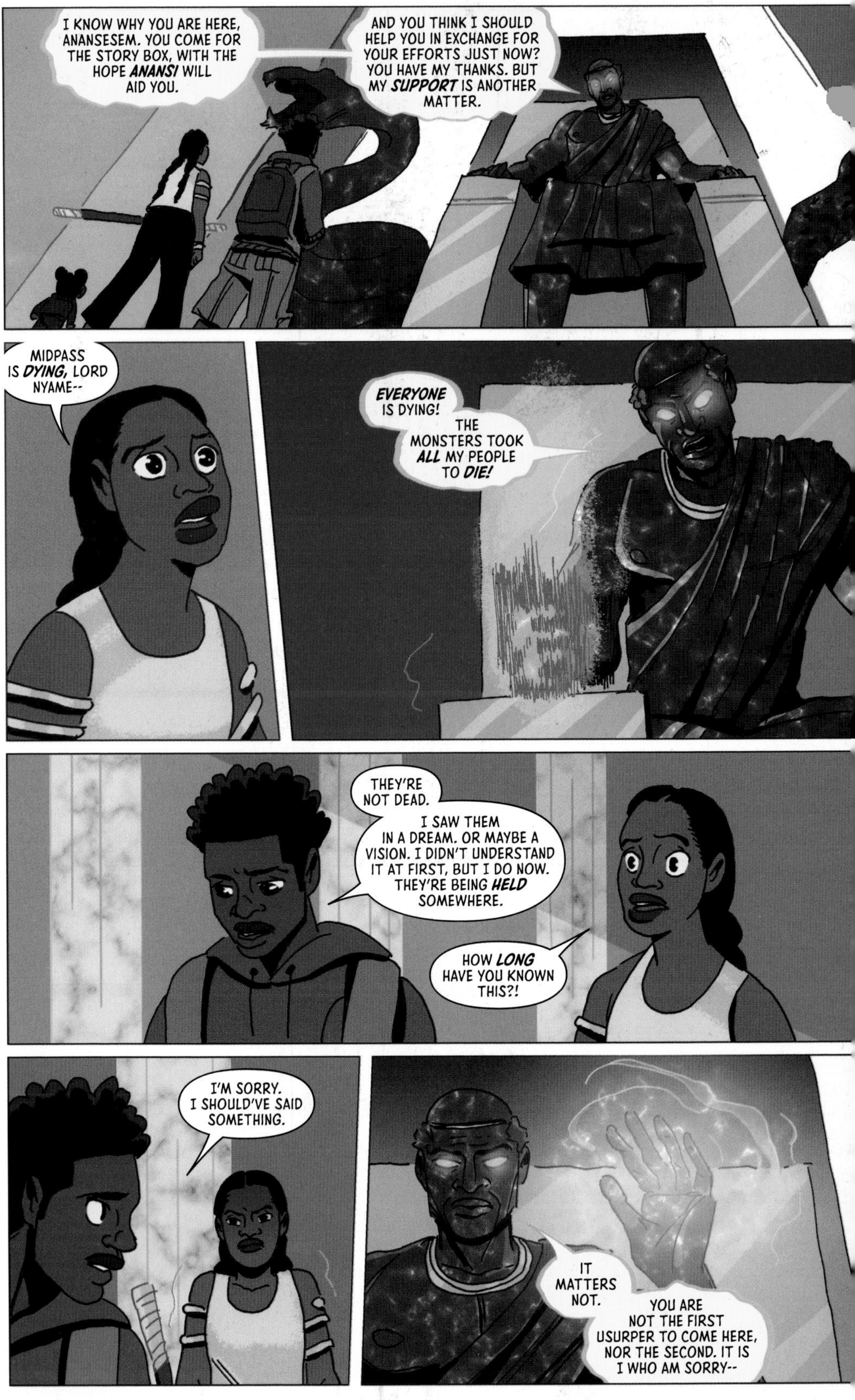
I KNOW WHY YOU ARE HERE, ANANSESEM. YOU COME FOR THE STORY BOX, WITH THE HOPE ANANSI WILL AID YOU.
AND YOU THINK I SHOULD HELP YOU IN EXCHANGE FOR YOUR EFFORTS JUST NOW? YOU HAVE MY THANKS. BUT MY SUPPORT IS ANOTHER MATTER.
MIDPASS IS DYING, LORD NYAME--
EVERYONE IS DYING!
THE MONSTERS TOOK ALL MY PEOPLE TO DIE!
THEY'RE NOT DEAD.
I SAW THEM IN A DREAM. OR MAYBE A VISION. I DIDN'T UNDERSTAND IT AT FIRST, BUT I DO NOW. THEY'RE BEING HELD SOMEWHERE.
HOW LONG HAVE YOU KNOWN THIS?!
I'M SORRY. I SHOULD'VE SAID SOMETHING.
IT MATTERS NOT.
YOU ARE NOT THE FIRST USURPER TO COME HERE, NOR THE SECOND. IT IS I WHO AM SORRY--

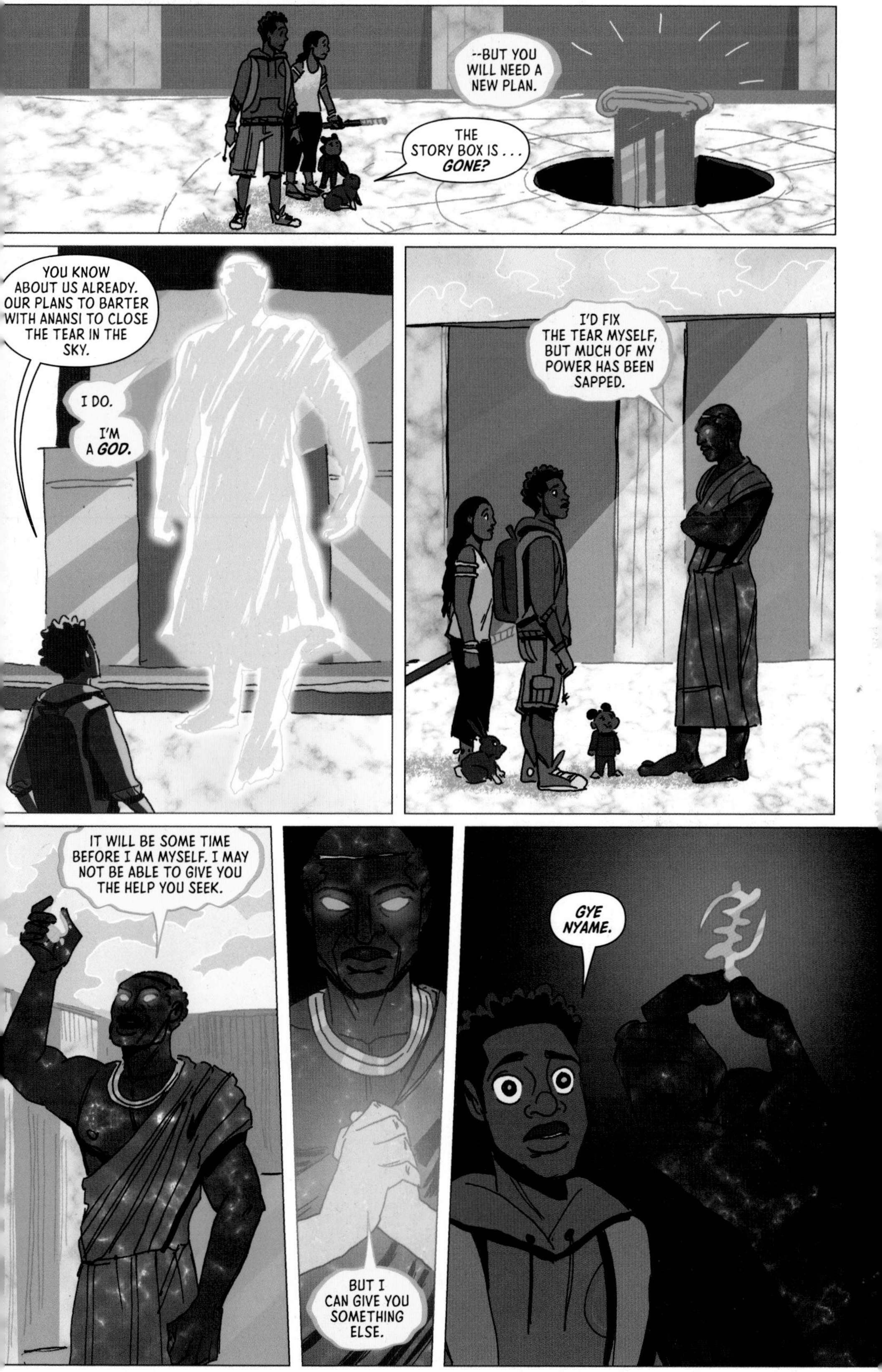
--BUT YOU WILL NEED A NEW PLAN.
THE STORY BOX IS . . . *GONE?*
YOU KNOW ABOUT US ALREADY. OUR PLANS TO BARTER WITH ANANSI TO CLOSE THE TEAR IN THE SKY.
I DO.
I'M A *GOD.*
I'D FIX THE TEAR MYSELF, BUT MUCH OF MY POWER HAS BEEN SAPPED.
IT WILL BE SOME TIME BEFORE I AM MYSELF. I MAY NOT BE ABLE TO GIVE YOU THE HELP YOU SEEK.
BUT I CAN GIVE YOU SOMETHING ELSE.
GYE NYAME.

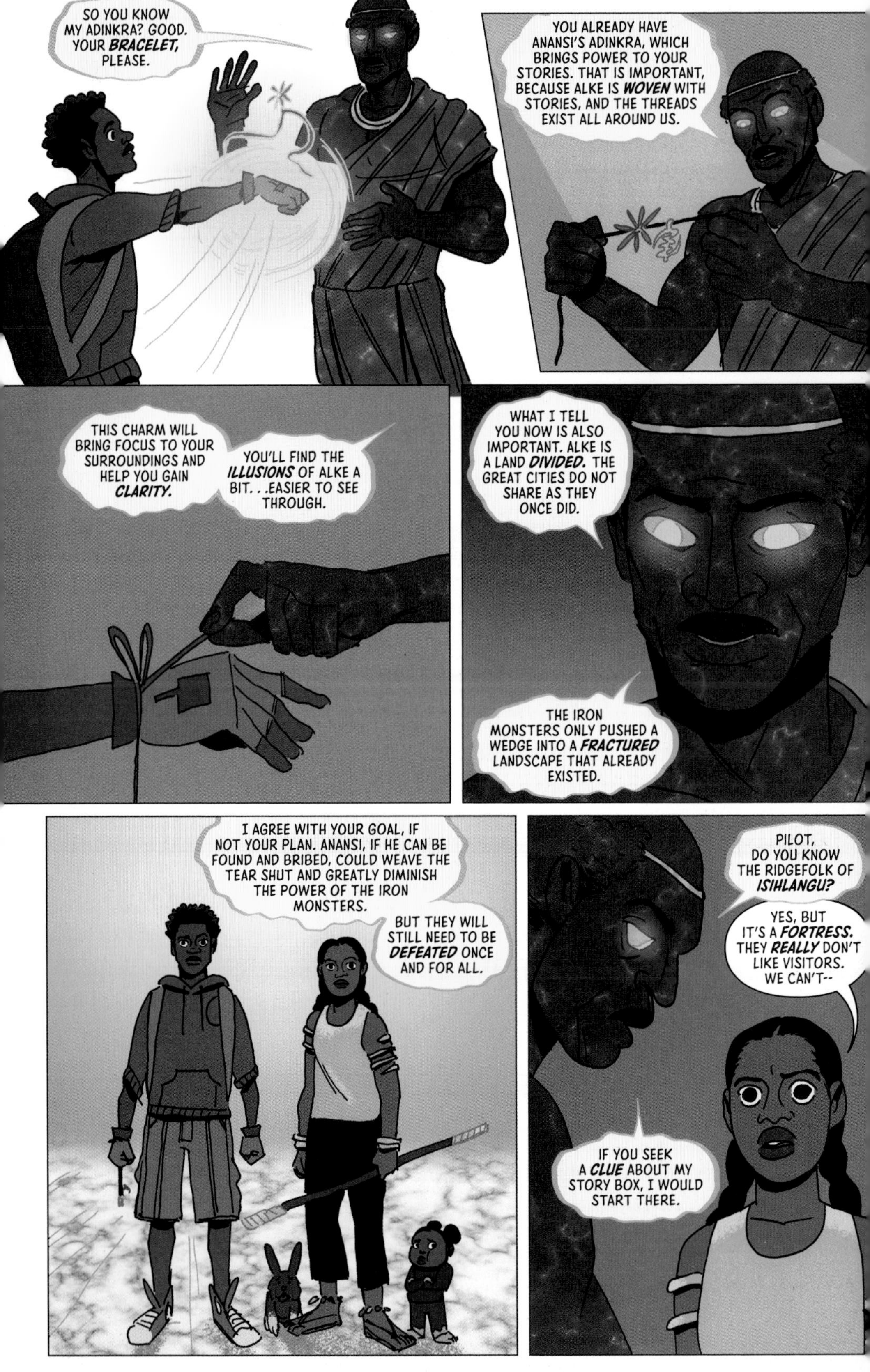
SO YOU KNOW MY ADINKRA? GOOD. YOUR BRACELET, PLEASE.
YOU ALREADY HAVE ANANSI'S ADINKRA, WHICH BRINGS POWER TO YOUR STORIES. THAT IS IMPORTANT, BECAUSE ALKE IS WOVEN WITH STORIES, AND THE THREADS EXIST ALL AROUND US.
THIS CHARM WILL BRING FOCUS TO YOUR SURROUNDINGS AND HELP YOU GAIN CLARITY.
YOU'LL FIND THE ILLUSIONS OF ALKE A BIT. . .EASIER TO SEE THROUGH.
WHAT I TELL YOU NOW IS ALSO IMPORTANT. ALKE IS A LAND DIVIDED. THE GREAT CITIES DO NOT SHARE AS THEY ONCE DID.
THE IRON MONSTERS ONLY PUSHED A WEDGE INTO A FRACTURED LANDSCAPE THAT ALREADY EXISTED.
I AGREE WITH YOUR GOAL, IF NOT YOUR PLAN. ANANSI, IF HE CAN BE FOUND AND BRIBED, COULD WEAVE THE TEAR SHUT AND GREATLY DIMINISH THE POWER OF THE IRON MONSTERS.
BUT THEY WILL STILL NEED TO BE DEFEATED ONCE AND FOR ALL.
PILOT, DO YOU KNOW THE RIDGEFOLK OF ISIHLANGU?
YES, BUT IT'S A FORTRESS. THEY REALLY DON'T LIKE VISITORS. WE CAN'T--
IF YOU SEEK A CLUE ABOUT MY STORY BOX, I WOULD START THERE.

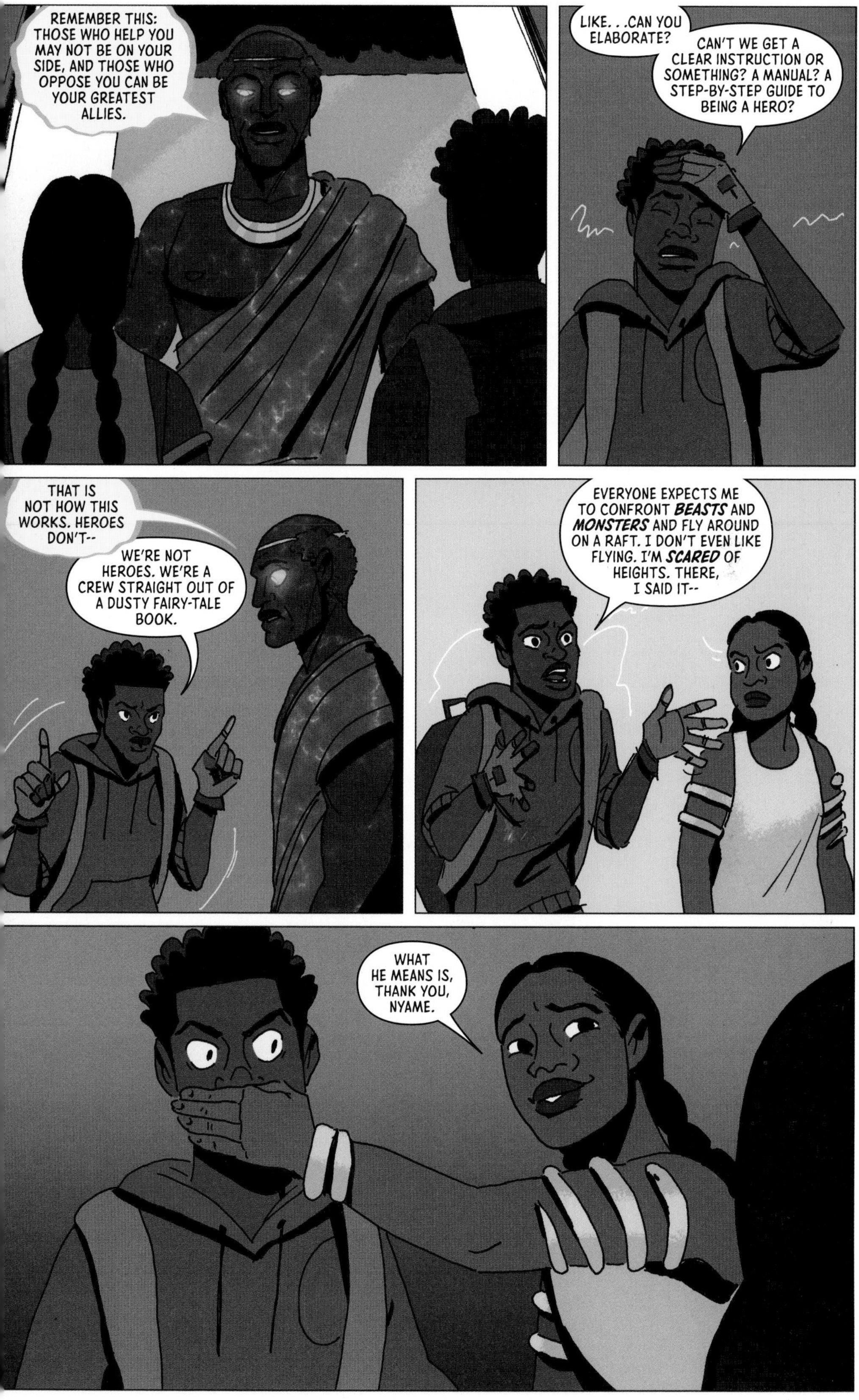
REMEMBER THIS: THOSE WHO HELP YOU MAY NOT BE ON YOUR SIDE, AND THOSE WHO OPPOSE YOU CAN BE YOUR GREATEST ALLIES.
LIKE. . .CAN YOU ELABORATE?
CAN'T WE GET A CLEAR INSTRUCTION OR SOMETHING? A MANUAL? A STEP-BY-STEP GUIDE TO BEING A HERO?
THAT IS NOT HOW THIS WORKS. HEROES DON'T--
WE'RE NOT HEROES. WE'RE A CREW STRAIGHT OUT OF A DUSTY FAIRY-TALE BOOK.
EVERYONE EXPECTS ME TO CONFRONT *BEASTS* AND *MONSTERS* AND FLY AROUND ON A RAFT. I DON'T EVEN LIKE FLYING. I'M *SCARED* OF HEIGHTS. THERE, I SAID IT--
WHAT HE MEANS IS, THANK YOU, NYAME.

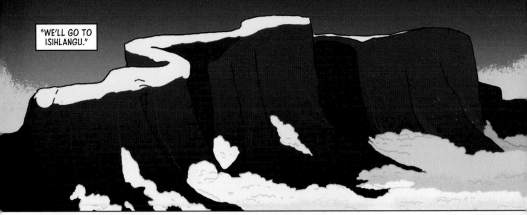

"WE'LL GO TO ISIHLANGU."

YOU STILL THINK HIDING IN THE *TRASH CAR* WAS A GOOD IDEA?

WE MADE IT *INSIDE*, DIDN'T WE?

THIS IS *INCREDIBLE.* NO RABBIT HAS EVER MADE IT THIS FAR. IF I CAN BRING NEW INFORMATION ABOUT THE RIDGE BACK TO THE WARREN SOCIETY...

...THEY'LL *HAVE* TO MAKE ME A MEMBER.

WHILE Y'ALL WERE *JAWING,* GUM BABY FOUND A BACK DOOR.

MOVE!

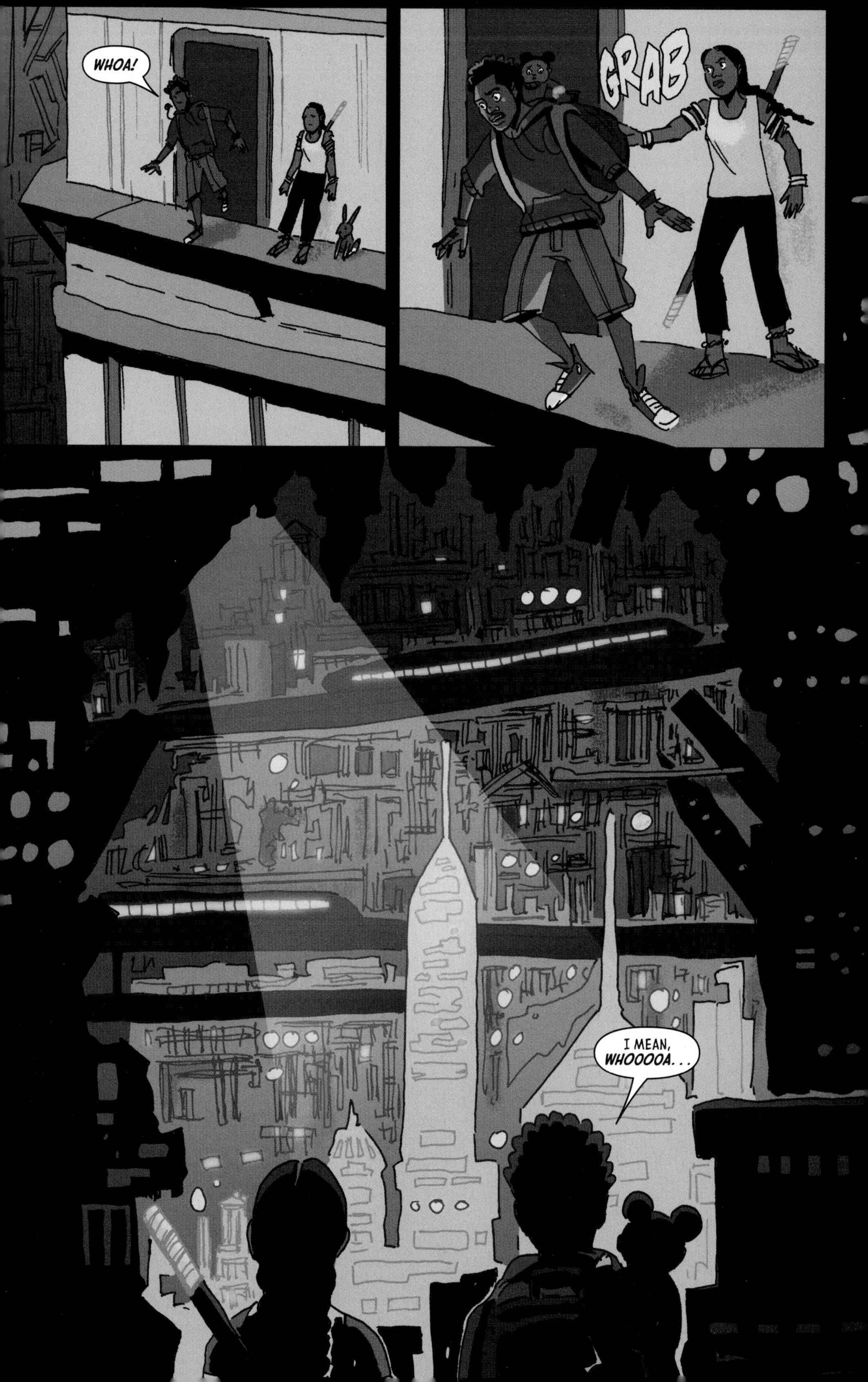
WHOA!
GRAB
I MEAN, WHOOOOA...

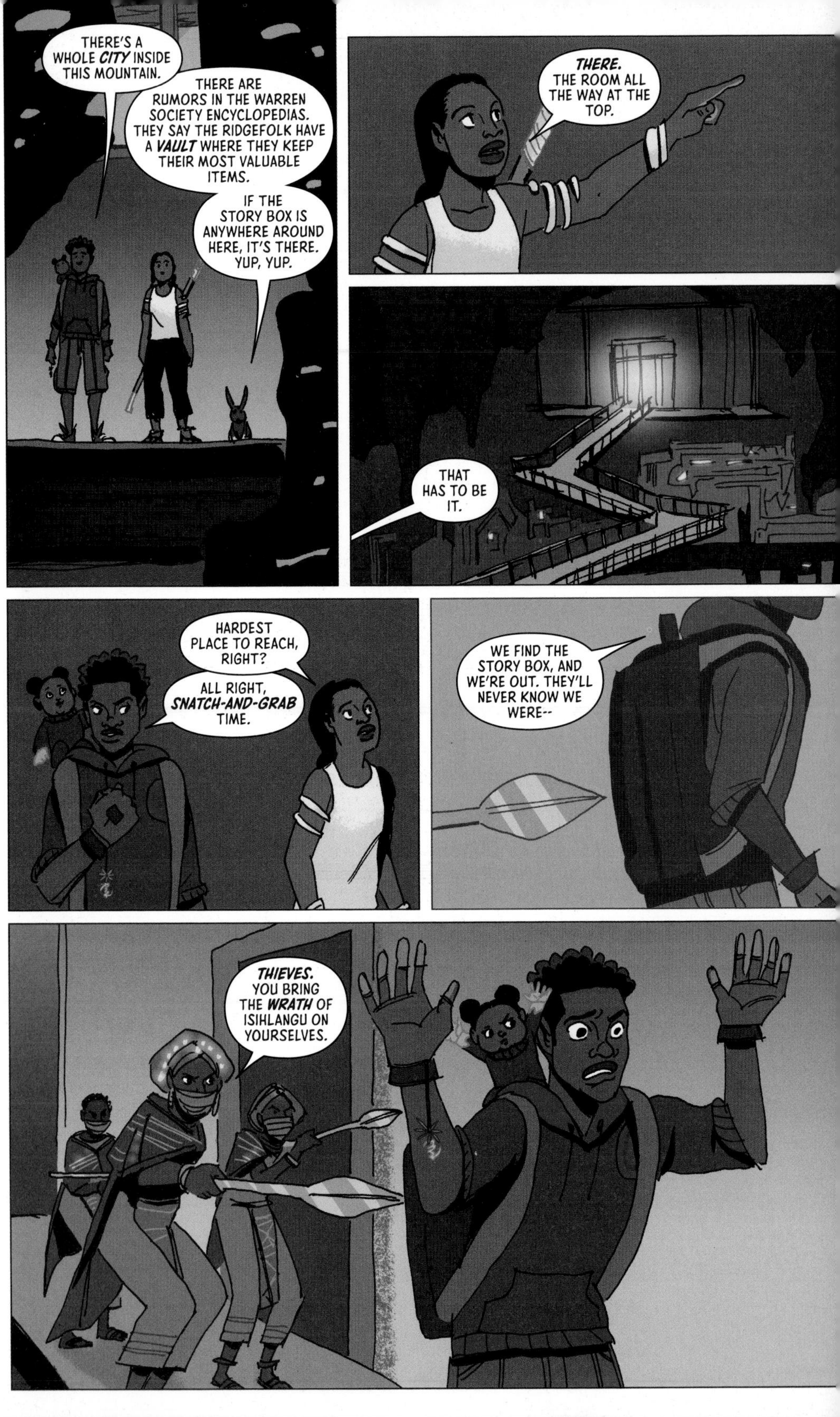
THERE'S A WHOLE *CITY* INSIDE THIS MOUNTAIN.
THERE ARE RUMORS IN THE WARREN SOCIETY ENCYCLOPEDIAS. THEY SAY THE RIDGEFOLK HAVE A *VAULT* WHERE THEY KEEP THEIR MOST VALUABLE ITEMS.
IF THE STORY BOX IS ANYWHERE AROUND HERE, IT'S THERE. YUP, YUP.
THERE. THE ROOM ALL THE WAY AT THE TOP.
THAT HAS TO BE IT.
HARDEST PLACE TO REACH, RIGHT?
ALL RIGHT, *SNATCH-AND-GRAB* TIME.
WE FIND THE STORY BOX, AND WE'RE OUT. THEY'LL NEVER KNOW WE WERE--
THIEVES. YOU BRING THE *WRATH* OF ISIHLANGU ON YOURSELVES.

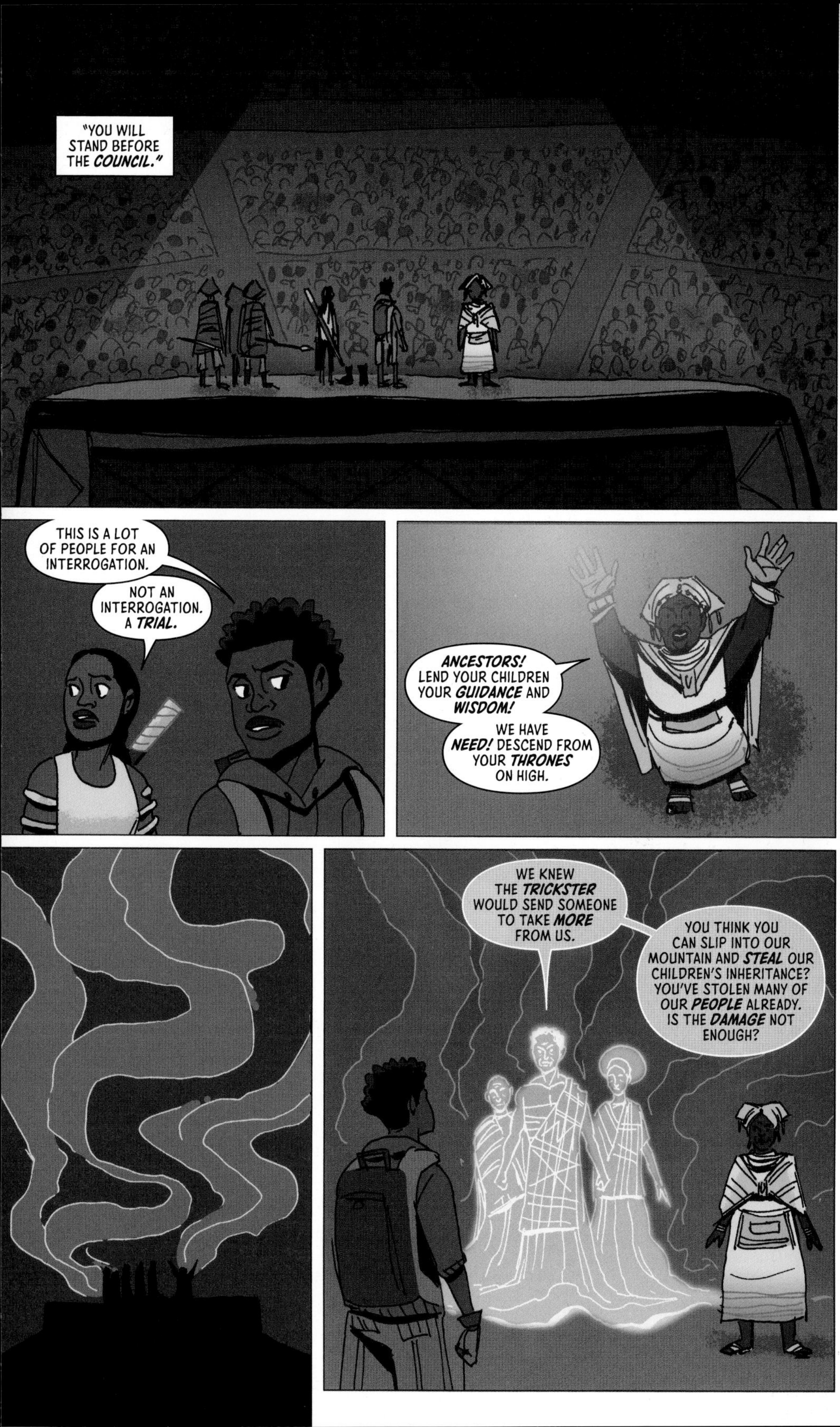
"YOU WILL STAND BEFORE THE COUNCIL."
THIS IS A LOT OF PEOPLE FOR AN INTERROGATION.
NOT AN INTERROGATION. A TRIAL.
ANCESTORS! LEND YOUR CHILDREN YOUR GUIDANCE AND WISDOM!
WE HAVE NEED! DESCEND FROM YOUR THRONES ON HIGH.
WE KNEW THE TRICKSTER WOULD SEND SOMEONE TO TAKE MORE FROM US.
YOU THINK YOU CAN SLIP INTO OUR MOUNTAIN AND STEAL OUR CHILDREN'S INHERITANCE? YOU'VE STOLEN MANY OF OUR PEOPLE ALREADY. IS THE DAMAGE NOT ENOUGH?

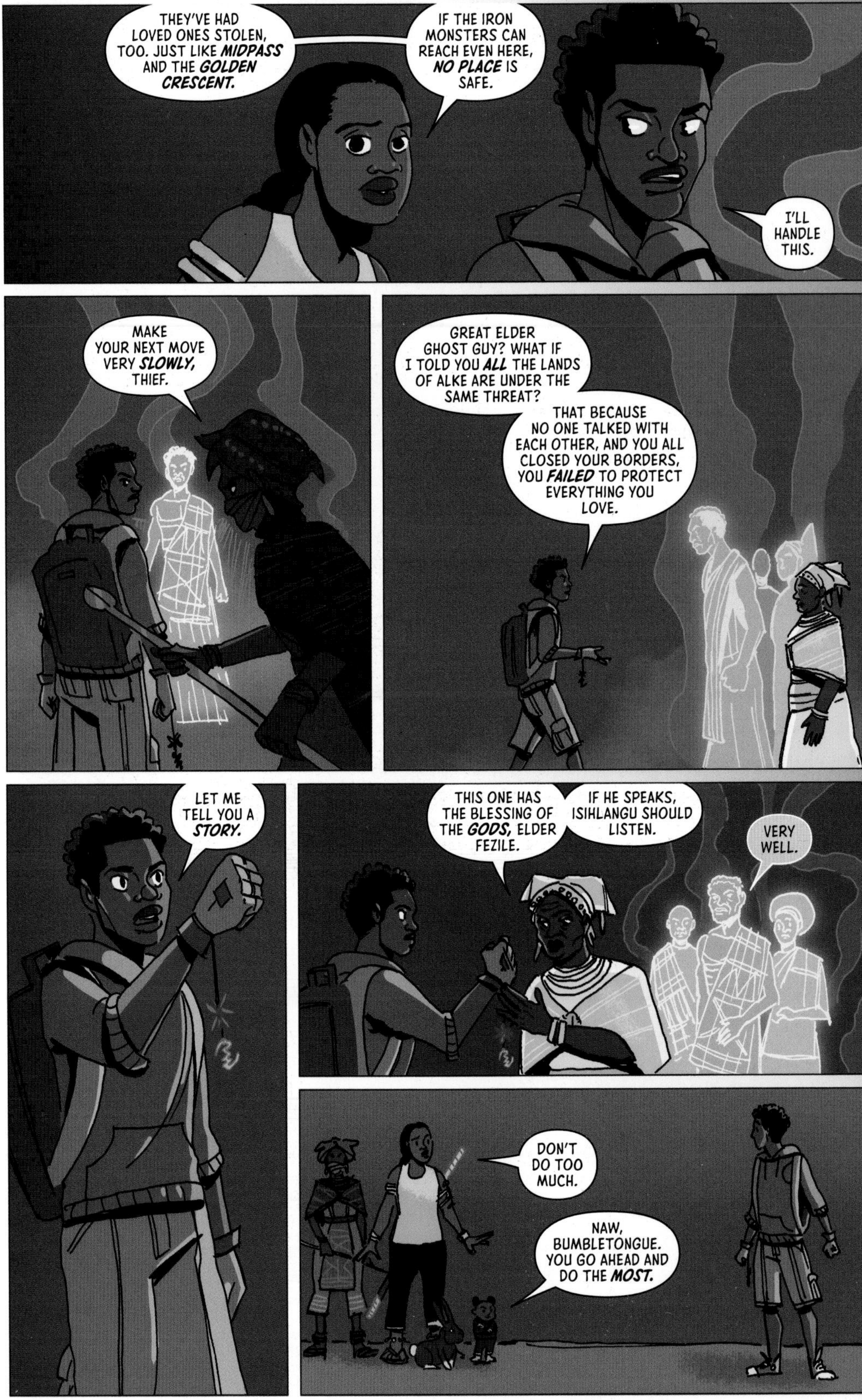
THEY'VE HAD LOVED ONES STOLEN, TOO. JUST LIKE *MIDPASS* AND THE *GOLDEN CRESCENT.*
IF THE IRON MONSTERS CAN REACH EVEN HERE, *NO PLACE* IS SAFE.
I'LL HANDLE THIS.
MAKE YOUR NEXT MOVE VERY *SLOWLY,* THIEF.
GREAT ELDER GHOST GUY? WHAT IF I TOLD YOU *ALL* THE LANDS OF ALKE ARE UNDER THE SAME THREAT?
THAT BECAUSE NO ONE TALKED WITH EACH OTHER, AND YOU ALL CLOSED YOUR BORDERS, YOU *FAILED* TO PROTECT EVERYTHING YOU LOVE.
LET ME TELL YOU A *STORY.*
THIS ONE HAS THE BLESSING OF THE *GODS,* ELDER FEZILE.
IF HE SPEAKS, ISIHLANGU SHOULD LISTEN.
VERY WELL.
DON'T DO TOO MUCH.
NAW, BUMBLETONGUE. YOU GO AHEAD AND DO THE *MOST.*

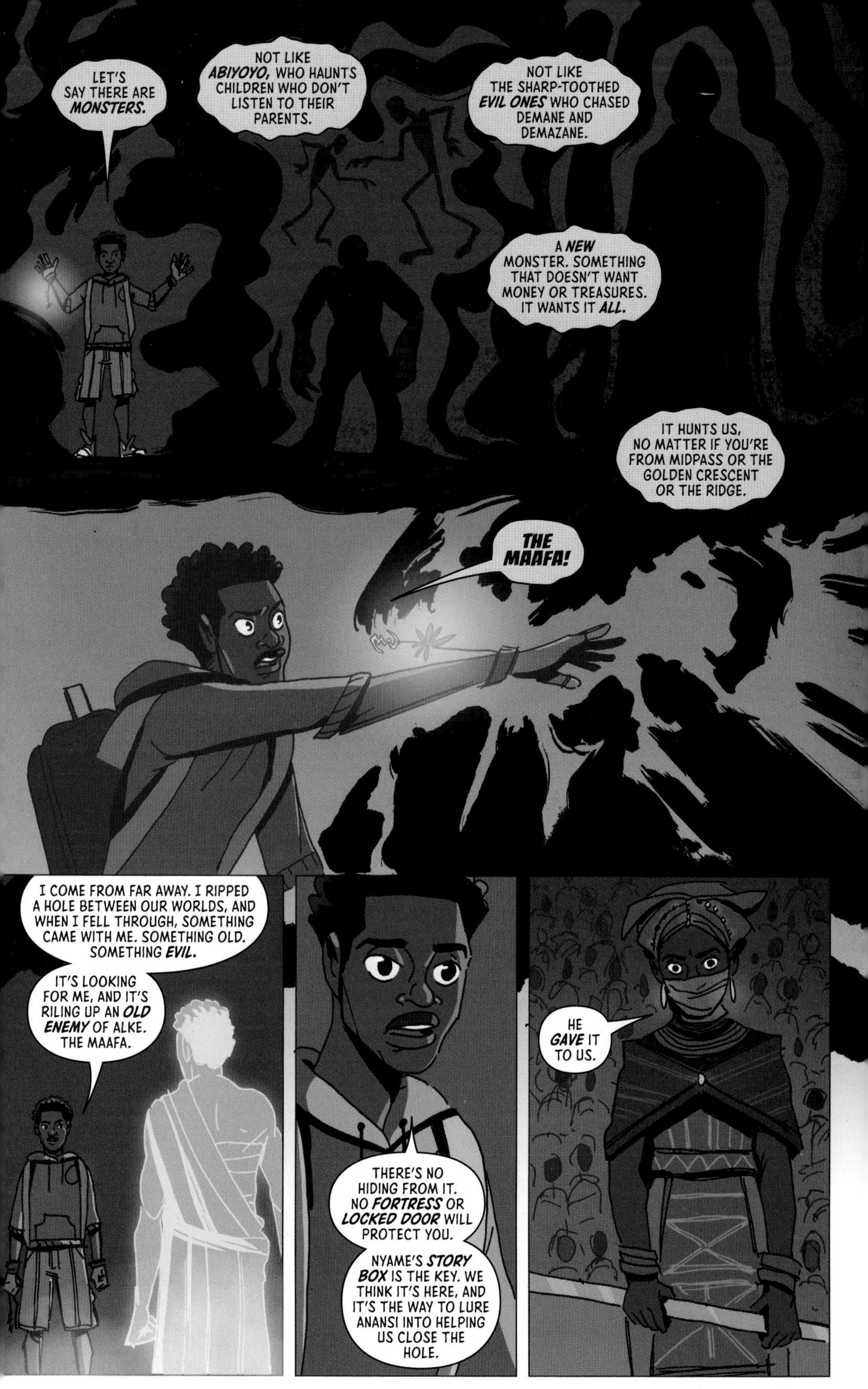
LET'S SAY THERE ARE MONSTERS.
NOT LIKE ABIYOYO, WHO HAUNTS CHILDREN WHO DON'T LISTEN TO THEIR PARENTS.
NOT LIKE THE SHARP-TOOTHED EVIL ONES WHO CHASED DEMANE AND DEMAZANE.
A NEW MONSTER. SOMETHING THAT DOESN'T WANT MONEY OR TREASURES. IT WANTS IT ALL.
IT HUNTS US, NO MATTER IF YOU'RE FROM MIDPASS OR THE GOLDEN CRESCENT OR THE RIDGE.
THE MAAFA!
I COME FROM FAR AWAY. I RIPPED A HOLE BETWEEN OUR WORLDS, AND WHEN I FELL THROUGH, SOMETHING CAME WITH ME. SOMETHING OLD. SOMETHING EVIL.
IT'S LOOKING FOR ME, AND IT'S RILING UP AN OLD ENEMY OF ALKE. THE MAAFA.
THERE'S NO HIDING FROM IT. NO FORTRESS OR LOCKED DOOR WILL PROTECT YOU.
NYAME'S STORY BOX IS THE KEY. WE THINK IT'S HERE, AND IT'S THE WAY TO LURE ANANSI INTO HELPING US CLOSE THE HOLE.
HE GAVE IT TO US.

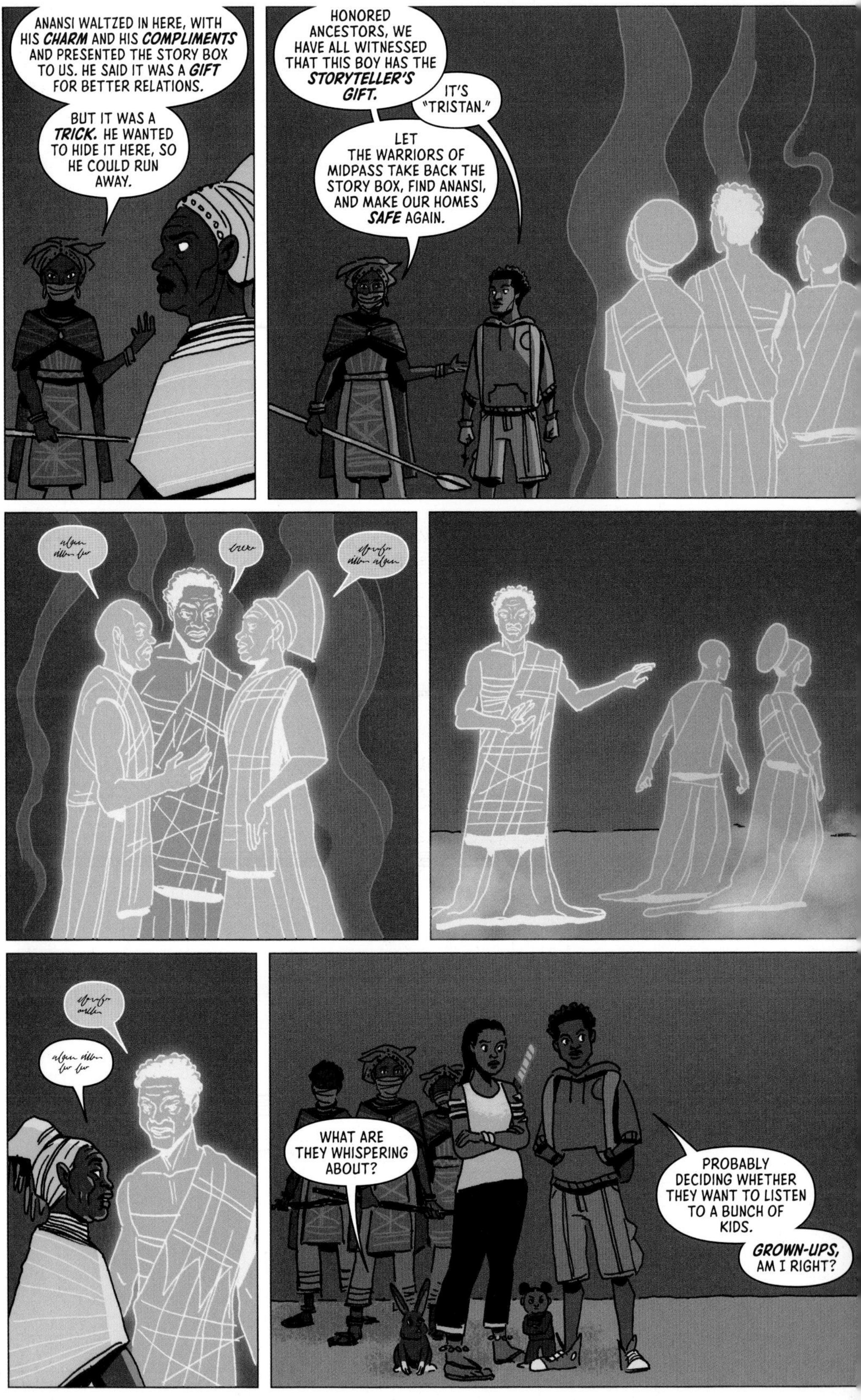
ANANSI WALTZED IN HERE, WITH HIS CHARM AND HIS COMPLIMENTS AND PRESENTED THE STORY BOX TO US. HE SAID IT WAS A GIFT FOR BETTER RELATIONS.
BUT IT WAS A TRICK. HE WANTED TO HIDE IT HERE, SO HE COULD RUN AWAY.
HONORED ANCESTORS, WE HAVE ALL WITNESSED THAT THIS BOY HAS THE STORYTELLER'S GIFT.
IT'S "TRISTAN."
LET THE WARRIORS OF MIDPASS TAKE BACK THE STORY BOX, FIND ANANSI, AND MAKE OUR HOMES SAFE AGAIN.
WHAT ARE THEY WHISPERING ABOUT?
PROBABLY DECIDING WHETHER THEY WANT TO LISTEN TO A BUNCH OF KIDS.
GROWN-UPS, AM I RIGHT?

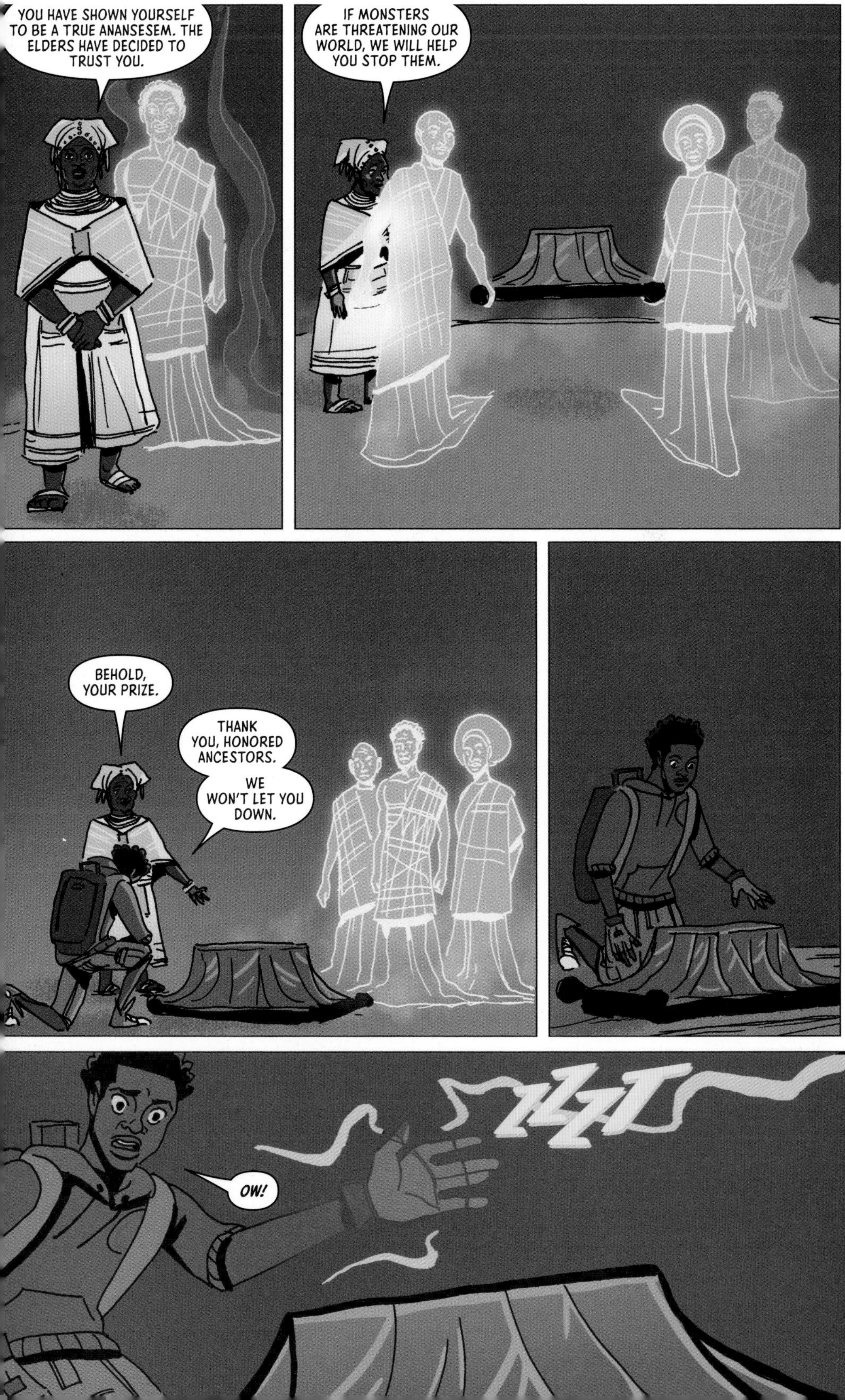
YOU HAVE SHOWN YOURSELF TO BE A TRUE ANANSESEM. THE ELDERS HAVE DECIDED TO TRUST YOU.
IF MONSTERS ARE THREATENING OUR WORLD, WE WILL HELP YOU STOP THEM.
BEHOLD, YOUR PRIZE.
THANK YOU, HONORED ANCESTORS.
WE WON'T LET YOU DOWN.
ZZZT
OW!

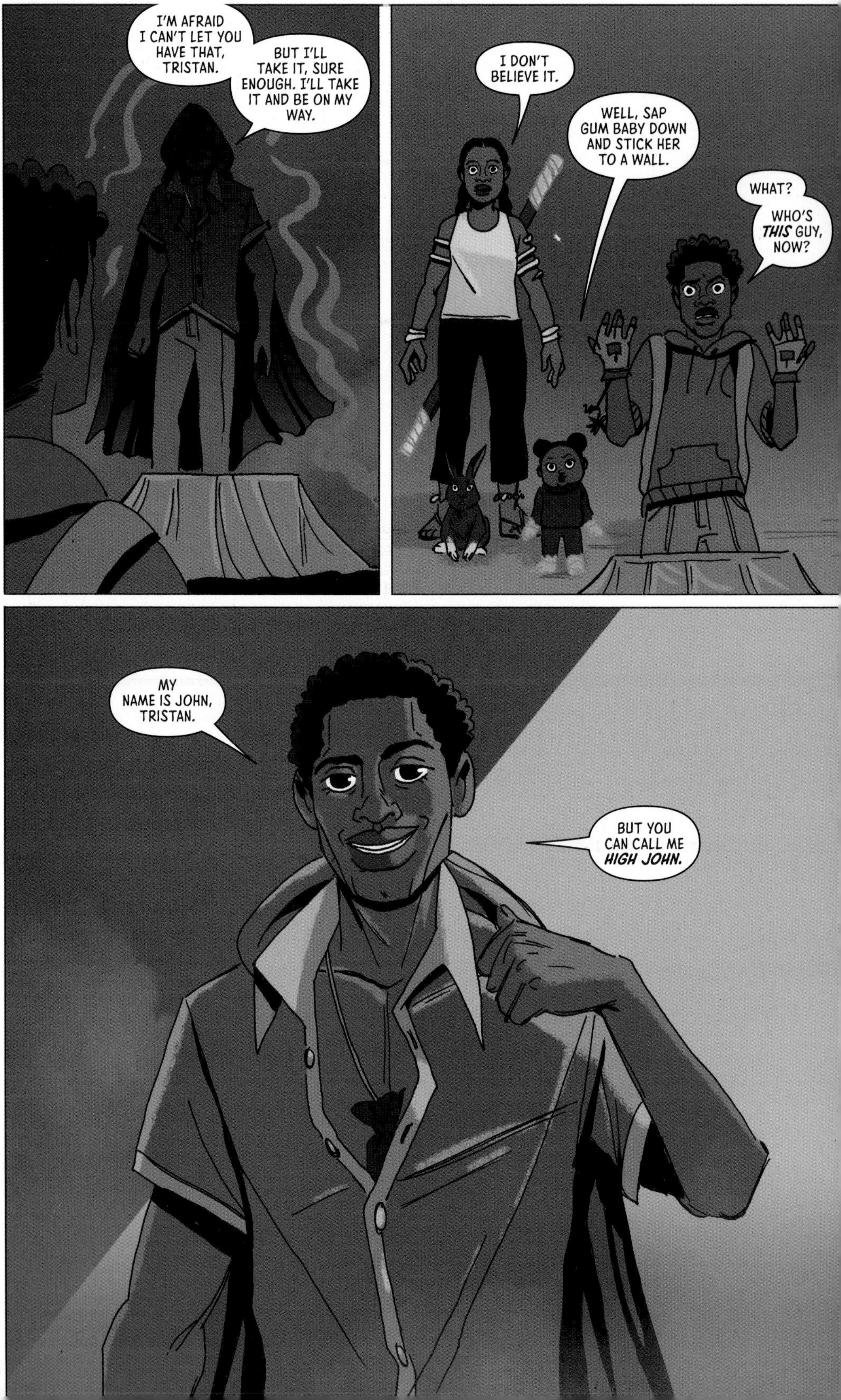
I'M AFRAID I CAN'T LET YOU HAVE THAT, TRISTAN.
BUT I'LL TAKE IT, SURE ENOUGH. I'LL TAKE IT AND BE ON MY WAY.
I DON'T BELIEVE IT.
WELL, SAP GUM BABY DOWN AND STICK HER TO A WALL.
WHAT?
WHO'S *THIS* GUY, NOW?
MY NAME IS JOHN, TRISTAN.
BUT YOU CAN CALL ME *HIGH JOHN.*

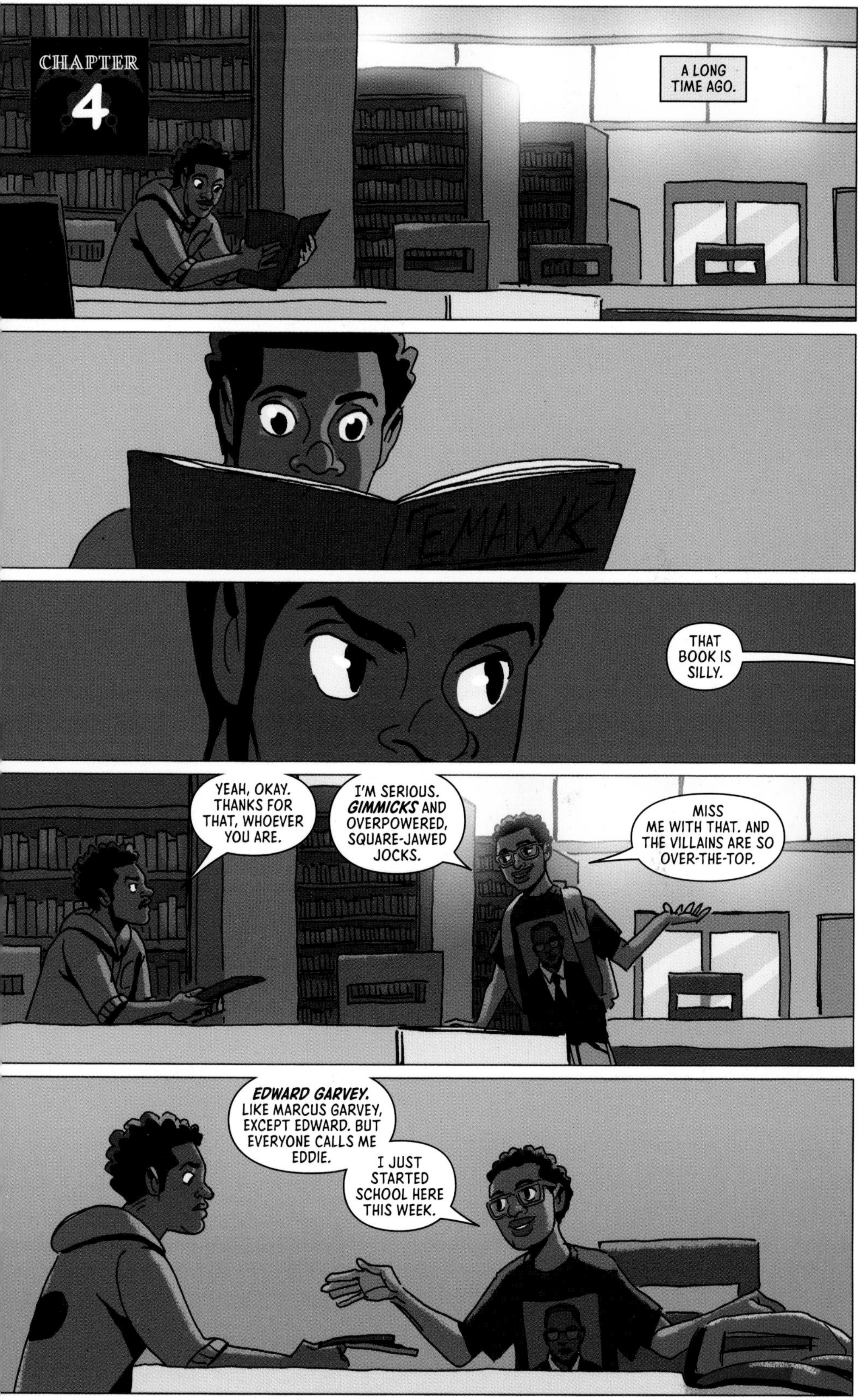
CHAPTER 4
A LONG TIME AGO.
EMAWK
THAT BOOK IS SILLY.
YEAH, OKAY. THANKS FOR THAT, WHOEVER YOU ARE.
I'M SERIOUS. **GIMMICKS** AND OVERPOWERED, SQUARE-JAWED JOCKS.
MISS ME WITH THAT. AND THE VILLAINS ARE SO OVER-THE-TOP.
EDWARD GARVEY. LIKE MARCUS GARVEY, EXCEPT EDWARD. BUT EVERYONE CALLS ME EDDIE.
I JUST STARTED SCHOOL HERE THIS WEEK.

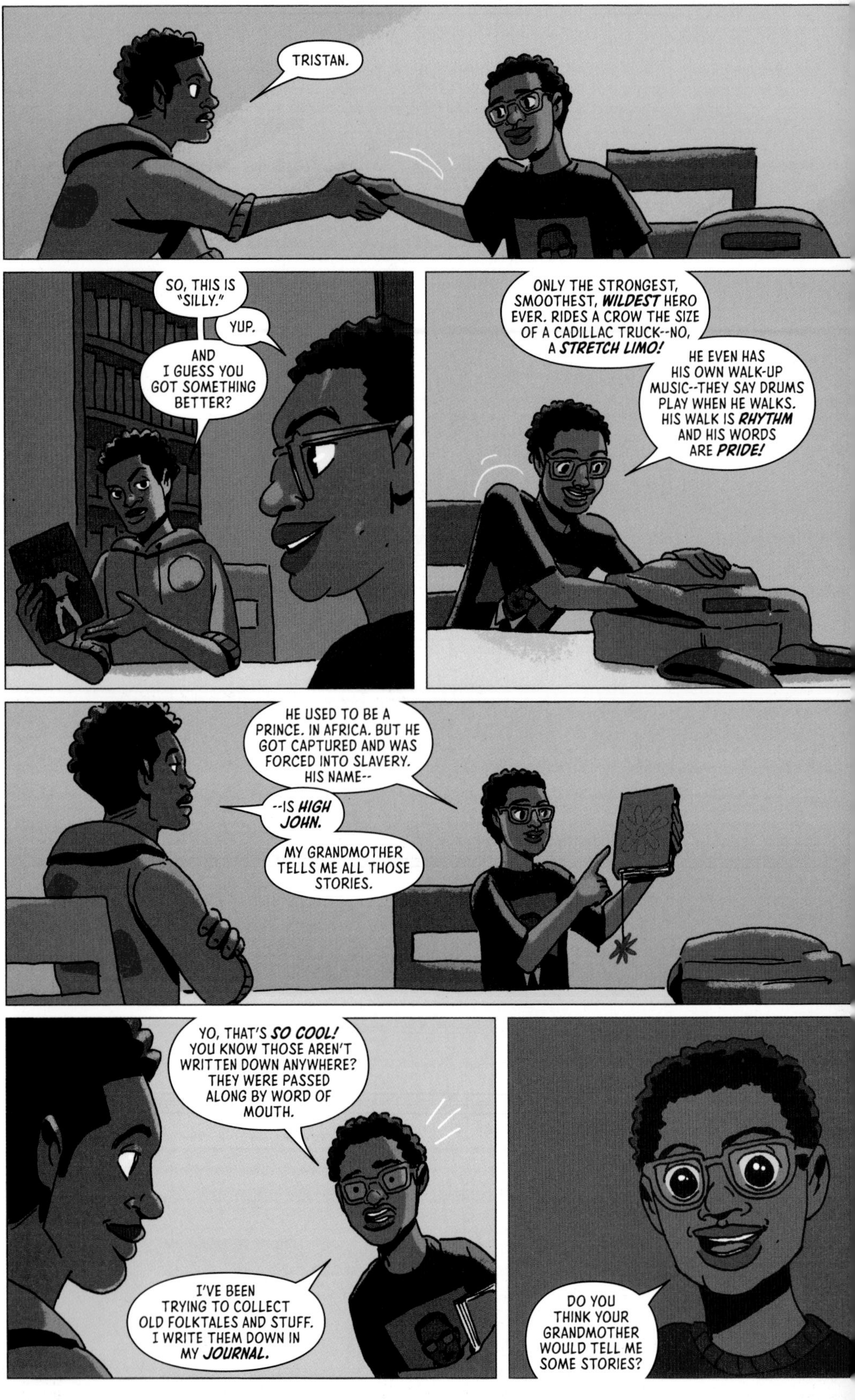
TRISTAN.
SO, THIS IS "SILLY."
YUP.
AND I GUESS YOU GOT SOMETHING BETTER?
ONLY THE STRONGEST, SMOOTHEST, **WILDEST** HERO EVER. RIDES A CROW THE SIZE OF A CADILLAC TRUCK--NO, A **STRETCH LIMO!**
HE EVEN HAS HIS OWN WALK-UP MUSIC--THEY SAY DRUMS PLAY WHEN HE WALKS. HIS WALK IS **RHYTHM** AND HIS WORDS ARE **PRIDE!**
HE USED TO BE A PRINCE. IN AFRICA. BUT HE GOT CAPTURED AND WAS FORCED INTO SLAVERY. HIS NAME--
--IS **HIGH JOHN.**
MY GRANDMOTHER TELLS ME ALL THOSE STORIES.
YO, THAT'S **SO COOL!** YOU KNOW THOSE AREN'T WRITTEN DOWN ANYWHERE? THEY WERE PASSED ALONG BY WORD OF MOUTH.
I'VE BEEN TRYING TO COLLECT OLD FOLKTALES AND STUFF. I WRITE THEM DOWN IN MY **JOURNAL.**
DO YOU THINK YOUR GRANDMOTHER WOULD TELL ME SOME STORIES?

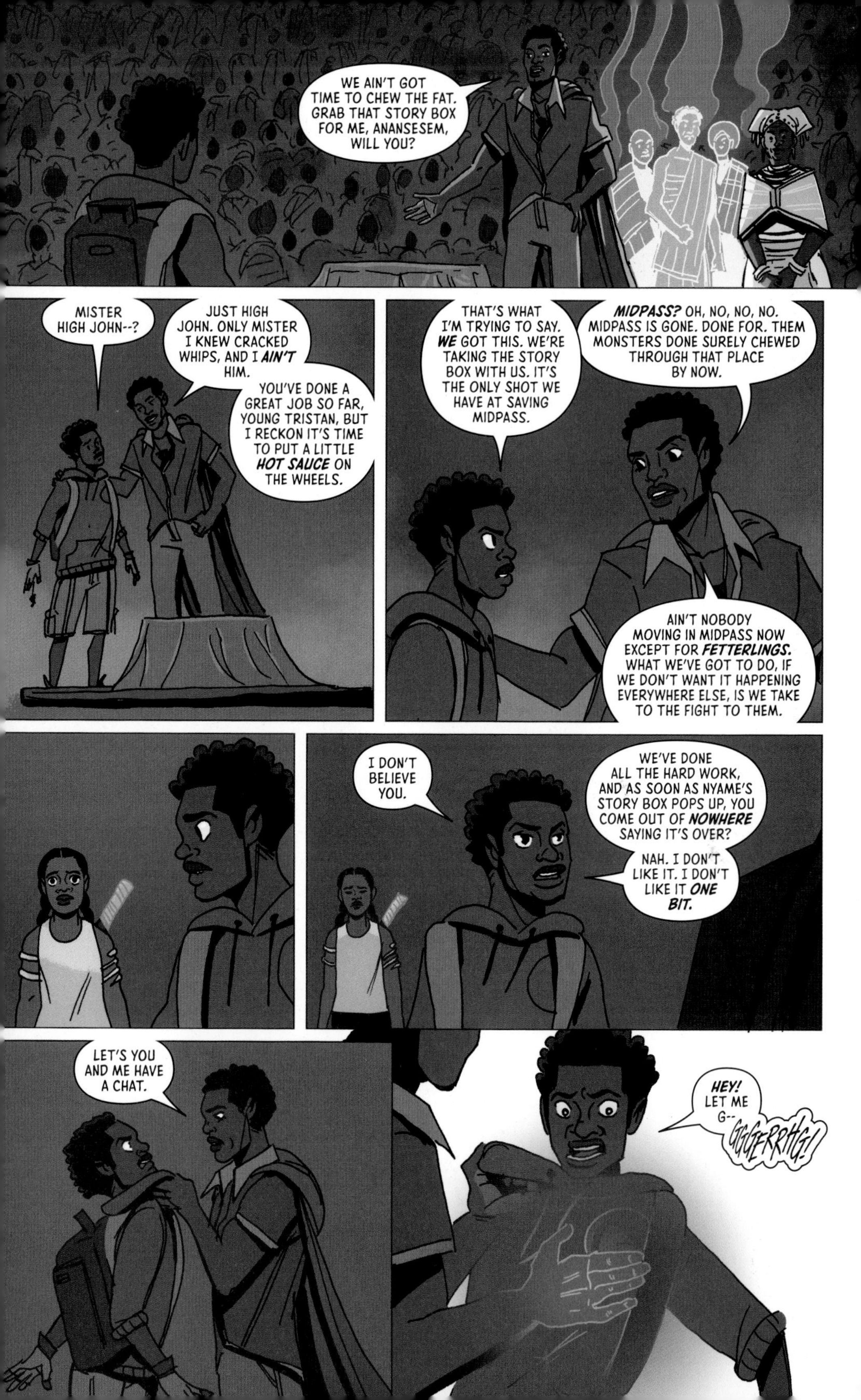
WE AIN'T GOT TIME TO CHEW THE FAT. GRAB THAT STORY BOX FOR ME, ANANSESEM, WILL YOU?
MISTER HIGH JOHN--?
JUST HIGH JOHN. ONLY MISTER I KNEW CRACKED WHIPS, AND I AIN'T HIM.
YOU'VE DONE A GREAT JOB SO FAR, YOUNG TRISTAN, BUT I RECKON IT'S TIME TO PUT A LITTLE HOT SAUCE ON THE WHEELS.
THAT'S WHAT I'M TRYING TO SAY. WE GOT THIS. WE'RE TAKING THE STORY BOX WITH US. IT'S THE ONLY SHOT WE HAVE AT SAVING MIDPASS.
MIDPASS? OH, NO, NO, NO. MIDPASS IS GONE. DONE FOR. THEM MONSTERS DONE SURELY CHEWED THROUGH THAT PLACE BY NOW.
AIN'T NOBODY MOVING IN MIDPASS NOW EXCEPT FOR FETTERLINGS. WHAT WE'VE GOT TO DO, IF WE DON'T WANT IT HAPPENING EVERYWHERE ELSE, IS WE TAKE TO THE FIGHT TO THEM.
I DON'T BELIEVE YOU.
WE'VE DONE ALL THE HARD WORK, AND AS SOON AS NYAME'S STORY BOX POPS UP, YOU COME OUT OF NOWHERE SAYING IT'S OVER?
NAH. I DON'T LIKE IT. I DON'T LIKE IT ONE BIT.
LET'S YOU AND ME HAVE A CHAT.
HEY! LET ME G--
GGGERRHG!

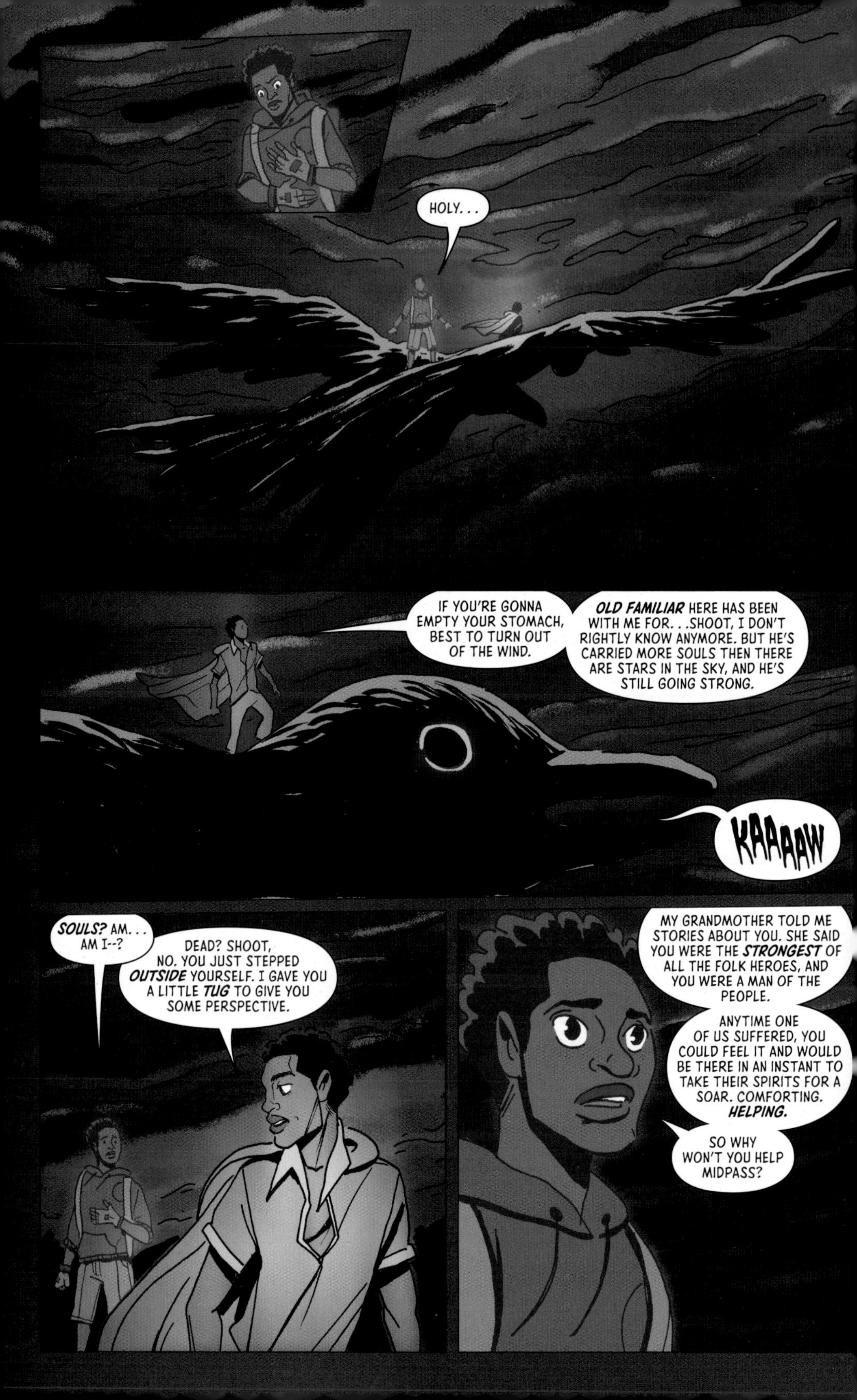
HOLY. . .
IF YOU'RE GONNA EMPTY YOUR STOMACH, BEST TO TURN OUT OF THE WIND.
OLD FAMILIAR HERE HAS BEEN WITH ME FOR. . .SHOOT, I DON'T RIGHTLY KNOW ANYMORE. BUT HE'S CARRIED MORE SOULS THEN THERE ARE STARS IN THE SKY, AND HE'S STILL GOING STRONG.
KAAAAW
SOULS? AM. . . AM I--?
DEAD? SHOOT, NO. YOU JUST STEPPED OUTSIDE YOURSELF. I GAVE YOU A LITTLE TUG TO GIVE YOU SOME PERSPECTIVE.
MY GRANDMOTHER TOLD ME STORIES ABOUT YOU. SHE SAID YOU WERE THE STRONGEST OF ALL THE FOLK HEROES, AND YOU WERE A MAN OF THE PEOPLE.
ANYTIME ONE OF US SUFFERED, YOU COULD FEEL IT AND WOULD BE THERE IN AN INSTANT TO TAKE THEIR SPIRITS FOR A SOAR. COMFORTING. HELPING.
SO WHY WON'T YOU HELP MIDPASS?

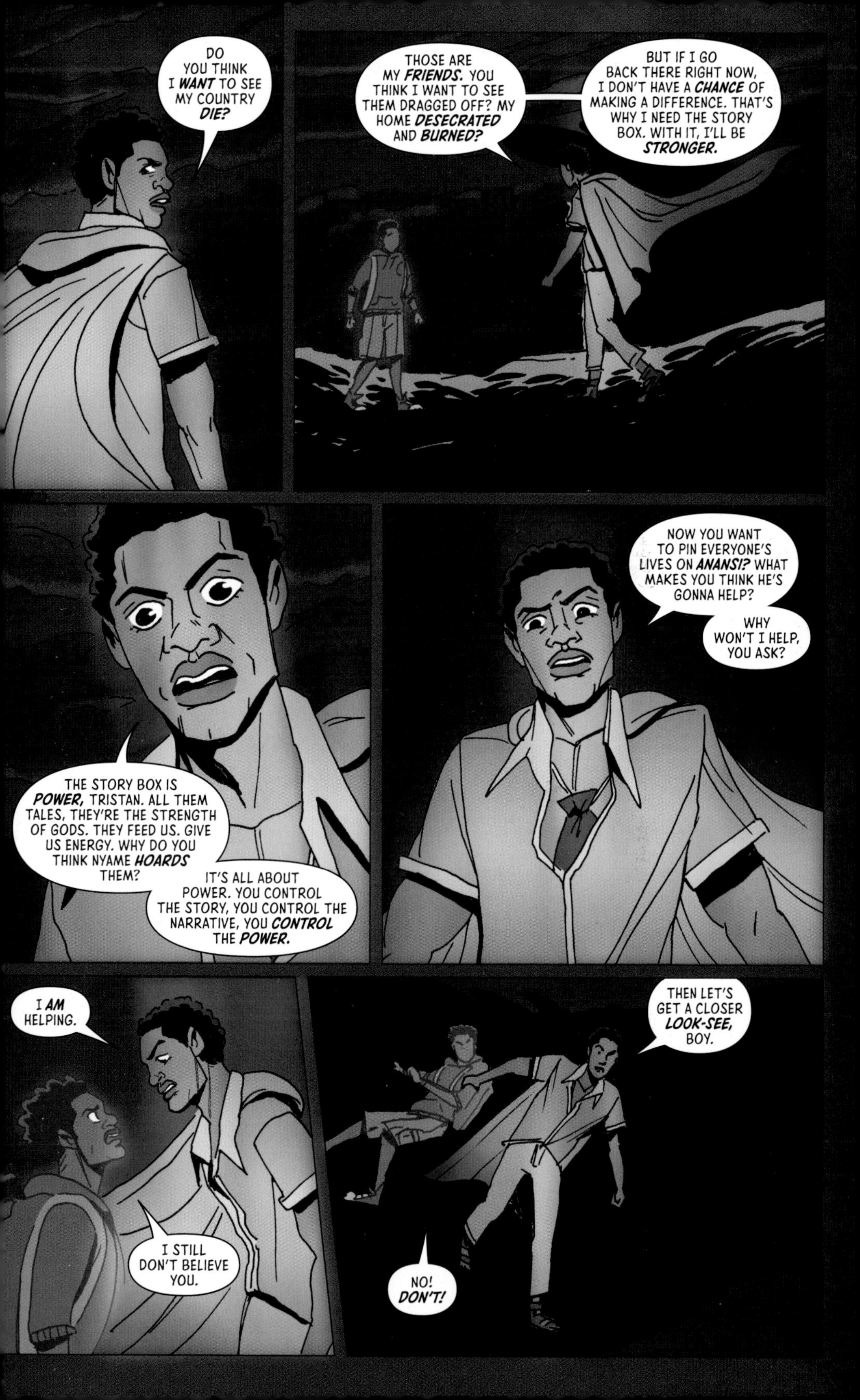

DO YOU THINK I WANT TO SEE MY COUNTRY DIE?
THOSE ARE MY FRIENDS. YOU THINK I WANT TO SEE THEM DRAGGED OFF? MY HOME DESECRATED AND BURNED?
BUT IF I GO BACK THERE RIGHT NOW, I DON'T HAVE A CHANCE OF MAKING A DIFFERENCE. THAT'S WHY I NEED THE STORY BOX. WITH IT, I'LL BE STRONGER.
NOW YOU WANT TO PIN EVERYONE'S LIVES ON ANANSI? WHAT MAKES YOU THINK HE'S GONNA HELP?
WHY WON'T I HELP, YOU ASK?
THE STORY BOX IS POWER, TRISTAN. ALL THEM TALES, THEY'RE THE STRENGTH OF GODS. THEY FEED US. GIVE US ENERGY. WHY DO YOU THINK NYAME HOARDS THEM?
IT'S ALL ABOUT POWER. YOU CONTROL THE STORY, YOU CONTROL THE NARRATIVE, YOU CONTROL THE POWER.
I AM HELPING.
I STILL DON'T BELIEVE YOU.
THEN LET'S GET A CLOSER LOOK-SEE, BOY.
NO! DON'T!

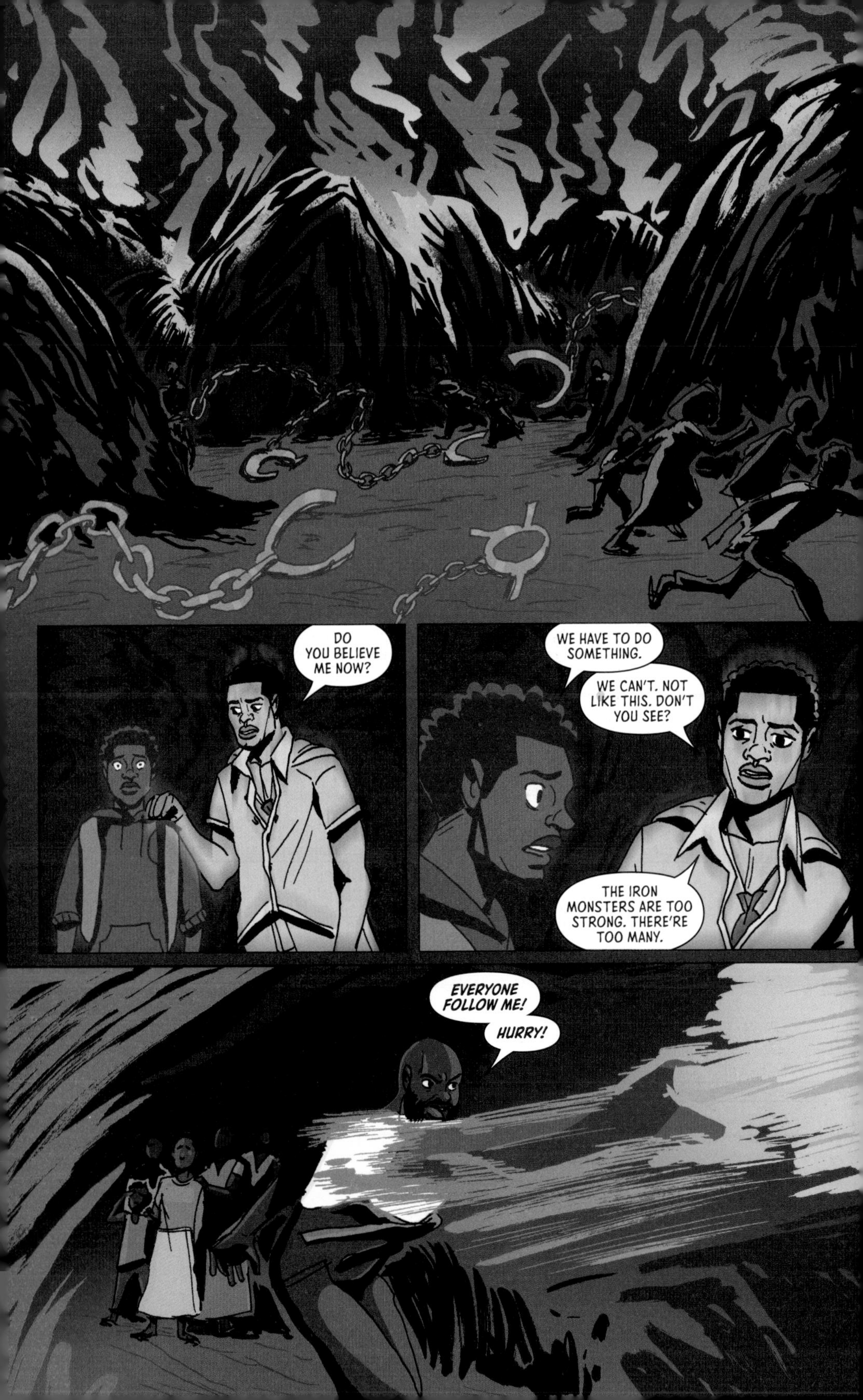
DO YOU BELIEVE ME NOW?
WE HAVE TO DO SOMETHING.
WE CAN'T. NOT LIKE THIS. DON'T YOU SEE?
THE IRON MONSTERS ARE TOO STRONG. THERE'RE TOO MANY.
EVERYONE FOLLOW ME!
HURRY!

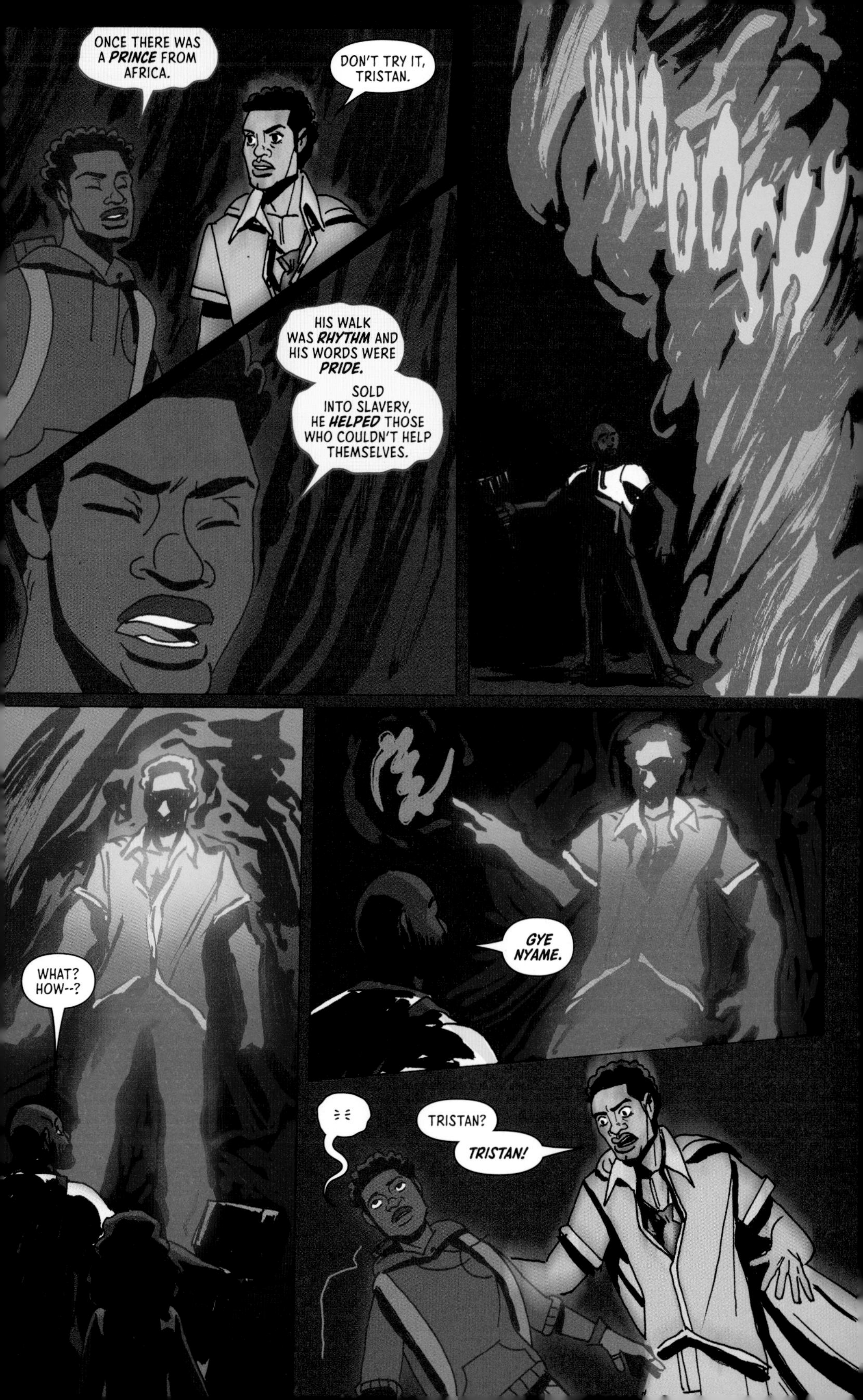
ONCE THERE WAS A *PRINCE* FROM AFRICA.
DON'T TRY IT, TRISTAN.
HIS WALK WAS *RHYTHM* AND HIS WORDS WERE *PRIDE.*
SOLD INTO SLAVERY, HE *HELPED* THOSE WHO COULDN'T HELP THEMSELVES.
WHOOOSH
WHAT? HOW--?
GYE NYAME.
TRISTAN?
TRISTAN!

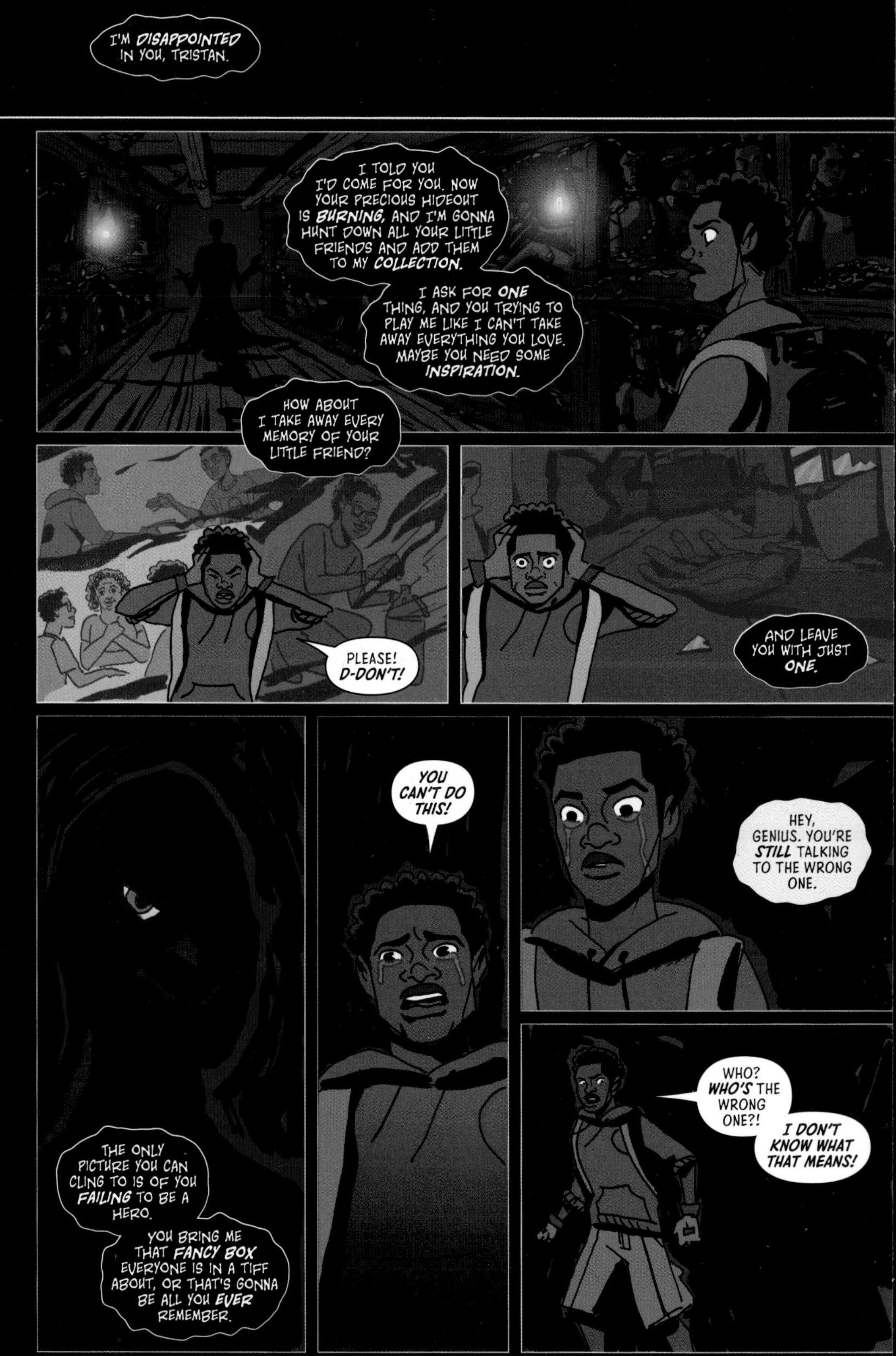
I'M DISAPPOINTED IN YOU, TRISTAN.
I TOLD YOU I'D COME FOR YOU. NOW YOUR PRECIOUS HIDEOUT IS BURNING, AND I'M GONNA HUNT DOWN ALL YOUR LITTLE FRIENDS AND ADD THEM TO MY COLLECTION.
I ASK FOR ONE THING, AND YOU TRYING TO PLAY ME LIKE I CAN'T TAKE AWAY EVERYTHING YOU LOVE. MAYBE YOU NEED SOME INSPIRATION.
HOW ABOUT I TAKE AWAY EVERY MEMORY OF YOUR LITTLE FRIEND?
PLEASE! D-DON'T!
AND LEAVE YOU WITH JUST ONE.
THE ONLY PICTURE YOU CAN CLING TO IS OF YOU FAILING TO BE A HERO.
YOU BRING ME THAT FANCY BOX EVERYONE IS IN A TIFF ABOUT, OR THAT'S GONNA BE ALL YOU EVER REMEMBER.
YOU CAN'T DO THIS!
HEY, GENIUS. YOU'RE STILL TALKING TO THE WRONG ONE.
WHO? WHO'S THE WRONG ONE?!
I DON'T KNOW WHAT THAT MEANS!

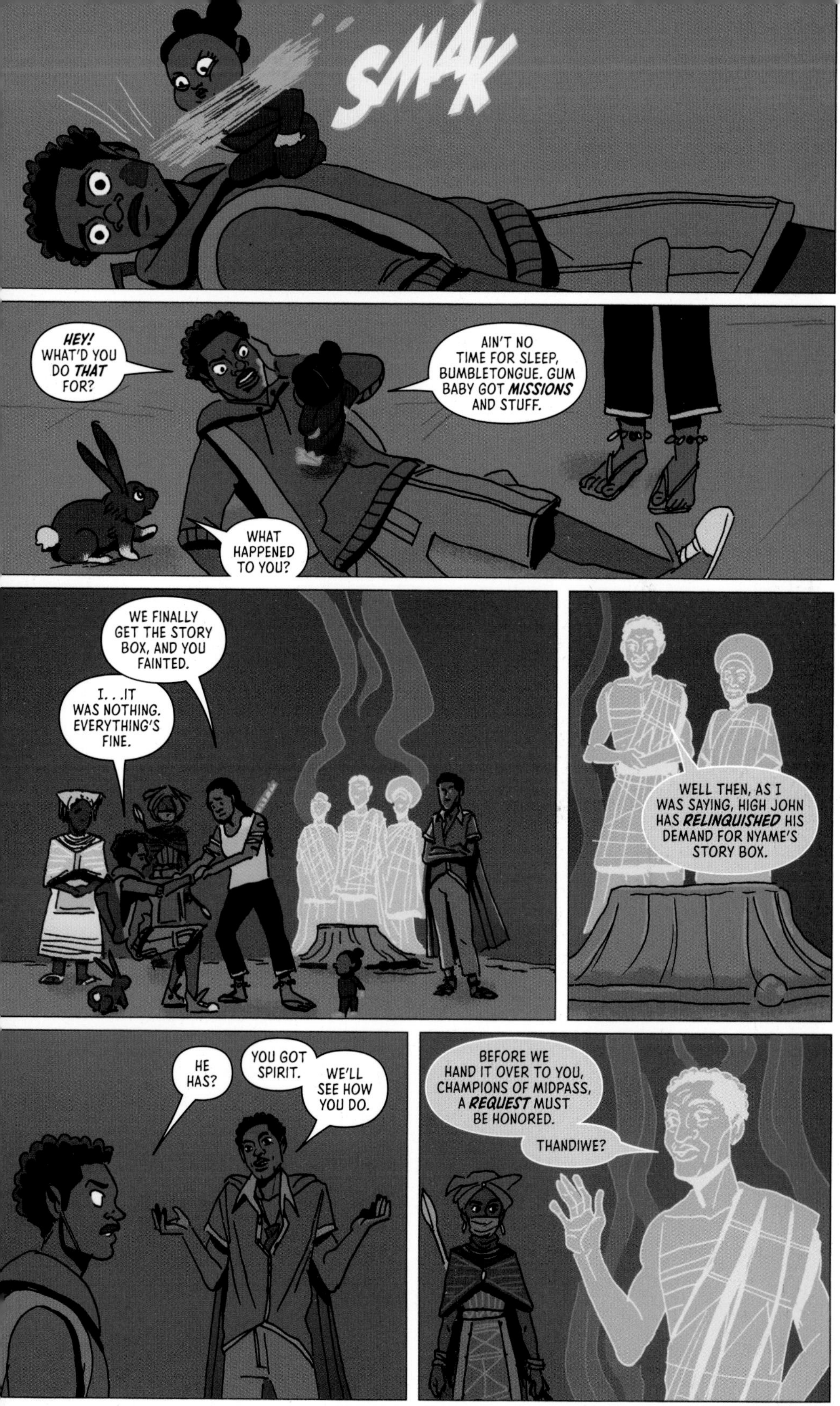
SMAK
HEY! WHAT'D YOU DO THAT FOR?
AIN'T NO TIME FOR SLEEP, BUMBLETONGUE. GUM BABY GOT MISSIONS AND STUFF.
WHAT HAPPENED TO YOU?
WE FINALLY GET THE STORY BOX, AND YOU FAINTED.
I. . .IT WAS NOTHING. EVERYTHING'S FINE.
WELL THEN, AS I WAS SAYING, HIGH JOHN HAS RELINQUISHED HIS DEMAND FOR NYAME'S STORY BOX.
HE HAS?
YOU GOT SPIRIT.
WE'LL SEE HOW YOU DO.
BEFORE WE HAND IT OVER TO YOU, CHAMPIONS OF MIDPASS, A REQUEST MUST BE HONORED.
THANDIWE?

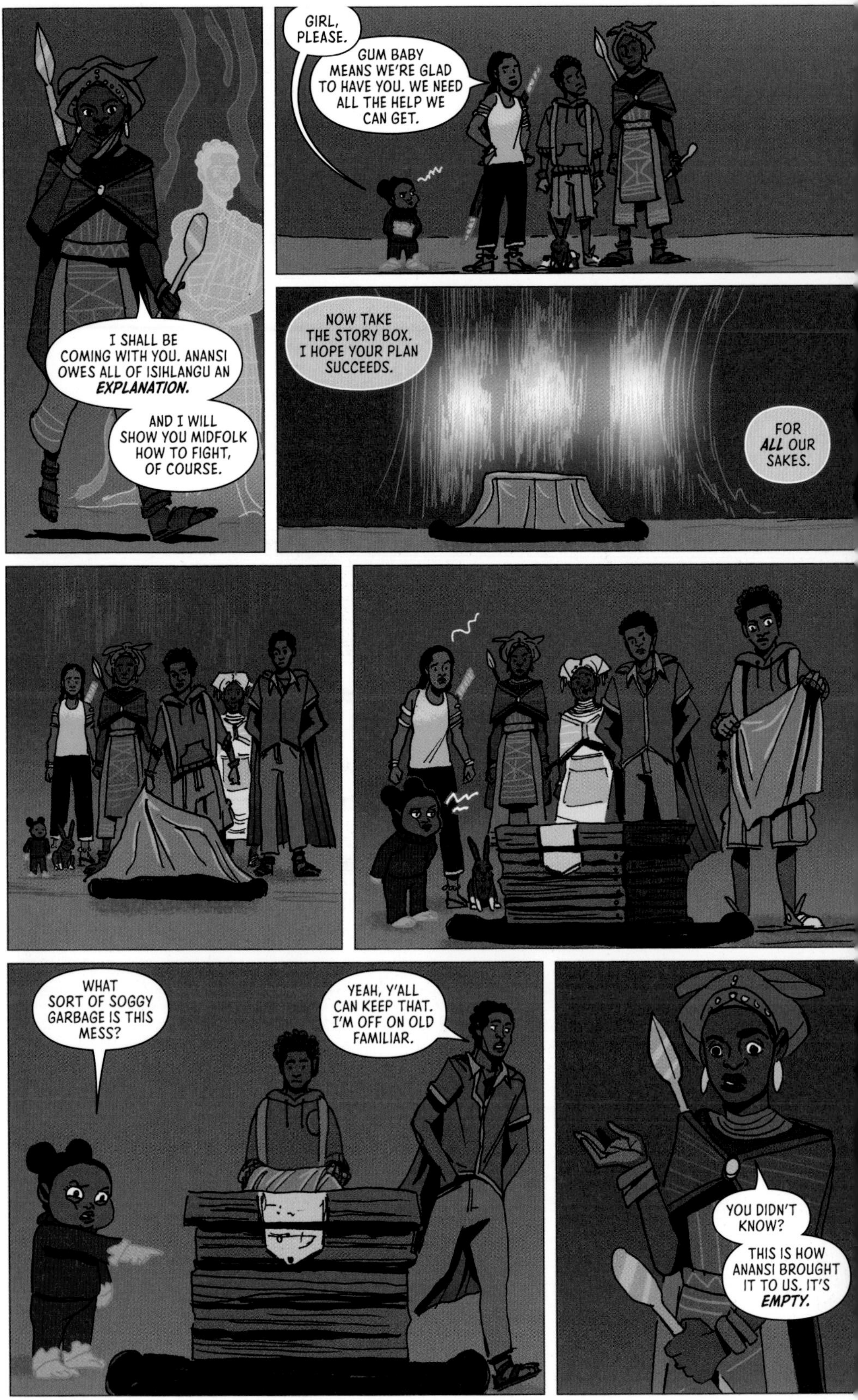
I SHALL BE COMING WITH YOU. ANANSI OWES ALL OF ISIHLANGU AN *EXPLANATION.*
AND I WILL SHOW YOU MIDFOLK HOW TO FIGHT, OF COURSE.
GIRL, PLEASE.
GUM BABY MEANS WE'RE GLAD TO HAVE YOU. WE NEED ALL THE HELP WE CAN GET.
NOW TAKE THE STORY BOX. I HOPE YOUR PLAN SUCCEEDS.
FOR *ALL* OUR SAKES.
WHAT SORT OF SOGGY GARBAGE IS THIS MESS?
YEAH, Y'ALL CAN KEEP THAT. I'M OFF ON OLD FAMILIAR.
YOU DIDN'T KNOW?
THIS IS HOW ANANSI BROUGHT IT TO US. IT'S *EMPTY.*

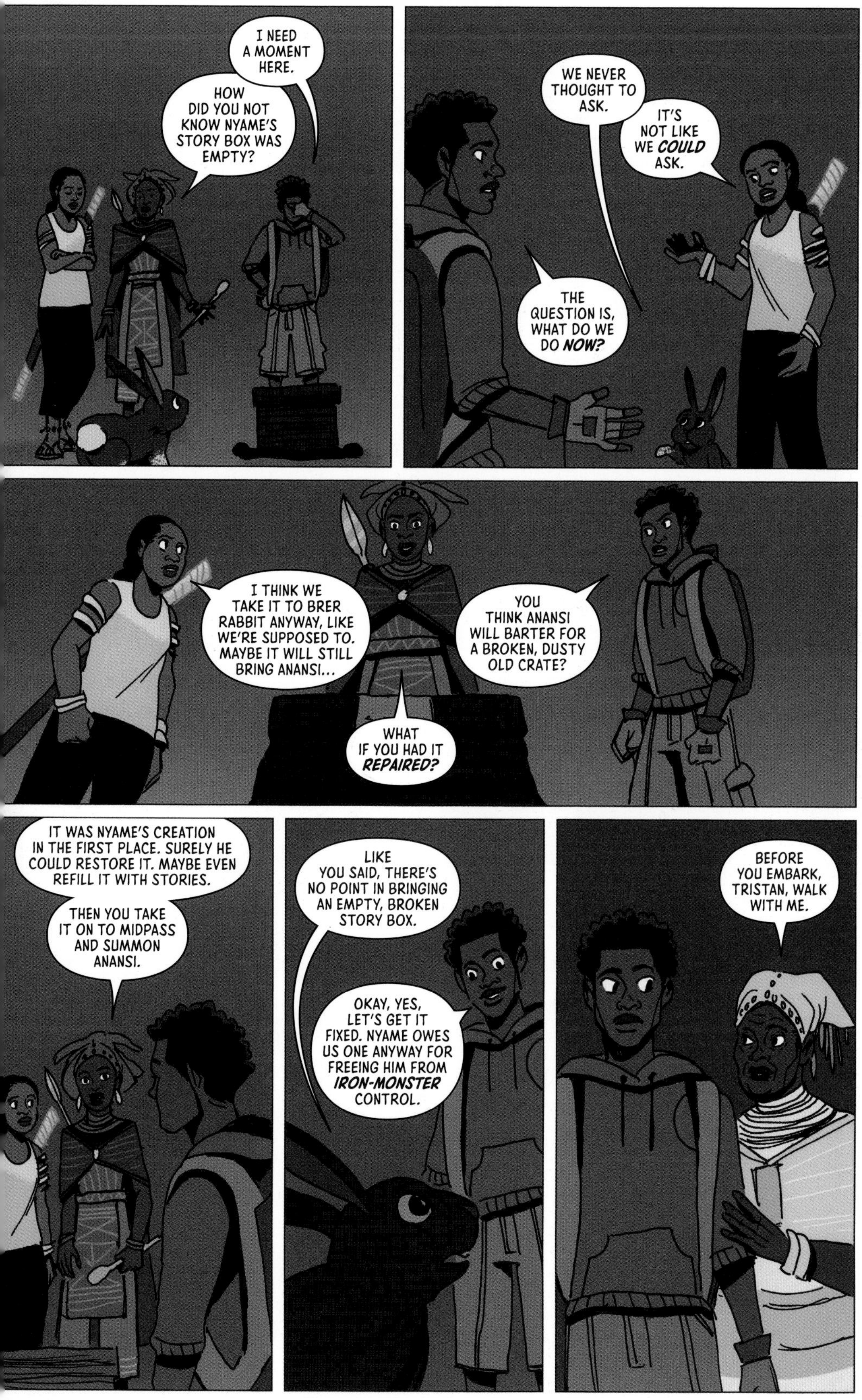
HOW DID YOU NOT KNOW NYAME'S STORY BOX WAS EMPTY?
I NEED A MOMENT HERE.
WE NEVER THOUGHT TO ASK.
IT'S NOT LIKE WE COULD ASK.
THE QUESTION IS, WHAT DO WE DO NOW?
I THINK WE TAKE IT TO BRER RABBIT ANYWAY, LIKE WE'RE SUPPOSED TO. MAYBE IT WILL STILL BRING ANANSI...
YOU THINK ANANSI WILL BARTER FOR A BROKEN, DUSTY OLD CRATE?
WHAT IF YOU HAD IT REPAIRED?
IT WAS NYAME'S CREATION IN THE FIRST PLACE. SURELY HE COULD RESTORE IT. MAYBE EVEN REFILL IT WITH STORIES.
THEN YOU TAKE IT ON TO MIDPASS AND SUMMON ANANSI.
LIKE YOU SAID, THERE'S NO POINT IN BRINGING AN EMPTY, BROKEN STORY BOX.
OKAY, YES, LET'S GET IT FIXED. NYAME OWES US ONE ANYWAY FOR FREEING HIM FROM IRON-MONSTER CONTROL.
BEFORE YOU EMBARK, TRISTAN, WALK WITH ME.

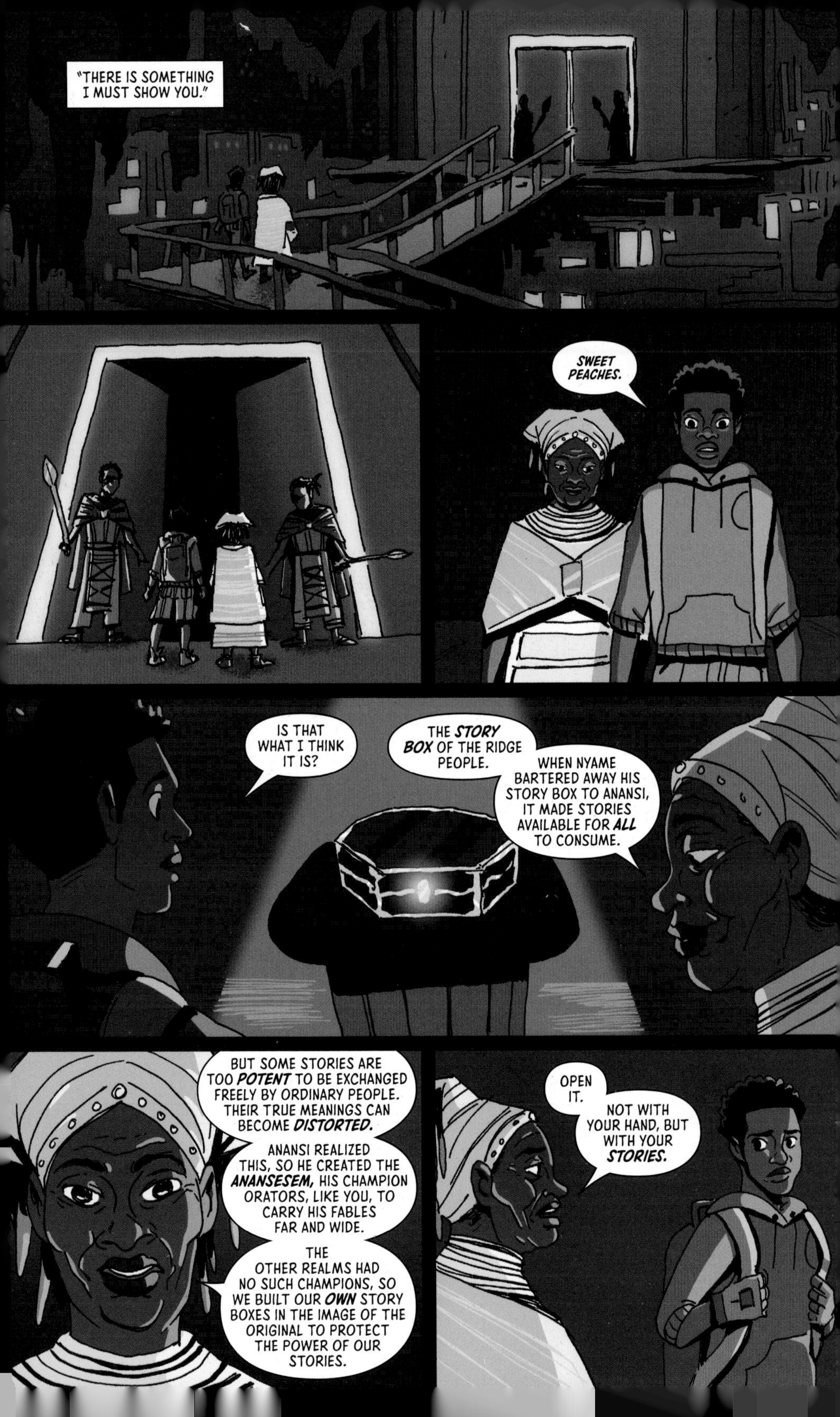
"THERE IS SOMETHING I MUST SHOW YOU."
SWEET PEACHES.
IS THAT WHAT I THINK IT IS?
THE STORY BOX OF THE RIDGE PEOPLE.
WHEN NYAME BARTERED AWAY HIS STORY BOX TO ANANSI, IT MADE STORIES AVAILABLE FOR ALL TO CONSUME.
BUT SOME STORIES ARE TOO POTENT TO BE EXCHANGED FREELY BY ORDINARY PEOPLE. THEIR TRUE MEANINGS CAN BECOME DISTORTED.
ANANSI REALIZED THIS, SO HE CREATED THE ANANSESEM, HIS CHAMPION ORATORS, LIKE YOU, TO CARRY HIS FABLES FAR AND WIDE.
THE OTHER REALMS HAD NO SUCH CHAMPIONS, SO WE BUILT OUR OWN STORY BOXES IN THE IMAGE OF THE ORIGINAL TO PROTECT THE POWER OF OUR STORIES.
OPEN IT.
NOT WITH YOUR HAND, BUT WITH YOUR STORIES.

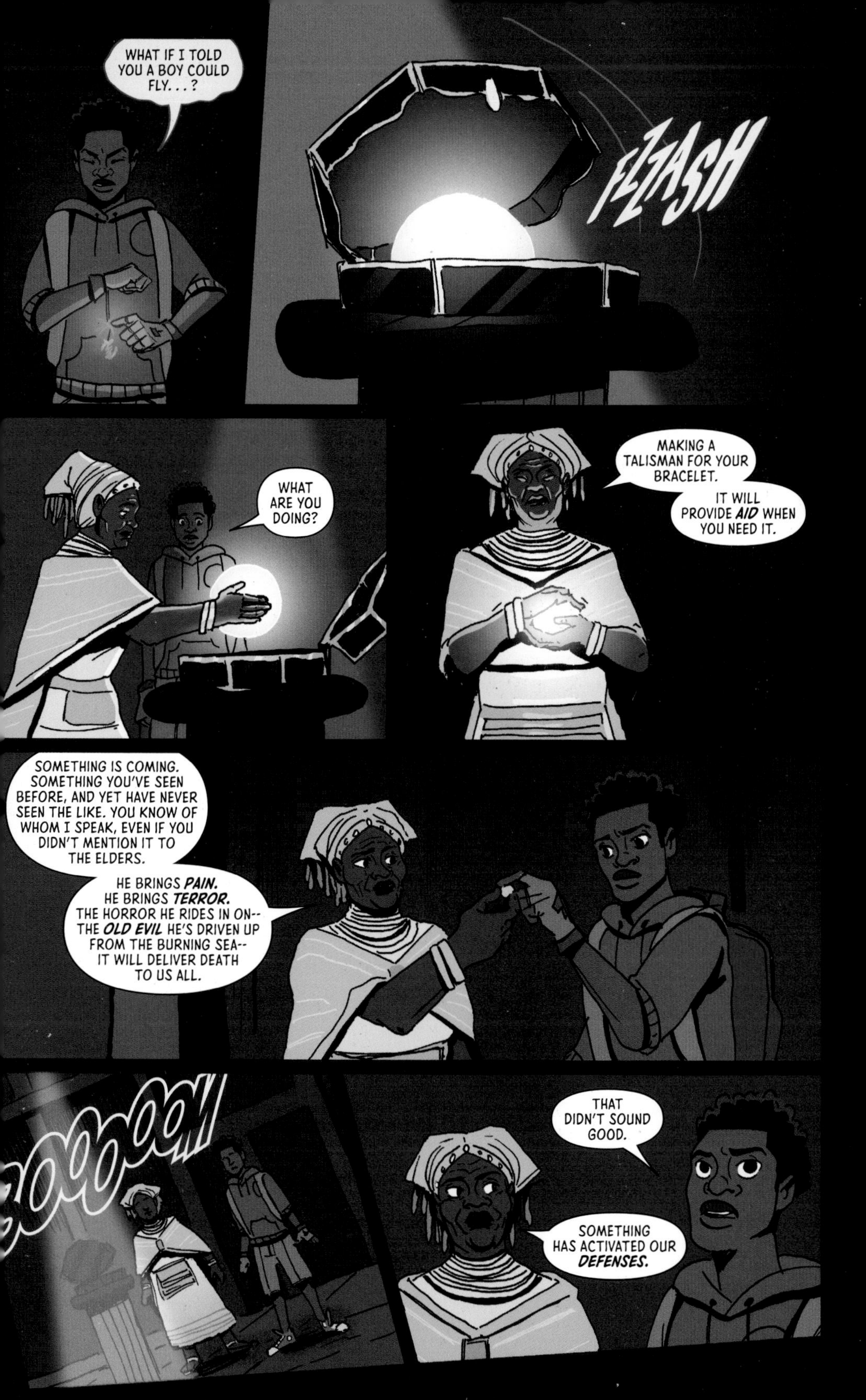
WHAT IF I TOLD YOU A BOY COULD FLY. . . ?
FFZZASH
WHAT ARE YOU DOING?
MAKING A TALISMAN FOR YOUR BRACELET.
IT WILL PROVIDE AID WHEN YOU NEED IT.
SOMETHING IS COMING. SOMETHING YOU'VE SEEN BEFORE, AND YET HAVE NEVER SEEN THE LIKE. YOU KNOW OF WHOM I SPEAK, EVEN IF YOU DIDN'T MENTION IT TO THE ELDERS.
HE BRINGS PAIN. HE BRINGS TERROR. THE HORROR HE RIDES IN ON-- THE OLD EVIL HE'S DRIVEN UP FROM THE BURNING SEA-- IT WILL DELIVER DEATH TO US ALL.
BOOOOOOM
THAT DIDN'T SOUND GOOD.
SOMETHING HAS ACTIVATED OUR DEFENSES.

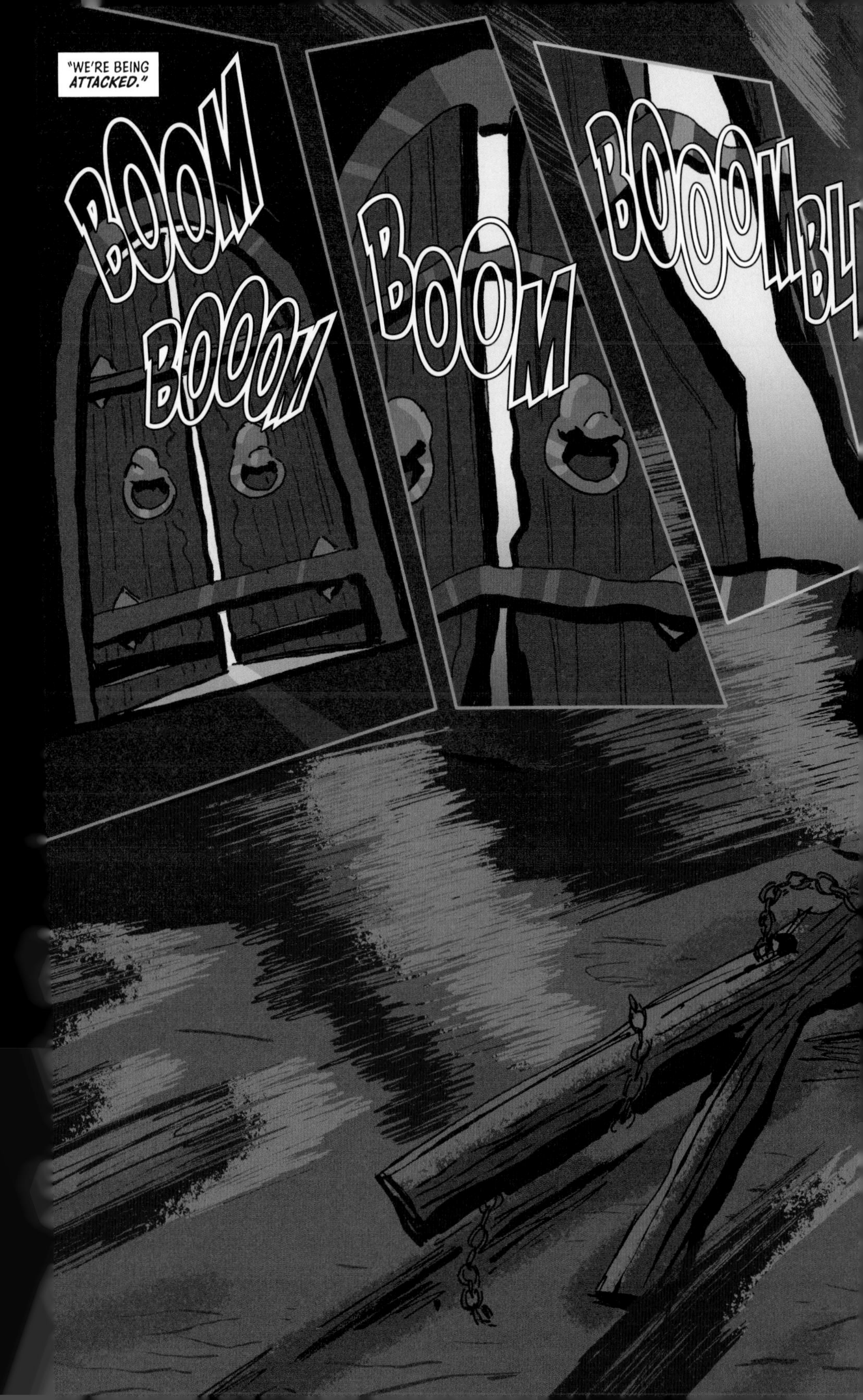
"WE'RE BEING *ATTACKED.*"
BOOM
BOOOM
BOOM
BOOOOMBL

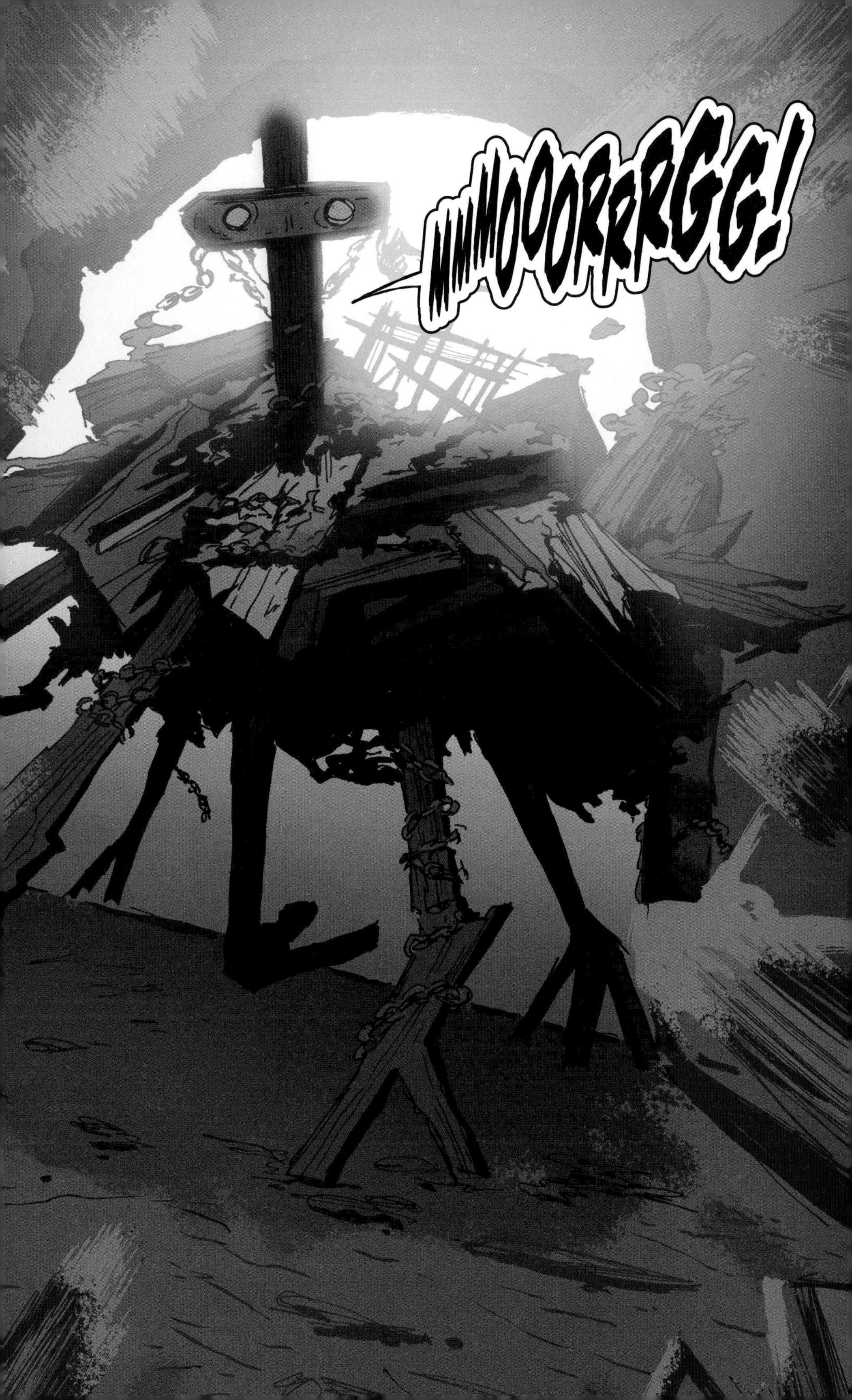
MMMMOOORRRGG!

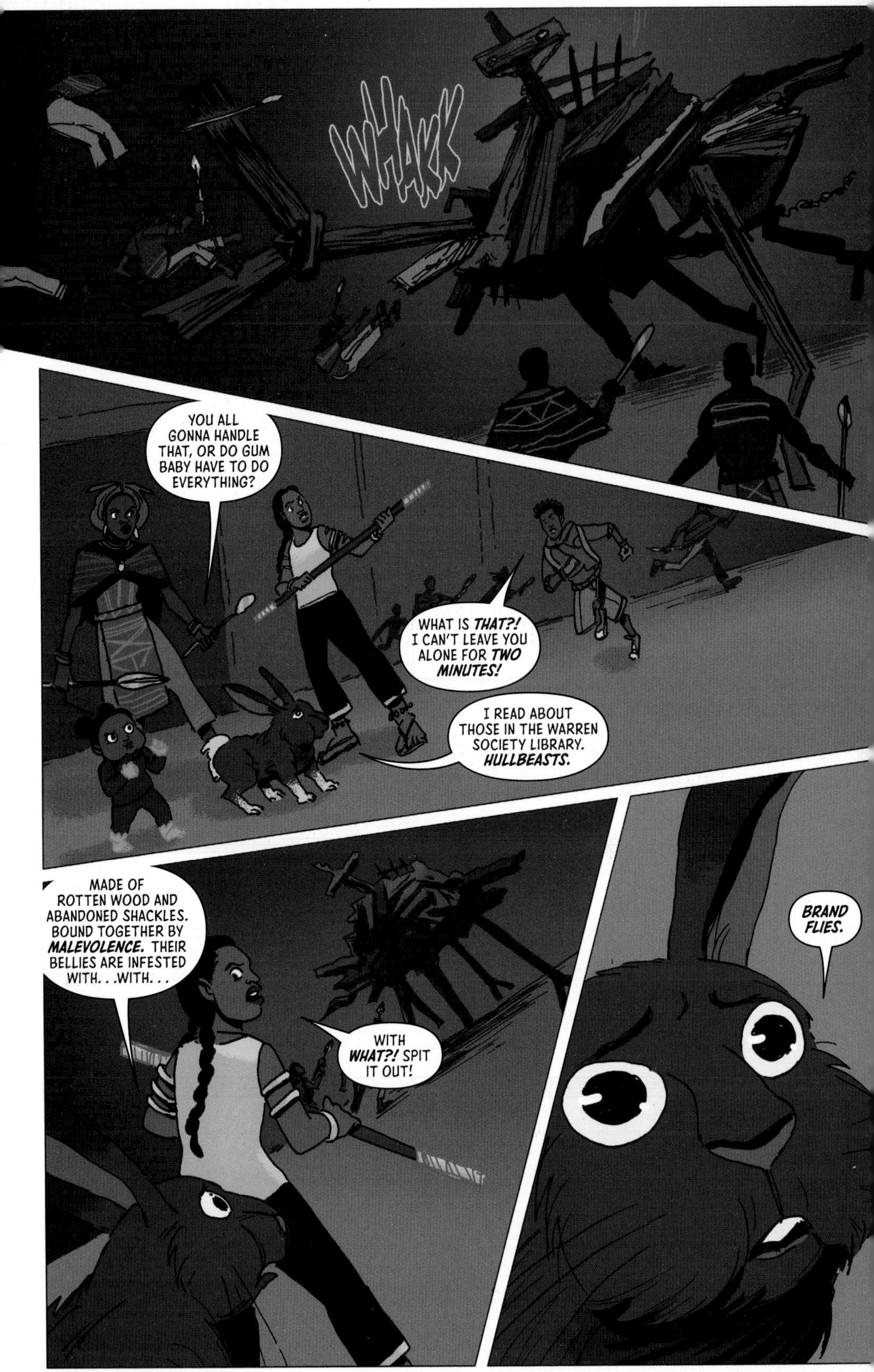
WHAKK
YOU ALL GONNA HANDLE THAT, OR DO GUM BABY HAVE TO DO EVERYTHING?
WHAT IS *THAT?!* I CAN'T LEAVE YOU ALONE FOR *TWO MINUTES!*
I READ ABOUT THOSE IN THE WARREN SOCIETY LIBRARY. ***HULLBEASTS.***
MADE OF ROTTEN WOOD AND ABANDONED SHACKLES. BOUND TOGETHER BY ***MALEVOLENCE.*** THEIR BELLIES ARE INFESTED WITH. . .WITH. . .
WITH *WHAT?!* SPIT IT OUT!
BRAND FLIES.

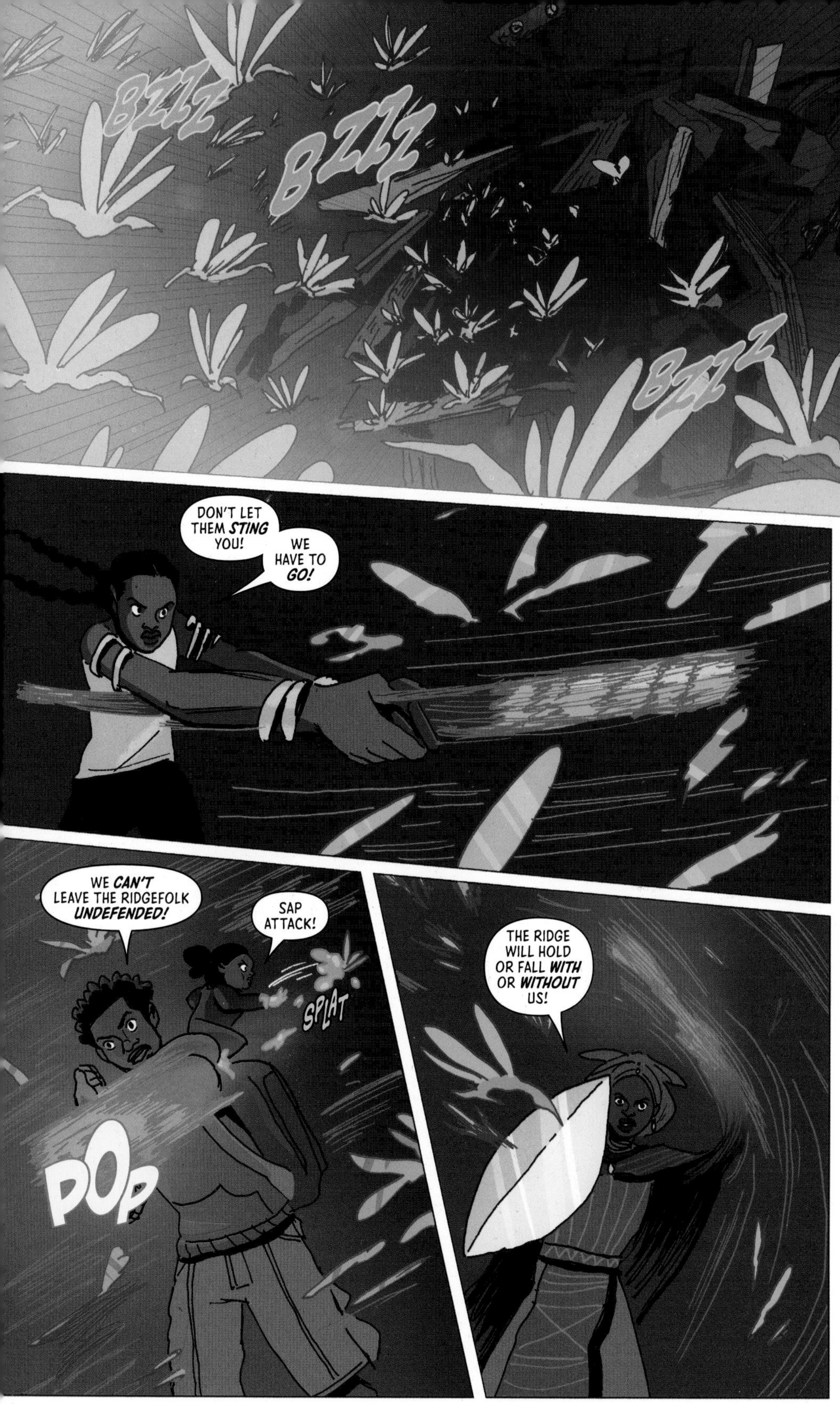
BZZZ
BZZZ
BZZZ
DON'T LET THEM STING YOU!
WE HAVE TO GO!
WE CAN'T LEAVE THE RIDGEFOLK UNDEFENDED!
SAP ATTACK!
SPLAT
POP
THE RIDGE WILL HOLD OR FALL WITH OR WITHOUT US!

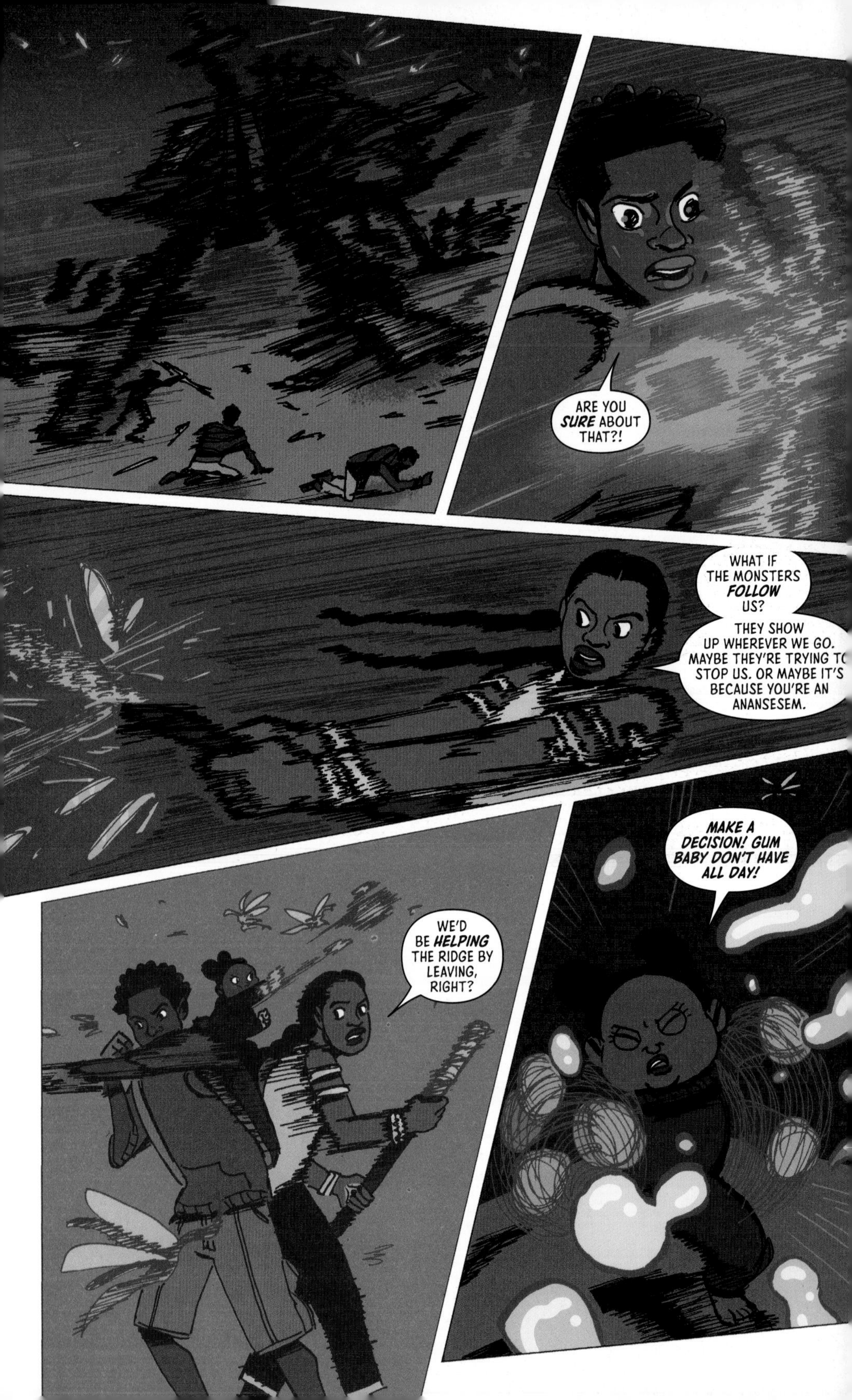
ARE YOU SURE ABOUT THAT?!
WHAT IF THE MONSTERS FOLLOW US?
THEY SHOW UP WHEREVER WE GO. MAYBE THEY'RE TRYING TO STOP US. OR MAYBE IT'S BECAUSE YOU'RE AN ANANSESEM.
WE'D BE HELPING THE RIDGE BY LEAVING, RIGHT?
MAKE A DECISION! GUM BABY DON'T HAVE ALL DAY!

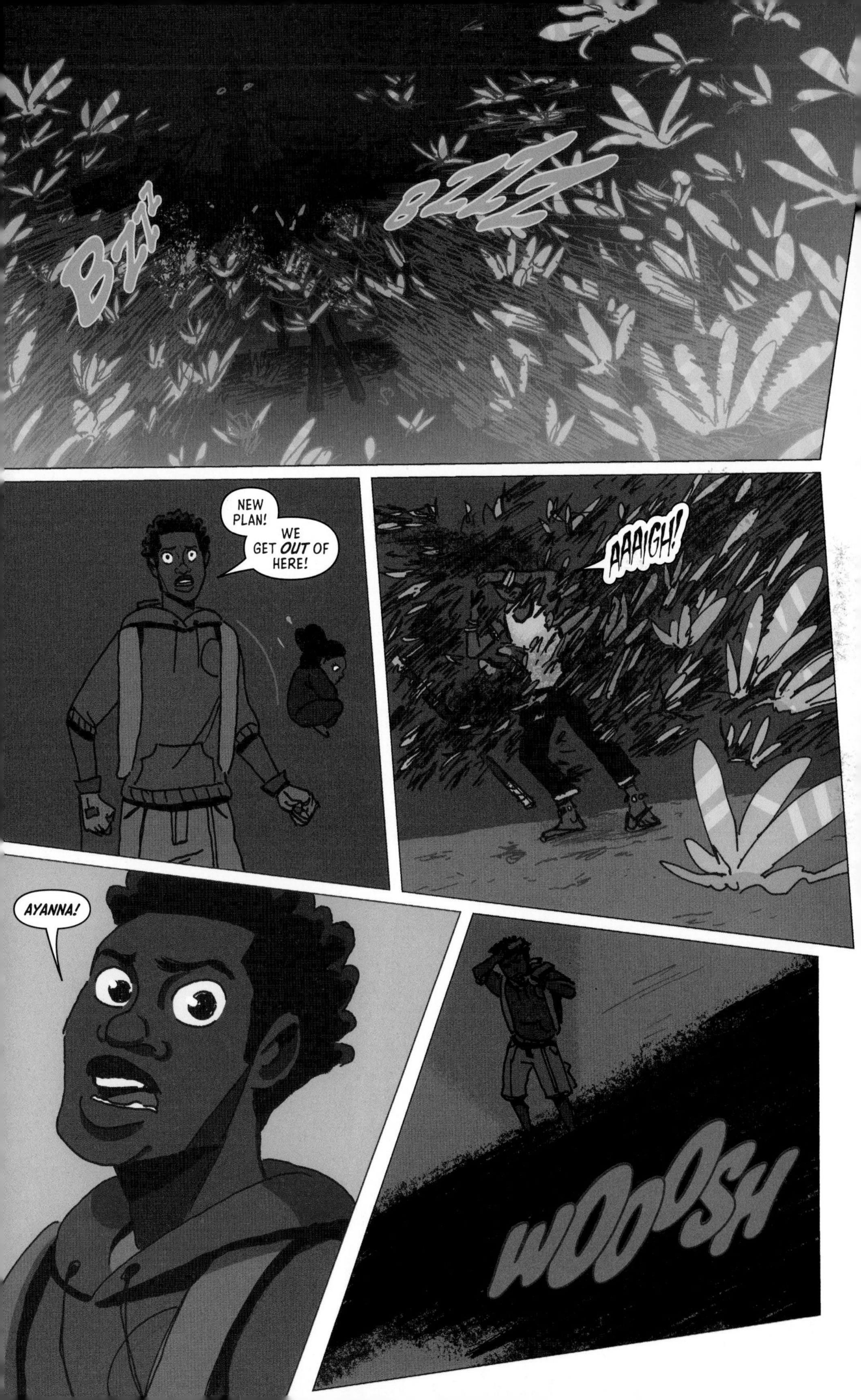
Bzzz
BZZZZ
NEW PLAN! WE GET OUT OF HERE!
AAAIGH!
AYANNA!
WOOOSH

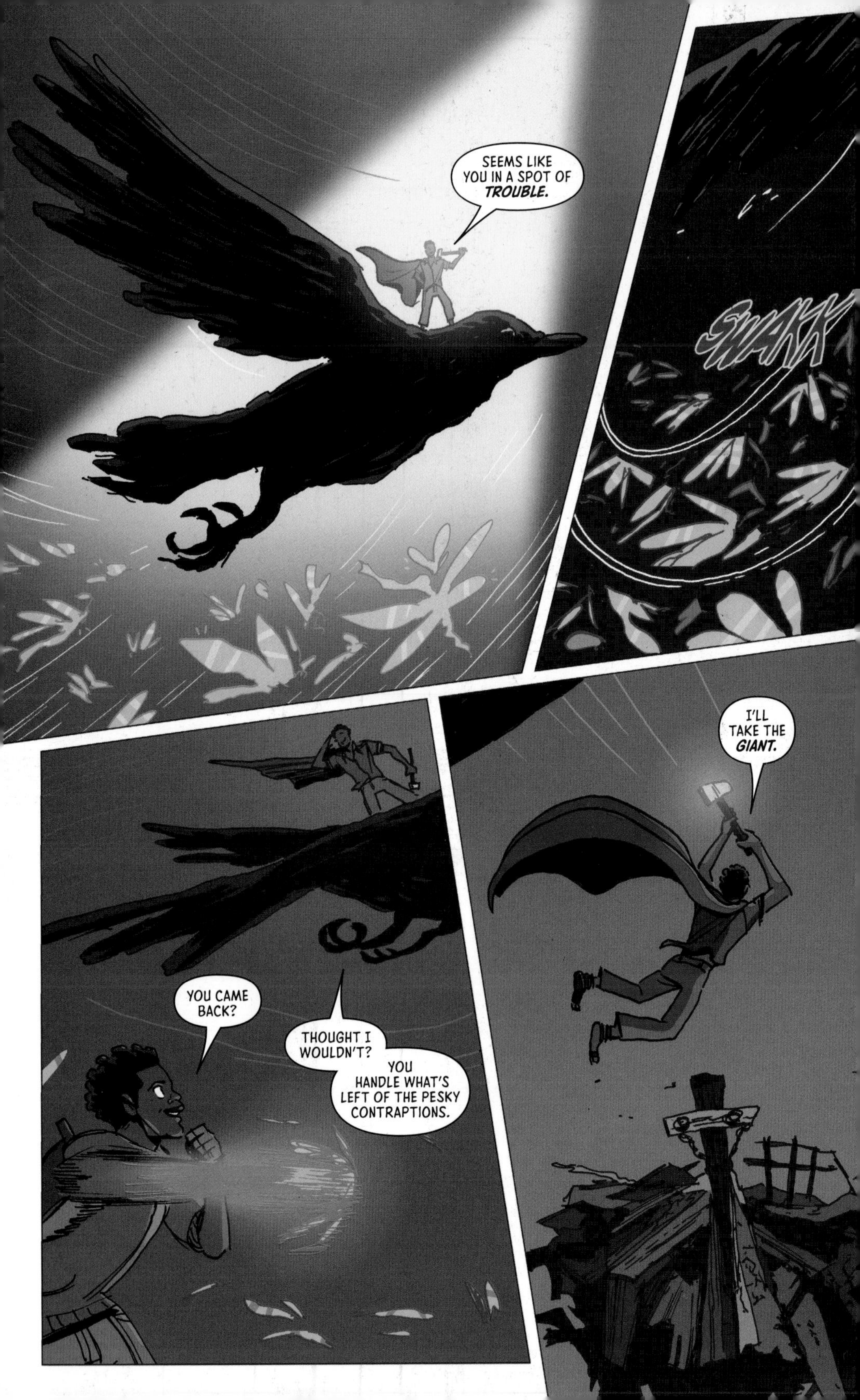
SEEMS LIKE YOU IN A SPOT OF *TROUBLE.*
SWAKK
YOU CAME BACK?
THOUGHT I WOULDN'T?
YOU HANDLE WHAT'S LEFT OF THE PESKY CONTRAPTIONS.
I'LL TAKE THE *GIANT.*

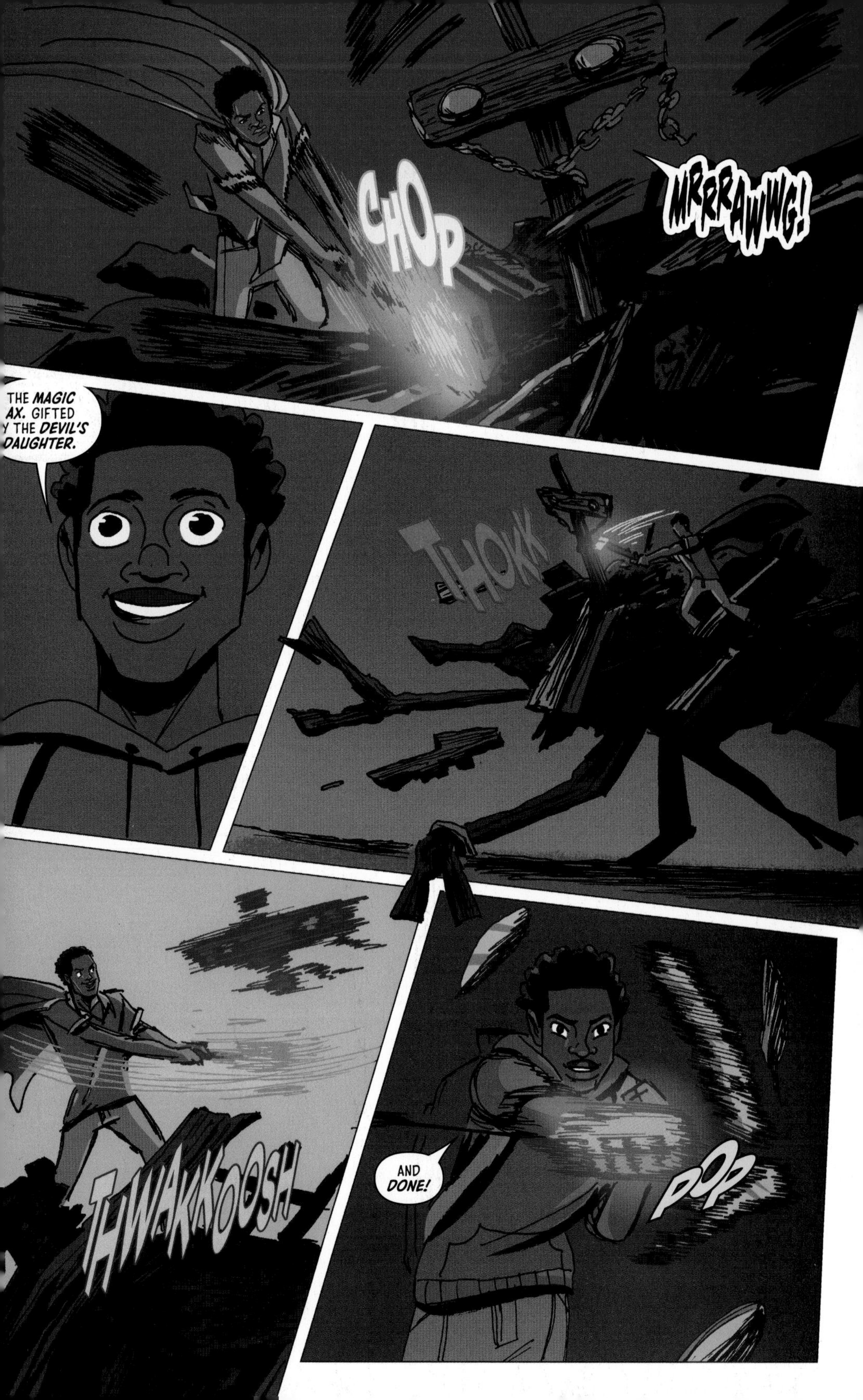
CHOP
MRRRAWWG!
THE *MAGIC AX.* GIFTED Y THE *DEVIL'S DAUGHTER.*
THOKK
THWAKKOOSH
AND *DONE!*
POP

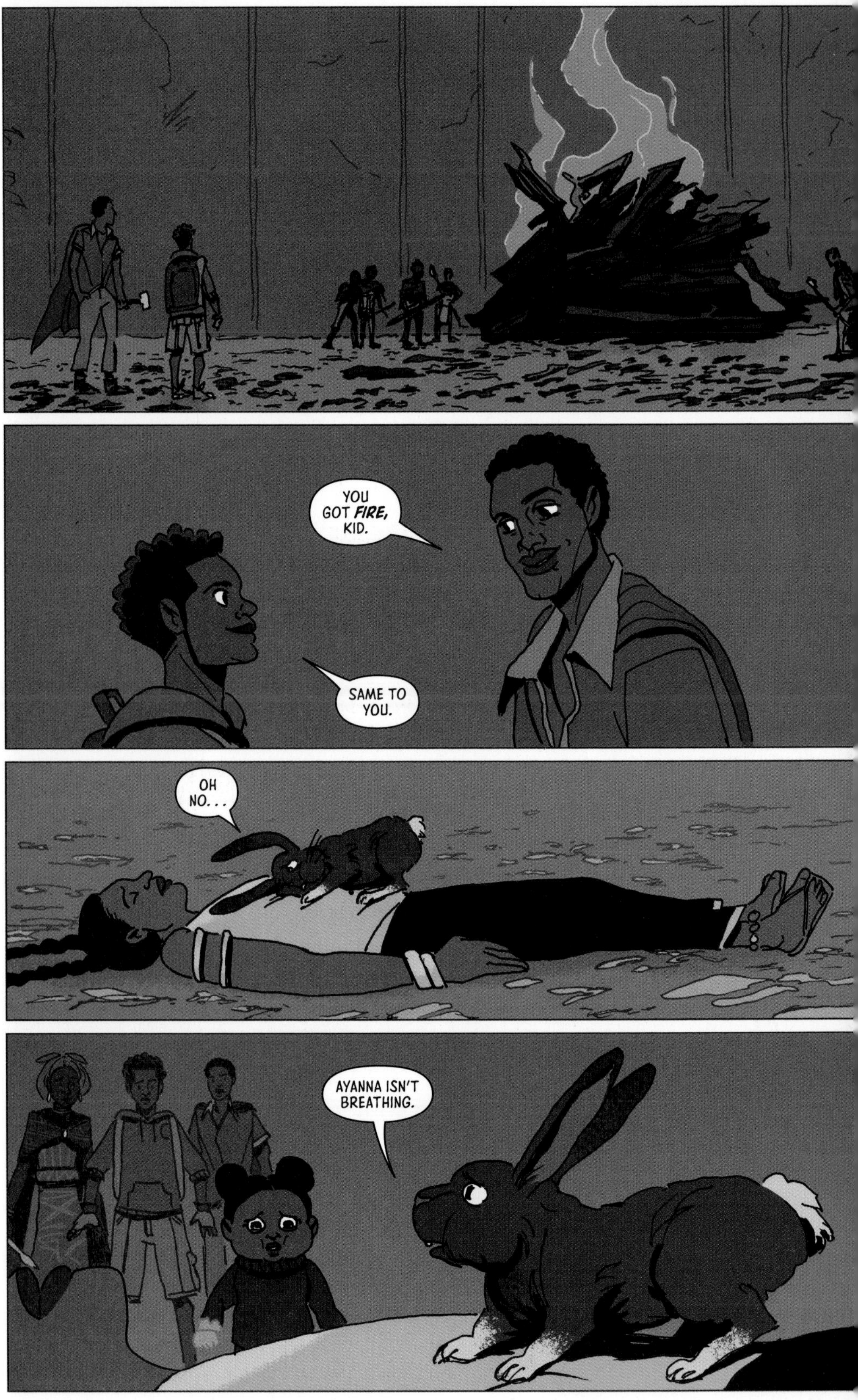
YOU GOT FIRE, KID.
SAME TO YOU.
OH NO. . .
AYANNA ISN'T BREATHING.

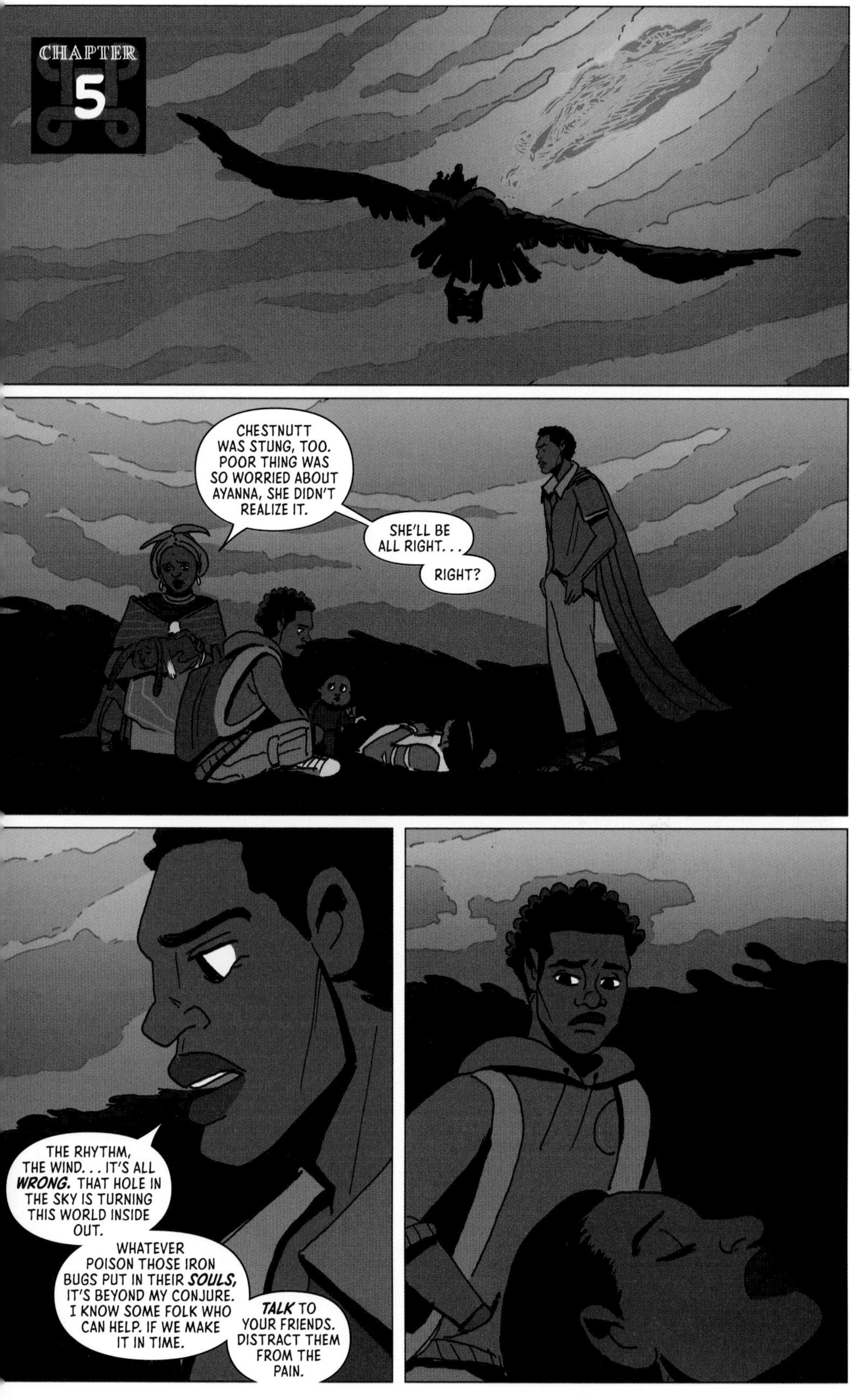
CHAPTER 5
CHESTNUTT WAS STUNG, TOO. POOR THING WAS SO WORRIED ABOUT AYANNA, SHE DIDN'T REALIZE IT.
SHE'LL BE ALL RIGHT. . .
RIGHT?
THE RHYTHM, THE WIND. . . IT'S ALL **WRONG.** THAT HOLE IN THE SKY IS TURNING THIS WORLD INSIDE OUT.
WHATEVER POISON THOSE IRON BUGS PUT IN THEIR **SOULS,** IT'S BEYOND MY CONJURE. I KNOW SOME FOLK WHO CAN HELP. IF WE MAKE IT IN TIME.
TALK TO YOUR FRIENDS. DISTRACT THEM FROM THE PAIN.

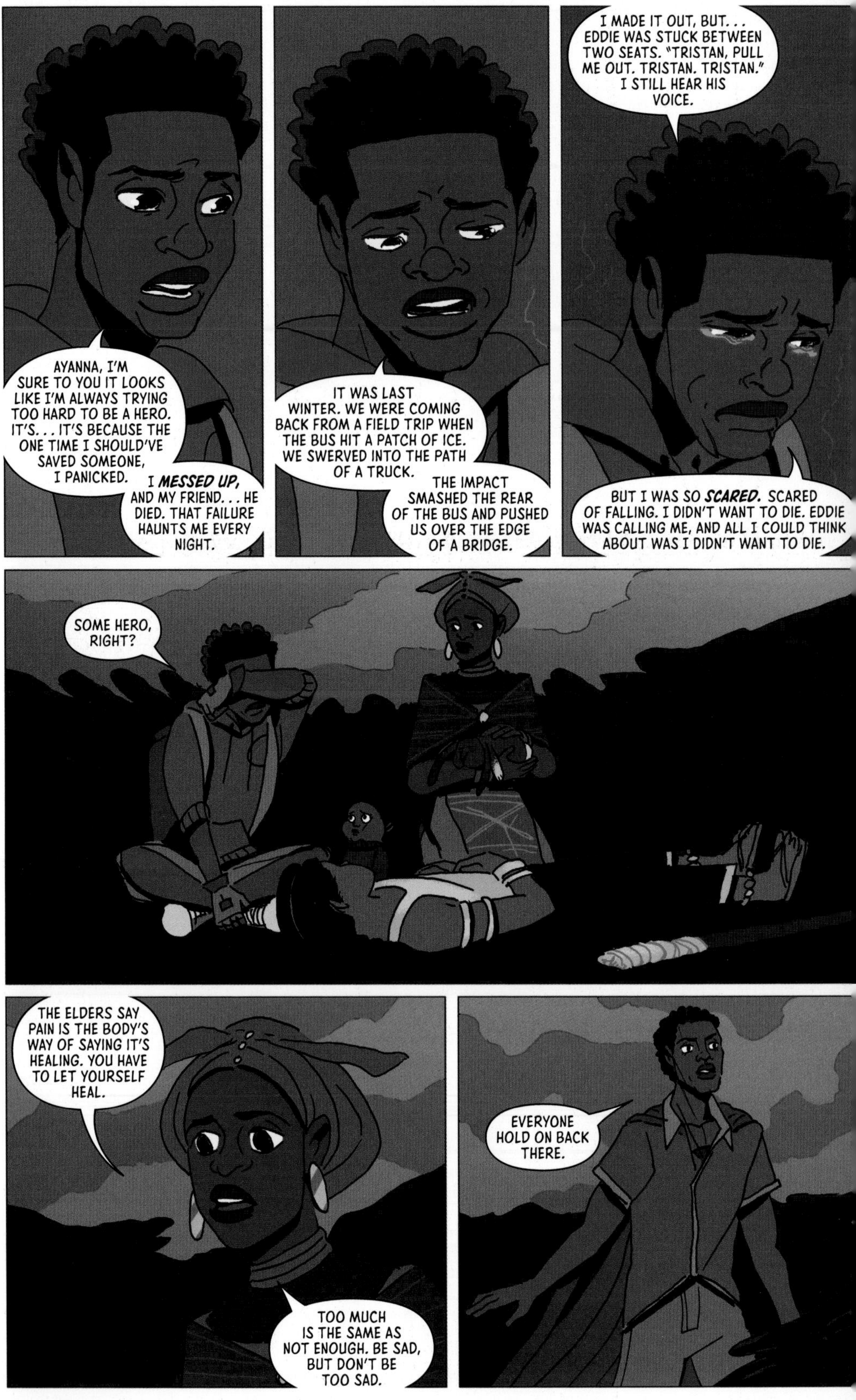
AYANNA, I'M SURE TO YOU IT LOOKS LIKE I'M ALWAYS TRYING TOO HARD TO BE A HERO. IT'S. . . IT'S BECAUSE THE ONE TIME I SHOULD'VE SAVED SOMEONE, I PANICKED.
I ***MESSED UP,*** AND MY FRIEND. . . HE DIED. THAT FAILURE HAUNTS ME EVERY NIGHT.
IT WAS LAST WINTER. WE WERE COMING BACK FROM A FIELD TRIP WHEN THE BUS HIT A PATCH OF ICE. WE SWERVED INTO THE PATH OF A TRUCK.
THE IMPACT SMASHED THE REAR OF THE BUS AND PUSHED US OVER THE EDGE OF A BRIDGE.
I MADE IT OUT, BUT. . . EDDIE WAS STUCK BETWEEN TWO SEATS. "TRISTAN, PULL ME OUT. TRISTAN. TRISTAN." I STILL HEAR HIS VOICE.
BUT I WAS SO ***SCARED.*** SCARED OF FALLING. I DIDN'T WANT TO DIE. EDDIE WAS CALLING ME, AND ALL I COULD THINK ABOUT WAS I DIDN'T WANT TO DIE.
SOME HERO, RIGHT?
THE ELDERS SAY PAIN IS THE BODY'S WAY OF SAYING IT'S HEALING. YOU HAVE TO LET YOURSELF HEAL.
TOO MUCH IS THE SAME AS NOT ENOUGH. BE SAD, BUT DON'T BE TOO SAD.
EVERYONE HOLD ON BACK THERE.

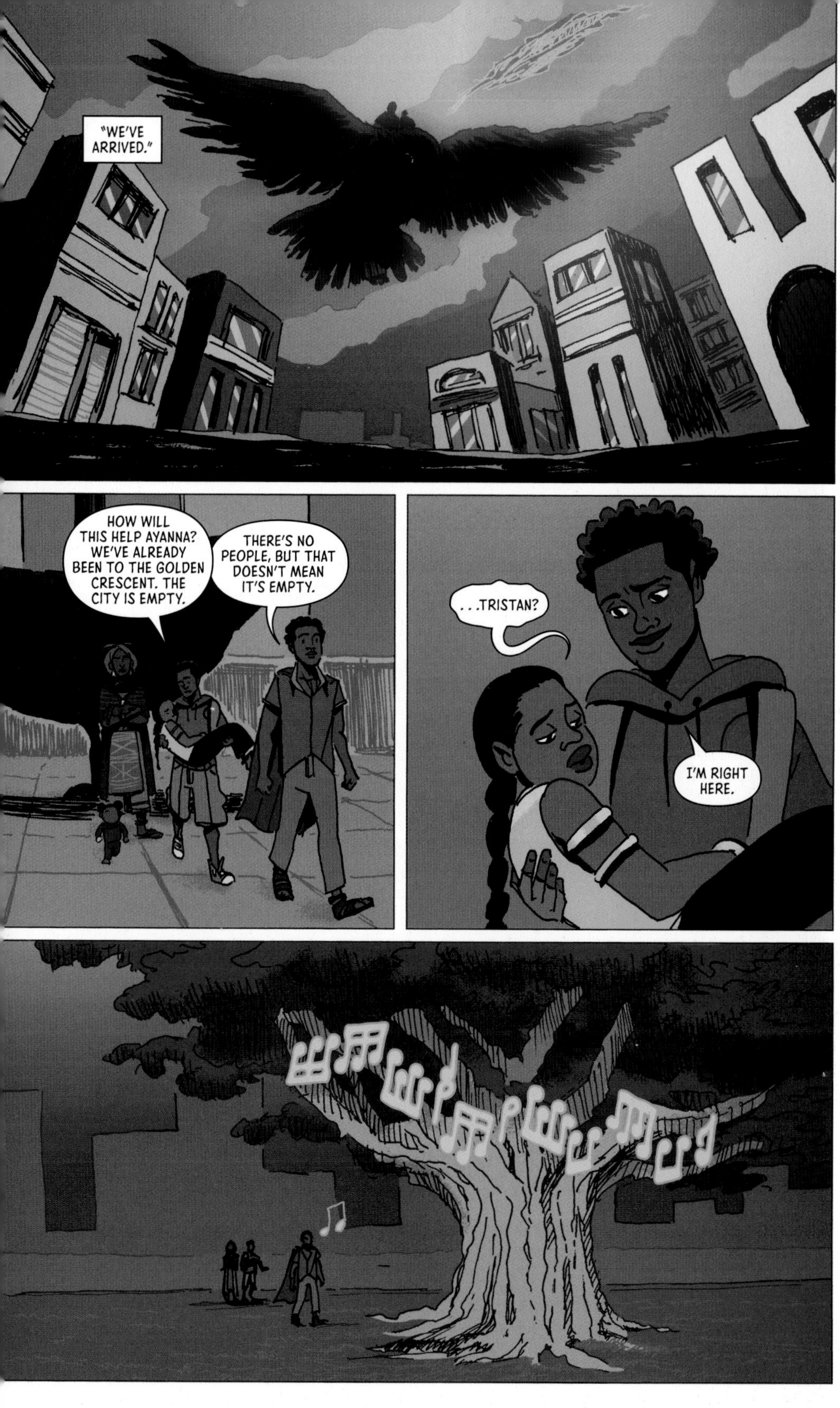
"WE'VE ARRIVED."
HOW WILL THIS HELP AYANNA? WE'VE ALREADY BEEN TO THE GOLDEN CRESCENT. THE CITY IS EMPTY.
THERE'S NO PEOPLE, BUT THAT DOESN'T MEAN IT'S EMPTY.
. . .TRISTAN?
I'M RIGHT HERE.

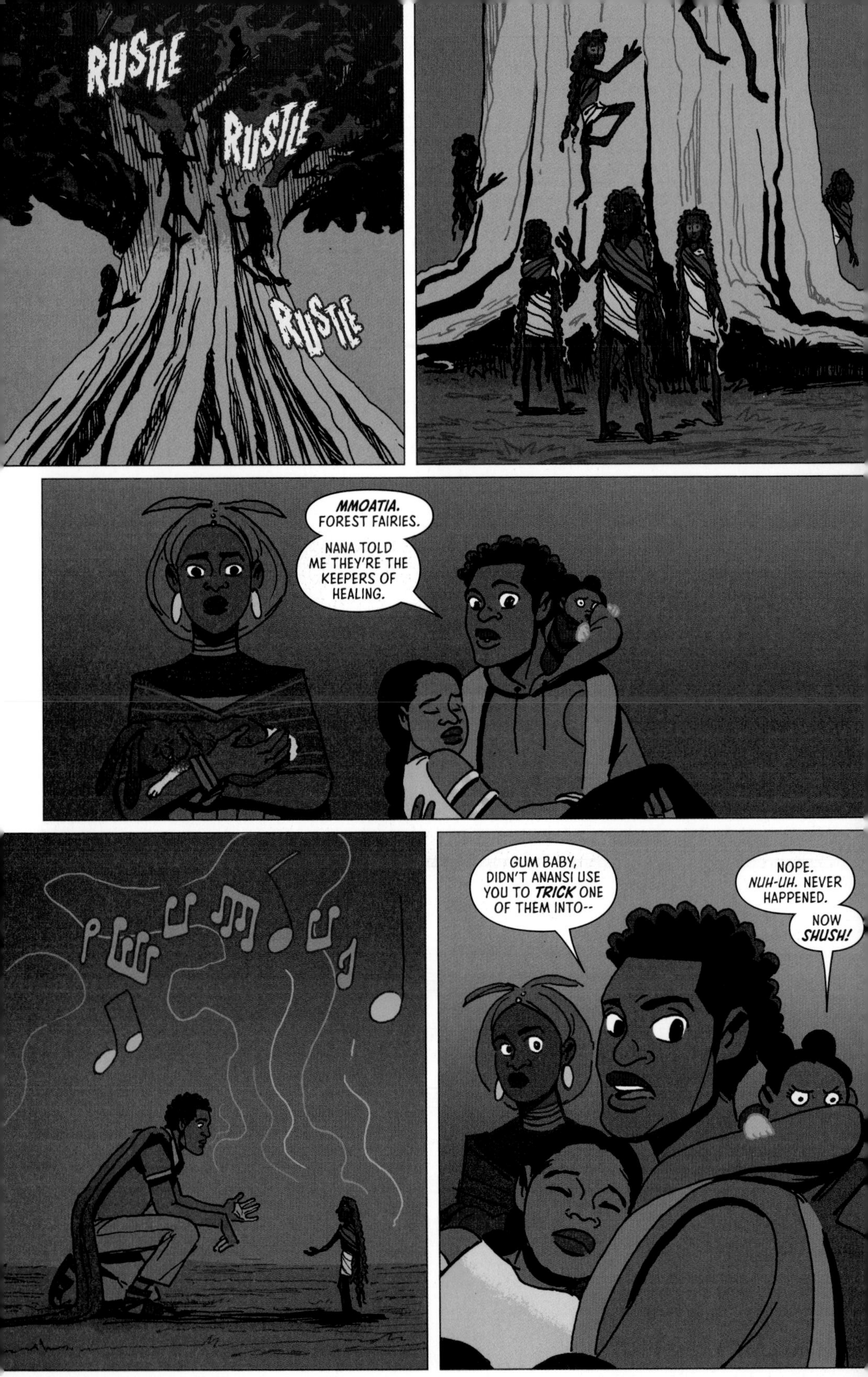
RUSTLE
RUSTLE
RUSTLE
MMOATIA. FOREST FAIRIES.
NANA TOLD ME THEY'RE THE KEEPERS OF HEALING.
GUM BABY, DIDN'T ANANSI USE YOU TO TRICK ONE OF THEM INTO--
NOPE. NUH-UH. NEVER HAPPENED.
NOW SHUSH!

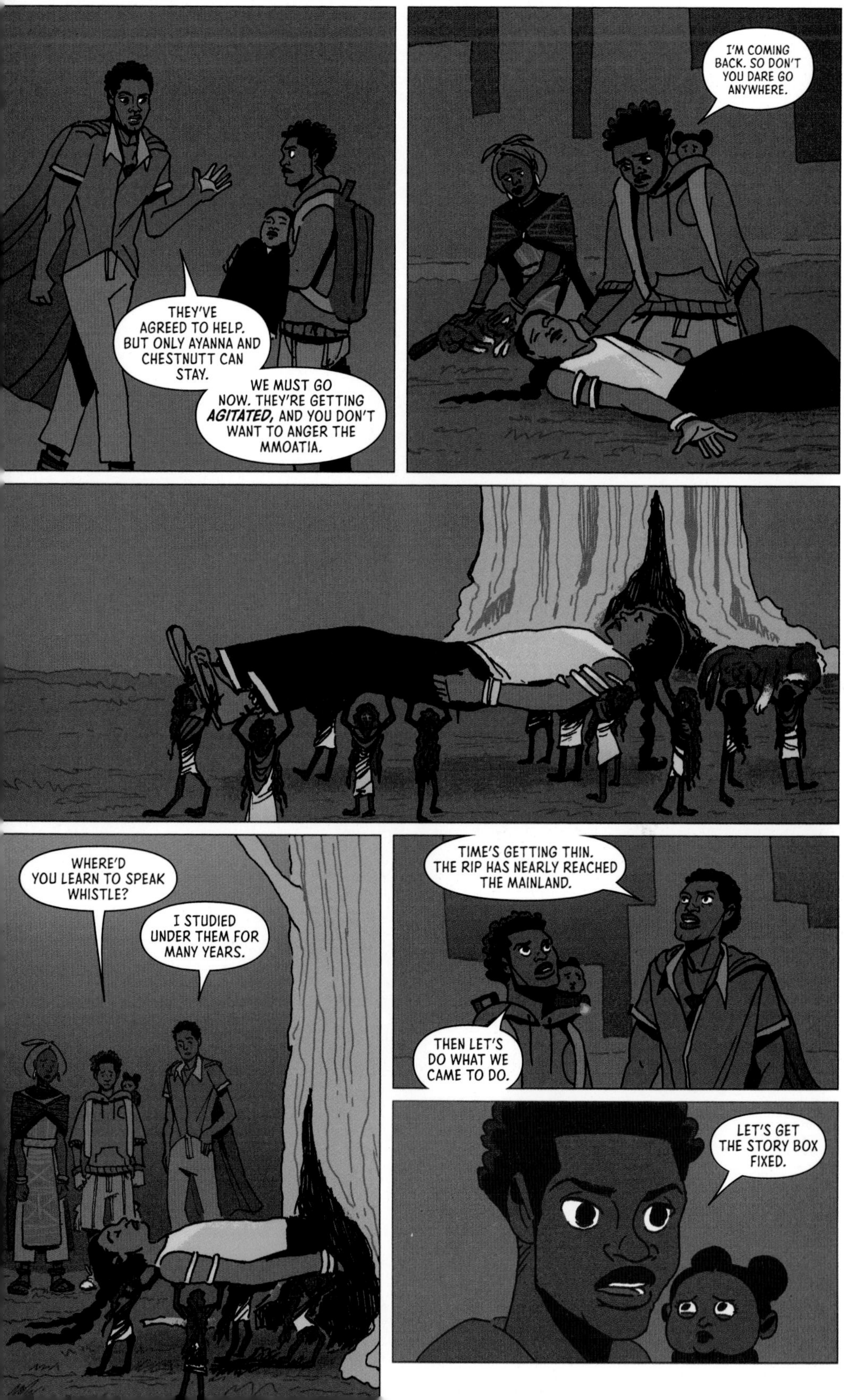
THEY'VE AGREED TO HELP. BUT ONLY AYANNA AND CHESTNUTT CAN STAY.
WE MUST GO NOW. THEY'RE GETTING *AGITATED,* AND YOU DON'T WANT TO ANGER THE MMOATIA.
I'M COMING BACK. SO DON'T YOU DARE GO ANYWHERE.
WHERE'D YOU LEARN TO SPEAK WHISTLE?
I STUDIED UNDER THEM FOR MANY YEARS.
TIME'S GETTING THIN. THE RIP HAS NEARLY REACHED THE MAINLAND.
THEN LET'S DO WHAT WE CAME TO DO.
LET'S GET THE STORY BOX FIXED.

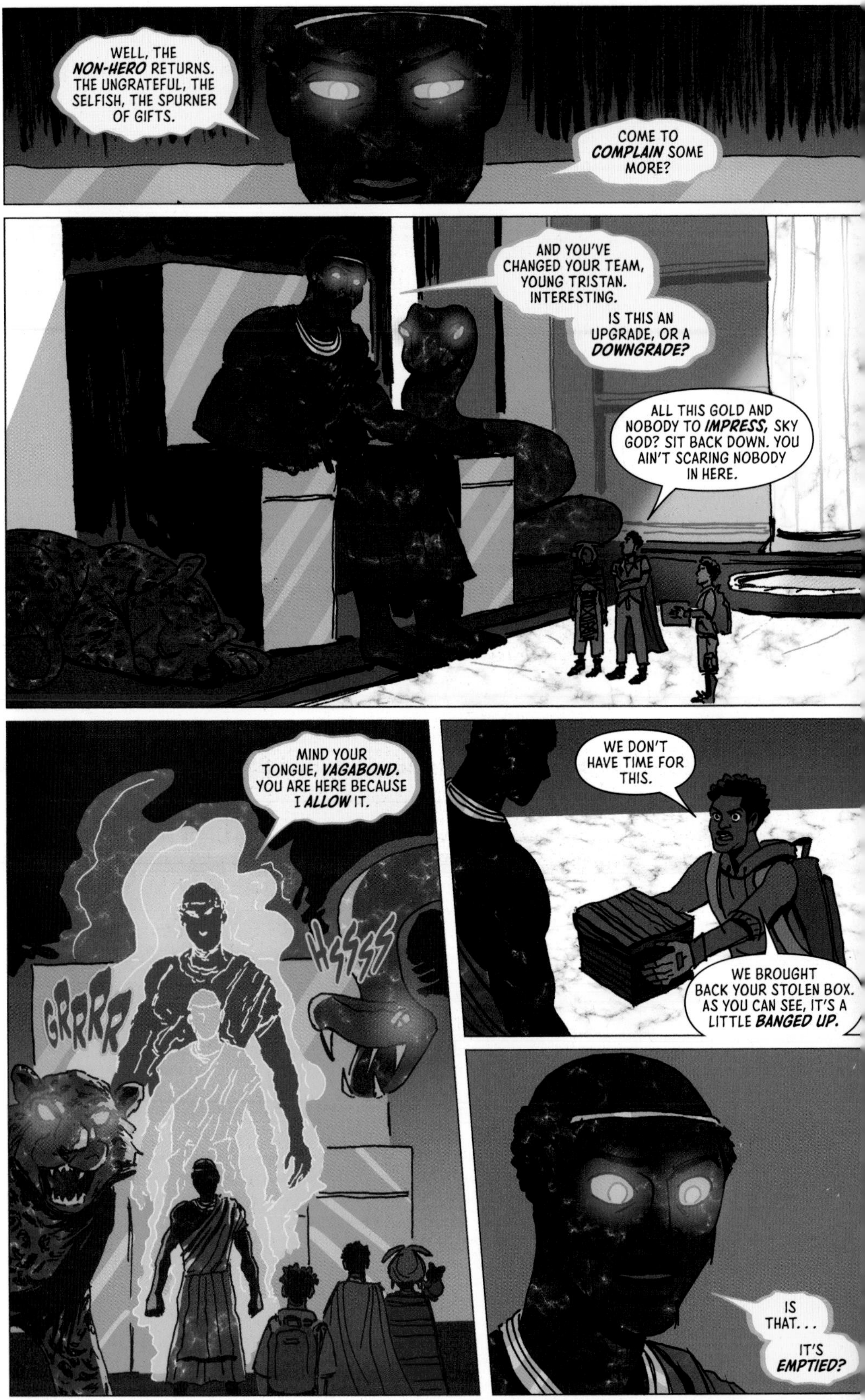
WELL, THE NON-HERO RETURNS. THE UNGRATEFUL, THE SELFISH, THE SPURNER OF GIFTS.
COME TO COMPLAIN SOME MORE?
AND YOU'VE CHANGED YOUR TEAM, YOUNG TRISTAN. INTERESTING.
IS THIS AN UPGRADE, OR A DOWNGRADE?
ALL THIS GOLD AND NOBODY TO IMPRESS, SKY GOD? SIT BACK DOWN. YOU AIN'T SCARING NOBODY IN HERE.
MIND YOUR TONGUE, VAGABOND. YOU ARE HERE BECAUSE I ALLOW IT.
HSSSS
GRRRR
WE DON'T HAVE TIME FOR THIS.
WE BROUGHT BACK YOUR STOLEN BOX. AS YOU CAN SEE, IT'S A LITTLE BANGED UP.
IS THAT. . .
IT'S EMPTIED?

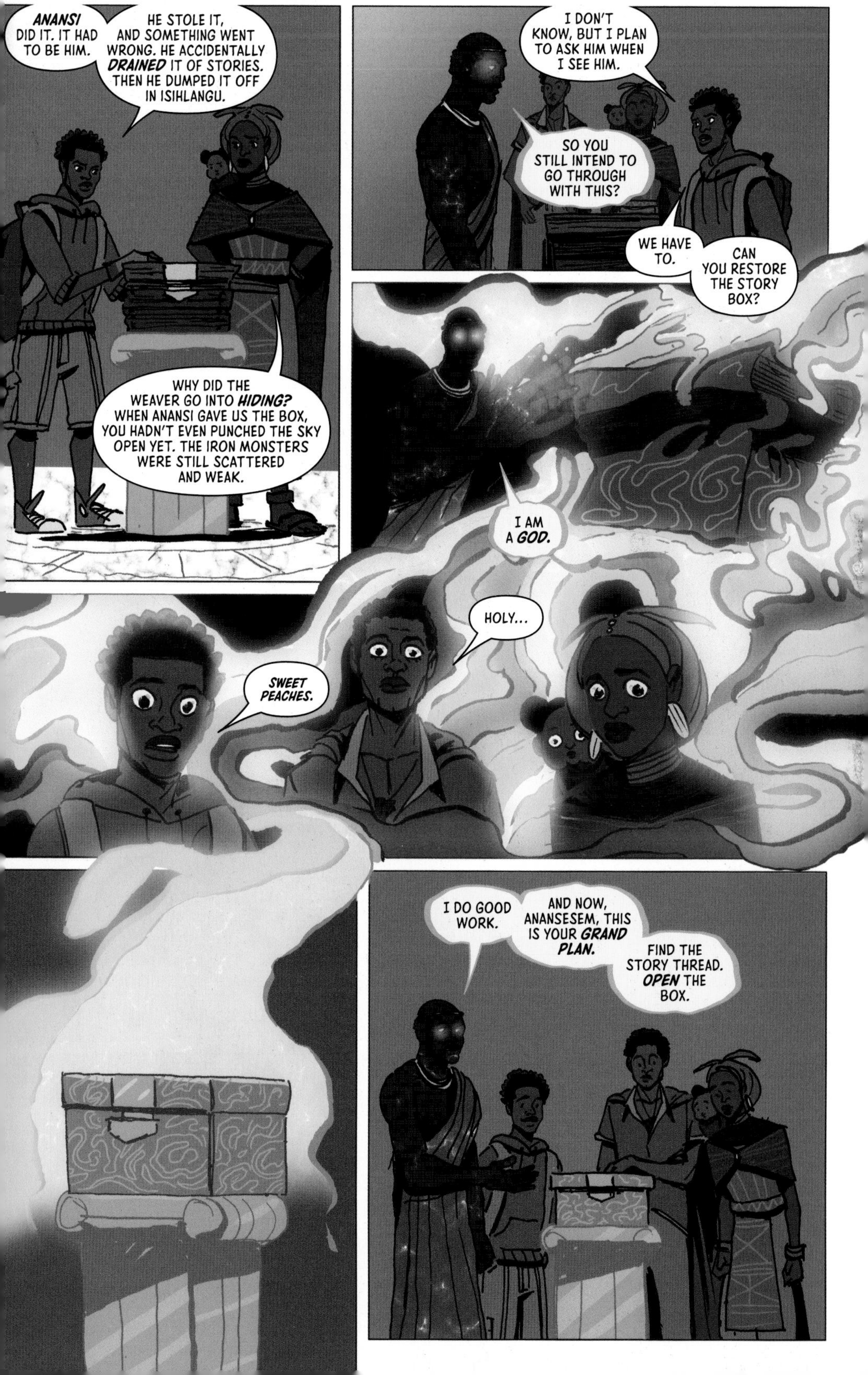
ANANSI DID IT. IT HAD TO BE HIM.
HE STOLE IT, AND SOMETHING WENT WRONG. HE ACCIDENTALLY DRAINED IT OF STORIES. THEN HE DUMPED IT OFF IN ISIHLANGU.
WHY DID THE WEAVER GO INTO HIDING? WHEN ANANSI GAVE US THE BOX, YOU HADN'T EVEN PUNCHED THE SKY OPEN YET. THE IRON MONSTERS WERE STILL SCATTERED AND WEAK.
I DON'T KNOW, BUT I PLAN TO ASK HIM WHEN I SEE HIM.
SO YOU STILL INTEND TO GO THROUGH WITH THIS?
WE HAVE TO.
CAN YOU RESTORE THE STORY BOX?
I AM A GOD.
SWEET PEACHES.
HOLY...
I DO GOOD WORK.
AND NOW, ANANSESEM, THIS IS YOUR GRAND PLAN.
FIND THE STORY THREAD. OPEN THE BOX.

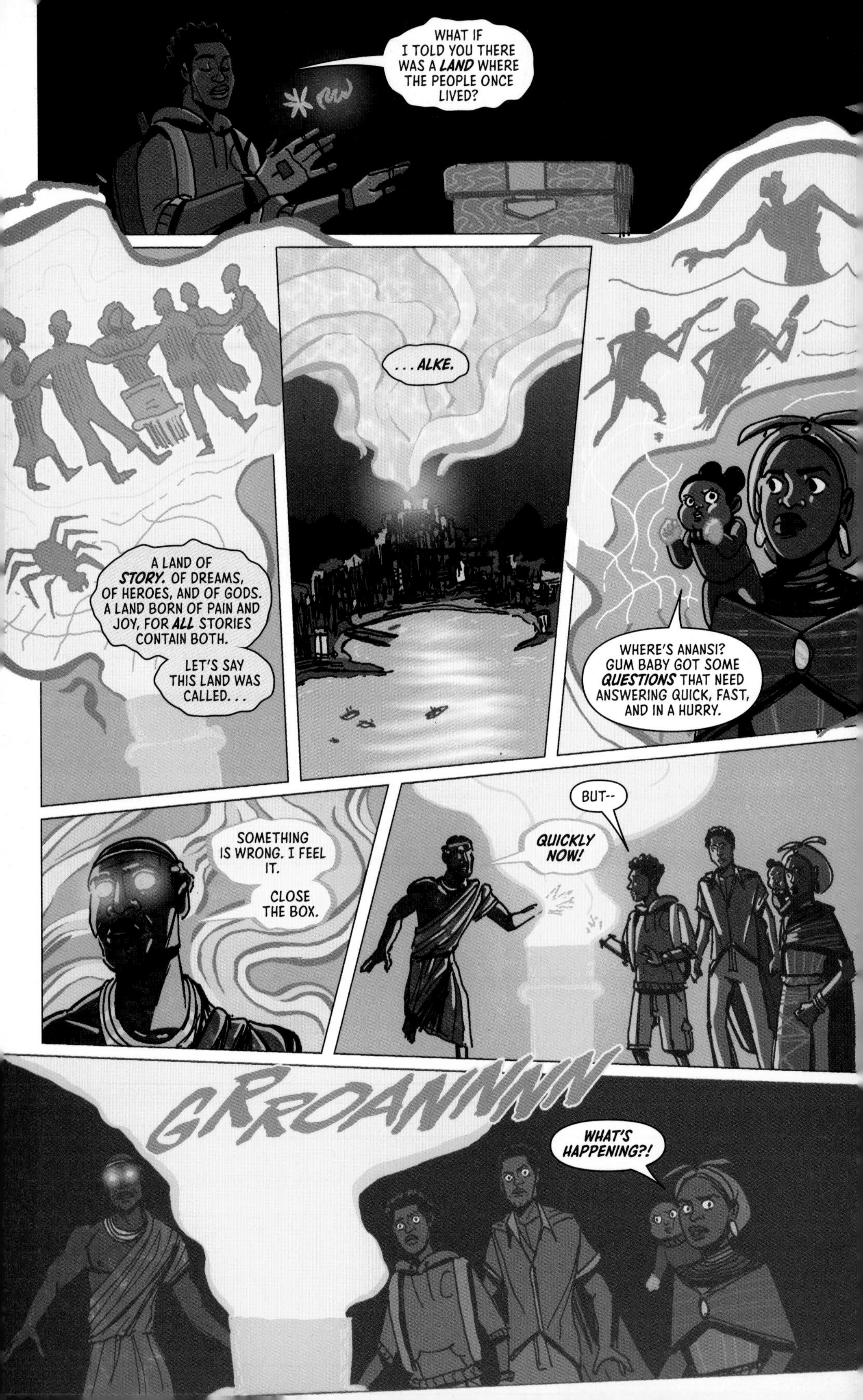
WHAT IF I TOLD YOU THERE WAS A LAND WHERE THE PEOPLE ONCE LIVED?
A LAND OF STORY. OF DREAMS, OF HEROES, AND OF GODS. A LAND BORN OF PAIN AND JOY, FOR ALL STORIES CONTAIN BOTH.
LET'S SAY THIS LAND WAS CALLED...
...ALKE.
WHERE'S ANANSI? GUM BABY GOT SOME QUESTIONS THAT NEED ANSWERING QUICK, FAST, AND IN A HURRY.
SOMETHING IS WRONG. I FEEL IT.
CLOSE THE BOX.
QUICKLY NOW!
BUT--
GRROANNNNN
WHAT'S HAPPENING?!

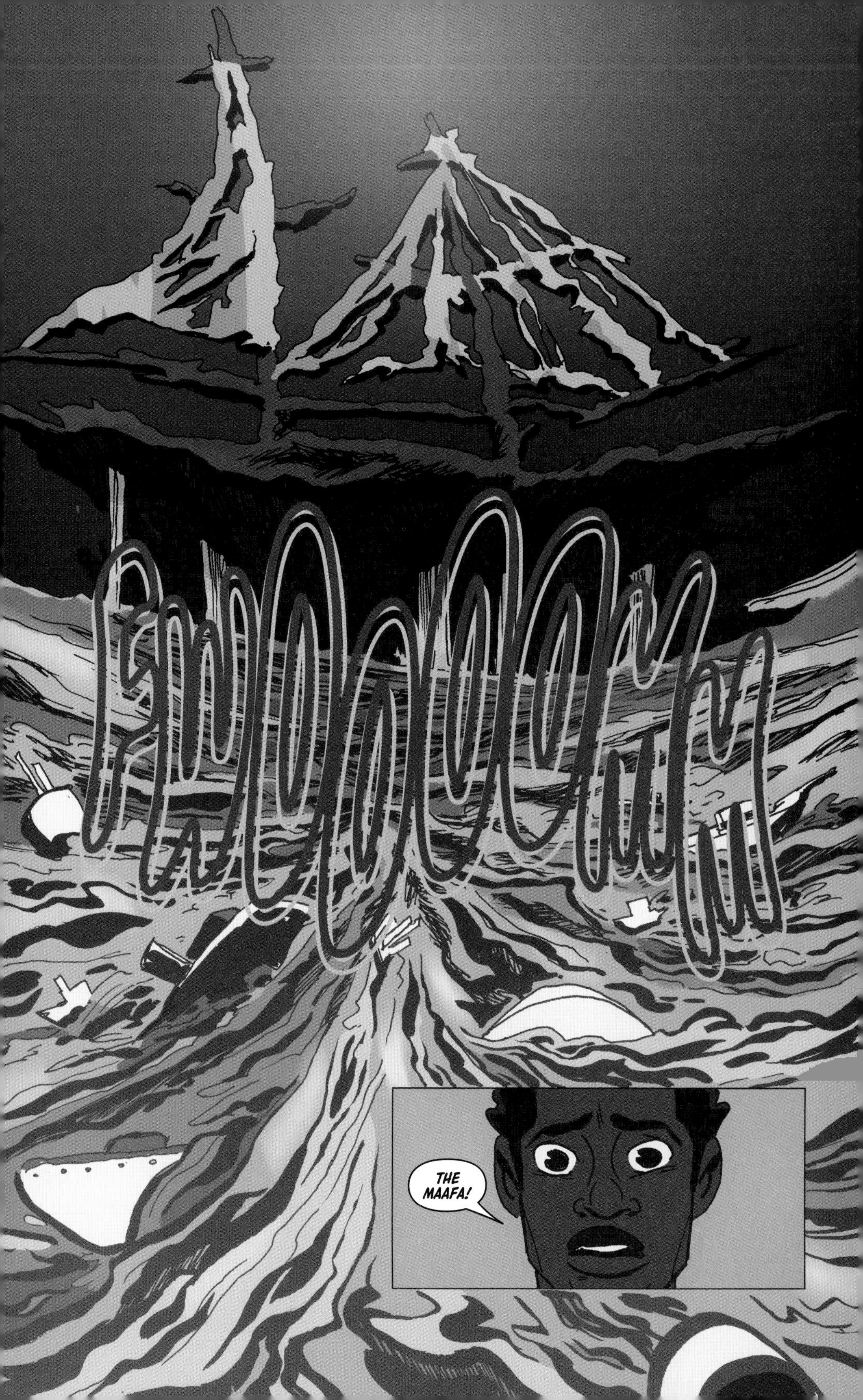
THE MAAFA!

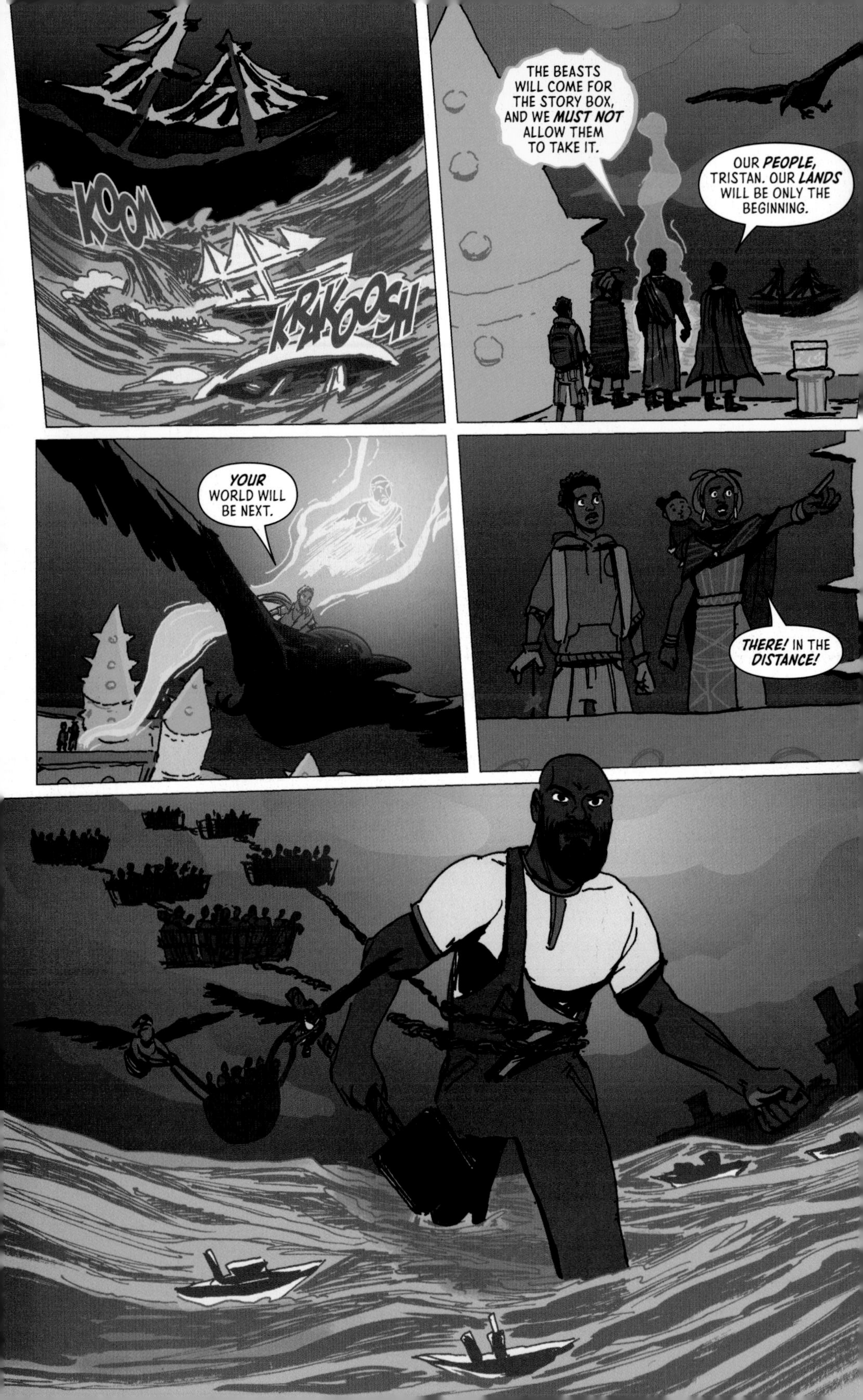
KOOM
KRAKOOSH
THE BEASTS WILL COME FOR THE STORY BOX, AND WE *MUST NOT* ALLOW THEM TO TAKE IT.
OUR *PEOPLE,* TRISTAN. OUR *LANDS* WILL BE ONLY THE BEGINNING.
YOUR WORLD WILL BE NEXT.
THERE! IN THE *DISTANCE!*

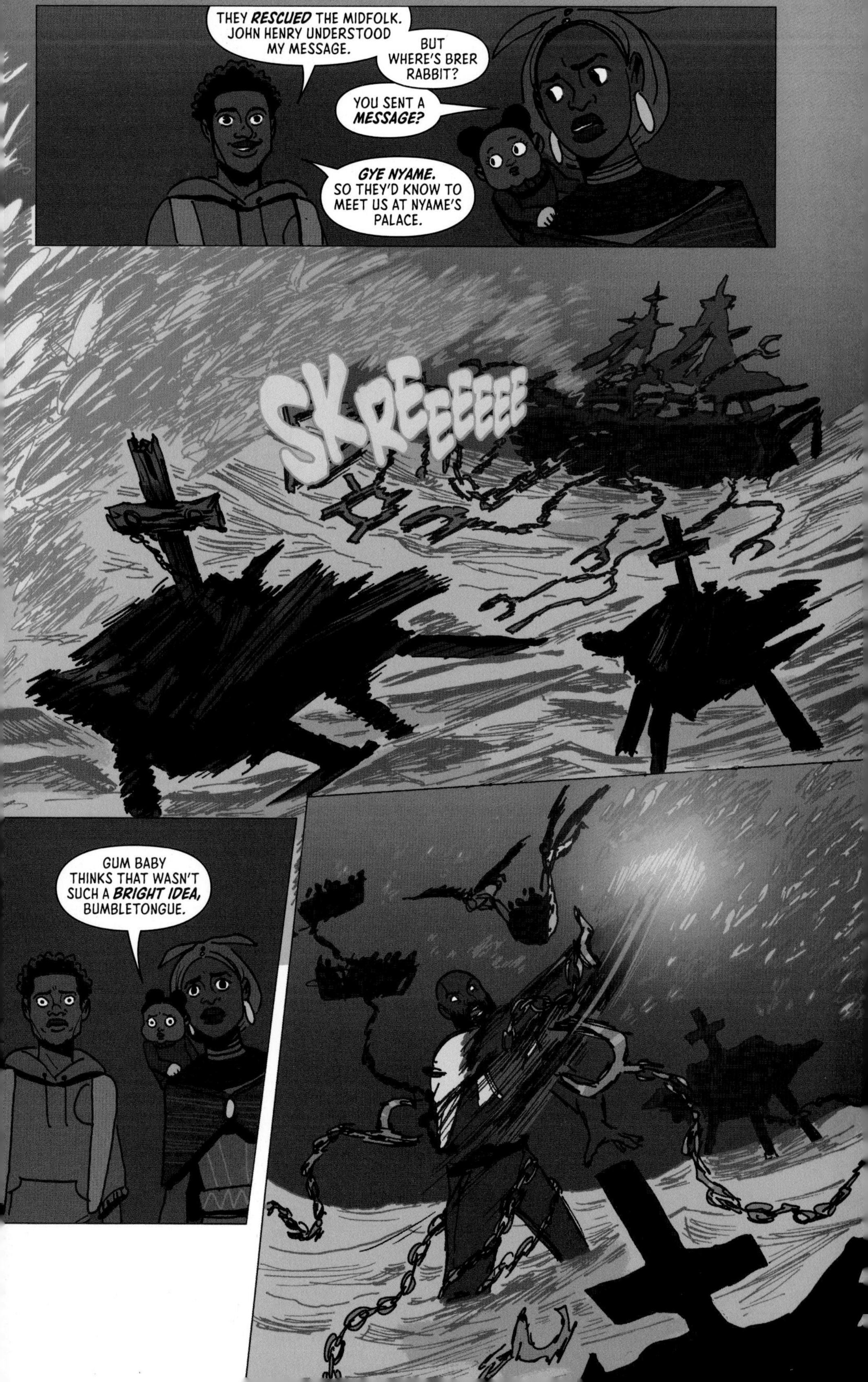
THEY RESCUED THE MIDFOLK. JOHN HENRY UNDERSTOOD MY MESSAGE.
BUT WHERE'S BRER RABBIT?
YOU SENT A MESSAGE?
GYE NYAME. SO THEY'D KNOW TO MEET US AT NYAME'S PALACE.
SKREEEEEE
GUM BABY THINKS THAT WASN'T SUCH A BRIGHT IDEA, BUMBLETONGUE.

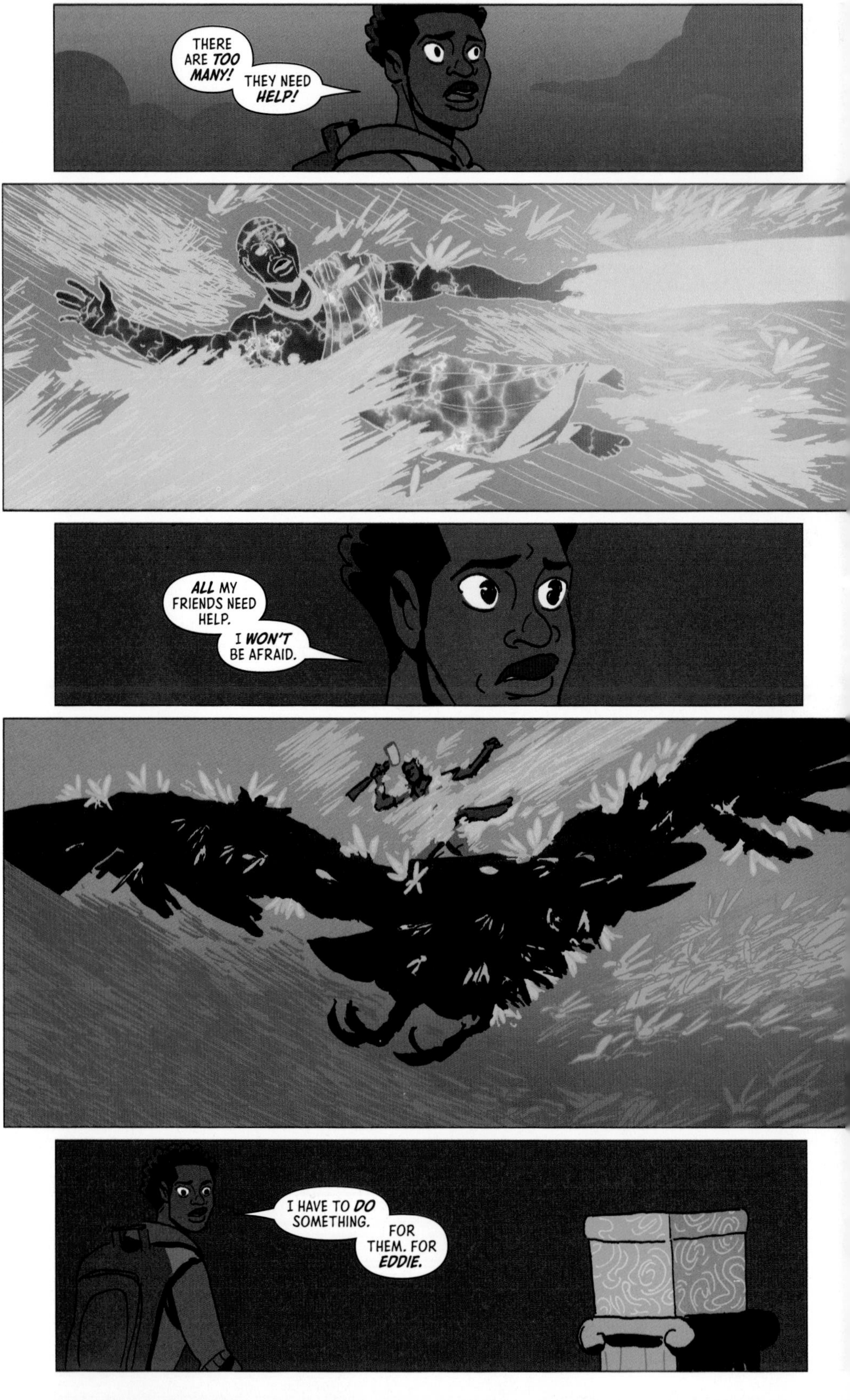
THERE ARE TOO MANY!
THEY NEED HELP!
ALL MY FRIENDS NEED HELP.
I WON'T BE AFRAID.
I HAVE TO DO SOMETHING.
FOR THEM. FOR EDDIE.

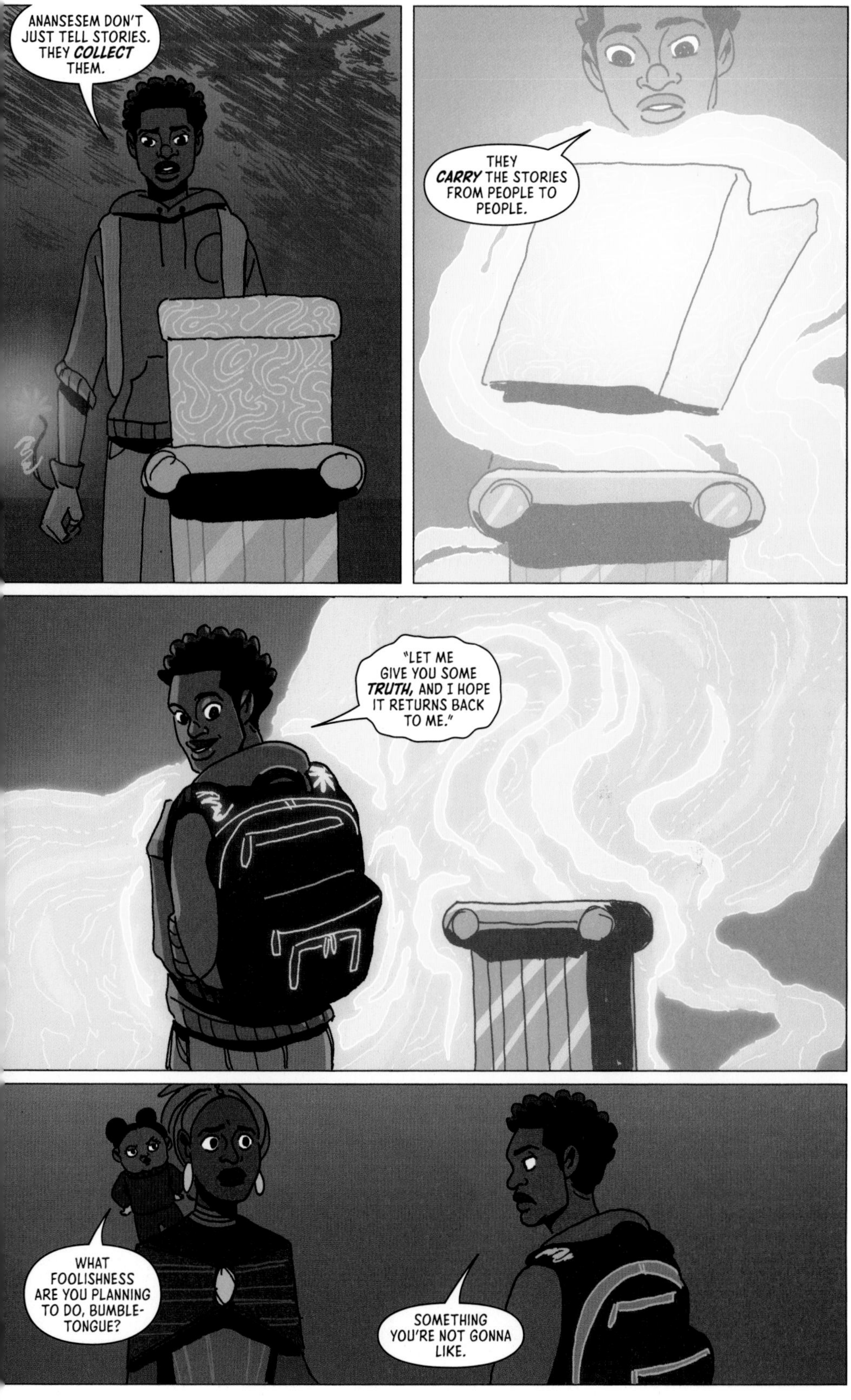
ANANSESEM DON'T JUST TELL STORIES. THEY ***COLLECT*** THEM.
THEY ***CARRY*** THE STORIES FROM PEOPLE TO PEOPLE.
"LET ME GIVE YOU SOME ***TRUTH,*** AND I HOPE IT RETURNS BACK TO ME."
WHAT FOOLISHNESS ARE YOU PLANNING TO DO, BUMBLE-TONGUE?
SOMETHING YOU'RE NOT GONNA LIKE.

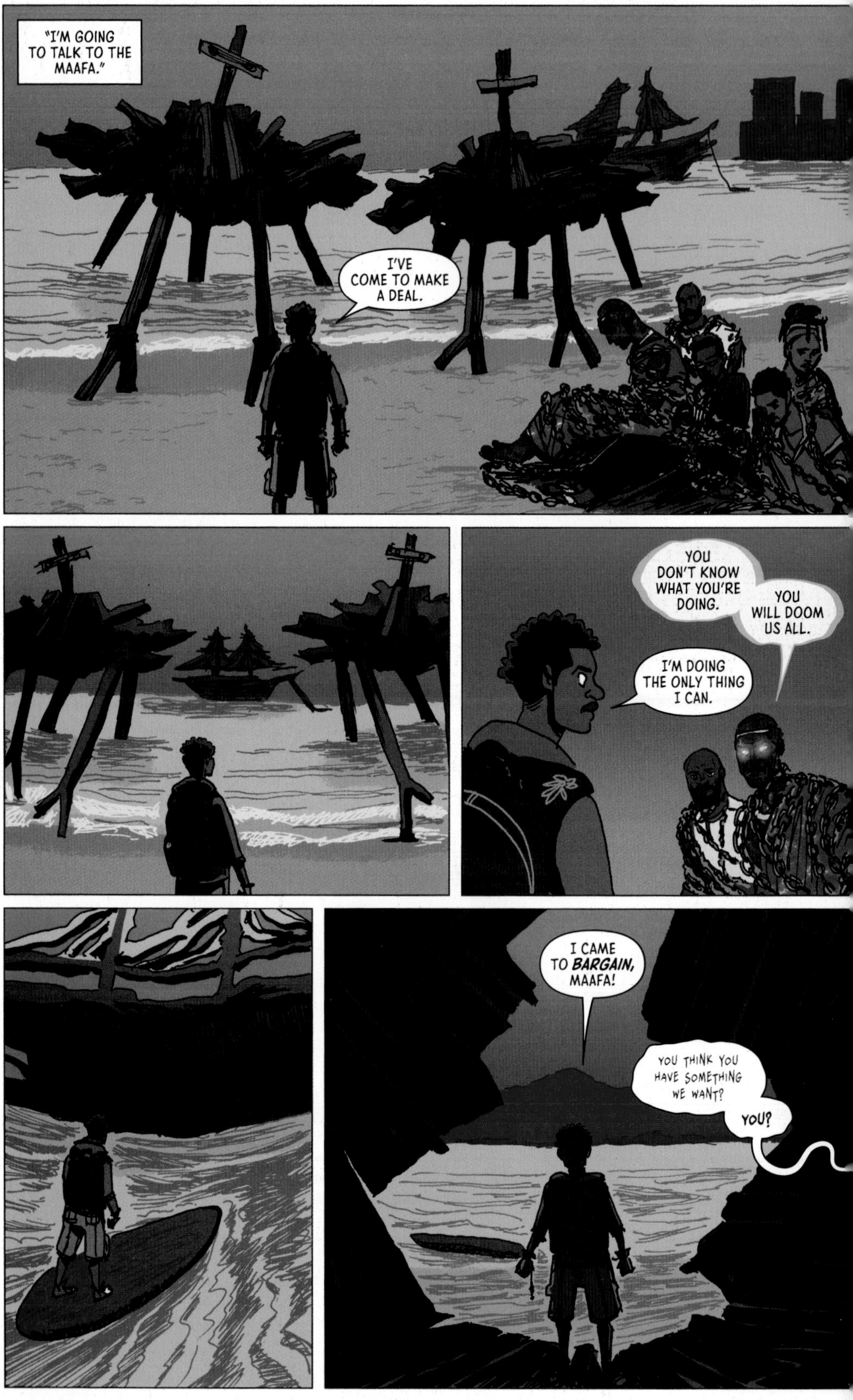
"I'M GOING TO TALK TO THE MAAFA."
I'VE COME TO MAKE A DEAL.
YOU DON'T KNOW WHAT YOU'RE DOING.
YOU WILL DOOM US ALL.
I'M DOING THE ONLY THING I CAN.
I CAME TO BARGAIN, MAAFA!
YOU THINK YOU HAVE SOMETHING WE WANT?
YOU?

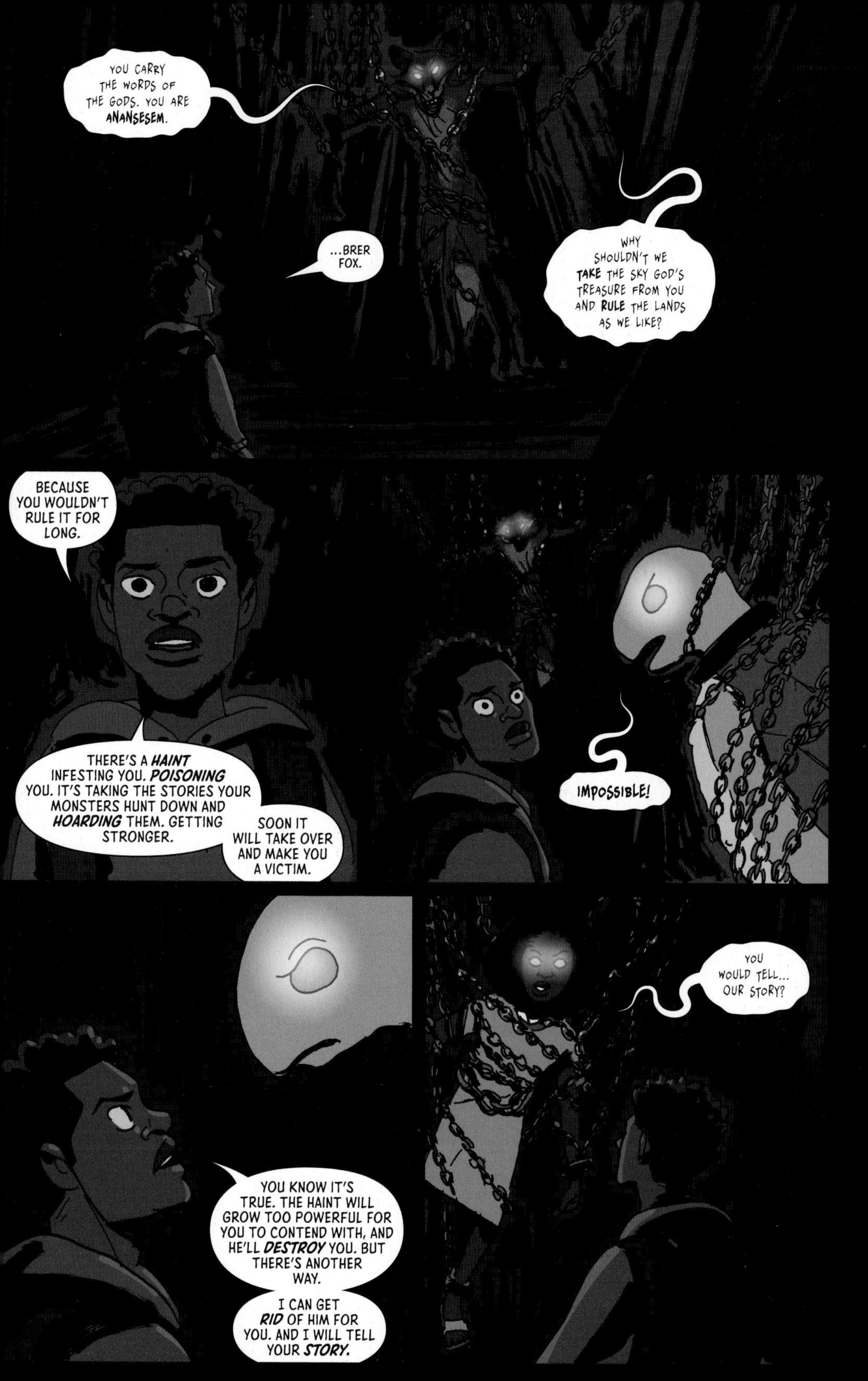
YOU CARRY THE WORDS OF THE GODS. YOU ARE ANANSESEM.
...BRER FOX.
WHY SHOULDN'T WE TAKE THE SKY GOD'S TREASURE FROM YOU AND RULE THE LANDS AS WE LIKE?
BECAUSE YOU WOULDN'T RULE IT FOR LONG.
THERE'S A HAINT INFESTING YOU. POISONING YOU. IT'S TAKING THE STORIES YOUR MONSTERS HUNT DOWN AND HOARDING THEM. GETTING STRONGER.
SOON IT WILL TAKE OVER AND MAKE YOU A VICTIM.
IMPOSSIBLE!
YOU KNOW IT'S TRUE. THE HAINT WILL GROW TOO POWERFUL FOR YOU TO CONTEND WITH, AND HE'LL DESTROY YOU. BUT THERE'S ANOTHER WAY.
I CAN GET RID OF HIM FOR YOU. AND I WILL TELL YOUR STORY.
YOU WOULD TELL... OUR STORY?

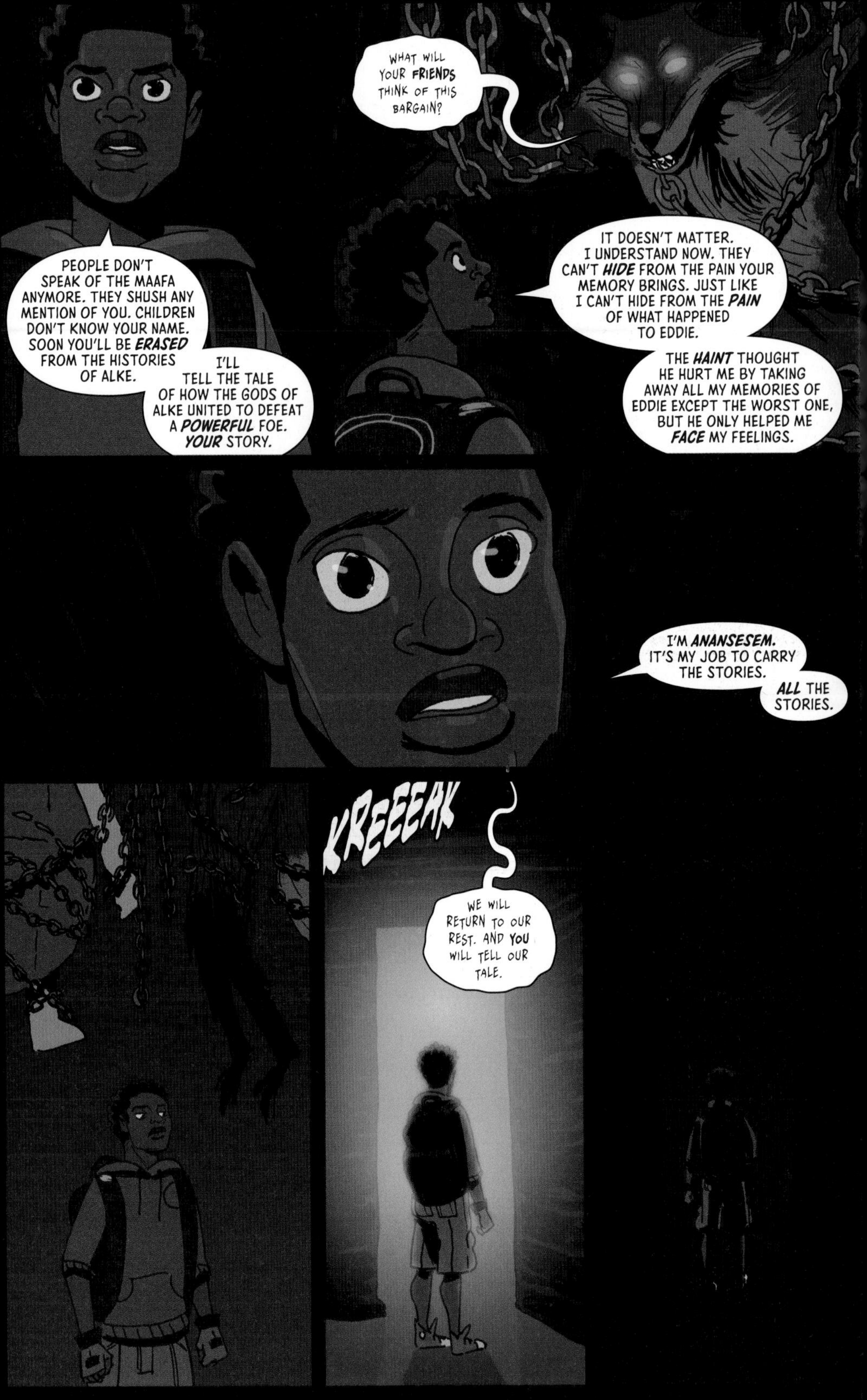
WHAT WILL YOUR FRIENDS THINK OF THIS BARGAIN?
PEOPLE DON'T SPEAK OF THE MAAFA ANYMORE. THEY SHUSH ANY MENTION OF YOU. CHILDREN DON'T KNOW YOUR NAME. SOON YOU'LL BE ERASED FROM THE HISTORIES OF ALKE.
I'LL TELL THE TALE OF HOW THE GODS OF ALKE UNITED TO DEFEAT A POWERFUL FOE. YOUR STORY.
IT DOESN'T MATTER. I UNDERSTAND NOW. THEY CAN'T HIDE FROM THE PAIN YOUR MEMORY BRINGS. JUST LIKE I CAN'T HIDE FROM THE PAIN OF WHAT HAPPENED TO EDDIE.
THE HAINT THOUGHT HE HURT ME BY TAKING AWAY ALL MY MEMORIES OF EDDIE EXCEPT THE WORST ONE, BUT HE ONLY HELPED ME FACE MY FEELINGS.
I'M ANANSESEM. IT'S MY JOB TO CARRY THE STORIES.
ALL THE STORIES.
KREEEAK
WE WILL RETURN TO OUR REST. AND YOU WILL TELL OUR TALE.

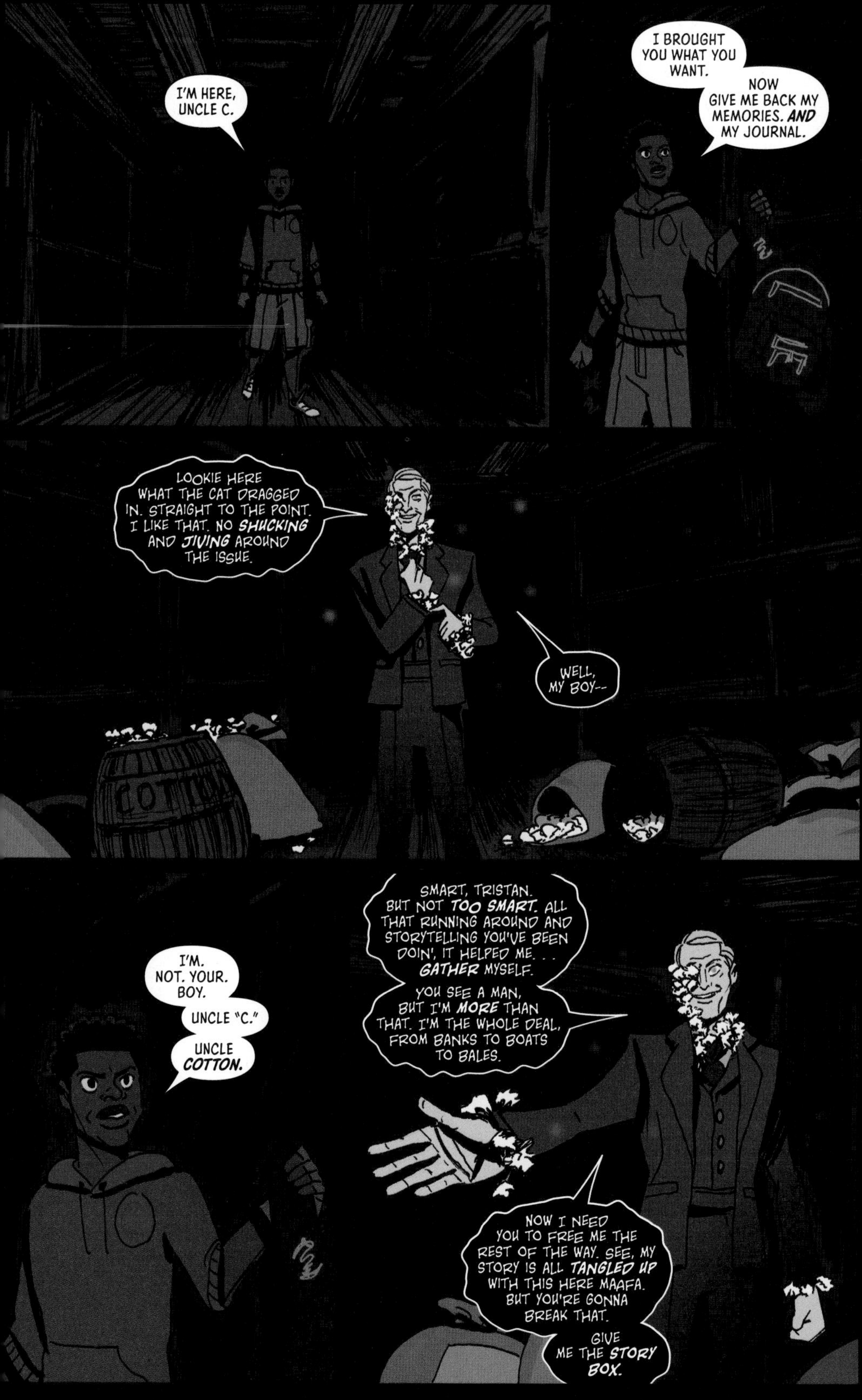
I'M HERE, UNCLE C.
I BROUGHT YOU WHAT YOU WANT.
NOW GIVE ME BACK MY MEMORIES. AND MY JOURNAL.
LOOKIE HERE WHAT THE CAT DRAGGED IN. STRAIGHT TO THE POINT. I LIKE THAT. NO SHUCKING AND JIVING AROUND THE ISSUE.
WELL, MY BOY--
COTTON
I'M. NOT. YOUR. BOY.
UNCLE "C."
UNCLE COTTON.
SMART, TRISTAN. BUT NOT TOO SMART. ALL THAT RUNNING AROUND AND STORYTELLING YOU'VE BEEN DOIN', IT HELPED ME. . . GATHER MYSELF.
YOU SEE A MAN, BUT I'M MORE THAN THAT. I'M THE WHOLE DEAL, FROM BANKS TO BOATS TO BALES.
NOW I NEED YOU TO FREE ME THE REST OF THE WAY. SEE, MY STORY IS ALL TANGLED UP WITH THIS HERE MAAFA. BUT YOU'RE GONNA BREAK THAT.
GIVE ME THE STORY BOX.

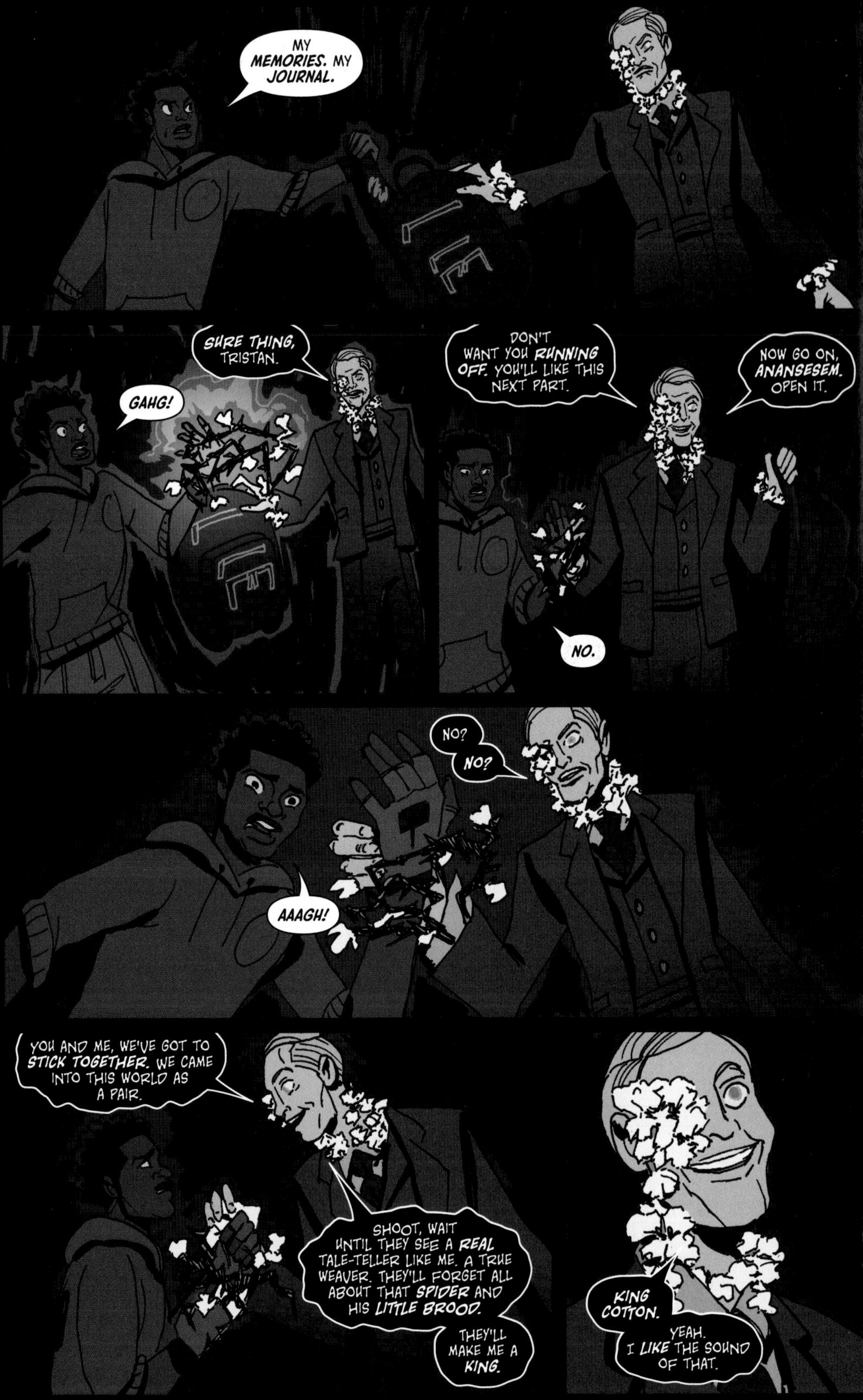
MY MEMORIES. MY JOURNAL.
SURE THING, TRISTAN.
GAHG!
DON'T WANT YOU RUNNING OFF. YOU'LL LIKE THIS NEXT PART.
NOW GO ON, ANANSESEM. OPEN IT.
NO.
NO?
NO?
AAAGH!
YOU AND ME, WE'VE GOT TO STICK TOGETHER. WE CAME INTO THIS WORLD AS A PAIR.
SHOOT, WAIT UNTIL THEY SEE A REAL TALE-TELLER LIKE ME. A TRUE WEAVER. THEY'LL FORGET ALL ABOUT THAT SPIDER AND HIS LITTLE BROOD.
THEY'LL MAKE ME A KING.
KING COTTON.
YEAH. I LIKE THE SOUND OF THAT.

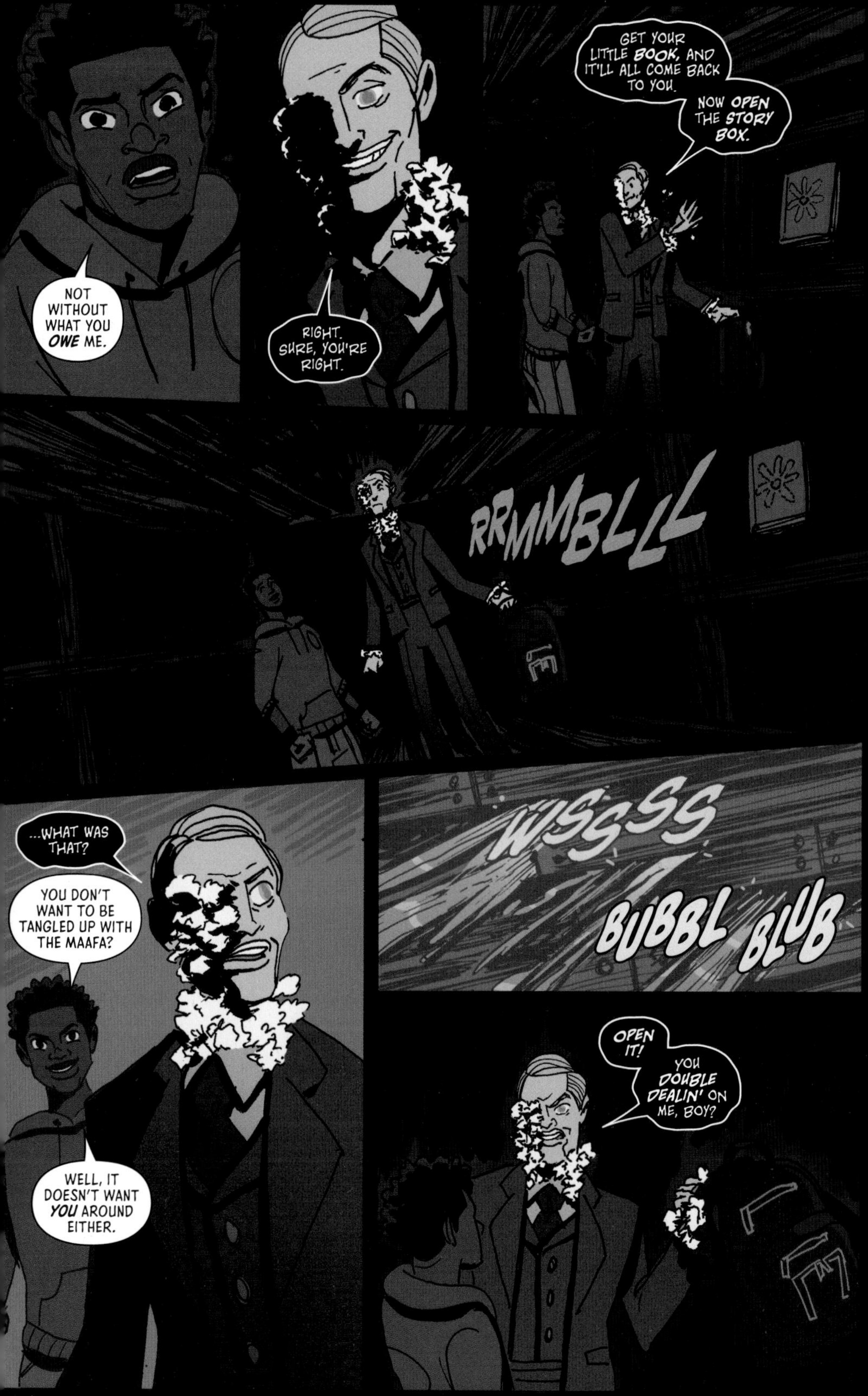
NOT WITHOUT WHAT YOU OWE ME.
RIGHT. SURE, YOU'RE RIGHT.
GET YOUR LITTLE BOOK, AND IT'LL ALL COME BACK TO YOU.
NOW OPEN THE STORY BOX.
RRMMBLLL
...WHAT WAS THAT?
YOU DON'T WANT TO BE TANGLED UP WITH THE MAAFA?
WELL, IT DOESN'T WANT YOU AROUND EITHER.
WSSSS
BUBBL BLUB
OPEN IT!
YOU DOUBLE DEALIN' ON ME, BOY?

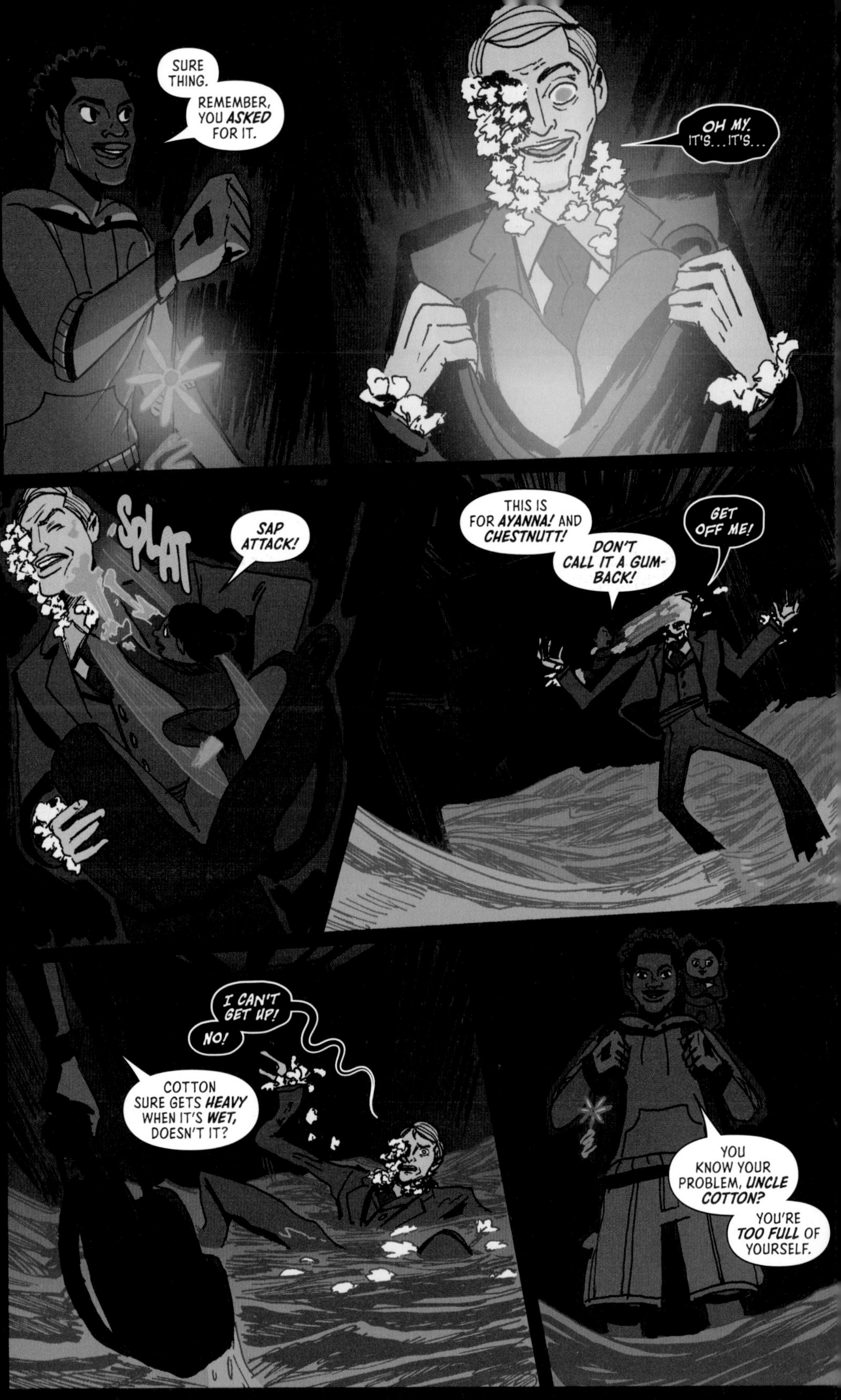

SURE THING.
REMEMBER, YOU ASKED FOR IT.
OH MY. IT'S...IT'S...
SPLAT
SAP ATTACK!
THIS IS FOR AYANNA! AND CHESTNUTT!
DON'T CALL IT A GUM-BACK!
GET OFF ME!
I CAN'T GET UP!
NO!
COTTON SURE GETS HEAVY WHEN IT'S WET, DOESN'T IT?
YOU KNOW YOUR PROBLEM, UNCLE COTTON?
YOU'RE TOO FULL OF YOURSELF.

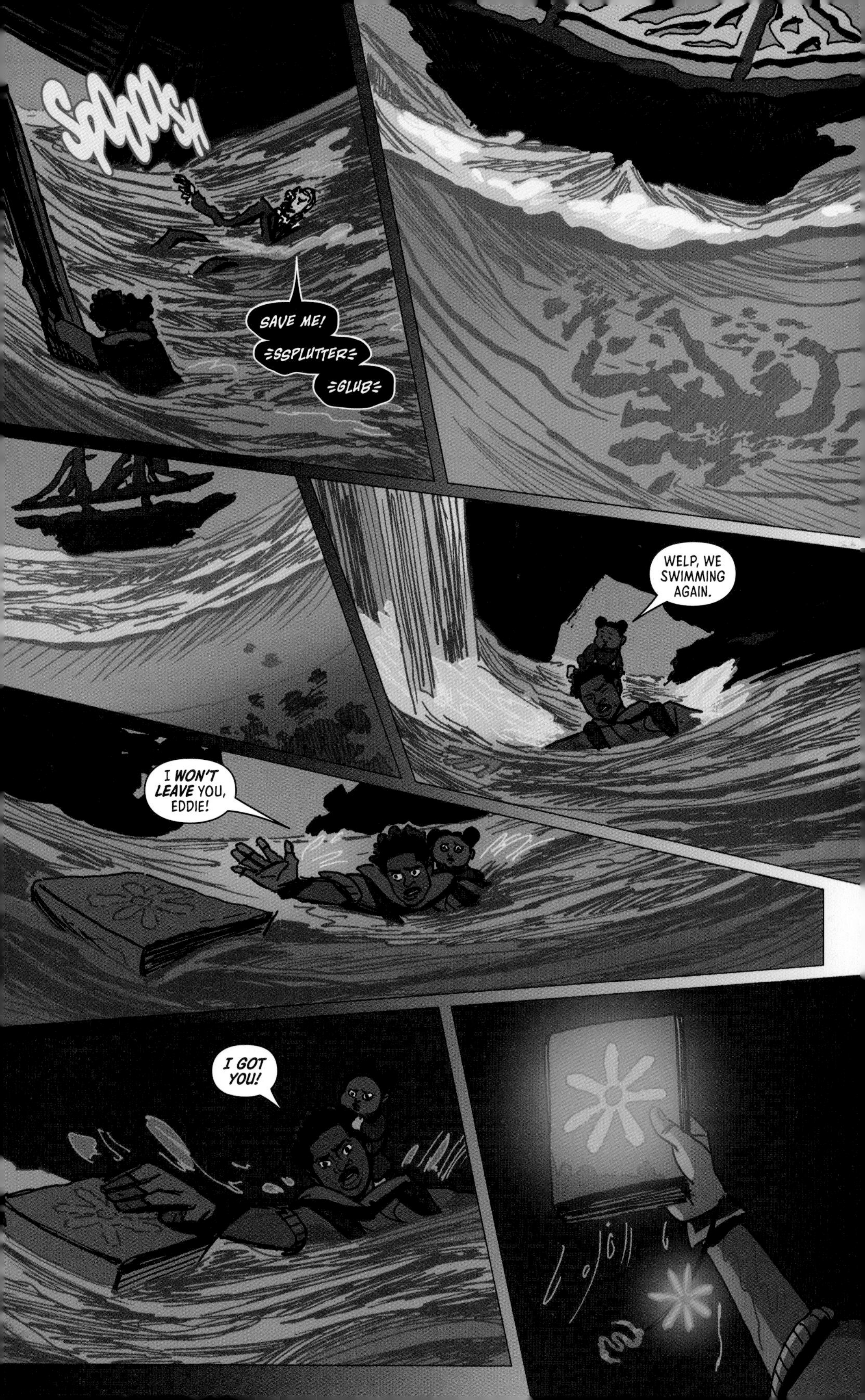
SPOOOSH
SAVE ME!
SSPLUTTER
GLUB
WELP, WE SWIMMING AGAIN.
I WON'T LEAVE YOU, EDDIE!
I GOT YOU!

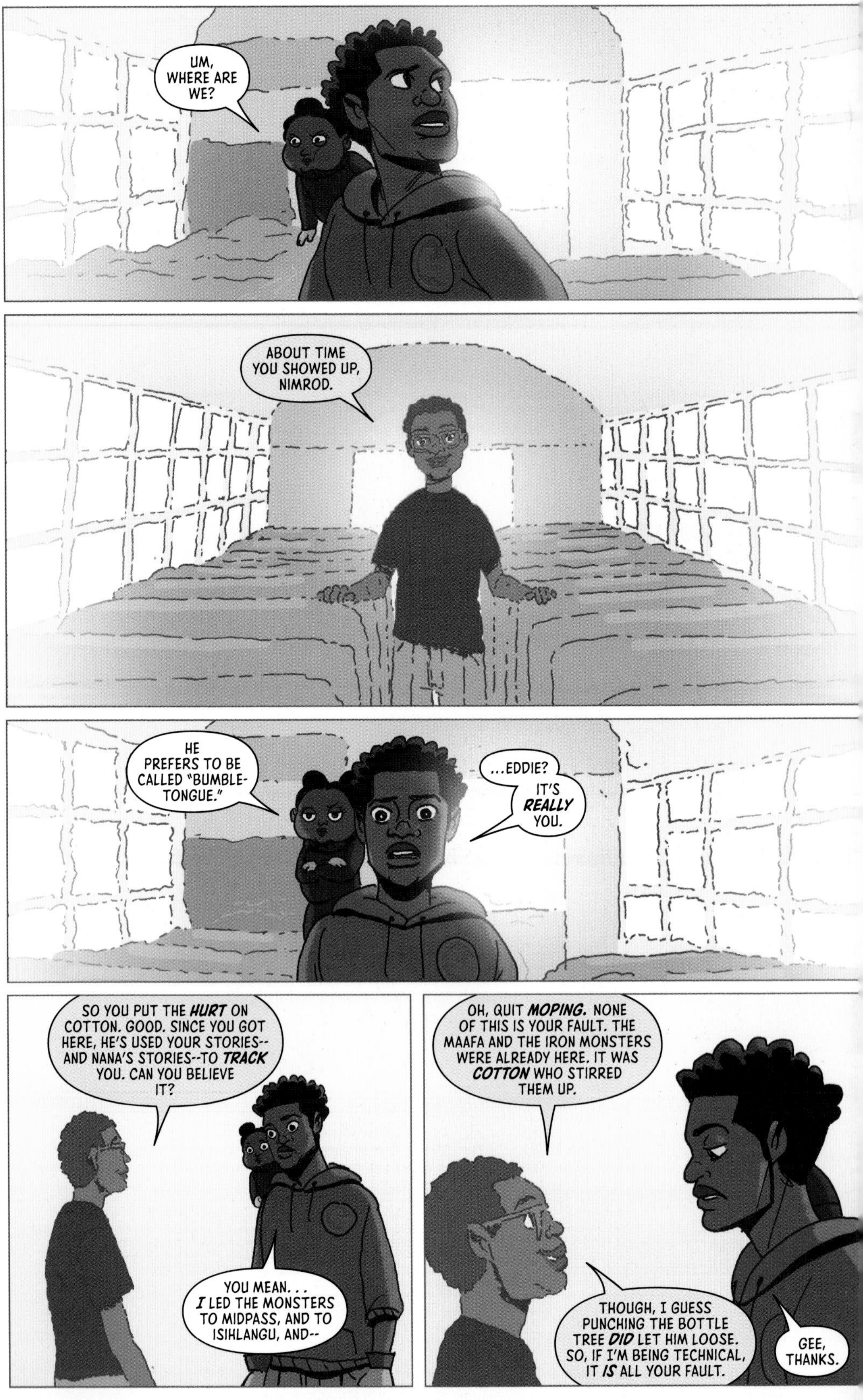
UM, WHERE ARE WE?
ABOUT TIME YOU SHOWED UP, NIMROD.
HE PREFERS TO BE CALLED "BUMBLE-TONGUE."
...EDDIE?
IT'S *REALLY* YOU.
SO YOU PUT THE *HURT* ON COTTON. GOOD. SINCE YOU GOT HERE, HE'S USED YOUR STORIES--AND NANA'S STORIES--TO *TRACK* YOU. CAN YOU BELIEVE IT?
YOU MEAN. . . *I* LED THE MONSTERS TO MIDPASS, AND TO ISIHLANGU, AND--
OH, QUIT *MOPING.* NONE OF THIS IS YOUR FAULT. THE MAAFA AND THE IRON MONSTERS WERE ALREADY HERE. IT WAS *COTTON* WHO STIRRED THEM UP.
THOUGH, I GUESS PUNCHING THE BOTTLE TREE *DID* LET HIM LOOSE. SO, IF I'M BEING TECHNICAL, IT *IS* ALL YOUR FAULT.
GEE, THANKS.

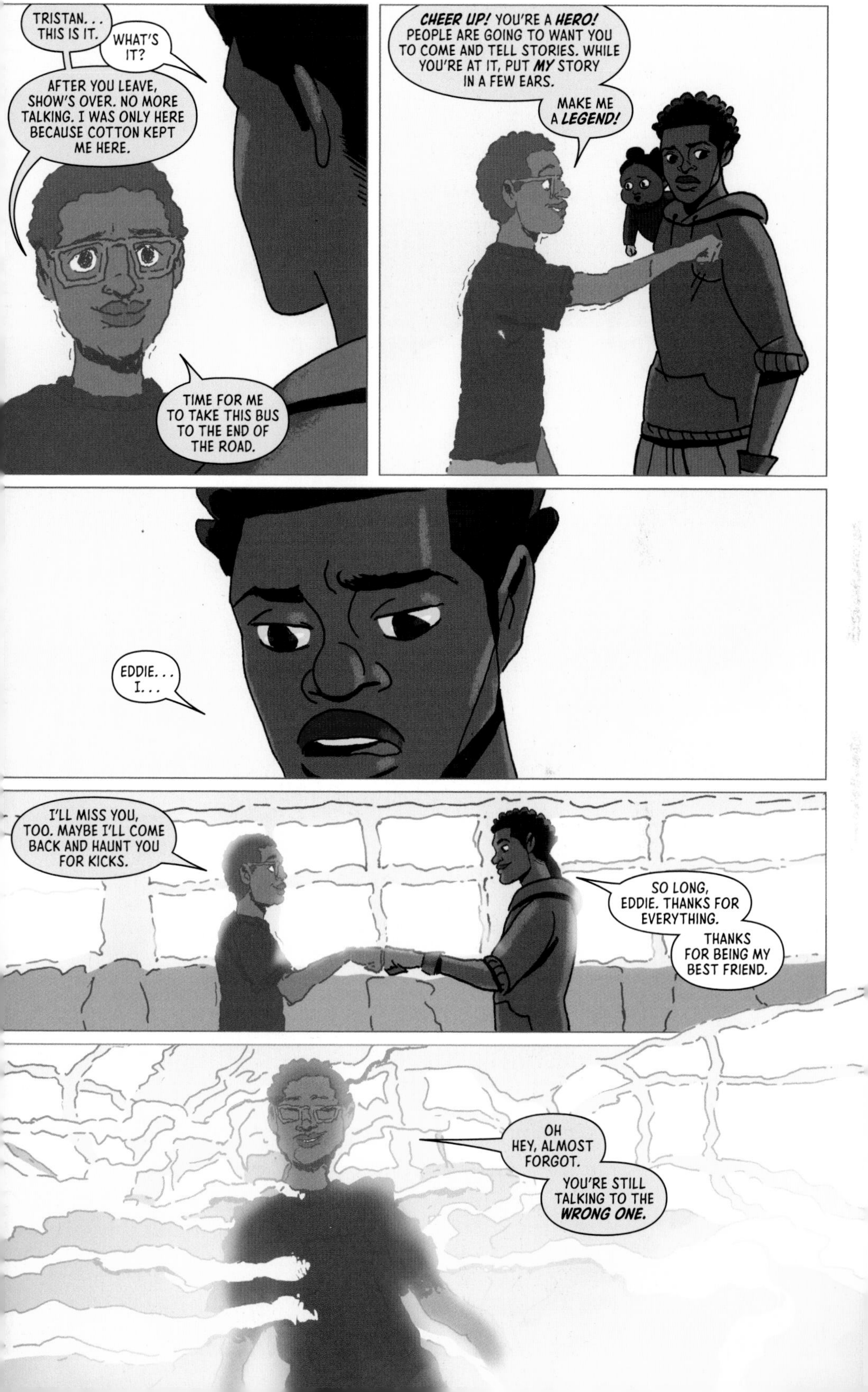
TRISTAN... THIS IS IT.
WHAT'S IT?
AFTER YOU LEAVE, SHOW'S OVER. NO MORE TALKING. I WAS ONLY HERE BECAUSE COTTON KEPT ME HERE.
TIME FOR ME TO TAKE THIS BUS TO THE END OF THE ROAD.
CHEER UP! YOU'RE A HERO! PEOPLE ARE GOING TO WANT YOU TO COME AND TELL STORIES. WHILE YOU'RE AT IT, PUT MY STORY IN A FEW EARS.
MAKE ME A LEGEND!
EDDIE... I...
I'LL MISS YOU, TOO. MAYBE I'LL COME BACK AND HAUNT YOU FOR KICKS.
SO LONG, EDDIE. THANKS FOR EVERYTHING.
THANKS FOR BEING MY BEST FRIEND.
OH HEY, ALMOST FORGOT.
YOU'RE STILL TALKING TO THE WRONG ONE.

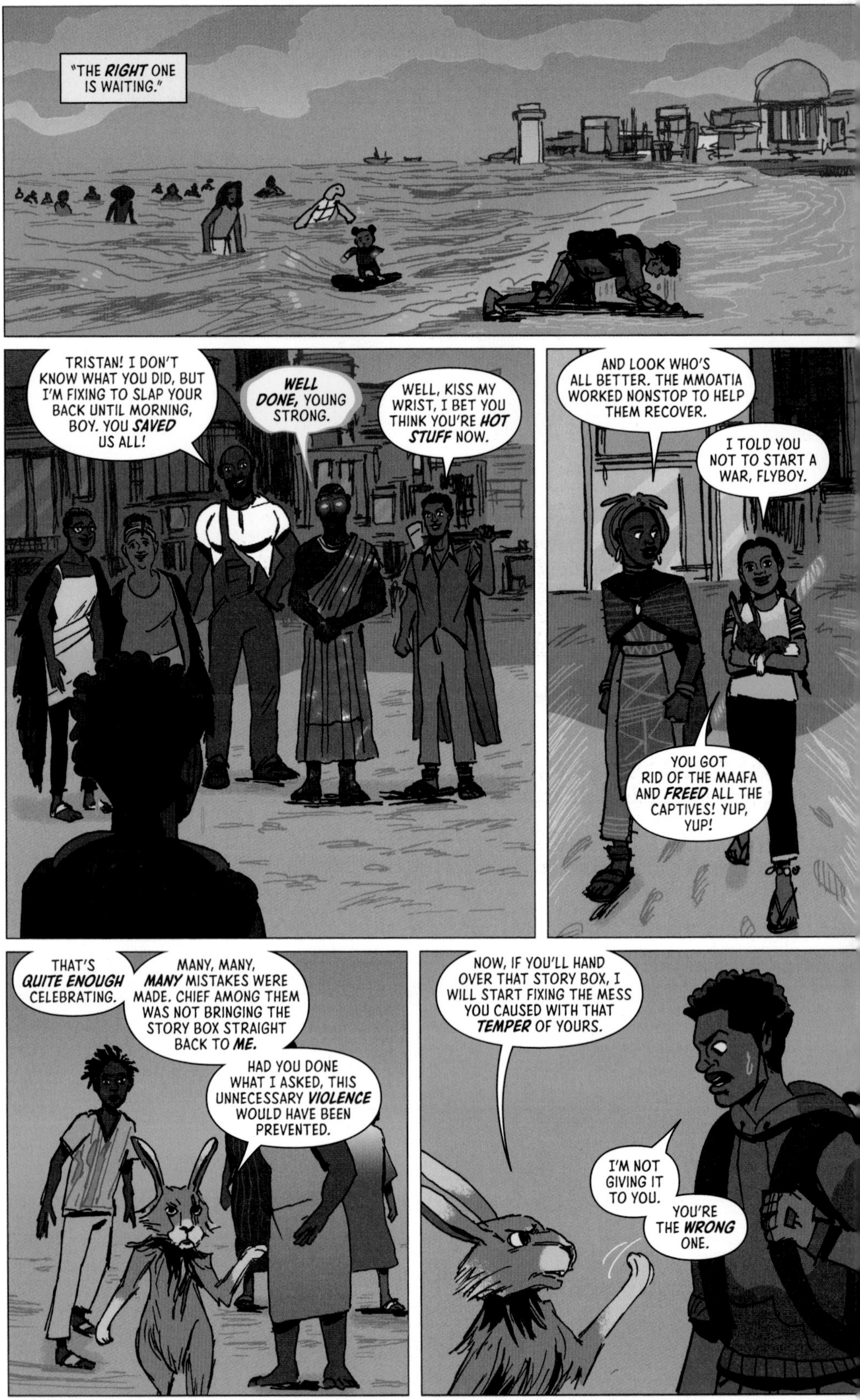
"THE *RIGHT* ONE IS WAITING."
TRISTAN! I DON'T KNOW WHAT YOU DID, BUT I'M FIXING TO SLAP YOUR BACK UNTIL MORNING, BOY. YOU *SAVED* US ALL!
WELL DONE, YOUNG STRONG.
WELL, KISS MY WRIST, I BET YOU THINK YOU'RE *HOT STUFF* NOW.
AND LOOK WHO'S ALL BETTER. THE MMOATIA WORKED NONSTOP TO HELP THEM RECOVER.
I TOLD YOU NOT TO START A WAR, FLYBOY.
YOU GOT RID OF THE MAAFA AND *FREED* ALL THE CAPTIVES! YUP, YUP!
THAT'S *QUITE ENOUGH* CELEBRATING.
MANY, MANY, *MANY* MISTAKES WERE MADE. CHIEF AMONG THEM WAS NOT BRINGING THE STORY BOX STRAIGHT BACK TO *ME.*
HAD YOU DONE WHAT I ASKED, THIS UNNECESSARY *VIOLENCE* WOULD HAVE BEEN PREVENTED.
NOW, IF YOU'LL HAND OVER THAT STORY BOX, I WILL START FIXING THE MESS YOU CAUSED WITH THAT *TEMPER* OF YOURS.
I'M NOT GIVING IT TO YOU.
YOU'RE THE *WRONG* ONE.

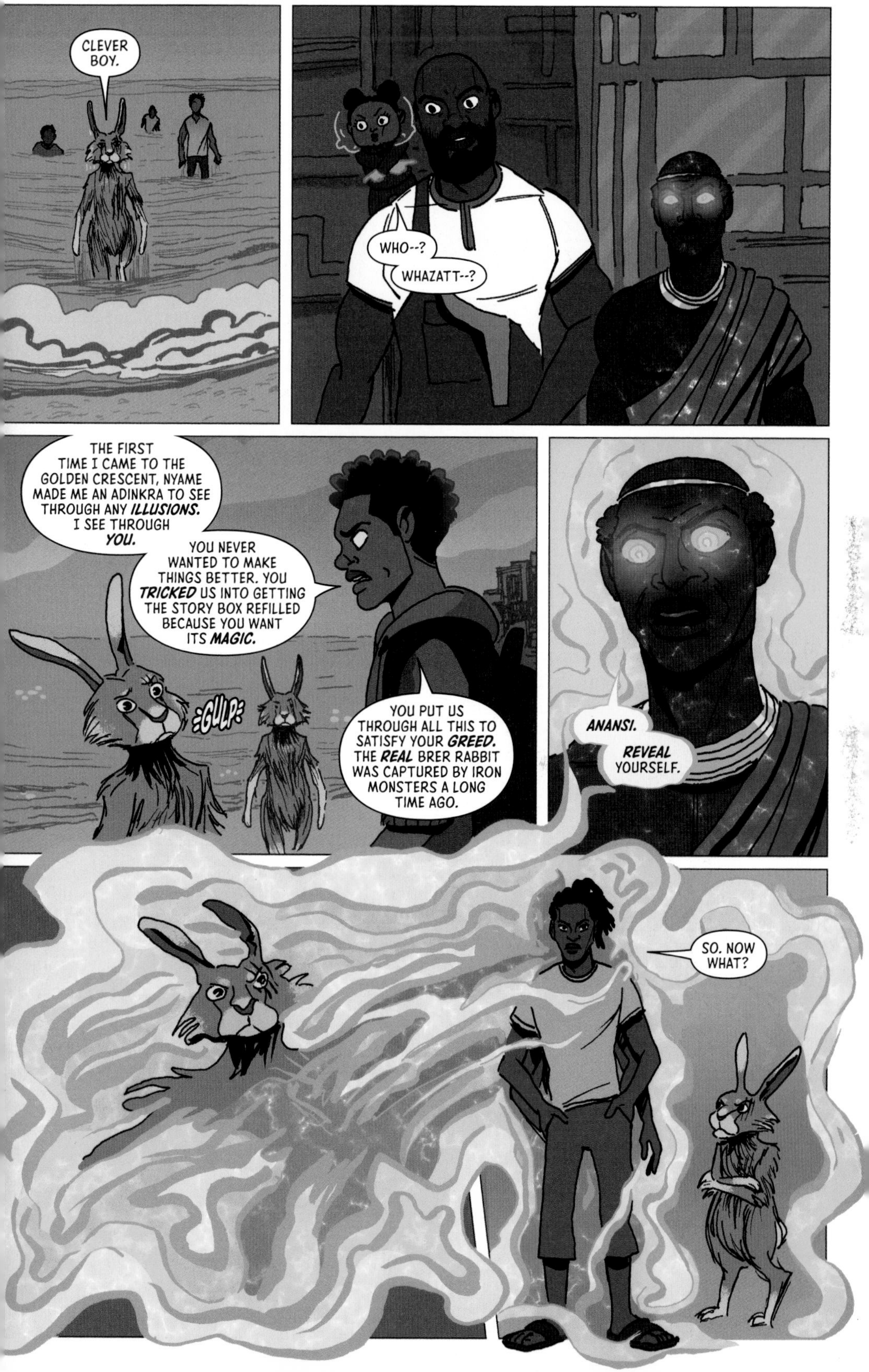
CLEVER BOY.
WHO--?
WHAZATT--?
THE FIRST TIME I CAME TO THE GOLDEN CRESCENT, NYAME MADE ME AN ADINKRA TO SEE THROUGH ANY ILLUSIONS. I SEE THROUGH YOU.
YOU NEVER WANTED TO MAKE THINGS BETTER. YOU TRICKED US INTO GETTING THE STORY BOX REFILLED BECAUSE YOU WANT ITS MAGIC.
GULP
YOU PUT US THROUGH ALL THIS TO SATISFY YOUR GREED. THE REAL BRER RABBIT WAS CAPTURED BY IRON MONSTERS A LONG TIME AGO.
ANANSI.
REVEAL YOURSELF.
SO. NOW WHAT?

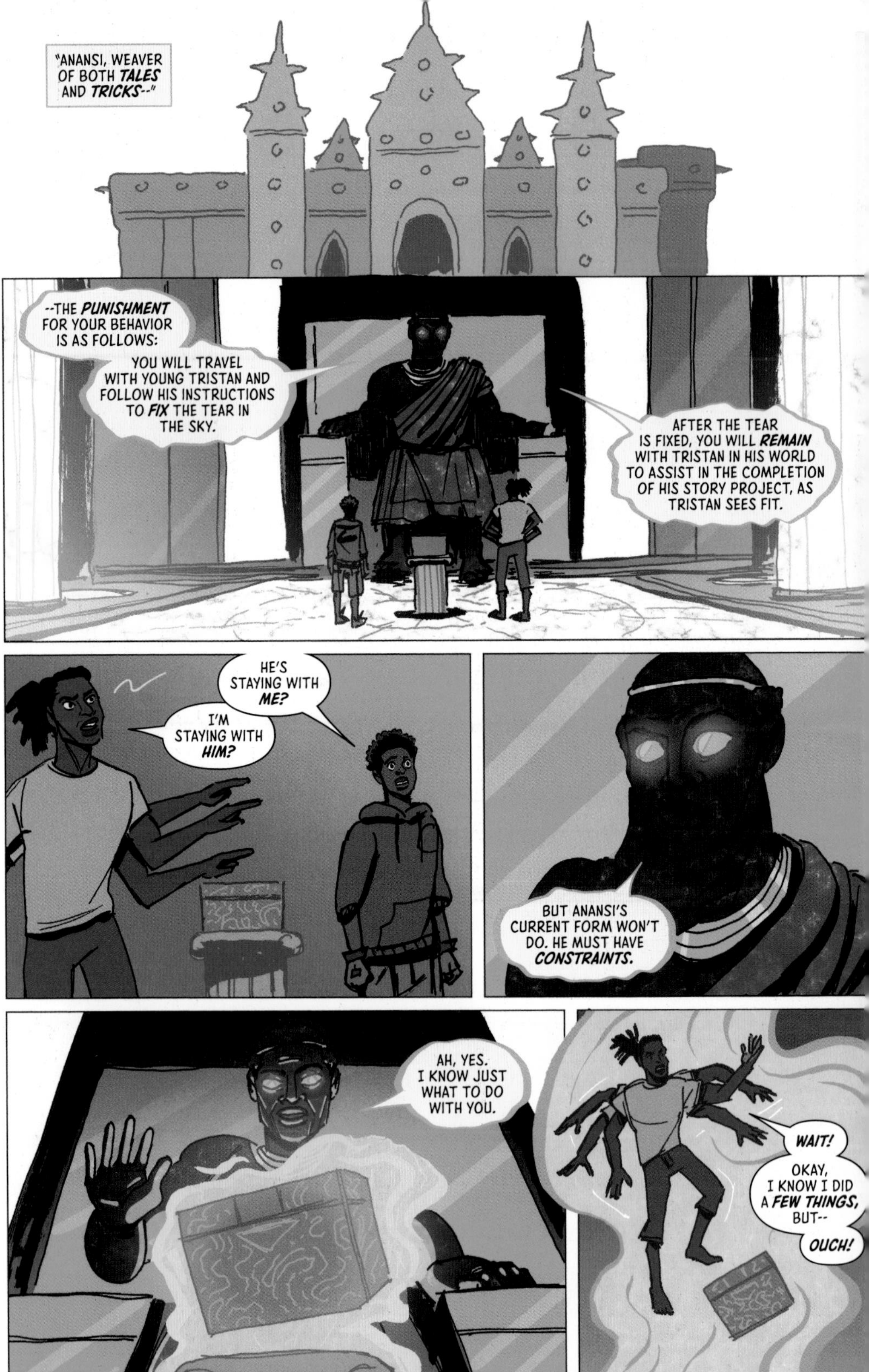
"ANANSI, WEAVER OF BOTH TALES AND TRICKS--"
--THE PUNISHMENT FOR YOUR BEHAVIOR IS AS FOLLOWS:
YOU WILL TRAVEL WITH YOUNG TRISTAN AND FOLLOW HIS INSTRUCTIONS TO FIX THE TEAR IN THE SKY.
AFTER THE TEAR IS FIXED, YOU WILL REMAIN WITH TRISTAN IN HIS WORLD TO ASSIST IN THE COMPLETION OF HIS STORY PROJECT, AS TRISTAN SEES FIT.
I'M STAYING WITH HIM?
HE'S STAYING WITH ME?
BUT ANANSI'S CURRENT FORM WON'T DO. HE MUST HAVE CONSTRAINTS.
AH, YES. I KNOW JUST WHAT TO DO WITH YOU.
WAIT!
OKAY, I KNOW I DID A FEW THINGS, BUT--
OUCH!

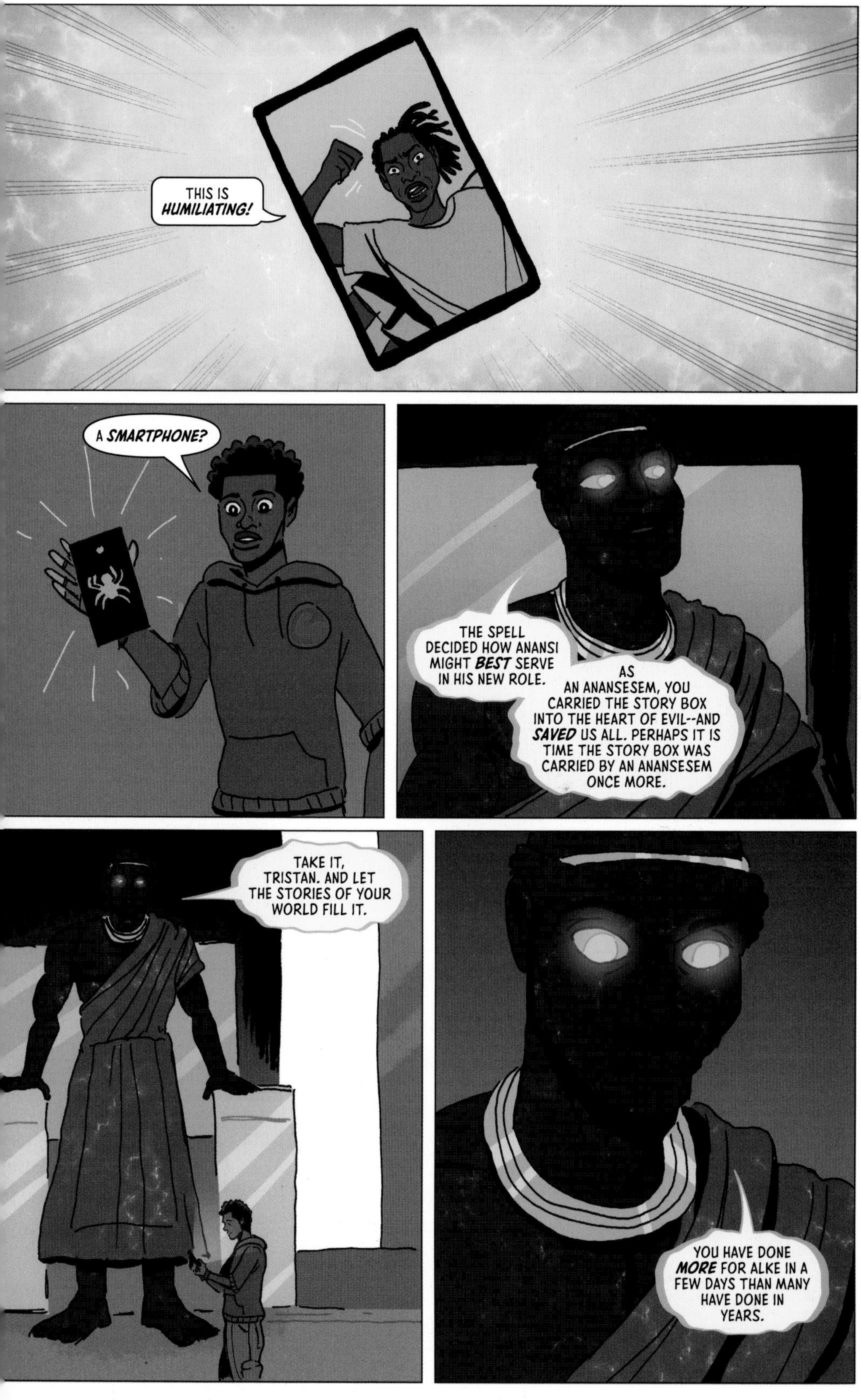
THIS IS **HUMILIATING!**
A **SMARTPHONE?**
THE SPELL DECIDED HOW ANANSI MIGHT **BEST** SERVE IN HIS NEW ROLE.
AS AN ANANSESEM, YOU CARRIED THE STORY BOX INTO THE HEART OF EVIL--AND **SAVED** US ALL. PERHAPS IT IS TIME THE STORY BOX WAS CARRIED BY AN ANANSESEM ONCE MORE.
TAKE IT, TRISTAN. AND LET THE STORIES OF YOUR WORLD FILL IT.
YOU HAVE DONE **MORE** FOR ALKE IN A FEW DAYS THAN MANY HAVE DONE IN YEARS.

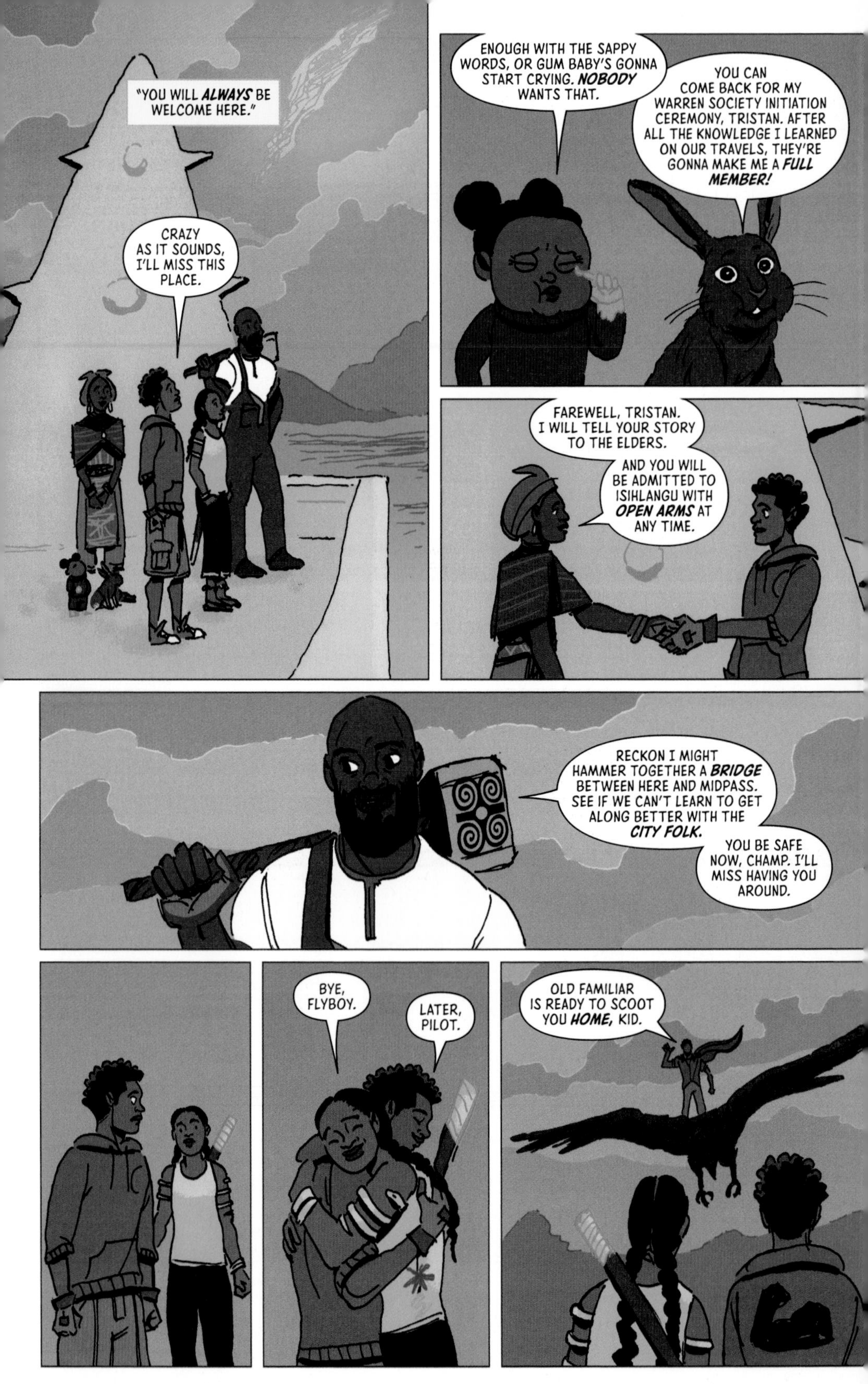
"YOU WILL ALWAYS BE WELCOME HERE."
CRAZY AS IT SOUNDS, I'LL MISS THIS PLACE.
ENOUGH WITH THE SAPPY WORDS, OR GUM BABY'S GONNA START CRYING. NOBODY WANTS THAT.
YOU CAN COME BACK FOR MY WARREN SOCIETY INITIATION CEREMONY, TRISTAN. AFTER ALL THE KNOWLEDGE I LEARNED ON OUR TRAVELS, THEY'RE GONNA MAKE ME A FULL MEMBER!
FAREWELL, TRISTAN. I WILL TELL YOUR STORY TO THE ELDERS.
AND YOU WILL BE ADMITTED TO ISIHLANGU WITH OPEN ARMS AT ANY TIME.
RECKON I MIGHT HAMMER TOGETHER A BRIDGE BETWEEN HERE AND MIDPASS. SEE IF WE CAN'T LEARN TO GET ALONG BETTER WITH THE CITY FOLK.
YOU BE SAFE NOW, CHAMP. I'LL MISS HAVING YOU AROUND.
BYE, FLYBOY.
LATER, PILOT.
OLD FAMILIAR IS READY TO SCOOT YOU HOME, KID.

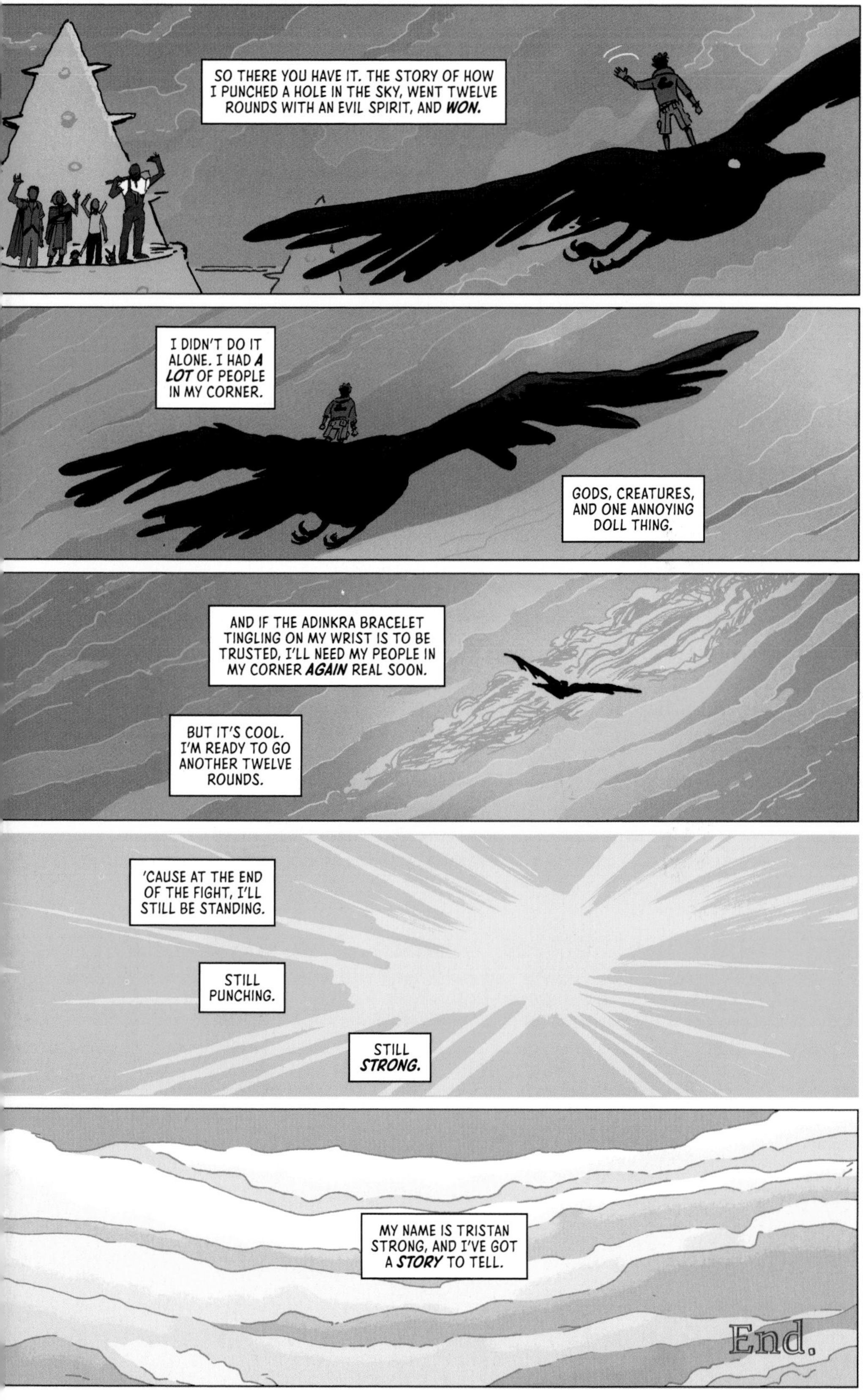
SO THERE YOU HAVE IT. THE STORY OF HOW I PUNCHED A HOLE IN THE SKY, WENT TWELVE ROUNDS WITH AN EVIL SPIRIT, AND ***WON.***
I DIDN'T DO IT ALONE. I HAD ***A LOT*** OF PEOPLE IN MY CORNER.
GODS, CREATURES, AND ONE ANNOYING DOLL THING.
AND IF THE ADINKRA BRACELET TINGLING ON MY WRIST IS TO BE TRUSTED, I'LL NEED MY PEOPLE IN MY CORNER ***AGAIN*** REAL SOON.
BUT IT'S COOL. I'M READY TO GO ANOTHER TWELVE ROUNDS.
'CAUSE AT THE END OF THE FIGHT, I'LL STILL BE STANDING.
STILL PUNCHING.
STILL ***STRONG.***
MY NAME IS TRISTAN STRONG, AND I'VE GOT A ***STORY*** TO TELL.
End.

First Edition, August 2022
10 9 8 7 6 5 4 3 2 1
FAC-038091-2132
Printed in the United States of America

This book is set in Ask for Mercy, Sans Sanity BB, and Dearly Departed/Fontspring
Designed by Tyler Nevins
Illustrations by Olivia Stephens
Color by Laura Langston, with additional color by Paris Alleyne
Lettering by Ariana Maher

Library of Congress Cataloging-in-Publication Control Number: 2022932651

Hardcover ISBN 978-1-368-07280-9
Paperback ISBN 978-1-368-07500-8

Reinforced binding for hardcover edition

Visit www.DisneyBooks.com
Follow @ReadRiordan